WOLFWOOD

MARIANNA BAER

AMULET BOOKS · NEW YORK

PUBLISHER'S NOTE: This is a work of fiction. Names, characters, places, and incidents are either the product of the author's imagination or used fictitiously, and any resemblance to actual persons, living or dead, business establishments, events, or locales is entirely coincidental.

Cataloging-in-Publication Data has been applied for and may be obtained from the Library of Congress.

ISBN 978–1–4197–3371–0

Text © 2023 Marianna Baer
Book design by Chelsea Hunter

Printed and bound in U.S.A.
10 9 8 7 6 5 4 3 2 1

Amulet Books are available at special discounts when purchased in quantity for premiums and promotions as well as fundraising or educational use. Special editions can also be created to specification. For details, contact specialsales@abramsbooks.com or the address below.

ABRAMS The Art of Books
195 Broadway, New York, NY 10007
abramsbooks.com

In memory of my mother

There aren't any wolves in Wolfwood, but there are monsters. I'm six years old when they find me.

Night after night, they trap me in the Wolfwood jungle. Roots like giants' fingers grab my ankles. Grotesque flowers knock me down with fleshy pink petals, slice open my gut with machete-sized thorns. Python-thick acid-green vines wind around my neck, squeezing tight, tight, tight . . . And always, just as I'm about to die, the Wolfwood girls circle around, their own bloody wounds bandaged with fabric torn from their brightly colored dresses. I never understand why they won't help, why they're so angry with me. The rage in their eyes is enough to wake me up screaming.

Don't be scared, Indigo, my mother says, as I crumple my sweaty, shaky body onto her lap. She hugs me close, whispering me back to sleep. *I made it all up. What isn't real can't hurt you.*

Her guilt is as heavy around me as her warm arms. She didn't mean for me to see her Wolfwood paintings, those torn-up girls, guts decorating the jungle like scarlet streamers. But the exhibition catalogue looked like a kids' book. I'd spotted its colorful spine on a high shelf, climbed on the couch to reach it.

Don't be scared, Indigo. What isn't real can't hurt you.

She says it with such conviction, over and over. For years. And at some point, when I'm too big for her lap, I finally believe her. I know enough of what *is* real that nightmares don't seem so scary.

I let down my guard. I believe her.

There aren't any wolves in Wolfwood, but there are monsters. I'm seventeen years old when I find them.

Chapter One

The Nordhaus Gallery in Manhattan is as far from the bloody chaos of Wolfwood as you can get. A cavernous space with an all-glass front and that echoey emptiness only fancy places can afford. Pristine white walls. Polished concrete floor. Staff always dressed in the almost-black to very-black spectrum. And—today, at least—large black-and-white photographs hanging. No color in sight.

Well, not for the moment.

I sweep open the door and breeze inside.

Red silk dress, wide yellow belt, turquoise heels. The only black: my long, wavy hair and the artist's portfolio I'm carrying. At six-foot-three in the four-inch pumps, with what my friend Grace calls my diva strut, I know how I look: confident, fierce, unflappable. The girl who's got everything, except reasons to worry.

Ha.

"Good morning," I say to the assistant at the reception desk. "I'm here to see Annika Nordhaus." My voice is steady, no sign I ran the last three blocks to get here on time.

She glances up from her laptop with a polite smile that stiffens when she spots the portfolio. "So sorry," she says, clearly *not* sorry about whatever's coming next. "The gallery isn't looking for new artists." Her eyes are back on her screen before she's finished the sentence.

I straighten up even taller. A bead of sweat slips down my spine. "I have an appointment. I'm Zoe Serra's—"

"Oh!" she interrupts, attention on me again. "Ms. Serra, apologies." And before I can correct her, she picks up the desk phone and tells someone that Zoe Serra is here. Seriously? She must be an intern or new to the gallery—anyone who works here for real would know I'm about thirty years too young to be my mother. Her first gallery show was before I was even born.

"Ms. Nordhaus will be right out," the girl says.

"Thanks." No reason to correct the misunderstanding now. Annika will see it's me soon enough.

I stand still instead of wandering the exhibition because of a killer blister I got walking here from the East Village in these heels, which I found last week abandoned in front of a church on Elizabeth Street—either a gift from God or an offering to her, I guess. When I chose them this morning I was in a hurry, thinking that if I was going to wear my one good dress and snub the art gallery black, I wanted to go extra: head-to-toe, in-your-face color. Didn't think about how long the walk was, or the fact I'd never worn them before. Rookie mistake.

A minute later, Annika emerges from the doorway that leads to the office and storage areas. Even from across the sprawling room, I can tell that everything about her is as precise and perfect as the gallery. Slim-fitting dress folded around her like origami. Pearls melting into the white skin of her collarbone. Signature ash-brown bob all sharp and shiny. I'm glad I fixed my lipstick as I waited to cross Tenth Ave. Perfection is fleeting with this cheap stuff.

"Indigo?" she calls, the *clack-clack* of her steps punctuating the air. "Where's your mother?" She turns to the girl at the desk. "You said Zoe Serra was here. Does this look like Zoe Serra?"

The girl's mouth opens, but nothing comes out.

"Zoe has a migraine," I explain. "I brought her drawings. Am I too late?"

"No, no," Annika says. "The collectors aren't even here yet."

At least running was worth it.

She gives my forearm a brief squeeze. "Sorry about Zoe, but lovely to see you, darling. You look gorgeous." Her grayish-blue eyes are filled with genuine warmth. One thing about Annika: She doesn't say what she doesn't mean.

"Thanks. You, too."

"Come on back." She starts toward the offices. "Please tell me you took a car here, lugging that big portfolio."

"It's a nice day," I answer vaguely.

I follow her through the gallery into a hallway and then through an office with white desktops built in along the length of the walls. I force myself not to limp as we pass by two men and a woman working at oversized monitors. There isn't a speck of dust in the air or smudge of dirt on any of the surfaces. Sterile as an operating room. One of the men makes eye contact with me. For a second I worry he can sense the dankness of our basement apartment clinging to my skin and dress, like I'm contaminating the room with my presence. A walking smudge.

I throw him a blasé smile: *I'm all that, who are you?*

Annika's spacious office is at the very back of the building. A glass wall looks out on a courtyard where geometric sculptures sit on a carpet of white rocks. A skylight shows the June blue above. It's so bright in here I almost need my sunglasses.

"We can lay out Zoe's sketches on the flat files," Annika says, seemingly referring to two low metal cabinets with shallow drawers that are covered with framed drawings of what look like spaceships. She holds down a button on her intercom, says, "I need help in the office." Then says to me, "Someone will clear them for us."

I slide the portfolio's strap off my shoulder and rest it against her desk.

"Pellegrino?" she says.

Overpriced water. We sell it at Stanton Füd, the prissy gourmet grocery store on the Lower East Side where I'm working this summer. (AKA "the Fud" among us cashiers.) "Do you have Coke?" I ask hopefully. I haven't eaten today—calories would be good. And caffeine is my lifeline.

"Coke? No. Kombucha?"

We sell that, too. I've never had it, but I'm pretty sure it has vitamins or minerals or something. "Sure. Thanks."

I check out the spaceships while Annika's over by a stainless steel minifridge in the corner. "What do you think of them?" she asks a moment later, handing me a tall, thin glass and gesturing at the drawings.

"It'd be fun to live in that one," I say, pointing at one that looks like a sci-fi luxury camper.

She smiles. "I meant as art."

Oh. Right.

My mother and I used to visit galleries and museums all the time, and she'd talk to me about the exhibitions—teaching me about composition and color and gesture—but my mind is blank. I run my tongue along the edge of my false front teeth while I think. "I like the quality of the line," I finally say. "There's a sensitivity to it that contrasts with the imagery. They're mechanical, but also humanistical." I take a sip of kombucha (disgusting, so definitely healthy), satisfied with what I came up with, even if I'm not positive "humanistical" is a real word.

Annika nods. "A young artist from Venezuela. We sold two yesterday." She pauses, her gaze on me now. "Such a pretty dress. It's familiar . . ."

"Oh," I say, touching the smooth silk—poppy red with a hot-pink chevron pattern. "It's one of Zoe's. Vintage, from the nineties or something." Annika probably remembers it because it's immortalized in a photo of my mother in *New York* magazine from before I was born. She's at a party, dancing barefoot on top of a large cube-shaped sculpture by the famous artist Richard Serra (no relation), arms above her head, hair hanging long and wild, eyes closed, glowing like a neon sign. I'm sure she was higher than an astronaut, but I still love the picture. And the dress. It's the only one of her designer things I've let myself keep, instead of selling it at the consignment store. Proof my mother used to be happy and electric. *Powerful.* Armor that makes me feel like I am.

"It's that old?" Annika says. "It's so fresh, the way you've styled it."

A knock comes at the open door, and a guy in a black knit beanie and faded gray tee—not as slick as the rest of the staff—enters the office. "Sorry that took a while," he says. "I was on top of the ladder, the big one, and—"

"Could you take the Suárez Díaz drawings back to the stacks?" Annika says, cutting him off. "And mark the ones that are sold."

"Which are those?" He reaches for a frame.

"Check with Tom."

"I can help," I say. I need this whole meeting to go as fast as possible so I can get to the Fud on time. I already had to scramble to get someone to cover the first half of my shift, which I hated doing.

"Don't be silly," Annika says as I put down my drink.

Ignoring her, I take two—they're heavier than I expect—and follow the guy into the hallway. He's shorter than me but solidly built, no hair peeking out of the beanie, strong, smooth forearms lightly tanned to a golden color.

"You really don't need to help," he says, setting his two frames on the floor. "Leave them here. I'll take them to the stacks."

"Just trying to speed things up." *Wasn't implying you can't do it yourself, Mr. Man.* I rest mine down and lean them against the wall.

As I start to turn around he says, "Wait . . . Indigo?"

I turn back. He's studying me with narrowed eyes. Not unfriendly. Curious. Then something clicks. "Kai?" I say. "Wow. I didn't recognize you." One of Annika's two sons. His face is less full than I remember, his lips fuller. The bright brown eyes under the arched eyebrows have a familiar spark, though, now that I'm paying attention. And there's a sprinkle of dark freckles along his angled cheekbones that I recognize, too.

"Me neither," he says. "I mean, not at first. You're . . . taller."

I smile down at him. "You're not."

He laughs and shakes his head, crosses his arms. "Oh, no. You're exactly the same."

"I assume that's a good thing, considering the way you used to follow me around."

"I was scared of turning my back on you! You had elbow lasers."

"Elbow lasers?" I say, no memory of this anatomical power.

"Don't ask me. You're the one who told me you had them."

We head into the office again. "You work here?" I ask. All I really remember about Kai—aside from how he followed me around gallery openings when we were little—is that he's a year above me in school, so would have just graduated, and that he ate a lot of cherry tomatoes that sometimes exploded when he bit them, pissing off his mother and making both of us laugh our heads off. And that he has a super cute older brother, Hiro, who I had a major crush on.

"Not really," he says, in a way that seems to imply there's more to the story. "I mean, sort of." He takes the last two drawings and, with a "Great to see you," disappears into the hallway.

"You, too," I call after him.

The cabinet tops now clear, I unzip the portfolio and carefully take out the sheaf of sketches that are the basis of the much larger paintings that will be in my mom's show at the gallery this September. The drawings are done on thin, rough paper that's slightly dingy and yellowed from age—she drew them over twenty years ago. As I lay them out, I check the numbers penciled in the lower right corners to make sure the sheets are in the correct order. The *Wolfwood* series tells a story in sequence, a story about a group of girls in a tropical jungle where the oversized plants are an army of brutal monsters who torture and try to kill them. The monsters are led by the one male character, a longhaired guy called the Wolf. These drawings are of the final "chapters" in the story. My mother had the first of her three *Wolfwood* exhibitions in the nineties. Until this year, she hadn't made new paintings in the series since before I was born.

I don't let my eyes linger on the graphic images. I haven't had nightmares about Wolfwood for years, but that doesn't mean I like to dwell on the violent world that came out of my mother's brain. She's told me the paintings don't have any real meaning. That she was young and doing a lot of drugs and wanted to be controversial. Somehow, that doesn't make it any less disturbing.

"How long do you think this will take, once the collectors are here?" I ask Annika. Before my shift at the Fud, I need to cash my paycheck from last night and pay a bill that's due today. And I have to go home first to change. It's not that I mind helping my mom with stuff like this—I just like to have more warning, so I can arrange things. (To be fair, my mom didn't ask me to come to the meeting. She was going to cancel it.)

Annika frowns at the sketches instead of answering my question. "Is this all of them?"

I count. There are seven: #25 through #31. There should be eight.

"No," I say, inwardly cursing. "Not the final one. Zoe . . . has that at the studio still." I guess? I didn't ask her if they were all in the portfolio. I assumed they were.

"Smart. No one should know how the story ends before the show."

"Right," I agree immediately. "Preserve the suspense."

Her cell phone pings. "Is Zoe okay, aside from the migraine?" she asks, typing something brief. "She never answers my calls. Makes arrangements difficult."

"She's fine. Just gets caught up in the work." This is true, but my mother is also the worst at taking care of business stuff, especially if it involves talking on the phone. Totally stresses her out. "Why don't you contact me from now on, and I'll make sure to get back to you? I'm kind of like her assistant."

"Fine with me." Annika tilts her head slightly. The light catches the wrinkles on her forehead and around her eyes, making her look less perfect, more human. "Zoe is so lucky to have a daughter like you. I remember when you two used to come here together, having so much fun . . ."

I brush away a pang of sadness. "Yeah, we did have fun." Hopping between gallery shows, exploring the marble halls of the Met, painting at my mother's sun-filled studio where she had more paint colors than we had at my whole school . . . We weren't rich then, either, but it felt like we were—our days were so rich with *doing*. I shift on my feet; sharp pain stabs up from my blister.

"Remind me how old you are now?"

"Seventeen."

"Really? You seem older." She pauses. "If you'd ever like to intern here, let me know. We have the space on Sixty-Ninth Street, too."

"Thanks," I say, knowing I wouldn't take her up on it even if I could. I'd want to intern in a fashion designer's studio, not a gallery. Moot point, though. Unpaid internships aren't for people like me.

Her phone pings again. "The Millers are just about here."

"Great."

"I'm excited about this." She picks up a small silver mirror and Chanel lipstick off her desk to reapply. "The art world is ready to go back to Wolfwood. I can feel it."

"So are we," I say, but my chest constricts, like one of those python-thick vines is wrapped around it, squeezing tight.

Chapter Two

Annika shoos me out of the office as soon as the front desk girl buzzes to say the collectors are here. I need to bring the drawings home with me, though, so I can't leave the gallery until the meeting's over. There's an alcove across from her office, where a printer and some supplies are kept. I figure it's as good a place to wait as any, and the door to the office isn't shut, so I can eavesdrop.

Checking the time, I see I have a text from the guy I've been hanging out with recently.

Josh: Chill later?

Despite the zing that vibrates through me, I write: Sorry babysitting

I'm working two jobs today: the Fud, then watching a toddler in our building. (Usually, I wouldn't be babysitting; I'd be sewing various bags and accessories for this lady Trinity's Etsy store. But sitting pays better.) After sending the text, and one to my mom letting her know I got to the gallery on time, I calculate that I should leave here in about thirty minutes. At the most. Annika never answered my question about how long the meeting will take.

I don't even want to think about the issue of actually getting home. I ease my heel out of my shoe, wincing. It's raw, covered in screaming-red blood, a thick flap of skin hanging off. Gross. I open my bag and take out the small zippered pouch where I keep money and cards. Occasionally a hair elastic or Band-Aid ends up in it. I dump it out on the table next to the printer and sift through: student ID, EBT card, library card, safety pin . . .

"Ouch," Kai says. *Shit*—I didn't notice him coming up next to me. He's staring down at my bloody heel.

I hurry to gather up my stuff, fumbling in my rush, praying he didn't see the EBT card. "It's not so bad," I say. "I was looking for a Band-Aid." Even if he saw the card, he probably wouldn't know it was for food benefits. Still, my face burns. Everyone makes the same assumptions about people on public assistance: lazy, useless, parasitic. My mother would *die* if Annika found out. I almost mean that literally.

"There are some in the bathroom," Kai says. "Want me to get you one?"

"Thanks," I say. "I'll go myself." As I zip my pouch closed, one of the collector's voices, the man's, broadcasts out of Annika's office, saying something about an "art fair," whatever that is.

"They're twins," Kai tells me quietly. "Did you notice?"

"Twins?"

He nods toward the hallway. "Those collectors. Not actual twins. They're married, and they always wear matching outfits. Like, they have some tailor make his and hers versions."

"For real?"

He nods again and lowers his voice even further. "And . . . they're both named Kris."

"No." I'm smiling now.

"With a 'K.'"

I laugh, quickly covering my mouth, as Kai keeps talking.

"And it's like, which came first, the names or the outfits, right? Like, did they go on a first date and say, 'Hey, we have the same name. We should get married and dress like twins.' Or did they show up at the date in matching outfits and decide to change their names?" He says this all in a whispered rush that gets less whispery as it goes.

"Shh!" I say, still laughing, but keeping it in as much as possible.

He glances into the hallway again. "I should get back to work, I guess."

"Yeah. I should take care of . . ." I gesture at my foot.

We give each other a final brief smile and I limp off. In the bathroom, after I push the silver trash can up against the locked door, I use wet toilet paper to clean my heel and find Band-Aids in the cabinet under the sink. I take a big one and smooth it on—one of the really good, waterproof kinds that last for days. I consider taking a few extra since the ones we have at home barely even stay on your skin for ten minutes, but the box isn't very full, so I take only one more, somehow worried that if I take several Kai will notice and think it's weird, which I also realize is a silly worry. I'm sure he has better things to do than inventory bathroom supplies.

I freshen my lipstick and check my teeth, making sure there's nothing in them or on them, nothing to draw attention. I've had my false front ones since I was thirteen, and they still feel too big, like they belong in someone else's mouth. (That someone else being a horse, ideally.)

When I return to the hallway, Kai's nowhere to be seen. I take up my spot by the printer.

Annika is talking about the paintings now. "You already know how influential the *Wolfwood* series has been," she says. "And from the recent auction result, it's obvious the work is as relevant as ever, twenty-five years after the first exhibition. That's because it speaks the truth, in the voice of an enormously talented artist."

I have no idea what auction result she's talking about, but I feel a swell of pride at the part about my mother's talent. Hating Wolfwood doesn't mean I think it's bad art. No, I think the paintings are *too* good. That's part of the problem.

"Do you know how you're pricing the pieces yet?" the woman asks.

"And what can you do for us if we reserve one now?" adds the man.

"Since you were early supporters of her work, I can do... twenty percent. So, let's see ... that would bring it to ... ninety-six."

Ninety-six. That can't mean ninety-six dollars, obviously, so it must mean ... wait ... ninety-six *hundred* dollars? My hand flies to my mouth. That's almost ten thousand dollars! Half of that would go to the gallery—the gallery always gets 50 percent, my mother once told me—but still ... Almost five thousand dollars! Five thousand dollars would be huge! More than I'll make all summer. It would mean we could catch our breath for a few months. And if these people are interested—after only seeing the drawings, not even the real watercolor paintings—maybe other people will be, too. Eight paintings in the show ...

Holy shit.

"That's reasonable," the man says. "We'd definitely like a reserve on this one. We'd also like to be the first to see the final work in the series."

"I have to give the Whitney first look," Annika says. "Although ... it *would* make sense for the final image to be in your collection. Maybe I can steer the museum toward another one."

"Please do," the woman says.

Jesus. They might want a second one? And the Whitney Museum is interested?

After they walk out—yes, in matching white linen suits—I find Annika making notes at her desk. Before I can say anything, her phone rings. She holds up a *give me a minute* finger and answers.

I begin putting the drawings back into the portfolio while she talks, my mind speeding like an express train. *I was right. I was right to tell my mother to do the show!*

Last fall, when Annika called out of the blue and asked her to finish the *Wolfwood* series for an exhibition on the twenty-fifth anniversary of the first show, my mother resisted. She told me she was worried about me because of my old nightmares. She said she didn't want to bring Wolfwood back into our lives. I was shocked. I told her not to worry, that I *wanted* her to do it. That we needed the money. (Duh!) Worst-case scenario, I'd have a couple of bad dreams.

"If I did it, there's no guarantee anything would sell," she said, not even looking away from the pot of macaroni or spaghetti or whatever was cooking on the hot plate.

"But something might. *Please* don't worry about me," I said again, more firmly. "It's going to be great."

And I was right!

"Absolutely not, Bruce." The volume and sharpness of Annika's voice draw my attention. "Reread the consignment agreement, then honor it and send me the money. Unless you want to hear from my lawyer." She hangs up. "Bastard," she snaps. "Sorry, Indigo. But it's always something. I have to fight for every penny to keep this place going. If you ever own a business, you'll see. It's a battle. Especially for a woman. You wouldn't believe the shit people try to get away with."

"That's awful," I say. "But the meeting went well, right?"

She furrows her brow, now typing on her laptop.

"The meeting," I repeat. "With the collectors."

"Oh," she says. "Yes. Very."

"What does it mean exactly, they want to reserve it?"

She looks up. "With the Millers, I'd say it's a firm promise to buy the piece, assuming it's as good as the older paintings—which, of course, it will be. And I get the sense they'll buy the other one, too. They'll wait until they see all the works hung in the show to make a final decision, but I think we can count it as an eventual sale."

I resist shrieking, instead saying, "And the price sounds good?" trying to keep my voice all *no big deal.*

Annika nods. "I hope Zoe understands that the primary market is different from auctions. But still, yes, it's a good price, ninety-six thousand."

"What?"

"I had to give them a discount," she explains. "The final price is ninety-six thousand."

Kai walks me out to get a cab home, carrying the portfolio for me.

I don't even protest.

I'm strangely numb. My whole body. My lips. Everything. Numb with numbers. *Ninety-six thousand. Forty-eight thousand to Mom. Ninety-six thousand to Mom if two sell. Three hundred and eighty-four thousand if all sell.*

Three hundred and eighty-four thousand dollars.

It's only when Kai begins to hail a cab that I snap back. I'm counting these huge numbers, but the reality is that I don't have even one dollar to get home. I'm cashing my paycheck today. For the moment, I'm down to loose change.

"Actually . . . I think I'll just walk," I say. "We don't live far."

"Where?"

"Uh . . . East Village."

He holds my gaze. We both know that the East Village doesn't count as "not far," especially in heels with a big-ass blister. It's a couple of miles away.

"My mom will kill me if I don't put you in a car," he says, reaching into his pocket. "She gave me money to pay for it, so . . . here." He brings out two worn, crinkled twenties.

My hand tingles with the urge to take the bills, but I smell bullshit. "Nice try," I say, voice light despite my fear that he's offering because he saw my EBT card. "If your mom even *uses* cash, it's crisp and unfolded."

He grins. "Okay, maybe, Sherlock. But I'll get reimbursed, if that's the problem. And since your mom just made the gallery a chunk of change, you can, you know"—he shrugs—"take the measly forty."

Kai's right, of course. Even if he did see the benefits card—*please, no*—this isn't charity. And there's no way I'll make it to work on time if I walk. Still, my fingers pluck only one of the bills and I hear myself saying, "It's not a forty-dollar ride." A taxi swoops up to the curb as I speak.

"You always were stubborn," he says, and then opens the cab's door for me. "Slide in. I'll hand you the portfolio."

"Thanks." I scoot across the vinyl seat, cursing myself for not just swallowing my pride and taking the forty, because no matter how much money might come to us in the future, that extra twenty would still make a difference now. Right on cue, my empty stomach grumbles loudly. *Could've bought a burger with the extra.* Not to mention, when was the last time I took a cab? Maybe it *is* a forty-dollar ride! I'll just have to get out early if I see the meter going too high. My heel throbs at the thought.

I settle the portfolio next to me. "East Seventh Street, please."

The cab takes off. The meter is already at $2.85. I rest my hands on my lap and lean back against the squishy seat, trying to relax. And then I remember.

Forty-eight thousand dollars. Each.

As we swerve and lurch crosstown, any other feelings are replaced by a steadily swelling excitement and thoughts, one after another, of what this might mean.

Even selling just one painting could mean a real apartment with an actual lease, a fridge full of food, a computer and internet at home . . . No more sneaking extra Band-Aids or handfuls of tampons from the bathroom at school or packets of sugar and condiments from McDonald's . . . My mother could pay off some of her debt, start climbing out of the impossibly deep hole.

And if all of them sell? Jesus. Maybe we could *buy* an apartment—no more landlords or fear of eviction, ever.

I close my eyes and feel the warm breeze coming through the taxi's open window, not sure whether I'm about to laugh or cry. *The show—it might be a success. An enormous fucking success.* And I can't stop my thoughts from going somewhere else, a deeper crevice of my mind. Because as much as I care about the concrete things the money can do for us, there's something even more important at stake here.

Ever since Annika called last fall, I've been pushing away worries about what will happen if the show *isn't* successful. I have this feeling that it's some sort of last chance for my mother. The last chance for her to get her life back.

She used to have a real life. An *amazing* life. She had her first gallery show at twenty-one; was in the Whitney Biennial—a super important museum exhibition—a couple of years later; sold every painting in her first three shows, some to major museums. For around eight or so years she danced on sculptures, was written about in *New York* magazine . . .

Then she got pregnant.

The way she tells it, once she had a daughter, she couldn't bring herself to fill the world with more paintings from Wolfwood, images that showed girls being treated so brutally. Couldn't protect a baby girl at home and then tear them apart in her paintings. She says it was visceral, a physical need to stop. She didn't stop painting; she just stopped painting Wolfwood. Some critics and museum people (and me!) loved her new works: a series called *Home Safe*—large watercolors of imaginary dollhouse interiors with all angles slightly softened, as if everything were made of marshmallow, and two little doll figures that represented the two of us. But the new paintings weren't what Zoe Serra was known for, and the collectors moved on. All they wanted from her was the end of *Wolfwood*.

When I was eleven, she got what we thought was a bad flu and didn't go to the doctor because she had no health insurance. Ended up in the emergency room; almost died from what was actually meningitis. Her outrageous bills from a week in the hospital crushed her with debt. She tried to work when she recovered—got a series of minimum-wage jobs in hotel housekeeping and fast food, because she never graduated from high school. She'd work two at once to try to make up some of what she owed. But she had lasting effects from the illness—migraines and fatigue—and something always went wrong. She'd miss too many days, or she'd have to leave midshift . . . and she'd be fired. Soon, her applications were being denied. We lost our apartment, were homeless for one nightmare stretch, until I started making cash working under the table. With that and public assistance, we were able to move into the basement room where we live now.

For the couple of years before Annika called, my mom was like a gray pencil-sketch version of herself—all the color of her personality faded away. No painting career. No job offers. The only things that got her up were cleaning the building we live in (part of our rent deal with the landlord) and stuff she did for me: cooking meals, washing my clothes . . . She loves being a mother. But that makes me worry: What will happen if I leave home someday and she has *no* reason to get out of bed? She needs something else to live for, and not just vacuuming a hallway. Something that makes her *happy*.

She needs painting.

Sometimes I imagine what her life would be like if she hadn't gotten pregnant or if she'd had a boy instead of me. Would she still have stopped painting Wolfwood? Or would she have had that final triumphant show and ridden the success to another series that people loved? She says the years I was growing up were the best years of her life. That everything went wrong because of the illness. But that's hard to believe. A week in the hospital didn't kill Zoe Serra's career. Having me did.

1988/89

Zoe Serra is seventeen years old and sketching in Grand Central Station the first time she sees Colin Wolf.

He's unmissable: long blond hair, swimming pool eyes, jeans hanging low on his hips. Best of all, an artist's portfolio in his hand. Zoe's cheeks flame as he squats down and asks if he can see what she's drawing. Dumbstruck, she flips through the pages where she's been trying to capture the blurry bustle of commuters. He murmurs all sorts of things about how much he likes them and how talented she is, each word fanning the fire of her blush. Over coffee, she finds out he's older (twenty), taking a break from college, and in the midst of choosing a gallery to represent him. He asks if she wants to go to the David Hockney retrospective at the Met with him later in the week.

David Hockney leads to Jeff Koons leads to Georgia O'Keeffe leads to kisses and clothes peeled off in his loft on Canal Street, surrounded by his huge canvases—abstract explosions of paint that remind Zoe of natural disasters: floods, fires, earthquakes. Everything about Colin is as passionate as his paintings. Even his moodiness is romantic to Zoe. They've been together for five months when he tells her he's heading down to the Yucatán Peninsula for an indefinite time, to paint and get a breather from the hustle of the New York art world. Does she want to go with him?

There's no decision to be made. The only thing she's scared of losing in life is him.

On the plane to Cancún, Zoe grips the armrests, bracing herself for tragedy. At the very least, she expects the pilot to make an announcement that they have to turn around and go back to real life. Ever since her parents died (mother of cancer when she was nine, father of a heart attack when she was eleven), she's gotten used to the idea that God has it in for her. Clearly, Colin is too good to be true, and this adventure is too big and beautiful to be her life! But the plane lands. And they survive hitching a ride from Cancún about eighty miles to the tiny town of Tulum, on the water at the edge of the jungle, where they rent a thatched-roof hut with two hammocks and nothing else.

Their first morning in Mexico, Zoe stands on the soft white sand under a cobalt sky in a sort of shock. Twenty-four hours ago she was living with her aunt Donna, who basically hates her, in an apartment in Queens with a plastic-covered living room set, going to an uptight Catholic school where she was the weird orphan girl with no friends. Now she's living in a cabana on the beach in Mexico with a gorgeous, talented boyfriend who loves her. Is she even the same person?

And Tulum! The glowing turquoise ocean, the infinite greens of the jungle, the Mayan ruins perched on the bluff . . . She's electrified by the thought of painting it all. A couple of years earlier, when Zoe told her aunt she wanted to be an artist, Donna said that it was an egotistical, self-indulgent thing to be. But Zoe doesn't want to be like that. She wants to be inspired by places like this, so that her art will add to the beauty and wonder in the world. Losing herself in her father's collection of art books pretty much saved her after he died. Before Colin saved her, that is.

Zoe doesn't know what she did to deserve this fresh start and perfect life, but she's going to do everything she can to be worthy of it. She's not going to screw anything up.

Chapter Three

When the driver pulls up at our building, I have enough money to pay him and a little left for a tip. I hurry down the short set of stairs behind the building's trash cans and unlock the door to the basement as quietly as possible, despite my excitement, in case my mother's migraine is in full force. I scan our cramped room—with its sagging couch (my mom's bed), twin mattress (my bed), coffee table, and makeshift kitchen area—but I don't see her. "Mom?" I call, setting down the portfolio. No answer, meaning she's not in the bathroom, either. I wait a few minutes, using the time to change into my Fud uniform and mop up water that's pooled in the slightly sunken area of the unfinished concrete floor near my mattress. As I do, I see a note that must have fallen off the coffee table: *At studio. Phone dead. Can't find charger. xo.*

Crap. While I'm glad she was able to cut short the migraine, I'm going to explode if I can't tell her the news.

All during my shift at the Fud, I'm spinning like an overwound windup toy, scanning containers of handmade lobster ravioli and insulated bags of steaming hot rotisserie chickens while thinking,

We'll be able to afford you, and you, and you . . . The kind of fantasies I never let myself have. Planning meals we can cook and imagining the juicy fresh fruit that I'll bite into whenever I want, sweetness dripping down my chin and making me feel like I'm on a tropical island—

"Indigo?" my co-cashier Naomi says, as I sway my hips to the beachy music in my head. "You here, girl?"

"Nope," I say, smiling widely.

When my half shift is over, my mom's still not home. I get a text from Marcus, the father upstairs, saying I don't need to show up for babysitting until an hour later than I thought, which means I have enough time to take the subway out to Brooklyn and find her at the studio.

I can't afford train fare, but there are other ways.

Luck is with me. A crowd is pouring out of the turnstile area when I get to the subway station, and my casual plea of "Could anyone swipe me in? My card isn't working," gets me quick entrance. It's the one situation where I don't feel that bad asking for handouts—lots of people have MTA accounts with unlimited rides, so they aren't even paying for my fare. I turnstile jump, too, but the fine if you get caught is huge. And asking for a swipe works pretty often. It probably helps that I'm white, female, and not strung out.

I get on the M train headed to Brooklyn. The studio my mother's using is on loan from the gallery. Annika usually gives it to out-of-town artists who need a place in New York to get ready for a show, but she's been letting my mom use it for this past year. I haven't been out here since I first helped her move her stuff in and prepare her materials last fall, and when I emerge from the subway station, it takes me a moment to get my bearings in the neighborhood and find my way to the old brick warehouse building. (I've probably been to Brooklyn five times in my life. It's basically a foreign country.) The door downstairs isn't locked; I go right in and clomp up the metal stairs, which clang and tremble under my knock-off platform Chucks.

I feel a sudden rush of guilt that I haven't been out here to see the work yet. I used to love hanging out at her old studio, back before her illness. She showed me her techniques, set me up with my own easel, gave me drawing and painting lessons—always so excited, like she was sharing her juiciest secrets with me. But I've been busy this year, focused on keeping my own things afloat, balancing jobs and school. Plus she hasn't invited me out here, so there's that. Probably she doesn't want me looking at Wolfwood, paranoid about those stupid nightmares.

The space is on the third floor. I knock on the grimy metal door. No answer. I knock harder. Still, nothing. I came all the way out here and missed her? Shoot.

I brought the portfolio with me since she needs the drawings as reference for the paintings. Might as well drop it off.

My mother is a disaster when it comes to losing stuff—keys especially—so I've kept an extra set of hers since I was a kid. After fishing them out of my bag (and finding the phone charger hiding there, too—oops), I unlock and pull open the door. Late afternoon light washes the room in an orangey glow. It smells like stale coffee. The studio has two rooms: this smaller one is more of an office, with a couch and desk; the larger inner room, where she paints, is through another door that's closed at the moment.

"Mom?" I call out, knocking on it. Silence.

As I turn the doorknob, I have a moment of wondering whether this is okay, going into the studio where she's been working, seeing the paintings for the first time without her. But my hands are moving faster than my brain, and before I make a decision, I've already pushed the door open and flipped on the light.

The room gleams. White. Bright white.

I look back and forth, blinking in the glare of fluorescence.

White because . . . the walls are empty.

There's a big wooden worktable with paints and brushes on it, a utility sink in the corner with rags draped over the side, and an enormous roll of watercolor paper on the floor. But the walls are empty.

Then—*thank god*—I spot a giant folder made of white foam-core, the kind she keeps her paintings in before they're framed. I release the breath I was holding, wrangle the folder onto the table, undo the tape around the edges, and flop open the front piece of foamcore. On top is a large sheet of the watercolor paper with a grid penciled lightly on it—probably one of the ones I prepared for her months ago, when we were getting her set up. The sheet behind it is the same—blank except for the grid. I look at the next and the next and the next. None of them have any actual painting done on them. Just the grids. There are five sheets altogether. When I helped her make them we made eight, so there must be three that are painted on somewhere.

I assumed she'd be much further along by now. She's been working out here for nine months already. The show opens in only ten weeks.

I moisten my dry lips and head back into the other room.

I search the small space—under the desk, behind and under the couch—and don't see anywhere the three paintings could be hidden.

Maybe she took them to the framer? I'd be surprised if she did that before finishing all of them, but I can't think of any other reason they wouldn't be in the studio. So that must be it. She finished three paintings and they're at the framer.

You sure about that?

I turn my attention to a heap of mail on the desk. Mostly junk mail for people I've never heard of—previous tenants, I guess. Catalogues for art and craft supply stores. Postcards announcing exhibitions. Among the junk, though, are a few envelopes from the gallery, addressed to my mother. Unopened. Addressed to her at home, so she must have brought them out here.

I open one. It's from last year. At first I don't quite understand what I'm reading, just that it's something to do with the studio. Then I realize: it's a bill for one month of studio rent. For $1,500. Wait . . . what?

I shuffle through the other mail, finding all the previous unopened bills, rip one open, pull it out, read the total, find another, rip, pull, read, rip, pull, read, waiting to see one that lists the amount owed as $0, because this was all a mistake. But the only thing they show is a steady accumulation of charges. I thought the studio was free. I didn't know we'd have to pay! These *must* be a mistake.

I'm standing, clutching the most recent one, a pit in my stomach, when my phone goes off. The alarm, reminding me about babysitting.

This isn't happening.

My mother has made some paintings. They're at the framer. And there's an explanation for the bills. There's an explanation for all of this.

Chapter Four

I try to stay focused on toddler Jaden—not very successfully, despite how adorable he is. We play with his elaborate wooden train set and read books, but I keep getting up and looking out the floor-to-ceiling windows to the sidewalk below.

The view from this spot is painfully familiar. This was actually *our* apartment until I was thirteen. When we lived here, it was a homey, unrenovated tenement apartment with an old clawfoot bathtub in the kitchen, hissing steam radiators, and chipped, lumpy bright yellow paint on the walls. After my mother kept losing all those jobs, and we had trouble with the rent, the landlord kicked us out and converted it into this sleek, modern place. Now we live in the building's mildewy basement, off the grid and totally illegal. Every time the landlord (AKA "the Asslord") calls, I'm petrified that he's kicking us out again.

Finally, I see my mother coming up the street. She's as tall as I am, with dark hair, a swanlike neck, and long, bare arms decorated with scattered tats from her early East Village days. When she's at the stoop, I tap on the window until she notices me. She waves. I gesture for her to come upstairs, somewhat reluctantly. I want answers, but I also don't, because right now I can still believe my own version. *The paintings are at the framer. The paintings are at the framer.*

Minutes later there's a knock on the door. I leave Jaden playing on the living room rug and let her in.

"Hi, honey." She hugs me tight, the way she always does, as if she hasn't seen me in years. The strength of it calms me. I squeeze her back.

"You're okay?" I say, leading her to the living room. "The migraine didn't get bad, I guess?" There are dark circles under her eyes, but that's not unusual for her.

"Caffeine helped." She holds out a small crinkled plastic bag. "For you. I saw it in the window and Parker let me trade my ugly jacket for it. She said to say hi."

"Mom, you need a jacket." I reach into the bag and discover an army-green tee that says FEMINIST in shiny gold letters from our favorite secondhand store nearby. I've wanted one like this since they were first popular.

"I love it. Thanks." I give her another quick hug.

"Zo-wee!" Jaden squeals.

"Hi, little man." She kisses him on top of his baby Afro. Jaden's mom died of cancer last year—I think that makes my mom feel a special bond to him.

"So . . . where've you been?" I ask carefully, as we both sit cross-legged on the carpet.

She drives a train car onto Jaden's pudgy foot. He giggles. "What do you mean?"

"I went to the studio. You weren't there."

She looks over at me. "You went to the studio?" I can't read the expression in her golden-brown eyes. "Why?"

"I thought you were there. So . . . you've made paintings, right? I didn't see any."

"You went *into* the studio? Without me?"

"Are they at the framer?" I ask, trying not to sound accusatory.

"That's my private space, Indigo."

"Sorry. But can you tell me where the paintings are?"

She turns her attention to Jaden again. "This isn't something for you to worry about. You have enough going on."

"Mom, you've made some of the paintings, right?"

Silence.

"Mom?"

She still doesn't look at me. "I'm not going to do it."

"Do what?"

"The show." She runs a train back and forth in front of Jaden. "What color's the choo choo, little man? Blue?"

I must be misunderstanding her. "What do you mean?"

"Wed!" he squeals. "Twain wed. Zoe siwwy."

"Ah, right," she says. "Red. Smart boy!"

"Mom, I don't . . . What do you mean? Of course you're doing it."

She shakes her head. "Artists don't go back in time."

"What?"

"*Wolfwood*. It's old. No one wants an artist to go back to old work."

"Mom, they do!" I say, reaching for her hand. Stupid me—I should have *started* with the news. "Listen! I haven't told you. The collectors—the ones from this morning?—they're going to buy a painting. For ninety-six *thousand* dollars! And maybe a second one, too! That's why I went to the studio—to tell you."

Her blank expression doesn't change.

"They want to buy one!" I say again, as if she's hard of hearing. "For ninety-six *thousand* dollars! Isn't that amazing?"

She shrugs. I let go of her hand.

"That money doesn't surprise you?" I say.

No response.

"Wait . . ." My thoughts flicker back to the gallery. "Do you know why Annika would have said something about an auction? About the price being different there?"

She doesn't want to answer. I can tell by the way she presses her lips together.

"You know I can probably look online and find out," I say.

"That's why Annika wanted to do the show," she finally admits. "One of the old paintings sold at auction."

"Did you get money from it?"

Hurt flashes in her eyes—the first sign of emotion I've seen. "Of course not. I'd have told you. Only the collector who sells the piece gets money. Well, and the auction house."

"Oh. Okay, so . . . how much did it sell for?"

"I don't know. Two hundred, or something."

"Thousand? Two hundred thousand?"

She doesn't correct me.

"So, you knew how much this show could earn you, and you still . . ." I can barely say it. ". . . you still don't want to do it?" I pause, but she doesn't respond. This is impossible. She can't really be saying this. "I don't understand. Because obviously people *do* want these paintings. Right? So . . . what's the problem? Please tell me this isn't about my nightmares." Jesus, I'll kill her if it is.

"No," she says firmly. "It has nothing to do with you." She picks up a piece of the wooden train track and connects it to another one. "I can't do them. I tried."

"What do you mean you tried?"

"Just that. Can we stop talking about this?"

"You've already done the drawings. You did them more than twenty years ago!" My voice rises. I struggle to bring it back down. "All you have to do is turn the drawings into paintings."

"I worked on a few. I did. But I got so tired. And concentrating that hard made my head hurt."

"Did you try working for just a little at a time?"

"I couldn't do it," she snaps, looking at me again. "I just told you."

It takes all my self-control not to snap back. But my mother, when she gets defensive like this, it's because she's actually mad at herself. Inside, she's beating herself up, and the wrong word can send her into a downward spiral where she thinks she's the worst person ever. Since we've lived in the basement, there've been stretches where she's barely gotten out of bed for weeks—as if her colorless pencil-sketch self is being erased completely. She doesn't call it depression—seems like that to me, though. And it's terrifying. I always try to be careful not to do or say anything that might set her off.

Jaden bangs the floor with a caboose. I pry it out of his hand. Usually I would drop whatever subject was making her feel bad or assure her that everything was okay. But this . . .

"You do realize how big a deal this money is, right?" My voice is as gentle as I can make it. I still hear the edge, though.

"Of course," she says. "But art isn't like that, Indigo. You can't force it. I was out of control, back when I made them. The drugs. Drinking . . ."

Nothing she's saying is adding up or making sense. "Who cares? You weren't high when you did the paintings, were you? It's not like you have to do drugs to paint well."

"No . . ."

"So what does it matter? Can't you just *do* them?"

"I already told you. No, I can't just do them. Now drop it, Indigo."

Frustration is threatening to overwhelm me. There's a low roar in my ears. I start arranging Jaden's train cars in color groups.

"Nine months," I say, placing a blue car next to another blue car. "You've supposedly been working out there for nine months. When were you going to tell me? Tell Annika?"

"It's Annika's fault," she says. "The stupid idea, going back in time. You can't go back to who you were. I'm sorry I didn't tell you sooner. I should have."

All of a sudden, I remember the other issue and look back up. "What about the rent for the studio? We don't owe that, do we? It's free, right?"

Those lips, pressed together again. "It's on account. The money will be taken out when she sells a piece."

"But there won't be any pieces to sell!"

No response.

"Book!" Jaden cries. "Book!"

"Mom, there won't—"

"Indigo, this discussion is over. I'm the parent here. I'll figure something out."

I inhale deeply and focus on Jaden, scared what she'll see in my eyes.

"Okay," I manage to say. "You know, it's late. I have to put Jaden to bed. You better go."

Chapter Five

By the time Jaden's dad gets home, I'm the kind of worked up that means I'll never fall asleep—a raging mix of furious, confused, panicky ... I don't want to be in the same room with my mother, lying awake, getting more and more anxious and angry. Even if I pull the curtain around my mattress, I'll still feel her breath in the air.

So I text Josh. And when I reach the first floor of our building, instead of going down to the basement, I go out the front door and down the stoop. It's a warm night. I jog the two blocks west, past groups of laughing twentysomethings going to bars and restaurants and a couple of familiar homeless men slumped against buildings, who I'd give my change to if they weren't passed out. I text again to tell Josh I'm here. He buzzes me in. I take the elevator to the sixth floor, and he's waiting in the hallway, outside the door to the comfortable one-bedroom apartment he lives in with his parents and brother and occasionally his daughter, who was born last year, when he was nineteen. Not that she's ever here when I am.

"Anyone awake?" I whisper.

He shakes his head. "Pop's at work. Mom and Kev asleep."

The living room is dark except for a Yankees game on the TV. I push him onto the couch and get on top of him, my knees on either side of his narrow hips, lean down and kiss him.

"Not wasting any time, eh, Serra?" he says quietly. But, as usual, I'm not here to talk. I'm here to not talk. To not think.

"Shh," I say.

He tastes like Doritos. It makes me hungry. When was the last time I ate? I should have eaten while babysitting, but I felt too sick.

He runs his hands up and down my sides, grabs my butt and rubs it with his thumbs.

You're screwed. She's not going to do those paintings. She's racked up thousands of dollars of new debt. You're going to lose the apartment, and there's no one to get you out of this. No one to help. No one, no one, no one.

I try to silence the voices in my head by pulling Josh's shirt up over his chest and watching as he takes it the rest of the way off. He's got nice muscles to distract me. I lean forward and kiss him again, press my hips against him. He lets out a soft moan. I move side to side slightly, building up more of a humming sensation, ignoring Josh for a minute to get myself where I need to be. I'm sitting up, eyes closed, putting all my focus between my legs. Mmm . . . that's it. The warmth pours through me like syrup, relaxing me. I bend down to kiss his lips or neck now and then, but mostly I let the sweetness build.

Eventually, Josh takes charge and smoothly maneuvers us so he's on top. I let him, because I like how confident and capable he is. My only other experience—with a boy who bussed at the same restaurant I did last winter—was a comedy of errors. Like puppies trying to do ballet. *Not* relaxing. With Josh, I can forget about everything and feel good for a little while—the whole reason I'm here.

I wriggle out of my underwear while he puts on a condom.

After we're done, we lie squished together on the couch, Josh's arm flung over me, uncomfortably heavy.

I toy with the idea of staying the rest of the night, but then I start to feel a painful pressure in my rib cage. My mother is home alone, knowing that she's disappointed me, knowing we're in big trouble. She pretends like she isn't worried, but she is. I know because I feel her emotions, physically. There's a string tied between our hearts, and when she's upset, it's like her heart is a spool and the string gets wound and wound around it, pulling at mine, pulling me toward her and making my own chest ache. I won't be able to sleep here any more than I'd sleep at home. All I'll do is worry. I'll keep picturing her there and keep feeling her desperation. I need to *do* something. I need to help her.

I wonder if her trouble painting is like stage fright. Performance anxiety. I have no doubt that her physical problems are an issue, but if it were just that, she'd have told me months ago. Maybe she's so scared that the paintings won't be good enough that she can't even bring herself to do them. I could see someone feeling that way in her position, with all this pressure and her not having picked up a brush in all these years. Annika's gallery is pretty prominent, and the show will get reviewed and talked about. I can see how overwhelming that would be, especially since her last exhibitions weren't successful.

I think back to her initial reluctance to do the show, her worry about my nightmares . . . I bet that was just an excuse. I bet she was just scared of failing. My heart clenches tighter at the thought.

Maybe I can figure out a way to ease her into it. There's still time before the opening. A couple of months. This show is going to happen—there is no other option—so those paintings need to be made. I need to sort of . . . trick her into forgetting about her anxiety.

What if you can't get her to do it? a little voice whispers in my ear.

Once my thoughts have gotten that push, I'm rolling downhill. No paintings. No show. No money. No way to pay back everything we owe. I'll have to drop out of school, won't I? For the last couple of years, because I was usually working two jobs, I routinely stayed up past 1:00 A.M. to finish homework, brain never processing right, falling asleep in class, barely passing even with all that studying. I can't work more than I have been during the week and still make it through senior year. And how soon will Annika want us to reimburse her for the studio rent? I remember her voice on the phone, talking to that guy, telling him she was going to call her lawyer. And my mother. Her guilt. It's going to consume her. If she can't do this show, if she digs us into this hole we can't get out of, even deeper than the hole we're in now, how is she ever going to look at herself? She'll *never* get out of bed. And what will happen if the Asslord kicks us out again?

A scene flashes in my head. The bathroom at the East Side Women's Shelter. I'm thirteen years old, sitting on the toilet peeing, pants around my ankles. That broken door slamming open. That woman—that woman I'd never even seen before—psychotic, who thought I was someone else, her fists coming at me, chunky metal rings glinting on them, coming at my mouth, my nose—

No.

I push Josh's arm off me and sit up. Touch my teeth, making sure they're there. Blink away the memory. I can't breathe here. I can't stay. I need to start fixing this. Now. An hour ago. A day ago. Months ago. I should have asked my mother more questions, should have made sure the work was going okay. I should have gone to the studio a long time ago. What was I thinking, letting this happen? I should have known. I should have been able to tell from the way my mother was acting. I usually read her so well. I was trying to give her space. Didn't want to bug her. (Although . . . was it wrong of me to want to believe she was actually taking care of things for once?)

"Hey," Josh says. "Don't go. We got time."

"I have to." I reach for my underwear. I hate taking the subway to Bushwick this late, alone, but at least it will be easy to jump the turnstile with no one around.

Josh sits up and shifts to face me. "Indigo?"

"What?"

He runs his hand through his short hair. "There's this thing . . . My cousin Tasha, she's getting married."

"Yeah?"

"Marrying a guy whose mom owns a ribs place, so good food, at least. Decent DJ, prob'ly. In the Bronx."

Oh. Wedding. *Good food, fun, music* ... But ... no. Going to a family event with a guy would be a whole other thing. And a wedding? Forget it. I'd love the meal, but not worth it.

"I'm really busy," I say as I pull on my shirt.

"We all are, right? Still gotta have fun."

"I know. But I have work and babysitting and other stuff." It's true. And I absolutely can't deal with this being more than an occasional hookup. Not now. "And to be honest, family stuff isn't really my thing."

"Whatever," Josh says. "It's cool. Kayla's been around. I'll ask her."

"Cool," I say, glad he got the point, even if it does sting a little.

This is why it works between us.

At the studio, running on adrenaline and coffee and a day-old bagel from the twenty-four-hour bodega across the street, trying not to be scared by being in this building alone at night, the first thing I do is re-read the studio rent bills, in case there's anything I missed, like a clause saying that if no paintings are sold the debt is erased. Of course, though, there's nothing like that. Just a steadily building number that will reach $18,000 by the time she's been using the studio for a year, in September. Eighteen thousand dollars more debt. *Breathe, Indigo.*

Next, I go into the room where she "paints." I pace around and around the table with her supplies, noticing now that the brushes and tubes of watercolors are covered with a layer of beige dust.

Okay. Like I was thinking earlier, what I need to do is figure out how to boost her confidence. Help her get past her fear of failure or whatever it is.

I need to . . . start one for her. Start a painting. Get it going. Make her see that it can be done. Maybe it's like climbing a mountain—it looks too high. But if I get her partway up, the rest won't seem so unimaginable.

I know her process. She wasn't doing Wolfwood paintings when I used to spend time at the studio, but the technique is the same, probably. First she does the detailed sketch, which I already have—those ones I brought to the gallery. The sketches are done on gridded paper, so she can use that as a guide when she copies the drawing onto the larger piece of watercolor paper. Then she does the painting with watercolor and gouache.

Anyway, I don't even need to do any actual painting. Just get the drawing transferred. Make her feel like she's partway up the mountain. All she'll have to do is fill in the colors.

Despite an almost manic energy coursing inside me, I need more coffee to keep my lead-heavy eyes open. I run back out to the bodega and get a large cup, which is only a little more expensive than a small, and fill it with half coffee/half milk and six sugars, to get some calories, too, all for the same price. I know I'm not sleeping tonight. Better keep up my energy.

Back in the studio, I lift one of the huge sheets of watercolor paper that's already gridded onto the worktable. I take out drawing #25 from the portfolio and pin it on the wall above the table, where it's easy to see, and scan the image.

In the first painting in the series—#1, done twenty-five years ago—four girls wake up in the Wolfwood jungle. From then on, each time one of them gets an injury from a monster attack, a clone of the girl appears in the next painting, bearing whatever injury the "original" girl got, and the original girl recovers. The clones have strips of their dresses wrapped around their wounds, holding their ravaged bodies together. By the end, an army of identical-looking girls—in varying states of bloodied, bandaged, and naked—is fighting back against the monsters, led by the four original girls. The monsters are led by that guy with long hair who looks sort of like Jesus. The Wolf.

In this image, #25, three of the clones are being roasted alive over a bonfire by an enormous orchid with petals as big as the girls' torsos. Nearby, two bloody clones are blindfolded and pinned to the ground by a thorny flowered vine. Another clone holds her own decapitated head, blood spouting out. In the foreground, a large group of them—held together by their bandages—is listening to the four original girls strategize. There are other scenes as well—lots of action happens in the one painting. Here and there are unobtrusive, handwritten comments: THE GIRLS MAKE A BUNKER. THE VINE LIES IN WAIT.

Copying the drawing in pencil shouldn't be *too* hard. I grew up taking those lessons from my mom, and she's helped me with my fashion sketches for years, teaching me about body proportions and gesture. Her style isn't very detailed—more like a comic or graphic novel illustration than a realistic image. So, copying the drawing seems doable. Right? Not to mention, what's the worst that can happen? I waste a piece of paper. Big deal.

I decide to start in the corner that has the girls being roasted alive. My hand is shaking a bit. I will it to stop. I concentrate on one square of the grid at a time, trying not to look at the whole image, instead breaking it down into shapes and negative space. Not thinking about charred flesh or sizzling skin. When I've drawn a group of four squares, I step back and see that it's not terrible, but it does have a bit of a disjointed quality. I think I need to work more as if I'm actually doing the drawing, not seeing it only as abstract shapes.

As I draw, I enter into a zone of focus, going back and forth between looking at the sketch my mother did and the larger version I'm creating. My breath evens out. I push away thoughts about what's happening in the picture.

I develop a steady rhythm, and it's working. I'm not sure I'd say it's in my mother's "hand," with all the subtleties of her gesture and stroke, but it looks like the drawing. And since she'll be the one to paint, it'll look even better later on. I feel more energized as the night passes, adrenaline coursing through me. I draw more quickly and confidently. The world of the story is coming to life. I don't even care that it's Wolfwood.

When I get to a section with the four original girls, I'm so in the zone that as I draw the tallest girl, I can almost feel the softness of her skin under my hand, can almost feel her tangled hair, and hear her talking to the other girls, discussing the plan for the next stage of the fight. In my frenetic, sleep-deprived state, words the tall girl might be saying echo in my head—"weapons," "danger," "flesh"— and then I wonder if I'm dreaming, and I shake my head a little and come back to the real world. Have to stay focused.

And I do. I work straight through until I reach the bottom right-hand corner and realize that it's finished. The entire three-and-a-half-by-five-foot drawing now exists. My eyes ache, my head is pounding. But stepping back to admire my work, I feel the satisfaction that comes with having been proactive. Holy shit—I *did* that!

When I walk into the outer room, I'm shocked to see the sky is a hazy morning blue. I check my phone. It's a little before 6:00 A.M. I was drawing for around six hours. No wonder my eyes hurt. I press my fingertips against them for a moment. *It's going to be okay*, I tell myself. *You took the first step. Mom will take it from here.*

The TV's quiet flicker is the only light in the basement, aside from the murky bit filtering in through our two tiny windows near the top of the front wall. My mother is lying on her side on the couch, facing the back of it, so I can't see her eyes. I can tell she's awake, though, from the tension in her muscles.

In the bathroom, I quietly move the dishes on the dish-drying rack out of the shower stall. I take a hot shower, change into boxers and a tank, and sit next to her in the dark, perched on the edge of the cushion. We stay there, both of us silent.

"I'm sorry," she whispers.

I lie down alongside her and put my arm around her and hold her tight. She's all bone and wiry muscles.

"I can't explain it," she says. "It's too hard. Everything is too hard."

"I know."

We're quiet for a long time, our breath syncing up. I think she's asleep. Then she says, "Where'd you go? I wanted to call—still can't find the charger."

I hesitate, not ready to tell her I did the drawing yet. I need to approach it carefully, when she's feeling stronger. "Friend's," I say. Not a complete lie. I was at Josh's for part of the time.

"Grace?"

". . . Mm-hmm." Okay, that is a lie. Grace is actually in California for the summer. But my mother's really protective when it comes to guys. Doesn't want the same thing that happened to her—a random pregnancy—to happen to me. She doesn't even know who my father is. Slept with guys she met at clubs while high during her partying days. Never saw any of them again. Not that she thinks I'd do that. But she thinks I'm too young to get involved. I try not to worry her.

"I should have told you I was having trouble," she says.

Yeah, I think. *You should have.*

"I kept hoping I'd figure something out," she says. "And then time just . . . passed."

I hold her a bit closer.

"I'm sorry I screwed this up. I'm so sorry I'm not a good mother anymore."

"Don't say that, Mommy." I press my face against her neck. She smells like sweat and unwashed clothes but also like that essential, impossible-to-describe mother scent. Comfort. "Don't ever say that. We'll be fine. Okay? We'll figure it out. I wouldn't want any other mother."

And I mean it, despite everything. The hardest times I've ever been through are the times I was separated from her: when she was in the hospital, and then after I got beat up at the shelter, when I stayed with Grace's family. I missed her so much during those months at Grace's. Sometimes when I saw her, it seemed like she hadn't slept or bathed in a long time, and she always had all her stuff with her. She said she was still staying at the shelter, but I was never really sure. I'd picture her sleeping on the subway or on a park bench . . . That string around my heart was pulled tight the entire time.

I haven't stopped worrying since.

As we lie here, my body spooned behind hers, I will myself to soak up her anxiety and self-doubt. I can handle it and she can't, and she's the one who needs to be strong. I need her to be okay and to do these paintings. So I hold her close and imagine it all seeping into me.

1989

Zoe and Colin's life in Tulum falls into a sunbaked rhythm.

Mornings are for painting. They bike to spots they've found while exploring and unfold their travel easels. Colin splits his time between his own painting and teaching Zoe watercolor techniques. Sometimes it's hard for her to concentrate, with his heat adding to the hot, wet jungle air. But Colin takes teaching her seriously, and in the end, luscious colors bleeding into paper seduce her, too.

Midday, they have lunch at Don Eduardo's, the cabana colony where they're staying. Tulum has almost no restaurants, just a few on the narrow highway that traces down the peninsula from Cancún, one taco cart in town, and snack stands outside the ruins. There's no choice of what to eat at Don Eduardo's, but the food is good and the small staff is friendly. After lunch, Colin is always productive: He rigs a better mosquito net or cuts down coconuts with a machete or goes spearfishing . . . He sleeps only a couple of hours at night and is never still during the day, like he's too full of life to waste a minute of it. Zoe mostly stays on the beach while he's gone, sketching and listening to George Michael or Prince tapes on her Walkman, daydreaming about their future together, trying not to feel lonely.

The time they spend together in the late afternoon and early evening is the magic time, for Zoe. Of course, painting is when she's most artistic. But there's something about the hours they spend exploring and discovering Tulum that makes her feel like an Artist.

One afternoon, while they're biking down a rutty dirt road, Colin notices an almost imperceptible break in a dense area of bushes. They hop off and push aside branches to uncover an overgrown path. Zoe follows him into the thicket, no idea where they're being led. Leaves and branches scrape her bare skin as they go deeper into the jungle. Just as she's getting nervous, a perfect blue cenote appears in the middle of all the green. A hidden water hole, like a sapphire dropped by a god. Long ropes hang from tall trees surrounding it, clearly there for climbing.

Colin immediately grabs one and starts up the tree, feet on trunk, hand over hand. It takes Zoe a moment to get the courage to climb one herself. But she does, and when she closes her eyes and jumps, there's a crystallized moment—airborne—of knowing the reward for bravery: Freedom. Invincibility. And then—splash!—giddy relief. She does it only once, but Colin climbs higher each time he goes up. Now jumping backward. Now flipping in the air. Fearless. Colin pushes everything he does as far as he can, even having fun. Zoe loves that about him.

Later that night, after their usual dinner at Don Eduardo's and drinking on the beach, they're lying in their separate hammocks in the dark, holding hands across the divide. As she drifts off to sleep, drunk on the day's romance, Zoe hears Colin say quietly, I'm never getting old, and she knows exactly what he means. If they keep living like this, being in love, flying like superheroes, making art—living like Artists—they'll feel young forever.

Chapter Six

I wake up to the sound of someone shrieking outside on the street. I'm disoriented, no idea what day or time it is. My mother's asleep, the TV off. I sit up and rest my throbbing head in my hands. Reorient myself. Check my phone: 10:43. Seems that after lying with my mom on the couch, I moved over to my bed and slept for three hours. I've trained myself to not need much sleep, but three hours is pushing it.

Today is Thursday. I'm working the closing shift. Need to be there at two.

I shuffle to the kitchen area. *Shit.* We're out of coffee. I can go without a lot of things, but I cannot exist without coffee. And I can't go to the store to buy it looking like this. No matter how tired I am, I never, ever leave the apartment without pulling together an outfit. Dressing like who I want to be that day. Who I want people to think I am.

After a quick scan of my clothing rack, I pull on a pair of wide, striped men's pajama pants that hang to the ground and a black bandeau that I made from an old Ramone's T-shirt. I cinch the pants paper-bag style with a gold belt. Twist up my hair and wrap a patterned scarf around my head. Add some sunglasses to hide the bags under my eyes. Today's look: East Village street meets Saint-Tropez. *On my way to chill with a mimosa, motherfuckers.*

I write a quick list of other groceries we need—almost everything, since it's the end of the month and our EBT balance is used up—and head out.

I have money from cashing my paycheck yesterday, but I still add up prices to the penny as I place items in my basket: milk, ramen, generic cornflakes, canned beans, rice ... The same things we always get that are cheap but filling and don't require much cooking. Even having done the math, I stiffen as the items are scanned at the register, watching the total go up and up and up. This happens every time I shop. I never relax until I'm outside, bags in hand.

Coffee, coffee, coffee ... a rhythmic chant with the slapping of my feet on the sidewalk on the way home. As I approach our building, someone is standing at the bottom of the stoop, staring up at it. Gray T-shirt, black knit cap. Kai? And some other guy is with him. I want to turn and run—I'm way too tired to deal with a conversation. But I'm also curious what the hell he's doing here. Although, *wait.* I stop walking. Maybe Annika knows there are no paintings. Maybe my mother called and told her. Called and canceled the show, and Kai is here to ... what? Demand money back for the studio rent or something? As I stand, frozen, I hear someone else shouting at me. Eddie, the super from the building across the street.

"Hey, hey! Lady Gaga!" he calls, waving.

I force a smile and wave back. Once—once!—when I was twelve or something, Eddie was sitting out front playing an old Gaga song, and I broke out in a lip sync and dance number that Grace and I had made up in her bedroom.

"No performance today?" he asks.

"Sorry!"

I wave again and turn toward our building. Kai is watching me, but I can't read his expression. I walk over, hiding my nerves behind the fixed smile and sunglasses.

"Hey," I say, casual. "What's up?"

"Don't worry," he says. "I'm not stalking you or anything."

"Didn't think you were. Till you said that."

"Right." He grins.

Okay, he's clearly not here as Annika's henchman. And—now I remember—I still have the phone charger, so my mother couldn't have called.

"So . . . what *are* you doing?" I ask, and glance at the other guy.

He's about my height or a little taller, lanky, with thick black hair flopping over his forehead and curling over his ears. Medium brown skin. Deep brown eyes and pink lips. Square jaw. Almost *too* good-looking, like he was made in a factory. Wearing a distinctive, silky navy tee with one neon-yellow sleeve.

"Hey," he says, with a tip of his chin.

"Friend Ravi," Kai says. "I was running errands for the gallery right around here, so figured I'd drop this off." He holds out an envelope addressed to my mom. "Couldn't find your buzzer or mailbox, though."

"Yeah, it's confusing." I don't explain that our buzzer says SUPER (and is broken, anyway) or that our mail goes under the stoop, not with the real tenants' mailboxes. "What is it?"

"What?"

"That." I flick the envelope. It's not the window type that those studio rent bills come in, thank god.

"Oh. Dunno. Saw it on the desk and knew I'd be right here, so . . ." Kai shrugs and hands it to me. "Could be a check? Diana was doing payments this morning, I think."

A check? Maybe those collectors already paid for one of the paintings?! But no, they clearly weren't about to do that without seeing the finished piece.

"Every time I see you you're giving me money," I joke.

"No surprise," Ravi interjects. "Kai always has to pay girls to talk to him." He drapes his arm around Kai's shoulders, emphasizing their height difference.

"Lucky you," I tell him, "getting to piggyback on it for free."

After a slight beat, he gives a half smile. "Ha. Truth."

I fold the envelope and slip it into my purse. "All right, so . . . thanks, Kai. See you." I start to head inside.

"We're going to lunch," Kai says. "Wanna come?"

I stop. "Lunch?" Even if I wanted to hang out with them, a restaurant meal would cost more than I budget for whole days. "Sorry. Gotta go to work in a bit."

"Where?" Kai asks. Ravi has turned his attention to texting.

"Stanton Füd?"

"Oh, no. The place with the umlaut?" His mock horror at the stupidity of the Fud's fake German word makes me smile.

"Unfortunately."

"We're getting pancakes at Clinton Street Bakery. Right nearby."

Ravi pockets his phone. "Forgot something at the house," he tells Kai. "We're walking back that way, yeah?"

"You live around here?" I ask him, surprised. He's the type of guy that's hard to miss.

"Moved in down there." He nods toward Avenue A.

"His mom bought a painting from the gallery," Kai explains. "I was over hanging it."

All of a sudden, something clicks. That distinctive T-shirt ... "Wait," I say to Ravi. "Tania Bawa's not your mother or something, is she?"

"You know her?"

Tania Bawa is this guy's mother?!

"I mean, no. Not her. But her clothes. Of course. And I knew she was moving into that place."

She's a totally famous fashion designer. Like, *legit* famous. One of the women in our building gets *Vogue* and I always take it from the recycling bin—Tania Bawa's stuff is pictured all the time. Everyone around here knew she bought a place at the end of the block. It was under construction for ages. She turned a small apartment building into one giant house.

"Yeah, only took a hundred years to finish the renovation," Ravi says, as if he read my mind. He studies me now with a little more interest. "Live on the block long?"

"Whole life."

"Like it?"

"Hey," Kai interrupts. "I'm hungry."

Ravi glances at him. "Relax. Just trying to figure out why you're scared of her."

"When I was a kid!" Kai says.

I snort. Ravi grins.

"Sorry about him," Kai says to me. "If you come to lunch, I promise he'll behave."

"Kai's treat," Ravi adds. "My mom gave him a fat tip." He pats the top of Kai's beanie. "And don't worry about the long wait at Clinton Street. I have ways."

"Um . . . let me take in these groceries, okay?" I can't believe I just said that, with the throbbing in my skull and the pain around my eyes and everything else. But I'm no dummy. I know how things work. And there's nothing bad about getting to know this guy who might be able to help me at some point, with all the people his mother must know. My big dream—on the rare occasions I let myself dream—is to have my own clothing brand. To make edgy, stylish stuff that normal people can afford, that doesn't exploit workers or kill the planet (hahaha—good luck, I know). This is the type of connection that most people in my situation would never get to make. And even though I probably have nothing in common with Kai and Ravi, I know how to talk to guys. Just have to avoid discussing anything real.

"Be right back," I say, as I head up the stoop, instead of using the outside basement door like normal. Our apartment can also be reached from the interior stairs.

"Oh," Kai calls after me, "if your mom's there, can you tell her to get in touch with Diana? I heard her complaining that Zoe hasn't answered something. She was really pissed."

"Diana?"

"The gallery director."

"Sure," I say. "No problem."

Inside, before going down into the basement, I sit on the staircase and call the gallery, knowing I'll keep worrying about it if I don't deal with it now.

As I wait for Diana to get on, I tear open the envelope. A check for nineteen dollars with a Post-it note: *Reimbursement for that studio light bulb. Sorry for delay.* Nineteen dollars. Well, it's not nothing.

"This is Diana," she says. "Indigo?"

"Hi. I heard you were trying to reach my mom," I say quietly. "She's at the studio, so can I help?"

"A couple of important things. I need an artist's statement so I can use it as reference for the press release. And an updated bio."

"Oh, okay."

"And we're doing an ad for the show in *ArtFocus* and need an image of a painting. When would be convenient for us to send a photographer to the studio? Maybe tomorrow?"

"An image of a painting?" I echo.

"We use a photographer named Ron. I can set it up or you can call him directly."

"Um . . . the thing is, my mom's working on a bunch of the paintings at the same time, so I don't think any are finished enough to be in an ad. Could you do an ad without a photo?"

"No," Diana says. "We use the same format for all our ads. Maybe a detail of one of the paintings? Not the whole thing? Or maybe a photo of your mother working? Sometimes we use studio shots like that."

I hesitate. "A detail might work." *What? No, it wouldn't!* "When would you need it by?"

"I'd have to have Ron there in the next few days."

"Oh. Well . . ." My mind starts spinning, thinking of ways to buy time. "The thing is, Zoe's really uncomfortable having people in the studio. Can she take the photo herself?"

"This isn't a selfie for Instagram." Diana sounds fully annoyed now. "It needs to be taken with a real camera by a professional. Maybe I should be speaking with Zoe about this."

"No, no. How about . . . She has a friend who's a photographer," I lie. "How about we get him to do it and send you some images? Is that okay?"

Silence. "Let me check." My head pounds while I wait. I lean against the wall, unbearably tired all of a sudden. Too tired to think about the impossibility of what I've just suggested. When she comes back, she says, "That should be fine, as long as they're good. I'll need to have them by Monday morning, in case we need a redo."

"Okay," I say. "No problem. I'll send you something by Monday."

Chapter Seven

After I tell Kai and Ravi I can't join them, I'm surprised to find my mother mending clothes instead of lying on the couch. She's wearing the same outfit from yesterday; still, out of bed and being productive is a good sign.

I wanted to give her more time to chill out before talking to her about going back to the studio, but if the gallery needs photos of a currently nonexistent painting by Monday, I need to figure out immediately how to make that happen. Thank god it can just be a detail.

"Indi?" she says, setting aside a sock she was darning. "Are you working for Trinity soon? There's a skirt seam that I can't really do by hand." Trinity has a workspace—a tiny room attached to a bar—with a couple of sewing machines to make the Etsy bags. If I'm there alone, I can use them for my stuff, too. It's the main reason I work for her.

"Yeah," I say, "leave it out."

"Thanks, honey. I'm going to wash my bras in a bit, if you want me to do yours."

"Sure."

I spend a few moments putting away the groceries and starting the coffee, but I can only stall so long. When the coffee's finished, I pour us both mugs and sit next to her on the couch.

"Hey," I say, "I need to ask you something."

"Mm-hmm?"

"You said you tried to make a couple of the paintings? Before you realized that it was hard to paint?"

She doesn't respond. Keeps her focus on the motion of the needle through fabric.

"The pieces you started, do they exist at all? I mean, even torn up or whatever?" Maybe enough of an image exists that we could use it for the ad.

"No."

I figured, but it still hurts to hear it.

"So, look," I say, animated. "I have an idea. Just . . . hear me out. What if I come out there and work as your assistant? I can do the drawings—you know, the outlines—and you can paint?" No response. "It'll be fun. And we can take a lot of breaks. I can give you massages and stuff." I rest my hand on her shoulder, but her eyes stay on her sewing.

"I told you already," she says. "I can't."

"But it would be fun, working on them together. I can do as much of it as you need me to."

"What did I just say?"

"I know, but if you got tired—"

"Indigo. I'm not talking about this."

My thin shell of patience is starting to crack. I take my hand off her shoulder.

"I know you might be scared, of the criticism and stuff. But this show has to happen."

Now she sets aside her sewing and looks at me. "We already had this conversation. And this is the last time I'm going to say it. I'm not doing the show. Do you understand?"

"But if I help—"

"I don't want your help!" she snaps. "I don't want anything to do with Wolfwood! Do you hear me? Don't ask me again!"

"This is such bullshit," I mutter, pressing my fingertips against my forehead. "Even for you this is crazy."

"What was that?"

"Nothing."

"If you have something to say to me, just say it."

"I said, this is bullshit!" The words explode through the thin shell, propelling me up to stand. "All you have to do is make some stupid paintings! Just stick a brush in some paint and put it on the paper! Do you understand that?" Silence. What the fuck is wrong with her? It's like she won the lottery and won't walk down the street to cash the ticket! "Forty-eight thousand dollars! At least! Forty! Eight! Thousand! Dollars! For ONE painting!" I can't stop. "You're always saying you're sorry you haven't done better for me. Well, here's your chance. Here's your chance to not have your teenage daughter pay all of the bills! Just get off the couch and *do* something for once!"

My words shatter the air.

But her expression doesn't change. It's like she's been waiting for me to say this.

"I'm so sorry, Mommy. I didn't mean that."

She nods. "Yes, you did."

We keep staring at each other, eyes locked, neither of us speaking. Both of us knowing that she's right.

I'm on the edge of tears throughout my entire shift at the Fud. When the shift is over, I go out to the studio instead of home. Once there, I give myself a minute. I sit on the couch with my head in my hands. No tears come, despite the exhaustion, frustration, and horrible, horrible guilt. I have the right to be angry at her, but I should have known better than to say those mean things. Not only did I hurt her, but I also destroyed any chance that she'll work on a painting before Monday.

It's good that I'm not crying, because the fact is that I don't have time for emotion. Of any sort. Nothing that happened changes the basic situation. Yes, I'll have to find a way to mend things with my mother. But I also have to deal with *Wolfwood*.

I can't dwell on this or second-guess myself. There's only one possible next step: I need to try to paint a section of the piece myself. A section that I can (somehow) photograph for Diana to use in the ad. This probably won't work, I realize that, but at the moment, it's the only option I see, so I'm just going to try. The worst that happens is that I ruin the drawing I already spent all that time on.

Telling Diana there's nothing to photograph is not an option.

This show is happening.

I scan the drawing for the section I think would work best, and my eyes immediately focus on an area with the four original girls. The girl with long, straight hair is holding the girl with a braid, who's injured. The tall one, with wavy hair, is slashing a monstrous vine, protecting the others. The one with bangs is pointing into the distance.

There's a large toolbox-like container on the worktable filled with tubes of watercolor and gouache in all different colors. There are also little plastic pots with paint in them (dry now), labeled with numbers. I study them for a moment, trying and failing to figure out what the numbers mean.

One of the most important things is that the colors I use have to match the colors my mom used in the old paintings. Like, each of the four girls wears a different-colored dress, and their clones are bandaged in matching ones. Obviously, since this painting is part of the series, the dresses need to look the same. Before I get frustrated about how I could ever match colors from memory, I remember that we brought a box of books out here when we moved my mom in last fall, and there were old exhibition catalogues in it.

Sure enough, one of the exhibition catalogues is on the shelf right underneath the table. *Zoe Serra*, the cover announces in big letters—the same catalogue I grabbed off our bookshelf when I was little and saw Wolfwood for the first time. When I crack the spine now, the pages fall open to a spread of one of the paintings with notes written in the margins. My mother's handwriting. There's also a scrap of watercolor paper wedged between the pages. I take out the scrap, which has blotches of various paint colors in rows, with handwritten notes next to each. It takes only a moment of deciphering before I inhale sharply, excited. This is a numbered chart of colors she's already mixed that are in the pots here on the worktable. The spread in the book is labeled with the same numbers, so it's extra clear what goes where.

I quickly realize that she didn't get around to mixing *all* the different colors in the painting. Not nearly. But she's mixed the colors of the girls' dresses, the acid green of a certain type of vine, the pink of a hibiscus-type flower. She even labeled the chart with notes about which colors she mixed together to make the final versions: *carthamus pink/purple lake* for one and *ultramarine/phthalo blue* for another . . .

I decide to begin with the plant monsters that surround the girls; that seems easier than doing one of the girls themselves. First, I set up my materials: a jar of water, a plastic palette with individual wells to mix the paints (like a baking tin for mini-muffins), more scrap paper to test the colors. I choose a brush with sable bristles that I know is my mother's favorite type because I was there when she bought it at the art store. I remember because it cost eighty dollars—for this tiny thing! I couldn't believe my mom was buying it, but she said that good brushes made a big difference, and Annika was paying for the materials. Yet another thing we'll probably owe her for.

I start swirling water and paint in a palette well for the stem of a giant orchid. My first tests are too watery and timid, but finally, I come up with what seems like a good base layer. I fill up my brush and rest the tip against the paper. All at once, paint pools across too big an area, spreading quickly past the borders of the stem onto everything around it. I fumble for a nearby paper towel, mop up as best I can. It still leaves a light green stain. Shit. Hopefully I'll be able to make it work anyway, painting over the slight stain with other colors. Taking a breath, I start again.

This time, I make sure the brush has less paint, place it on the paper, and stroke it down the stem. I do it as quickly as possible, to keep continuity of color in this one area. When the orchid stem has a first layer, I rinse my brush in the water jar and mix up the bluish green for the heart-shaped leaves on a different plant. I have a better feel about how much paint to load on my brush and blot off only two small areas where the color strays.

I develop a rhythm, and soon it's as if my hand is working on its own. Like my body knows something I don't: the right pressure of brush on paper, the way to pull the paint toward me in a smooth motion . . . I do all the different green areas first. Just the base layers, which I'll shade and make more vibrant after I have other areas painted in. Next, I move on to the petals, and as I paint, I imagine the thick, syrupy smell of the flowers—grotesque, just like they are. Almost rotten. The perfume hangs in the air around me.

By the time the plants and flowers are all filled in with the right base colors, I'm beginning to wilt, even with the adrenaline that's been keeping me going. But I can't break for a coffee run—I still have so much to do.

I need to move on to the girls.

I start with the one who has wavy hair and a white dress. After mixing her pale olive-yellow skin color, I load up the brush and place the pointy tip on her forehead and begin filling in her face, careful to paint around her eyes so they stay bright white. As the color soaks into the fibers, I smell something new: burning. It's so sharp and strong that I quickly check the other room to make sure nothing in there is on fire. Nothing is, of course, so I go back to work, wiping my forehead before starting. The air in here has turned hotter and more humid. I add purple for the bruise under the girl's eye, a touch of pink to her cheeks. My brush touches her skin like I'm putting blush on my own face. I feel the soft stroke of the sable. Next, the gold of her irises, delicate pinpricks of color. Shouts echo in my ears. She blinks at me. Wait, no—of course she doesn't. She couldn't. I close my eyes and pinch the bridge of my nose. Reset. The girl did not blink. But with my eyes closed, the shouts grow louder. The sharp burning smell fills my head and lungs. Coughing, I open my eyes. A burst of color flashes before me: green leaves, broken sunbeams, smooth gray palm tree trunks—the landscape flickers in and out. And then . . . it's all around me. Dense foliage. The leaves rustle. She's talking, the girl. No, *I'm* talking. *I'm* the girl. I'm shouting, calling out. The acrid fumes sting my nose and voices fill the air.

The girl in blue appears, the girl in purple limp in her arms. "Help!" Blue calls to me.

A vine surges toward them from above. Pure instinct, I lunge for it with my blade and—*thwack*—slice it clean off. It lands on the ground and convulses. I run to them.

"Where's she hurt?" I say, gathering a clean leaf to press on the wound. The girl in blue indicates the other girl's leg, slashed to the bone. I press the leaf against it to stop the bleeding, then reach for a thin dead vine on the ground and wrap that around it. We're in the shadow of a massive, anxious palm tree, its fronds trembling. To one side, a pink flower's petals surround a mouth with sharp yellow swordlike pistils. Liquid drips from the mouth. The flower shifts, and I keep my eyes on it while also tending to the girl's leg. The air is thick. Swampy.

The girl in red emerges from the foliage. "What are you doing?" she says in an angry whisper. "It's too dangerous to stop here." As if on command, another vine attacks and I thwack it off.

"See?" Red says.

"She was bleeding too much," Blue says.

Screams interrupt us. Inhuman wails pierce the heavy air.

"That's a lot of us," Red says. "We need to keep going. Stick to the plan." She points toward the horrible sounds.

I don't know what she means but know I shouldn't ask, should just go along, be helpful.

"Can you walk?" I ask Purple.

She shakes her head. Sweaty tendrils of reddish-blond hair stick to her face. "Not yet. Piggyback?" Her eyes light up.

I lean forward, bend my legs. As soon as Purple's warm weight is on top of me, I stand. Her arms wrap around my shoulders. "Okay," I say. "Let's go." I follow Red, running as best I can, Purple's body jostling against my back, no idea where we're going. The wails get louder. Foliage gets denser. *Smack, snap, snag,* the leaves and branches slap and catch us, even though these ones aren't monsters.

My nose fills with a sick perfume. Rot. Burning . . . The rancid smell squeezes the back of my throat. I gag, double over in disgust, the injured girl heavy on top of me. Charred flesh, that's the smell.

The ground wobbles under my legs. Carnival colors of leaves and petals swirl around me, closing in, dizzying. I have to pull myself together. No time to be sick.

Beep! Beep! Beep!

Siren. Fire alarm, for the flames under those poor girls whose flesh is burning. No. Not a fire alarm. *Beep! Beep! Beep!* I look up. No leaves, no flowers. A white room.

My phone. Ringing.

I blink, reach for the phone, ignore the call when I see it's an unknown number. Did I . . . did I fall asleep standing up? I struggle to make sense of things. Realize the brush is still in my fingers. I set it down. I'm so groggy, my brain feels sticky and swollen. Hazy memories of a weird dream—of jungle and running—evaporate before I can grab on to them.

I close my eyes and press my fingers against the lids. Rub my temples. When I open my eyes, they go straight to the painting on the worktable. My breath catches. A section about the size of a placemat is completely finished. All four of the girls, the monsters around them . . . I don't remember doing anything after the base colors of the girl in white's skin and the details of her face. I check the palette, and sure enough, all the colors I would have used are there in the wells. How . . . ? I must have been so in the zone, so caught up in the moment, I didn't even feel myself doing it. Maybe I really was asleep? No, that's impossible. Of course, being that "in the zone" feels impossible, too. But maybe . . . maybe this is what it's like, when you really focus on something artistic? I've seen my mother paint, seen her lose herself. She'd be so focused she'd block out everything else. Although . . . she never lost track of where she was and what she was doing. She'd block out a knock on the door, maybe, but not a question from me. Her mind always stayed in the studio.

No, that's not what this was.

This was exhaustion. The vivid hallucinations of total exhaustion. How much have I slept in the last forty-eight hours? Three hours, maybe? That's nothing. I'm surprised I can still stand.

And does it even matter? Does it matter what kind of weird headspace I found myself in? What matters is that I can paint. There, on the paper, is a painted area big enough for a magazine page.

The face of the girl in white looks back at me from the center of it.

Flushed, glowing. Almost alive.

Not only can I paint . . . I can paint just like my mother.

1989

One morning, Zoe comes out of the darkness of the cabana into the already strong sun, and instead of seeing the wide spread of empty sand as usual, she sees three girls with backpacks, asleep on the beach, their long hair fanned out like halos—two wheat blond, one strawberry blond. The other tourists in the cabanas aren't too friendly (they're mostly European or Canadian, and very cliquey), but something about these girls draws Zoe to them: their colorful clothes, a beat-up guitar case, the patches from other countries sewn on their packs . . . Zoe doesn't disturb them, just writes hi! in the sand.

Later that day, Itzel—a Mayan girl who works for Don Eduardo—tells Zoe that the three sisters arrived in the middle of the night, when the office was closed, and have now rented one of the cabanas.

The sisters are at Don Eduardo's for dinner. Zoe listens, entranced, as they describe their life to her and Colin. Lila is fifteen, Scarlet, seventeen, and Azul, eighteen. They've always been homeschooled, living with their parents in communal situations, first on one farm, then another, across the United States and overseas. Their mother is American and their father is Spanish, but Lila tells Zoe she's totally American. Her favorite things: Levi's, Tom Cruise, and Dairy Queen. Scarlet rolls her eyes and says Spanish culture is much more interesting. When the two start arguing, Azul puts an end to it: they're not American or Spanish, she says. They're citizens of the world.

Becoming friends with the sisters happens as naturally as Zoe's relationship with Colin did, as if she were waiting for them to arrive. They all sit together for meals now, and in the mornings, the sisters— who've rented a rusty old Jeep—drive Zoe and Colin anywhere they want, opening up a whole new range of places to paint. After lunch, when Colin likes to be productive, Zoe and the sisters hang out on the beach, and Zoe sketches them. She loves the challenge. Similar features—round eyes, long noses, pale skin with honeyed tans—but such different personalities. Azul: the quiet one, plays guitar and sings, is starting Oberlin College in the fall, and wants to spend every minute until then traveling; Scarlet: the bossy parent, in charge of sunscreen and budgeting and planning; and Lila: boy crazy and bubbly, with a huge sweet tooth, idolizes Zoe from the start. Scarlet and Lila bicker incessantly; Azul is the peacemaker—she doesn't say much, but when she does, everyone listens.

They're doing a project for their homeschooling while in Mexico, studying the Yucatán Peninsula. Because Zoe's been in Tulum for a couple of weeks, she's assigned the role of local expert, which is ridiculous, of course. But she does her best to tell them places to go that aren't written about in the guidebooks, like hidden cenotes and magical pockets of the Sian Ka'an preserve.

They all stay up late at night—with Colin, too—sometimes until dawn. Azul sings—Indigo Girls, Joni Mitchell, Carole King. Lila plays in the dark surf. Scarlet warns them all not to drink too much. One night, many beers in, Colin howls at the full moon. When Zoe tells the sisters that his last name is Wolf, Lila jumps to her feet in excitement. Lopez, the sisters' last name, comes from "wolf," too! From "lobo." They're *a wolf pack! For a split second, Zoe feels the sharp chill of being left out, but then Colin tells them all that Zoe is the real wolf, with her beautiful golden eyes. And he puts his arm around her, and the five of them howl at the moon until a man in a cabana yells at them angrily in Italian and they trade howling for (slightly quieter) laughter.*

As Zoe hugs Colin tight, she wonders if God made these wolf connections on purpose—a way to show her that, after years of being alone, she's finally found her pack.

Chapter Eight

I bring a cup of bodega coffee up to my lips, the subway rumbling beneath me as I head home for a much-needed shower after crashing on the couch at the studio for a few hours. I can't get the image of that girl's face out of my head, her eyes staring up at me from the paper. I can't stop thinking about the fact that *I* brought her to life.

My more logical mind is having a hard time reining in my thoughts, which are spinning out a wild scenario for what this might mean. Sure, all I was trying to do was paint an area big enough for the *ArtFocus* ad. But what if I don't stop there?

Look, my logical brain says, *it might have been a fluke, painting like that. You only did a small area. And you didn't even really do it on purpose—you were half asleep, almost hallucinating!*

But I wasn't asleep, clearly. Maybe it wasn't a fluke. Maybe I did know what I was doing. I spent all that time in her studio as a kid, took all those lessons from her. Art teachers at school have always said I'm talented. Maybe I just got in a zone and can do it again.

Well, even if you can paint like that, doesn't mean you can do what you're thinking of doing.

Why not?

Because that's nuts! She's the artist. You can't do her paintings for her.

Lots of artists have assistants help with their work. Even Da Vinci and Michelangelo did!

But you're thinking you might paint the paintings yourself, from start to finish. And lie about it to Annika. That's not "assisting." That's forgery. And when would you have time?

I'll make time. And I won't do all of them. I'll just keep painting until her mood changes. I can show her and she'll take over.

She won't ever go along with it. Not the way she's been acting. And she might have called Annika to cancel the show already.

Well, she hasn't called Annika, because I still have the charger in my bag. But the rest, I don't have an answer for. The way she's been behaving—so weirdly and illogically stubborn—I wouldn't be surprised if she refused to go along with it, if she refused to put her name on a *Wolfwood* exhibition even if she didn't have to make the paintings. And if she was worried about my nightmares before, what are the chances she'll let me do the paintings myself, knowing I'll be immersed in Wolfwood for weeks? She already said she didn't want my help.

Not to mention, who knows how she'll have reacted to those things I said to her yesterday. I've never been that mean to her in my life. *Just get off the couch and do something for once!* Whenever I think about it, I'm gripped by full-body nausea.

I take a long sip of coffee. Lukewarm and acidic.

I need to stay focused. Can't worry about the past. I said what I said. Repairing our relationship and convincing her to let me help aren't my immediate problems. First I need to figure out how to get a good enough photo of the painted area by Monday. One good enough that the gallery believes it's a professional photo of a painting by Zoe Serra.

She isn't home when I get there. No note or clues as to where she might have gone. I don't let myself dwell on the fact that she's probably not here because she doesn't want to see me. Hurts too much. Her phone is on the table—still dead, of course. I get the charger from my bag and plug the phone in, then, after a moment, flip it open and delete the gallery and Annika from her contacts and block the numbers, just to be safe.

What I really want to do now is go back to sleep, but my shift at the Fud starts in a few hours, and I have a lot to deal with before then.

As I hurry through showering and shaving before the meager hot water supply runs out, I mull over the problem of the photo for the *ArtFocus* ad. I can't afford to hire someone, obviously. And I don't have a camera to take it myself. I'm sure Josh doesn't have one I could borrow; he just uses his phone. The soapy water slides over the Band-Aid on my heel. I'm appreciating how smoothly it still lies against my skin when I think of Kai and Ravi. I wouldn't want to ask Kai—he's too connected to the gallery. But Ravi? Someone that rich definitely might have a camera. And he does live right here on the block, so maybe it's not that weird to ask, even though I barely know him. Weird, for sure. But *too* weird? The water goes cold.

I wrap myself in a towel, call the gallery, and ask for Kai.

"This is the first time the phone here has been for me," he says when he gets on the line. "I feel important."

"Glad to be of service," I say, smiling. "I was just wondering, could I have Ravi's number?"

There's a brief pause. "Aha," he says. "That request doesn't render my previous comment embarrassing at all."

I laugh. "Sorry. I'll call again about something else, if you want."

"No worries. Ravi's an irresistible force. I'm used to it. We've been friends since third grade."

"It's not that. I need to ask him a favor. Because he lives so close." For some reason I care that Kai believes me. Ravi's flashy good looks aren't my thing at all.

"Hmm . . . Well, hang on and I'll get it." He comes back a minute later and gives me the number.

"Excellent. Thanks."

"And, um, I'll give you mine, too. So you can text next time. You know, if you have gallery stuff I can help with."

"Oh," I say, feeling a hint of warmth at the offer. "Okay, yeah, that would be good."

After we hang up, I text Ravi, and before I know it he's on his way here, happy to loan me the camera he does indeed own. I wait out front under an ash-gray sky that's threatening rain, dressed in a navy jumpsuit, a hand-me-down from my friend Grace—the first thing I came across in my rush to be presentable. Concealer was the only makeup I had time for, and my hair is up in a wet twist. When I spot Ravi coming down the sidewalk, I realize how much I hate that I'm not as put together as I'd want to be for Tania Bawa's son. Like he's her proxy or something.

He's all right angles and comfortable rhythm as he walks, a combination of strength and ease. Clearly confident that this is *his* block, even though he just moved here. (If I didn't need to be nice, I'd have to point out that this is *my* block.) He has on another T-shirt designed by his mom, this one in deep magenta with a neon-yellow stripe down one side. A chunky black bag hangs on his shoulder.

He looks up at the sky when he reaches me. "About to rain. Should we go in?" He gestures up the stoop.

"Oh . . . no," I say, unprepared for the suggestion. "Our place is a bit messy right now. My mom wouldn't want anyone seeing it."

"Gotcha," he says. "My mom is so uptight, we finally had to hire a third housekeeper."

As he's talking, I notice someone walking up the street and remember that I have no idea where my mother is. She could turn the corner onto our block at any moment. "Actually," I say, "I think I just felt a drop. Let's go in the hallway."

I lead him up the stoop and in the front door, trusting that if my mom comes home she'll use the outside basement entrance as usual, instead of coming through here. We settle down on the narrow staircase that leads to the real apartments, close enough that I can smell his ample hair product. He unzips the bag, and a minute later I'm holding a heavy, professional-looking camera with enough buttons and dials for a command center at NASA. In the bag are three separate lenses, one of which is almost as long as my forearm, and a thick manual.

"Wow," I say, "you must be serious about photography." The camera feels precarious in my hands, like when I held Grace's tiny newborn sister.

"Not really. Just figured if I was gonna get a camera, might as well be a good one." He says it so casually, about something that's probably worth a few months of our rent.

"It looks super complicated. Think I'll be able to figure it out?"

"There's a function that makes it completely automatic." He points at a dial that has an "A" on it. "But you won't be able to make adjustments or anything. You know, focus, flash . . ."

"That would probably work," I say, having no idea if it would. Not like I have other options, though. "I'll give it a try. Thanks so much." I nestle the camera carefully in its bag, knowing that I'm going to be tense as hell until I've returned it in one piece.

I glance at him as I zip the bag up. "I love your shirt. I love all your mom's stuff. I'm really into fashion. I want to be a designer myself, eventually." *Subtle, Indigo.*

"You going to FIT or Parsons or somewhere?" He leans sideways against the wall as he asks. He has this way of tipping his head slightly so he's always looking down at me when he's talking.

"I'll be a senior this year. Not sure where I'm applying."

"Don't wait too long and pull a Kai."

"Hm?"

"Screwed up the college stuff. Although, wasn't his fault." An exasperated look crosses his face. "Don't get me started. Kai's like a little brother to me. I'm sick of people fucking stuff up for him."

Before I can say anything, a noise comes from above us on the stairs. The fourth-floor tenant who moved in a couple of months ago rounds the landing. I stand up and to the side, so she can get by.

"Oh, Indira." She smiles her smile that always looks like it hurts. "There's a stain on the carpet outside my place. If you could take care of it . . ."

Shit. What am I supposed to say with Ravi sitting right here? "Yeah, sure," I mumble.

"Today would be great."

After she's gone, Ravi gives a short, incredulous laugh. "What the hell? Why would she ask *you* that? She doesn't even know your name."

"She's kind of new," I say, scrambling for an answer that doesn't involve confessing that we do janitorial duties. "Anyway, sorry to borrow and run, or . . . send you running, I guess, but I've got work."

"Oh. Okay." He stands up and brushes off his pants, gives me a half smile.

I follow him outside and wait at the top of the stoop while he heads off.

"Thanks again," I say, when he's on the bottom step.

"No problem. You need to show me your favorite places in the hood sometime. Give me the tour."

"Sounds good," I lie.

"And whatever you do," he says with a grin, walking backward down the sidewalk, "don't clean that bitch's stained carpet."

My mother still isn't home by the time I leave for the Fud (having safely hidden the camera in the back of one of my drawers). Not knowing where she is makes me really uneasy. A leftover worry from the time she didn't come home when I was in sixth grade, and it turned out she'd fainted on the subway and was in the emergency room. People like to say, "I'm sure everything is fine," when you don't hear from someone. I learned back then that's not always true.

During my shift, the horrible things I said to her keep echoing in my head. By the end of work, my worry has snowballed into panic.

It's a humid night. The morning rain was only a slight squeeze of the sponge that's the sky. As I hurry home, sweat soaks the underside of my bra and the back of my tee. I made her feel so worthless. What if she went out and did something careless? Or what if she did something to herself on purpose? She wouldn't have, would she? My legs have a weird, rubbery feeling. A strange buzz.

I fumble with our locks. *Be here, be here, be here . . .*

And she is. Lying on the couch in the semidarkness, facing away from me.

Thank god. I squat down next to her and gently rest a hand on her arm. She shifts slightly and lets out a faint sound. She smells like alcohol. Usually, she drinks only on the anniversary of her father's death—an all-day binge followed by a couple days of recovery. I guess those things I said were mean enough for her to make an exception.

It's okay, I tell myself. *She's here. She's alive. It's okay.*

I let her sleep and get ready for bed myself. I pull the curtain we jury-rigged around my small area, turn on the little lamp next to my mattress, and lie down with the most recent issue of *Vogue*. As I slowly turn pages, tearing out good ones for a file I keep of clothes I like, I play a game, picking one dress for me and one for my mother to wear to the *Wolfwood* opening in September. Tonight, I choose a Rodarte for her and a Miu Miu for me. I imagine us walking into the gallery together, the space filled with fabulous people. We're arm in arm and everyone turns, and then I step back as everyone claps for my mother and she smiles, radiating light like in that old *New York* magazine photo. Then our eyes meet and I know she's saying thank you, because even though I've had to upset her along the way, I'm the one who spurred her to get going, who showed her she could do this. I'm the one who brought her back to life.

Chapter Nine

On the subway the next morning, I clutch Ravi's camera bag like it's going to make a break for it. The first problem, once I reach the studio, is that the section I painted doesn't look nearly as good as I thought it did. I do some touch-ups, which help a bit, and figure I can also fix stuff digitally if I need to. Set on automatic, the camera isn't as complicated as I feared. Still, the first photos don't turn out well. The light on the piece is uneven, with a glare on one area and one side darker. I experiment with turning on and off different ceiling lights, moving where the piece is hanging . . .

I get more and more frustrated. And the more frustrated I get, the more I get a bad feeling, like I shouldn't be doing any of this. Like I'm being delusional to think it could ever work. I keep thinking back to what happened earlier this morning and to the deeper hole I've dug for myself.

When my mother woke up, I'd already been awake for a couple of hours, anxious about talking to her for the first time since the fight. "Mommy," I began, "I'm so sorry."

"Don't apologize," she said, fishing under the couch for her slippers, clearly avoiding looking at me. "You were right."

"No, I was just upset."

She met my gaze then, eyes tinged red and shadowed by dark bags. "I can't do the stupid paintings, and I can't even pick up the phone and tell Annika. What do I think, she's going to forget about the show?" She folded her arms against her body and stared up at nothing. "It's like I'm . . . paralyzed. Useless."

As she spoke, my breath got tight. The fact that I deleted those contacts from her phone wouldn't put her off calling Annika forever, if she got up the nerve to do it. So I said the only thing that occurred to me: "I could talk to her for you."

"Talk to who?" She furrowed her brow.

"Annika," I clarified. "Tell her you want to cancel the show. You know, like when I brought over the portfolio. They know I'm like your assistant."

"Cancel the show for me?" She still looked skeptical, but there was a flicker of something else in her eyes, too. "Won't Annika think it's strange if I don't do it myself? Something so important. What excuse would you give?"

I shrugged. "You know me, I'm good at talking to people. And Annika likes me. I'll think of something. I mean, she needs to know as soon as possible. Like, today. So she can find another artist for the exhibition slot. And if you're not ready to do it . . ." I paused. "Unless maybe you *are* ready?" It felt terrible, how I knew just the right buttons to push.

She sat for a long moment, pressed her lips together and didn't say anything.

Eventually, she stood and headed to the bathroom. When she came out, we didn't say any more about it, which we both knew meant she agreed to let me do it but felt badly so didn't want to say it out loud. She squeezed my hand; her way of saying thank you.

Somehow, I feel much, much guiltier about the lie than about being here at the studio doing this. Forging paintings is one thing. Lying to my mother about something so big is far worse.

I just didn't see any way around it.

Finally, after hanging the sheet of paper in a spot directly between two of the ceiling lights, I get a photo that looks pretty good, I think. And I don't have more time, anyway, so I cross my fingers and head back to the city.

I drop the camera at Ravi's, leaving it with a uniformed woman who answers the door (one of the three housekeepers, I guess). He'll have to email me the pics—couldn't download them myself. When I realized he'd be seeing the images, I freaked out and sent him what probably seemed like a totally random and unnecessary text, with a bullshit story about how my mom had asked me to take test photos before a professional photographer came by her studio. Just in case he mentioned it to Kai.

By the time I'm done with my shift at the Fud, the library is closed, so I have to wait and go the following day. I'm there as soon as it opens, the first one at the computers. I get my email and nervously zoom in on the photos he sent, one after another. The resolution and quality of detail is amazing. Even seeing the painting this way, on a screen, there's a weird life in the girls' eyes. Somehow I captured that same creepy quality my mother gets. I use a free online photo editing program and do some manipulations on the best one, smooth out several areas where I messed up the paint, and save it as ZoeSerra-Artfocus.jpg, which sounds more professional than PleaseGodLetThisWork.jpg. Saying a prayer, I hit send on the message to Diana.

I bounce my legs up and down and try to distract myself with stuff online while I wait for her response. I scroll through Ravi's IG, which is mostly selfies. Kenya, Paris, Tokyo, Barbados . . . those are just the places he's been in the past year or so, sometimes with family, sometimes with friends. Despite my belief that it's fucked up for anyone to be this wealthy, it's hard to look at his pictures without feeling sharp pangs of envy. Not because they're so glamorous. It'd be fine with me if the beach was Coney Island instead of Barbados. It's all that time to relax. Have fun. Have friends. To do things for no other reason than because you want to. I know they're posing for the camera, but they all look so *happy*. There's that annoying saying that money doesn't buy happiness. And no, I get that it doesn't. But it does buy time. Freedom. Anyone who says different is a liar.

I've just found Kai's IG account and am staring at a picture of someone (him, I guess?) in swim trunks standing on his hands at the edge of a dock on a lake, back muscles flexed, when a message arrives in my inbox.

From Diana. I'm almost too nervous to open it.

Aren't there more options?

That's all it says. I bite my cheeks as I think of how to answer. Finally, I write:

This is the best. Zoe loves it! It's her choice for the ad.

I wait again. Hitting refresh and refresh and refresh.

Right as I'm about to have to turn the computer workstation over to someone else, another message pops into my box.

Would have rather had a variety to choose from, but ok, if Zoe feels strongly. Will pass along to our designer. Tx.

I read it over a few times. She's not thrilled, but . . . it worked. The photo is good enough and the painting is good enough. Holy shit. It worked.

Chapter Ten

My hand trembles as I hold the paintbrush. I set it back down and try to shake out the nerves. I open the door between the rooms so I get some of the daylight and open the window, too. Someone outside is blasting Eminem.

Knowing that I'm doing this—that I'm really going to try to paint this entire big piece myself—has made me more anxious about screwing it up. And there's no time for that. I worked out a schedule when I got here to the studio, and we have only around one week to spend on each piece in order to finish in time for the show. That doesn't include time for screwups. (Unless, of course, my mom takes over and paints much faster than I do, but I can't count on that.)

I decide to start with one of the flowers, which I can tell from the images in the catalogue should be a bright pink to deep red sunset color. I mouth words along with the music as I mix the paint on my palette, trying to make a good match. Every time I add a little more red, it looks like it needs a little more pink, and vice versa.

Finally, I'm reasonably sure it's okay and that I'm stalling because I'm nervous. I load up the brush and hold it over the area.

"You only get one shot . . ."

I put brush to paper, and immediately a big area floods with color, like last time. Swearing under my breath, I quickly blot up as much as I can.

Don't get frustrated. You can fix this. I shut the window in the outer room and the door between the two rooms so that it's quiet, no distractions. I brush the stained area with clean water and blot more—rubbing harder now—managing to remove enough of the color to try to keep going. It's too wet in that spot to paint right now, though, so I decide to move on to the girl in the white dress. I can do this. I know I can.

After adding water to her pre-mixed skin color, I stroke the soft brush tenderly over her face, with just the right amount of pressure and paint.

That smell is back, the burning one.

I reload the brush and carefully draw it down her arm.

Leaves rustle. The air is damp and hot, like an exhaled breath. The jungle pulses around me.

We're hiding behind a thicket of bushes with white flowers. I'm squatting, hunched, ready. Shoulder to shoulder with the girl in red on one side, the girl in blue on the other. Peering through the leaves and petals at a clearing. The flowers' perfume doesn't cover the smell of burning flesh. Three girls, trussed and roasted on a spit to the point of unrecognizable black shrivel. A massive vine surrounds the fire pit, undulating up and down like a sea serpent. Its thinner offshoots writhe in the air. An ugly orchid with an eyeball at its center tends the fire.

"Zoe," someone is saying. "Are you listening?"

I turn to the voice. The girl in red is looking at me.

Zoe?

I stare into her wide dark brown eyes, my head suddenly empty. Completely empty. Like I've been wiped clean as this white dress I'm wearing.

A cold, primal fear latches on to every cell.

I look around. Where am I? Who am I?

"Zoe?" another girl says. The one in blue. "Are you okay?" She rests a warm hand on my arm.

All of a sudden, it comes back.

She means me. Zoe.

Fear rushes out as memory rushes in. I'm Zoe. Right. And her name . . . her name is Azul, the one in the blue. The first one, in red, with a curtain of blond bangs, is Scarlet. Behind us, sitting with legs outstretched, is Lila, the one in purple who I carried piggyback. We're in Wolfwood. Yes. Thank god. I know who I am, where I am. It's okay. A shudder of relief passes through me.

"Sorry," I say. "I felt faint. The smell . . ." The strength of it does feel poisonous, concentrated in the wet air.

"We should've gotten here quicker," Scarlet says. "Now we've lost all of them." She means the girls on the spit, clones, burned beyond the point of recovery. The Others—that's what we call them.

They can recover from almost all injuries, but not something like this. Not when they're just charred husks.

"It wasn't my fault my leg was slashed," Lila says, defensive.

Azul and Scarlet's younger sister. The three look alike except Lila is reddish blond and the other two are more golden. Lila's rubbing her leg where the bandage is. Her eyes—a slightly greenish shade of brown—are clouded with remorse, and I reach to hand her a couple of berries from my pocket. We don't eat to survive here, but Lila still craves sweet stuff, so when I see the rare nonpoisonous berry, I collect them for her.

"She's not blaming you," Azul tells Lila gently.

"No, our route was wrong," Scarlet says. "Again." She draws in the dirt with a stick. "I don't understand. That area with the low trees was right over there." She points at a spot on the crude map she's drawn. "And we came through the area of other flowers here. But it looks like we've ended up back over there, even though we didn't loop around."

The landscape in Wolfwood is a live animal, always moving and shifting. Maps are mostly useless. But Scarlet always resists this. She takes on the role of leader and needs to feel like she can plan a route.

"From now on, maybe we shouldn't waste time making maps," Lila says.

"We can't just run randomly," Scarlet insists. "The only way we're getting out of here is by using our brains and figuring out which areas we haven't covered yet. There has to be a way out somewhere. And we haven't seen it yet."

"Well, what we've been doing isn't working. What do you suggest?" Lila asks, raising her eyebrows. Scarlet doesn't answer.

I look around, then point up at a nearby palm tree that's miles taller than any others. "I'll climb up and get a good view," I say. "At least figure out where to head from here." Some of the trees and plants and flowers here are monstrous, some aren't. The palm tree isn't.

I hand over my weapon—a blade of sharpened hard wood. Scarlet and Azul make stirrups with their hands and hoist me up as far as they can. I use all my strength to grasp the trunk with my arms and legs. "Okay, I'm good," I say, and I begin the climb, hauling with my arms, digging my feet in, scooching my thighs. My legs start trembling almost immediately. Why did I say I'd do this? I made the offer without really thinking about it, like I saw the tree and knew what had to happen next. Although, it is true that I have the sharpest senses of all of us.

To distract from my quivering muscles, I try to review what I know, let more facts fill my head—still a little disturbed by that strange, blank moment, when I didn't even remember who I was.

My name is Zoe. We are in Wolfwood. *Trapped* in Wolfwood. The earliest moment I can picture is when I first saw the sisters. They were sleeping in the middle of a circle of palm trees, about to be attacked. Between them, written in the dirt, it said: KILL THE WOLF.

We've been together ever since, though we're not sure how long it's been. The sun here never moves—it's fixed high overhead—so there is no measurable time or passing of days. We've been here long enough that it's taken its toll, though, that's for sure. No way to count how many attacks we've survived at this point. I can picture them in vivid, static images: Azul's leg torn off by a massive orchid; a woody vine hanging Scarlet from her neck; a branch like a sword, stabbed clear through Lila's eye and out the back of her head. An endless series of gore and pain. So much pain.

Finally, I break through the tree line and the landscape sprawls in front of me. It's greengreengreen, with open patches and denser patches and bursts of other colors dotted around.

My eyes key in on different details. A round turquoise water hole surrounded by spike-leafed mangroves. An area of chartreuse ferns, taller than we are, with a group of Others wandering between them, collecting bloody body parts that they'll reattach with torn strips of their red, purple, and blue dresses.

No white dresses, since I don't have any clones. When I get injured, I take a long time to heal, not like the sisters, who recover impossibly quickly from what should be fatal injuries, another clone joining the army of Others as it happens. We don't know why I'm different. Luckily, I don't get injured often, and never bad enough that I'm close to death. I've got a lightning-fast instinct for anticipating attacks, and I can usually sense when a tree or flower or vine is a monster and when it's harmless. Sometimes it's obvious— they have vicious mouths or searching, cyclops eyeballs—but not always. Some monsters are good at hiding their nature until it's too late. Like they're holding their breath.

My legs are trembling so violently now I can't climb any higher. I try not to think about how far up I am and how bad it would be if I fell, try to concentrate on the landscape. I spot a swampy, grassy area with a wooden walkway that we built to get across. Next to that, a section of bone-white flowers that burned us by spitting acid. Scenes of what's already happened here flash in my mind. Everywhere I look, it's just areas we've already been through. Nothing to show which way we should go next.

Will I even know what I'm looking for when I see it?

Then, in the distance, in the area with several water holes, something catches my eye.

I focus in on it more closely. It's a structure, not something natural. It doesn't look new—vines have grown around it. A roof of thatched palm leaves almost makes it invisible. Definitely something that was constructed. A shelter.

And we didn't build it ourselves.

A vision hits me: sharp face, long blond hair, bright blue eyes. Him.

Beep, beep, beep . . . beep, beep, beep . . .

The noise pulls me out, my brain struggling to make sense of what it is and where I am. Alarm. Studio. Right.

It's like coming out of a dream. For the briefest second, images and sensations linger: a map in the dirt, the smell of burned flesh, a green landscape. But they slip away almost immediately, water through my fingers. Gone, like the first time. And again, I stare in amazement at what I've done. I've completed two of the vignettes in the painting. One with the girls strategizing while watching the clones burn on the spit, and one where the girl in white climbs to the top of a tree to scout out the area. The landscape is a lush tangle of greens and pinks and yellows and oranges. The caption written under this vignette is: SHE SPOTS THE SHELTER. I painted the words in thin black letters that look eerily like my mother's handwriting.

I clean my brush, go into the other room, and sink onto the couch. It's time to head home—that's what the alarm meant—but I need a minute.

The more I think about it, the harder my blood pounds in my veins. It's not normal. Not at all. Weird is a total understatement. It's downright scary, like I don't have control over my own mind. Moments after my brush strokes the paper, I'm swallowed up by my imagination. It happened even quicker today.

I don't like it. I don't like it at all.

I stare out the window as a cloud drifts across the sky. What happens to me is strange, yes. Unbelievably strange. But it's not a problem, is it? It's not a reason to not do the painting. It's the reason I *can* do the painting. Because I'm entering this weird state, where I'm not nervous or overthinking the physical act. I'm so involved in the story I'm actually imagining I'm there. So if that's what it takes . . . I guess I should just accept it. And maybe it won't keep happening.

Somehow, though, I know that it will.

My anxiety about the experience doesn't go away during my sewing shift at Trinity's. I mess up an almost-finished clutch bag and have to hope she won't notice. Later, I can't sleep, can't get comfortable. I keep turning over and over, wishing I could get online to see if this happens to artists or just talk to my mother about it . . . talk to anyone about it. Maybe Jaden's father, Marcus? He's a psychiatrist and professor—maybe what's happening is a well-known psychological thing? But no, he'd think I was so weird, too weird to babysit his son. After getting myself more and more worked up, it finally occurs to me I could call Grace. She's not into art, but she's writing a fantasy novel and has always been open to sort of strange things, like really believes the stuff the five-dollar palm reader tells her. (She's going to meet her life partner on a Greyhound bus, apparently, even though I say she's way too glam for that.) Losing yourself in a dream state while awake seems like it could be a thing she'd know about, or at least could talk about without thinking I've lost it. Not that I can tell her I was painting Wolfwood . . .

I carefully get up from my mattress and find my phone in the dark, thinking I'm going to sneak outside, but as I turn the doorknob, my mother mumbles, "Indigo?"

"Sorry," I say, cursing our lack of privacy. "I told Grace I'd call. Going to sit outside."

"'K, love you, have fun," she mutters, clearly half asleep.

Settled on the stoop, I hesitate a minute before calling, wondering if I'm being foolish, if Grace is going to get suspicious about what's going on. I'll have to be careful about how I phrase it. Although, it's not like she could ever guess what's *actually* happening.

"Booboooo!" she says when she picks up, using her pet name for me. "You're alive!" We haven't been in touch at all this summer and only rarely during the school year.

"You're the one who disappeared to La-La Land," I joke. "How is it? Hanging out at the Peach Pit?"

She laughs. Before now, our main reference for LA was the reruns of *90210* we used to watch together.

We've been friends since we met in first grade at the Earth School. We were inseparable there and in middle school, but we've grown apart since I lived with her family. At the time, my mom told them I needed somewhere to stay because our building was being renovated and I'd fallen down the stairs, not that we were homeless and I'd been beat up at the shelter. Lying about my whole life was kind of like building a wall around myself. I couldn't talk to Grace about anything real, not even how worried I was about my mother or how terrified I was in public bathrooms. Then we got assigned to different high schools, and now . . . well, we see each other maybe once every couple of months, that's it.

"LA's wild," she says. "Totally different world."

She tells me about it: palm trees and cacti, too much time in the car, mind-blowing tacos, cute barista at the coffee shop near their rental house in a neighborhood called Silver Lake. She asks what she's missed here in the city, and I tell her a bit about the Fud, Josh . . .

Finally, in a completely casual tone, I say, "Hey, so . . . question: When you're writing, do you ever sort of lose track of where you are? Almost like you're inside your imagination instead of in the real world?"

She hesitates. "Uh . . . no. Why?"

"Just, you know, curious. I've been doing this project, and I'm having these sort of dreams about the story—"

"Wait, you're *writing?*"

"No, god no." I laugh. My dislike of any sort of writing-based task is well established. "Fashion stuff."

"Okay," she says, chuckling. "Sorry, keep going."

"Well, there's a story that I'm telling with the drawings, and sometimes it's like I'm dreaming about it, but I'm awake at the same time. Like my imagination takes over." Casual, casual. Nothing weird here!

"Sounds like you need more sleep, as usual. What's this for? Portfolio for college?!" She's clearly excited by the possibility.

"Maybe . . . Just messing around for now. And yeah, you're right about sleep. I'm sure that's it."

"I mean, damn, I just realized how late it is there. You working tomorrow?"

"Yeah."

"Hold up!" she calls to someone else. Then to me, "Hey, I'm so sorry, Booboo—I got people waiting for me here. So . . ."

"Of course," I say, a sudden hollow of loneliness opening up inside me. It's always like this when I see or talk to her now. So good to hear her voice, and then the emptiness of missing her. "Thanks for talking."

"Any time, girl. Get some sleep. Promise?"

"Promise."

I can hear people in the background calling her, but she doesn't hang up quite yet. "Is there something else you wanted to talk about?" she says. "How's Zoe? She . . . okay?"

I hesitate. "Great," I say. "She's great."

1989

Since her first morning in Tulum, Zoe has cocooned herself in her new reality: Colin and Zoe, expats in love, completely free, no other attachments or obligations. Colin, the talented one. Beautiful. Perfect. Zoe, the lucky one. The one anybody would envy.

It all seems like plain fact.

Then, in mid-April, Colin receives an airmail letter, handed to him by Itzel at lunch. (It hasn't even occurred to Zoe they could get mail at Don Eduardo's, mostly because there's no one who would write her.) Not a big deal, but a reminder: there are other people in Colin's life, a world outside of Tulum. Zoe is dying to know who it's from, but his closed-off expression tells her not to ask. He thanks Itzel and shoves it in his pocket, stands up from the table, and tells Zoe and the Lopez sisters that he'll see them later.

After he's gone, Zoe explains that he has plans to talk to someone about doing a mural on the side of a small building—another expat involved with the new construction. (There's buzz around town that Tulum's becoming more of a tourist destination.) Hearing about the mural, Lila's eyes light up. But Scarlet crosses her arms. It's so arrogant, she says. Like a dog wanting to piss on a territory. Does Colin think he's Diego Rivera? Mexican art—Mayan art—is the art that belongs here. Not Colin's. It's like artistic colonization. Bad enough that expats are building here, trying to capitalize on the beauty of someone else's land.

Zoe is taken aback. She hasn't thought about it like this, not at all, and her first instinct is to be defensive. After a moment, though, she has the uncomfortable realization that Scarlet may be right. (She also has the uncomfortable realization that Scarlet doesn't like Colin nearly as much as Zoe assumed she did—as much as she assumes everyone does.)

That afternoon, in the cabana, Zoe tries to discuss it with Colin without sounding like she's criticizing him. But his face gets more and more stony as she talks.

When she's finished, he gives a small, hard smile. He says, Thank you so much for enlightening me. I didn't know you were an art expert. And a cultural expert. Thank goodness you're here to set me straight.

The coldness of his tone makes Zoe shiver. She tries to explain, tries to backtrack.

But he just gets angrier, reminding her that she didn't even graduate from high school. He asks what she knows about the history of colonization in Mexico, what she knows about the history of art, aside from what he's taught her. Then he abruptly gets up and walks out, toward the water, throwing off his shirt and diving into crashing waves.

Zoe doesn't understand what just happened. They've never fought like this before. She's never heard that tone of voice or seen that look in his eyes. After his swim, he disappears and isn't at Don Eduardo's for dinner. Later he returns from town drunk with a couple of French guys he and Zoe don't even like. Zoe goes to bed alone while he's out on the beach drinking more. She can't sleep, sweaty and uncomfortable in her hammock, wondering why he got so upset. Hating herself for opening her mouth. Starting to panic that she's ruined everything.

Finally she drifts off, only to be woken hours later by the swing and dip of Colin getting into her hammock with her, curling his body around hers. I'm sorry, he whispers, breath heavy with beer and regret. I'm so sorry. I was such a jerk. Don't leave me, he says.

It takes a minute for Zoe to process what he's saying. Leave him?! Of course she won't leave him. Of course! She's always had to suppress worries that he'll leave her. There's nothing in the world that would make Zoe leave him.

She breathes into the comforting warmth of his body and pushes away thoughts that the fight or any of today's surprises changes anything. Life here is exactly what she thought it was. It was just a bad day. Tomorrow will be perfect.

Chapter Eleven

The next time I'm at the studio, I know what to do. Quiet room. Door shut. I set the alarm for only a couple of hours from now, not having much time before I need to be back in the city. After a few minutes testing colors, I hold the brush over the paper, the tip so close to touching. I pause for a moment. Why am I scared? It's like dreaming—nothing worse than that. I lower the brush.

Wolfwood is waiting.

I barely control my slide down the long trunk, the bark burning my thighs and arms, but my excitement to go find the little thatched hut almost masks the pain. There's something important about that place, I know it. I feel it. Nearing the bottom, I jump, my legs buckling when I hit the ground. The sisters turn. They're huddled together in a sheltered spot a short ways off, keeping close, unified. A family.

"I saw something," I call to them.

"What?" Lila asks, as all three hurry over to me.

"A shelter—like a little hut. Something someone built."

The sisters' eyes widen at the news.

The Others don't do anything but fight the monsters; none of them would have built it. And the only other person in Wolfwood is *him*.

There's a quiet moment as they let this sink in. I take my blade back from Lila.

"So . . ." Scarlet finally says, "he could be living right nearby. He could be watching us as we speak." She twists her head as she says it, scanning the area around us.

Scarlet has never seen the Wolf—none of them has. I'm the only one. I first glimpsed him when he was climbing a tree that had attacked us. He made it all the way to the top, no movement at all from the monster. If anything, it was using its leaves to *help* him climb. He got to the top and then he flung himself off, flipping in the air, whooping on the way down. When I told the sisters—when I described him—they immediately decided: he must be the Wolf. KILL THE WOLF—the instruction written in the dirt when I first found them.

Since then, we've been looking for him while also searching for a way out. Kill the Wolf or escape, whichever comes first—that's what Scarlet says. But whenever I've glimpsed him, he's disappeared by the time we've reached the spot. Scarlet says he's messing with us. That this is his domain, his monsters. He's letting them toy with us. Torture us.

"I want to see him!" Lila says. "Let's go there, to the shelter."

"Keep your voice down," Scarlet hisses.

"It's pretty far from here," I say.

"Where?" Azul asks.

I orient myself, then point. "Back that way. Past the big wetland. Near the water holes and the white poison-spitters. We should go now, before the landscape shifts too much."

"We've already been in that area," Scarlet says. "We'd have seen something like that."

Does she think I'd make this up? "Well, I saw it. So we must have missed it."

Out of nowhere, a branch lunges at us, grabs Lila's arm so hard she shrieks, but all at the same time my reflexes kick in and I stab the branch clear through and the monster pulls back, growling and coiling into itself. The whole thing happens in less than a second. Lila rubs the scrape on her biceps. We move farther away, Lila sticking close to me.

Not only do I have the best reflexes, but I'm the only one with a blade—a machete of razor-sharp hard wood. I've had it from the start. The girls use rocks or whatever else they can find as weapons.

"I'm not sure about this," Scarlet says. "Every time we go looking for him it's like a wild-goose chase."

"We're supposed to kill the Wolf," Lila says. "We can't *not* look for him."

"I don't care about killing him!" Scarlet says. "I just want to find the way home. The longer we're here, the more danger we're in."

"What danger?" Lila says. "We can't die, right? As long as we're here, we live forever."

"We don't know that for sure," Scarlet says. She's pacing around, smacking the ground with a long, thin stick. "We've had this discussion before. Maybe we're like the Others. They're hard to kill, but they can die. If one of us was decapitated, and the head was thrown away, I don't think we'd be fine. Or if we were burned as badly as those Others were, down to charred stumps, we wouldn't be fine. And what about Zoe?" She stops and gestures at me. "One bad attack and she'd probably die. She doesn't heal like us. We have to weigh the risks of everything we do. And I don't know if this one is worth it."

"I have a thought," Azul says, in her quiet, calm tone. Since she doesn't talk much, we all pay attention when she does. "What if the structure Zoe saw is a . . . a *portal*. Maybe it's the way out of here. Like in a book. Like the wardrobe entrance to Narnia."

Lila inhales a small gasp. "The way home?"

Scarlet looks at me. I shrug. "Could be," I say, even though, somehow, I don't think that's it. She rubs her jaw, frowning.

"Okay. Fine," she says. "We'll go there."

Scarlet leads the way, based on my direction. After some easy bushwhacking, we have to lizard-crawl under a woven tangle of vines, through mud that smells like it's made from decomposed bodies. We make it through safely, emerging from under the web of vines into a riot of color—fleshy flowers the pink of our gums. Petals as long as our bodies, edged with jagged teeth. Muscular stems as thick as our legs. There's a slow, subtle movement among them. A pulse. Following Scarlet, we forge a careful path between them, all of us with our weapons at the ready.

"This pink color reminds me of the house we lived in on the river," Lila says to her sisters, holding her sharp rock in the air.

As she says it, a strange realization comes over me. I can't remember *anything* from before the moment I discovered the sisters here in Wolfwood. I struggle to latch on to something—a face, a house, a voice—but it's all a big blank. Has it always been this way? Or is it somehow linked to that earlier moment of blankness, when I didn't know who I was?

"Quiet!" Scarlet stops suddenly. We all freeze. "Listen."

I hear the bass of the jungle's breath, like ocean waves. And then . . . a yowl. A chorus of yowls. The sound of pain. They can't talk, the Others, but they can scream.

The chorus grows. Something terrible is happening to them.

Lila blocks her ears.

"We have to get to these ones," Scarlet says. "Before it's too late."

I'm anxious to find the shelter, but we need the Others to help us fight the monsters. That's why we always try to save them, if we can. They fight for us, we fight for them. They're getting into battles all the time. The jungle is littered with body parts.

"Can you tell which way the sound is coming from?" Scarlet asks me.

The wailing is everywhere now, drenching the air. I close my eyes to hear better.

The minute my vision goes dark, a black-and-white image flashes before my eyes: our bodies, tossed in the air. Another: Lila's neck, broken.

Startled, I blink away the imagery.

"What's wrong?" Azul asks, lightly touching my wrist.

I shake my head. "Nothing. Sorry." No idea what that was. Memories, I guess. A past attack. Although . . . it felt more like a premonition.

"So, can you tell where the screams are from?" Scarlet sounds impatient.

I focus on listening, this time with my eyes open.

"That way." I point toward a dense area of glossy leaves.

We hurry toward the carnage.

Chapter Twelve

On Wednesday, I wake up painfully early and spend time sewing at Trinity's workspace before my midmorning Fud shift. Trinity is *pissed*. Not only did she notice that I fucked up that clutch, but I haven't been here as much as usual, which limits what she has to sell. So I concentrate extra hard and turn out even more work than I usually would before heading to the Fud.

It's a blessedly uneventful day at my register—just the usual stream of entitled "guests" wanting to make sure I apply today's two-dollar discount to their $45/lb chanterelle mushrooms. As I walk down the crowded sidewalk after my shift, I check my phone and find a text from Grace, asking if I want to come out to LA for a few days. Her parents will pay for the ticket. Chance to relax, catch up on sleep. First I call my mom and tell her I'm going to do some more work for Trinity (a lie, to buy myself time to go to the studio). Then I text Grace, explaining that I can't take time off from work and that I'm helping my mom get ready for her big show. Of course, I want to go, but aside from not having time, I get uncomfortable with letting her family pay for things. Some of the "hand-me-downs" she used to give me seemed brand-new and were suspiciously perfect for me. I appreciate their generosity, a lot, but can't stand feeling like they pity us.

It's her show. Not yours, Grace writes back, as if she read something between the lines.

Me: Obviously. I'm helping cause I want to

That's where we leave it. An old argument. She thinks I take on too much responsibility. Her parents are married and she has siblings. She doesn't get that I'm the only one, the *only one*, who can help my mother. And of course, she doesn't know how depressed my mom can get. I'd never betray my mother by telling her.

In addition to the texts, there's a voicemail from Kai, which is weird. Left an hour ago: "Hey, could you call me back when you get this? Too long a story for text. Or you can text if you'd rather. I don't know why I left a voicemail. Who does that? Either way. Cool. Thanks."

I have limited texts with this phone plan, so I call from outside the stairs down to the subway station. It's a brutally hot day and I'm dripping with sweat. Not to mention burned out from working all day.

"Thanks for getting back to me," Kai says. "Here's the thing. I'm usually very responsible, but we had a lot going on here this week."

"Okay . . ."

"I'm preparing some stuff for this presentation here tomorrow, and I was supposed to get a few of your mom's old catalogues from her. And I forgot. And the meeting is, um, first thing tomorrow morning. We're having this opening now and I can't leave. We usually don't serve food and stuff at these things, but the artist insisted and I'm stuck manning the table."

I fan the hem of my tee in and out to get some air on my damp skin, not liking where this is going.

"Would you be able to bring a few by?" he asks. "Either today or tomorrow morning at nine?"

I can't go in the morning. "You're still at the gallery now?"

"The opening goes till eight. It would really save my ass. Maybe your mom could? I think it's too late to get a messenger."

No way I'm going to a gallery opening in my Fud uniform, smelling of BO and rotisserie chicken fumes, so I'd have to go home, shower and change, go to the studio to pick up the catalogues, and *then* go to the gallery. Not doable by eight. Also, I'm supposed to paint for a few hours, to stay on schedule.

"I'm sorry, Kai. I could maybe just make it there, but I don't have time to go home first and I'm not dressed for an art opening."

"Don't worry about that," he says. "No one cares. Or I can meet you on the sidewalk if you don't want to come in. And if you take a car, you don't even have to get out, just pass me the catalogues through the window. Or you can ride in the trunk, with the catalogues on the seat. That would work. I don't need to see you at all."

I laugh and wipe sweat from above my upper lip. "It's important?"

"Seems like it. My mom's coming into the gallery early for it."

I think of how important that meeting with the twin collector couple turned out to be and sigh. "Okay," I say. "I'll be there by eight."

By 7:50 p.m., I'm standing on the sidewalk outside the gallery, holding the catalogues and looking in at the space. It's packed. People filling the whole huge room, and some out here on the sidewalk, smoking and vaping and drinking wine and talking. All either beautiful or stylish or both. Men with silver hair and round glasses with thick black frames, older women with skin stretched taut over their bones like Saran wrap, and younger women in short, silky dresses or wide linen palazzos. Some people in streetwear, but high end.

A memory surfaces: the opening reception for my mom's last show, when I was eleven. She'd recently bought a used sewing machine, and we altered one of her cool old dresses to fit me. I was painfully insecure about my height back then; that night, I felt like a glamorous superstar. And so proud to be the artist's daughter.

Flash forward to now: me in my cheap black pants and Fud shirt. Well, sort of. Before leaving the studio, I turned the shirt inside out, cut out the tag, cuffed the sleeves, and knotted it under my boobs so it shows the high waist of my pants and a strip of skin. God knows what it looks like, but anything would be better than a basic-shaped tee saying FÜD! And I forgot my makeup at home today, too, so that's another subpar situation, especially since my new breakout has gotten worse.

I call Kai, but he doesn't pick up.

I text: Outside. Can you come get them?

I wait. No response.

The opening doesn't look like it's ending any time soon, so I brace myself, head in and toward the back, looking for Kai as I go.

I work my way through the crowd, holding on to the box, slouching, smiling, and saying, "Excuse me," and "Sorry," ignoring the annoyed looks and telling myself I belong here as much as they do, no matter how I'm dressed. I'm still Zoe Serra's daughter.

I make it to the office area and find only one person back there, one of the guys who was on a computer when I was here for the meeting. He's on the phone, so I just pick a desk and put the box on it, with a note that says, *For Kai Nordhaus.* (After I write it I remember that's not his last name. He has his dad's Japanese last name, which I forget. Obviously they'll know who I mean, though.)

I'm on my way out when I spot the table of food at the edge of the main gallery area. It's pretty picked over at this point, but still edible and free, and I'm starving in that clawing way that comes with lack of sleep. Kai isn't manning it—no one is—so as subtly as possible, with my back to the room and hunching to be shorter and less conspicuous, I quickly eat a few things and then start filling a napkin full of crackers and cheese and vegetables—as much as I can hold. While I'm wrapping the napkin around it to put it in my bag, an older man stands beside me.

"Modigli-ahhh-nee," he says, in a voice right out of a PBS documentary about people who own yachts. He looks the part, too: old white man with a striped bow tie and fluffy white eyebrows like troll hair.

"Excuse me?" I say politely, even though the last thing I want to do is talk to him. I'm holding the food awkwardly, as if this is a normal amount to have taken. Putting it in my bag now would seem even weirder.

"You look like a Modigliani, my dear." He raises his cup of wine in my direction, sloshing it.

Oh . . . *Modigliani*. A painter whose work I've seen at the Met and MoMA. Portraits of women with long, narrow faces.

"He loved hips," the man continues, spitting a bit, and I think I heard him wrong, but then he says, "His nudes. Slim torsos and great, swelling hips. Ones you can grab on to." He says it with relish, sloshing his drink again as his stare reaches out toward *my* hips.

Are you kidding me, perv?

"Pity what happened to him," I say, then bite down hard on a baby carrot.

"Modigliani?"

"Mm-hmm. Arrested for sexual harassment."

The troll brows pull together in confusion. No wonder—I made it up.

"Had to go to jail," I continue, "because he was such a—"

"Ma'am?" The voice comes from my side. Kai. Materialized out of nowhere. "That piece you're interested in buying, I brought it out. It's in the back."

For a split second I think he's mistaken me for someone else. Then I catch on: rescue brigade. I don't need rescuing, but I appreciate the effort. "Oh, thank you so much," I drawl. "I did want to take another look before committing to it."

"A young collector," Troll Eyebrows says, sounding intrigued. "Whose work?"

"Zoe Serra," I say, without missing a beat. "She's brilliant. But"—I cock my head—"probably out of your price range." I give him a *too bad* smile and turn around to follow Kai, biting my bottom lip to keep from laughing.

We thread our way through the crowd and stop at the edge of the room, out of the old guy's vision.

"Ma'am?" I say to Kai. "I know I look older than seventeen, but you called me 'ma'am'?" I casually put the bundle of food in my bag.

"Forget that. Did you really say what I think you did to that guy?"

I smile. "I hope he's not important."

"No idea. Thank god I saved him when I did."

"Oh, so you were rescuing *him* from the conversation, not me?" I plant my hands on my Modigliani hips.

"One of my duties is making sure none of the gallery's clients get shot by elbow lasers."

Keeping a totally straight face, I lift both elbows and make *pew, pew!* shooting noises.

Kai chuckles. "I knew it. You haven't changed at all."

I grin, although what I'm really thinking is that's not "me" anymore. I don't even know where it came from.

"Anyway," he says, "thanks for bringing the catalogues. Sorry I didn't get your texts in time. But you look perfectly fine. Better than fine."

"Clearly we have different standards."

"Ouch," he says, looking down at his own outfit of (nicely snug-fitting) white tee and black jeans.

I laugh. "I didn't mean—"

"Kai." Annika swoops next to us, a man and woman at her side. "I need you to get the Knowles sketches from the flat files. Now."

He hurries off and she notices me. "Oh, Indigo, darling, so good of you to come. I was just telling Malcolm here that whenever Zoe is ready, he can go to the studio. Malcolm, this is Zoe Serra's daughter, Indigo. This is Malcolm Frain, a curator at the Whitney. A longtime supporter of your mother's work. And Paige Droste, head of the Young Collectors Council at the museum."

I sober up immediately and shake their hands. Crap. I should have left the catalogues on the sidewalk.

"Nice to meet you," I say. "It's so wonderful that you like my mother's work." God, that sounded weak. "I know the Whitney was instrumental in launching her career."

"Indeed it was," the curator says. He's pink-cheeked and bald with a dark fringe of hair and round wire-rimmed glasses. "I was so thrilled to hear that she's painting again. It always struck me as a great tragedy for the rest of us that she stopped." He pauses, smiles slightly. "My husband actually bought a small drawing she donated to a benefit auction, just one of the Wolfwood girls standing alone. It's genius. We hung it in the dining room and talk about her as if she's real. Such presence and intensity. Takes a lot of talent and heart to turn a piece of paper into a member of the family."

"I can't wait to see the new pieces," Annika says. "Zoe's been keeping them hidden, Malcolm."

A thin vine of doubt curls through my gut. Am I nuts to think people like this who know her work so well would fall for my forgery? I am, aren't I?

"They're beautiful," I say, as if by saying it I'll make it true. "Very powerful."

"Is she coming tonight?" Annika asks.

"Here?" I say. "No. She . . . um, she's painting all the time, really. I barely see her. I just came to drop something off."

"We'll get you to the studio," Annika says to the curator. "Nice for you to reconnect with her after all these years. See what she's up to before the show."

Well, *that's* not happening.

"Maybe it would be a good visit for the council," the woman with him says. She has luminous dark skin and is wearing a gold sleeveless top with an oversized, drapey hood.

"Wonderful idea, Paige," Annika says. "I'll call you to follow up."

"Sounds great," I say, when really all I'm thinking is that this conversation needs to end before Annika insists they go to the studio right now or something unhinged like that. "Very nice to meet you both."

As I walk away, I hear the curator say to Annika, "Lovely girl. Reminds me of her mother."

I make a beeline toward the door. Halfway there, I stop dead in my tracks. Ravi is coming in, his arms around two girls who even from here smell like money. He hasn't seen me, so I scoot over to the side, by a column. Shit. This whole event is like a video game that keeps leveling up.

I glance around the room. I could change course and maybe slip by unnoticed on the other side. But what if Ravi did see me and thought (correctly) that I was ditching him? Not good. Seeing no other option, I spin in a tight circle and hurry toward the back, dart into the bathroom, push the trash can against the door. I toss my hair to make it fuller and bite my lips to make them redder. Still don't look good enough to meet rich kids, not in these clothes. I need *something*.

I leave the bathroom and walk farther back into the offices like I belong there. "Just dropping something on Annika's desk," I say to the guy who I'm beginning to think is chained to his computer. Annika's office door is open and the room is empty. After taking one more look toward the hallway to make sure no one's coming, I hurry in, grab her Chanel lipstick and mirror off her desktop, and quickly apply it, marveling at how smooth and luxurious it is, at how satisfyingly heavy the case is. Lipstick like this can salvage a whole outfit. I replace it and the mirror on the desk and wander back out, like nothing at all.

Ravi and the girls are talking to Kai now. When Ravi sees me, he gives me a chin tip and says, "Didn't know you were here." He looks at Kai. "You guys have plans?"

"Just dropping something off," I say. "On my way home now."

One of the girls he's with has translucent white skin, huge dark eyes, and shoulder-length, natural flame-orange hair. Ethereal, like she should be a character in *Lord of the Rings* or something. She's got on pleated black leather short-shorts and a white tank top that's cut super low in the neck and armholes, with a wisp of a black bra under it. The other girl has brown skin a shade darker than Ravi's, with long ombre hair that's cherry red at the tips and black at the roots. Cheekbones that could maim. A small diamond stud in her nose. She's wearing ripped jeans and a T-shirt that I'm pretty sure I saw in the window of the Stella McCartney store.

I'm relieved their style isn't uptight Upper East Side rich, but I still feel ridiculous in this inside-out, knotted-up tee, and too tall and too big and too everything. I take a hip out, slouched position, but I'm still towering over them.

"Hey," I say to the girls, smiling in a way so my teeth don't show and they can be blinded by the expensive perfection of my lips.

"Fiona and Natalie," Ravi says, gesturing first at the redhead and then at Cheekbones. "Indigo's mother shows at the gallery," he explains to them. "She's known Kai forever. Even longer than us."

"Since he was a baby?" Fiona says. "He's playing a baby in my show. Or he was." She snags Kai's beanie and rubs his head, which I now see has only a slight shading of dark hair. Almost bald.

He grabs the hat back. "C'mon, Fee."

"Aww . . . cute baby," she says playfully, hugging him. "How come we've never met before?" she asks me. There's an effortless glamour to her. Her features are so precise and elegant, it's like she was drawn with the finest-tipped pen.

"Oh, I hadn't seen Kai in years," I say, "until recently."

"You should've invited her to the show," she says to Kai, arms still loosely around him, then says to me, "He was great. I couldn't afford to pay a whole cast, you know, already renting the theater. And he saved me." Wait, she rented a *theater*?

"He's in love with her," Ravi adds.

"For fuck's sake," Kai says. "Will you never let that die?"

"Dude, you shaved your head to be in her play."

"*Everyone* is in love with Fiona," Natalie says.

"You're all my babies," Fiona says, keeping one arm wrapped around Kai and hugging Natalie with the other.

They're so intensely familiar with one another, the way they touch and the way everything they're saying seems like lines they've said a million times before. I hope they realize how lucky they are.

"We're just here to pick up Kai," Ravi says to me. "If you want to wait a sec and ride with us, come hang at my place? The car's waiting outside."

"Oh," I say, calibrating. I'd rather ditch them completely. But since I already told them I was going home, not sure how I'd refuse a ride. There's no way I'm spending time with them at Ravi's, though—definitely not dressed like this, after working such a long day. "Um, yeah, sure. I can't come over. But a ride would be cool."

Chapter Thirteen

Ravi gets in the front seat next to the driver; the remaining four of us look at the back seat and then at one another. I'm about to happily offer to not go, when Fiona says, "I'll sit on Kai's lap."

So we crush in, my knees pressed hard against the driver's seat, legs folded up and entangled with Kai's and Fiona's. I can't help noticing how strong Kai's thighs are and how warm his body is, even after the chill of the gallery's air-conditioning. He seems confused about where to put his hands, since Fiona's very bare thighs are on his lap and there's no room on the seat next to him. (I wonder if Ravi was right, that he's in love with her . . .) He settles for reaching his arms up behind me and Natalie. I feel myself wanting to apologize, for taking up so much room, for smelling like grease and sweat. For being poor.

Ravi glances back at us. "Sometimes it pays to be a little guy," he says to Kai, holding his phone up and taking a selfie with us in the background.

"Does it ever pay to be an asshole?" Kai shoots back.

"Ravi," Fiona says, "I hope you have some good bubbles at your place to celebrate Nat." She leans to the other side and kisses Natalie on the top of her head.

"Nat just won a big essay contest," Kai explains to me.

"For high schoolers," Natalie adds.

"It's going to be in the *Washington Post*," Fiona says, sounding like a proud parent.

"Wow," I say. "Congratulations." Who are these people? They do stuff like rent spaces to put on shows and write essays that get published in national newspapers?

My phone vibrates with a text.

> Mom: Fridge broke again. Fix tricks arent working. Needs your magic touch

"Cute phone," Fiona says.

"I don't like being tethered to technology," I say, flipping it shut.

"I've been thinking about going that direction," Fiona says. "I admire your self-control."

Natalie snorts. "You'd get a flip phone as soon as you'd fly coach."

"Are you guys headed to the Hamptons tomorrow?" Kai asks.

"Ugh, I don't know." Fiona fiddles with a gold medallion hanging from a long chain around her neck. "We were all set, but then my aunt gave me tickets to that new show with Daniel Radcliffe on Broadway. But it's Sarah Ashford's big party in Sag . . ."

As she's talking, I'm trying to tuck my legs into a less obrusive position. I wish the windows were rolled down, for some air.

"Tough decision," Kai says. "Sorry life is so hard."

She smacks him on the thigh. "Do you guys want the tickets to the show, if I don't use them? It's the Saturday matinee." She looks between the boys.

"Can't," Ravi says. "Grandmother's birthday."

"Sure, I'll take one," Kai says enthusiastically. "Thanks."

"Want the other?" she asks, twisting to look at me. "They're comps, so no big deal."

"That's so nice," I say, taken aback. "I have to work, though."

"They're really good seats. Couldn't you take the afternoon off?"

I've never been to a professional play or musical of *any* kind, let alone one on Broadway that has well-known actors. But I can't afford to miss a shift. And if I'm not at the Fud, I need to be at the studio, painting. Or sewing at Trinity's. One thing I do not have is time. Still, Fiona's looking at me expectantly with her big doe eyes, and I have this weird sense of not wanting to disappoint her, and I hear myself saying, "Um, maybe."

"Great!" she says.

They segue into trading stories about some guy named Babar— yes, they confirm for me, Babar like the elephant—who Fiona knows from her theater program at Yale and who is apparently now dating the Sarah Ashford girl, and my mind wanders. I stare out the window, letting myself imagine being part of a tight-knit group like this, with a shared community and references and history. Like family you've chosen instead of been born into. Then I wonder what excuse I could give to my manager Shawna for flaking on my shift, if Fiona ends up giving me and Kai the tickets, even though I know I shouldn't do it. Know I *can't* do it. Can't. Capital "C."

"I'm sure this is all fascinating," Kai says to me, "the lives of people you don't even know."

"Oh, right!" Fiona says, looking at me again. "Sorry, Indigo. We're being so rude."

"No worries." I smile.

She studies me for a moment. "Can I ask, what happened to your face?" She has an expression of concerned curiosity.

I reach a hand up and brush my cheeks but feel nothing. Irrationally, I wonder if that gross old guy at the gallery spit on me or something. "What do you mean?"

"It looks like something happened at some point. Like, your nose has been broken and your teeth are, you know, off."

My blood stills.

"Fiona, what the fuck?" Kai says reproachfully.

"Not in a bad way!" she says. "Obviously, otherwise I wouldn't have said it. You remind me of Anjelica Huston when she was young. That great sort of edgy look."

No one has ever asked me this before. I try to believe that no one can tell, that I look fine, weirdly pretty, even, on a good day. And here she is, calling it out. And I think I might die. Because no matter what she said, is there a "good way" to look like your face was broken?

For a moment, I'm tempted to tell the truth—beat up in the bathroom of a homeless shelter—just for the shock of it.

"I fell down some stairs," I say, giving the excuse my mother and I gave back then. "Years ago."

"Ouch." Fiona winces. "Must've been scary."

There's a rush of blood in my ears, pumping hard to make up for the time it lost when it froze. Shame burns through me, knowing that they've been looking at me and wondering. Thinking I look weird. Different. Do they also see that I've colored in spots where the leather has worn off my shoes? Or that my thick eyebrows are self-plucked instead of professionally waxed? On top of that, I'm angry at myself for feeling shame about things that shouldn't be shameful. There is nothing shameful about my life, I know that. But sometimes it's hard not to *feel* like there is.

I should have told Kai I couldn't bring the catalogues. I never should have gone there looking like this. And I definitely shouldn't have come in this car. I have no superpower tonight, no glamour to disguise me. Adults are easier to fool—good posture and eye contact go a long way. But not peers.

My phone buzzes again.

Mom: Leftovers ruined. Could you pick up dinner? Thanks hon xo

"I'll just get out on A, at the bodega," I say, relieved we're almost there. Suddenly, my mother is the only person I want to be with.

"Sure you can't come over?" Ravi says.

"Yeah, sorry. Here," I say to the driver. "Right here. Yeah, this is good."

He pulls up to the curb, and I waste no time opening the door.

"I'll get your number from Kai," Fiona calls, "if I decide not to use the tickets."

"Thanks," I say with a wave, not even looking back as I step onto the pavement.

⌒

I take off my shirt the minute I walk into the basement, saying, "Hot out. I'm totally gross and sweaty," so my mother won't ask why my Fud tee is inside out and tied up like this. I hand her the bag from the bodega and go into the bathroom.

I stare at my face in the mirror, turn to both sides. Bare my teeth. Trying to see what Fiona saw. Damage.

A shiny brown roach scuttles from behind the mirror. I try to smash it, but it darts back before my hand hits the wall. The flimsy wallboard shakes, and the soap container clatters off the sink and onto the floor. When I reach to get it, I see another roach running under the shower stall. My eyes sting.

"You okay in there?" my mother calls.

"Yup, fine!"

After I replace the soap on the sink, I text Kai:

Sorry turns out I can't make show. Thanks to F for offer

⌒

As my mother places our bowls of ramen on the coffee table, I'm reminded of the food from the gallery in my bag. "They were throwing samples away at work," I say. "I snagged some." I take out the bundled napkin and set it between our bowls. The vegetables look even sadder here than they did at the gallery, but at least they're vegetables.

"I hope no one saw you, honey." She doesn't say it meanly.

"They didn't." I go to get a glass of water and pause at the fridge. Rattle it from side to side, turn the dial on and off, unplug and plug it, rattle it some more. Finally the light goes on again and it starts making a geriatric hum. Working, for now, but clearly on its very last legs.

"I'm surprised you didn't notice sooner that it stopped making noise," I say, sitting on the chair next to the coffee table. After I've said it, I regret it, blaming her for not realizing soon enough to save the food.

"I know," she says. "Sorry."

"That's okay."

I get a text. Glance at it.

> Kai: Sucks but I understand. Work matters

A second one comes right after.

> Kai: Sorry about Fiona. She's a playwright. Interested in people. Nosy

I flip the phone shut and concentrate on slurping down the noodles for a bit, before realizing that my mom is just staring at her bowl, stirring the ramen in circles.

"Not hungry?" I shouldn't have been mean to her about the fridge.

She looks over at me, takes a deep breath. "I started job hunting again."

I'm momentarily speechless. "Really?" I can't even remember the last time she tried. She got so discouraged before, so angry at herself that nothing worked out.

She nods. "I'm just so . . . I've been so weighted down, trying to make myself paint, and all the guilt." She purses her lips and averts her eyes. "I know that we need the money and that I blew my opportunity. I know that. I've let you down in a really big way. Everything you said to me that day, it was all stuff I'd tell myself all the time. I'd sit there at that studio, or just walking around the neighborhood, and I'd say all of those things. And I still couldn't do it. I can't explain why." She pauses. "It's just . . . those paintings are tied to a different time in my life. But I want to do what I can to make it up to you. I'm determined to."

"You don't need to make it up to me," I say reflexively. "I already told you, I was just angry when I said those things."

"I think the economy might be a little better now than when I last tried."

I bet she's saying this to convince herself. Still, it's huge that she's feeling strong enough to look. Not only because if she *can* get a job, it'll be huge, but because the stronger she feels in general, the sooner I can approach her about doing the paintings with me, which is definitely my plan. I'm only partway through the first painting, and I can already tell that combining full days at work with long shifts at the studio isn't sustainable.

"You should ask Daphne, the nice librarian," I say. "She'll help find listings online."

"Think anyone will hire a washed-up old lady?" My mom smiles, partly joking but mostly not.

"You're not *that* old. What are you now, eighty? Eighty-one?" I tease. She's not even fifty.

"Excuse me?" she huffs. "Only seventy-nine!" We both laugh. I lean over and give her a hug, inhaling the shampoo smell of her clean hair. As she hugs me back, my throat swells. It feels good to have her arms around me. "What would I do without you?" she murmurs.

We pull away, and before we turn back to our dinners, she says, "You look so pretty. Is that new lipstick?"

"Um, no," I say, averting my eyes and reaching for a limp red pepper. "I borrowed it."

"Suits you," she says. "My elegant girl."

1989

As much as Zoe tries to pretend that nothing has changed, Colin becomes especially moody after the fight about the mural. Not angry. Quiet. Withdrawn. She's perpetually sick to her stomach about it.

But then, one morning, it's like his light has been turned back on. He announces that he needs to make a trip to Cancún. He won't tell Zoe why—says it's a surprise—and arranges to pay Don Eduardo to borrow his ancient, hulking car the next day. He buys beers for everyone in the cabanas that night and entertains them by singing love songs to Zoe as Azul plays guitar. Lila grabs an Italian boy and makes him dance with her. The Canadians start singing along, and then a whole group is laughing and dancing and singing to Zoe.

In her lovedrunk happiness, a terrible idea occurs to her. Terrible because she wants it to be true, and it probably isn't. But maybe . . . maybe Colin wants to propose to her and is going to Cancún to buy a ring? Once the thought is buzzing like a mosquito, she can't get rid of it. He did ask her to run away to Mexico after knowing her only a few months. Is it that strange to think he'd get engaged as impulsively? True, she's heard him scoff at the importance of marriage and family, but he's so romantic. How could he not want to get married? Zoe knows she's young, but she also knows that she wants to spend her life with Colin Wolf.

He leaves for Cancún the next morning, still acting mysterious, those swimming pool eyes all lit up. Zoe goes with the sisters to Xel-Há to snorkel, and during the drive, they speculate on what he might be doing. Does he need new clothes? Art supplies? Pot? (Azul's hopeful suggestion.) Lila says it must be a present for Zoe, but Zoe keeps her engagement ring fantasy to herself.

Then Scarlet says that the only reason she'd go to Cancún is the airport.

The airport.

Scarlet wasn't even suggesting it as a real possibility, but still, Zoe goes cold. She thinks back to the fight about the mural, how angry he was. The week of moodiness. And he did get his passport from Don Eduardo's safe, to bring in case anything went wrong. No, she tells herself, of course that's not it. He begged her not to leave him, after the fight. He sang cheesy love songs! But now that Scarlet has said it, it's a second mosquito in Zoe's head, buzzing even more loudly. What if, what if, what if . . .

After all, she's always known this new life was too good to be true. That she doesn't deserve it.

Out of nowhere, she remembers the airmail letter. The letter Colin never even mentioned, just shoved in his pocket. That was the day his moodiness started. Zoe has never done anything like this before, but she knows she won't be able to stop herself. As soon as they get back to Don Eduardo's, she tells the sisters she needs to take a siesta and goes to the cabana to look for it.

Chapter Fourteen

t's early, early morning, the sun just rising. I'm already at the studio, a huge cup of coffee in my hand. This is where my focus needs to be—not on making friends with rich kids I have nothing in common with or going to some Broadway show. I keep hearing Annika and that museum curator talking about my mother's work. *Genius. Talent. Heart.* I'm about a third of the way through this first painting, and I need to make the rest even better, if people like that are going to fall for it.

The section I'm starting on today is a big action scene, with the girls being ambushed by snakelike roots that wrap around them, thrashing them in the air and beating them on the ground, crushing bodies and breaking necks. Studying the pencil outlines of the image, and one later scene where the dark-haired girl in white is taking care of the girl in purple, I have a strange sense that when I'm inside my imagination, I take on the role of the girl in white. I don't know that for sure, since the memories disappear so quickly and completely, but I feel more of a connection to her, or something.

Before starting to paint, I pin the *New York* magazine photo of my mother on the wall. I stare at her raised arms and defiant posture and imagine her as fierce and wild. Imagine myself as fierce and wild. Stronger than all the monsters.

I rest a finger against the photo, as if her neon energy from all those years ago can flow into me.

"It's a trap," I whisper. "We need to leave."

We've followed the sounds of those screaming Others and are now hiding near where they're being tortured, squatting under the cover of low trees with twisted branches, coming up with a plan to save them. From what we've seen, they're being sliced up by enormous palm plants whose leaf segments are razor-sharp blades. But even though we've made it this far, I'm now convinced we need to get out of here. I keep having those black-and-white visions that I had before: Lila's neck broken. Bodies in the air. I don't understand it, but I feel like they're definitely a warning. A premonition.

"A trap?" Scarlet says. "How can you tell?"

"I just know. I can feel it." Someone—or something—is waiting for us. It's in the air. Like we're inside a held breath.

The sisters look around. The leaves above us rustle gently. The images flash in my mind again, even clearer this time.

"We need to get out of here. Now." I stand up.

"Zoe's hunches are usually right," Lila says to her sisters.

An especially desperate scream rips through the jungle.

Scarlet turns to me. "Sometimes I think you don't care about saving the Others as much as we do because none of them are yours."

I don't have a chance to respond. With a seismic rumble, the ground erupts beneath us. I'm hurtled into the air. Something grabs me. It wraps around, snares me into a trench where the earth exploded. Monsters writhe on all sides. Above me, the sisters are being thrashed back and forth. Whipped into the air and slammed against the ground, over and over, gripped tight by the roots. I'm pinned down, can only watch as they're flung and slammed, blood pouring out of Scarlet's ears, Lila's neck broken. The air is full of soil and blood and screams, including my own.

I flail and fight like mad, biting the sinewy root that's wrapped around me like a boa constrictor. Finally something releases and I slide out of its grip, as if my sweat and the blood all around made me too slippery to hold. With a wild cry I raise my blade, slashing at anything I can, frenzied, not knowing what I'm doing or whether it's working, just stabbing my blade into anything that moves, getting the roots at their bases, not risking hurting the bodies they're holding at their tips.

Primal desire fills me. *Save them.*

Slash, turn, stab. Slash, turn, stab. Slash, turn, stab . . .

Frantic.

And then, after I don't know how long, I realize I'm the only thing moving. I'm the only one screaming.

The roots are limp on the ground, viscous white blood oozing out of their wounds, the smell like a carcass left in the sun.

In a daze, I climb out of the trench, search for the bodies lying in the dead monsters' coils. I clamber over the battlefield and come to Lila first. I manage to pull her, then Scarlet, then Azul, out of the muscular grips and drag them into an area under a safe bunch of low trees. They don't have the type of injuries I can help. No cuts to bandage or thorns to remove. Their necks and limbs are crooked at extreme angles. Rib cages crushed so their torsos are flattened. Skulls dented. Like broken dolls. No blood except what's dripping out of their ears and noses. I use a soft petal to wipe off their faces. I align their heads and limbs.

What if Scarlet's right and they are like the Others, and some injuries are too bad to come back from? What would I do here without them? I should have been more insistent it was a trap, should have gotten us away sooner.

I don't want to be alone.

A group of Others has gathered around us. Their strange, dead-eyed stares stay locked on me, as if I've done something wrong. I focus my attention on the sisters. A little voice inside me tells me that they'll be fine. That the ambush was supposed to happen. That I did good.

I don't know how long I sit and wait. And then . . . a twitch. Lila's hand. I sit up, lean over her, feel for a pulse. Yes, she's breathing. Her eyes flutter. Breath fills her chest and she expands again, ribs no longer crushed flat.

A sound comes from Scarlet; she's awake, too.

Thank god.

Soon, all three of them are sitting up. Battered, but whole.

"What happened?" Scarlet asks. "How did we even survive?" They scan the chaos around us. The monsters are chopped into pieces, their rancid white blood spilled like spoiled milk.

"They were totally slaughtered," Lila says.

For a moment, I consider lying, telling them that the Others who are standing around us got here in time to save us. But why would I lie? I want them to know it was me. That I saved them.

"One of them got me, but I escaped," I say. "Then I just . . . used my blade."

"You escaped?" Scarlet says, incredulous. "How? That grip. It felt like I was being liquidized inside."

I don't want to admit that my monster didn't thrash and slam me, that it just held me down in the trench. It seems strange that I wasn't attacked as violently as they were. I shrug.

"Thank god you *did* escape," Lila says to me. "I don't think we'd have made it. We should've listened to you earlier, when you said it was a trap."

"I still don't understand how you could've gotten out of that grip," Scarlet says.

"Scarlet, it doesn't matter," Azul says. She presses herself up to stand, clearly still feeling the effects of the attack. "We need to start following her hunches. They're always right. She's been here longer than we have. From here on out, if Zoe has a feeling about something, we listen. If she tells us it's a trap, we believe her." When Azul says something like this, it's a decree.

"Right," Lila says.

Scarlet's eyes tell me that even though she won't argue with her sisters, she doesn't agree with them. Her eyes tell me that instead of making her trust me more, this has done the opposite.

And despite having saved them, despite being happy that Lila and Azul want to do what I say, one clear emotion flares inside me. Guilt.

Chapter Fifteen

Over the next few days, I can tell I'm making steady headway bringing the graphite sketch to life, the white paper filling with color. Still, when the alarm pulls me out of Wolfwood and the first painting is finished, I can't quite believe it.

I pin it on the wall, carefully—it's hard to wrangle this enormous sheet of thick paper—step back and look at it. Seeing it like this is impressive at first. It's big and colorful and detailed, and my mother's composition is full of movement and tension.

Then my eyes snag on a mistake. Suddenly, it's hard for me to see anything other than the spots that aren't perfect. I can't see it as a whole work. I squint, and it looks better. A blur of fabulous, luscious colors. But when I let myself study the details, I can't tell whether it's good enough. It'll have to be, though, won't it? And framing will help. Even little Jaden's paintings look like real art in the nice frames his father uses.

I reward myself with a coffee and cheap chocolate from the bodega near the studio and consider the situation. One down, seven to go.

Not that I can keep doing this for seven more paintings. No way. I've barely had time to breathe for the past week, constantly on the go and losing track of my own life. Hardly sleeping. And things keep adding up that the gallery wants to talk to *her* about. One of these days, for sure, it's going to be something I can't fudge.

Aside from the logistical headaches, painting is taking an emotional toll on me, too. The memories from Wolfwood still slip away when my alarm pulls me out; what doesn't slip away is a thick, sticky layer of guilt that covers me every time. With my Wolfwood nightmares, when I was little, the emotion I was left with was terror. None of that now. Always guilt. I suppose it's because I know it's wrong of me to be doing this, to be doing the paintings and to be lying to my mother. Whatever the reason, I can't escape it. Not even a recent night at Josh's got me fully out of my head.

At some point soon, I'm going to have to tell her what's going on. Get her to take over or at least work on the paintings together.

I've been avoiding thinking about this. Because, honestly, how am I ever going to confess what I've done? How am I ever going to get her to want to paint? She's so relieved now that she thinks the show isn't happening. And she's focusing on her job hunt. Still, I don't have a choice.

I spend the next day transferring the drawing for the second painting onto the watercolor paper. It's a welcome break, since I don't get lost in Wolfwood when I draw the way I do when I paint. I'm concentrating in a different way, having to look back and forth from the sketch to the bigger version. Instead of starting to paint the second when I finish, I take the next days to draw the third and fourth, too. I figure it'll give my mother an added boost, if she sees a bunch of them are partway done. As I copy lines, I think about how to ease her into the idea of painting again and come up with the beginning of a plan to open her mind to it.

On Thursday evening, we're sitting at the laundromat, watching our clothes and towels and sheets spin in the dryer. To save money, we wash at home in the bathroom sink—or the shower for bigger things—and then bring everything here to dry. If we hang dry them at home, it takes forever and they smell like mildew.

Usually we sit out front, near the windows. Now I'm paranoid about running into Ravi when I'm with her, so I steered us toward a dryer in the back. (Since the whole broken-face thing, I've been keeping a polite distance from Kai and Ravi, responding to occasional texts but nothing else.) She's in an okay mood, because the last time she went to the library and checked job listings, a bunch of new positions had opened up at Target. Until now, she's seen almost nothing listed anywhere that she could even apply for. Always a requirement she doesn't meet: *Need car. Need bachelor's degree. Need experience . . .*

Someone left a copy of a travel magazine here, and I've been paging through it, showing her pictures and discussing where we'd rather go, critiquing hotel design, salivating over food porn. Procrastinating putting my plan into motion.

"What about Morocco?" I hold out the magazine, open to a spread of a tiled interior.

"Mm," she says. "Those colors and patterns are gorgeous."

"They remind me of that Philip Taaffe show we went to at Pace, the one that you loved so much?" I say, tentatively mentioning something art-related, which I wouldn't usually do.

"I can see that. God, I wanted to *eat* those paintings, they were so juicy. And wasn't that also the day—"

"We followed Keanu!" After I say it, we both laugh, remembering how we were in a gallery and realized that Keanu Reeves was in there with us, and we tried to be all subtle, following him down the street, which is totally not something New Yorkers do, but he was in my mother's favorite movie, so we made an exception.

The dryer buzzes. When I check, everything is still wet. Shoot. I add more quarters.

"This machine sucks," I say, as it starts to rumble and spin again.

I sit back down and flip slowly through boring ad pages, shoring up my courage to say what I need to. Finally, I begin. "My half-birthday is coming up soon."

She raises her eyebrows, amused. "Is that . . . an event?"

I smile, but my mouth has gone a bit dry. "I've decided it is. And I was wondering . . . there's something I want."

"Honey, you know we can't afford—"

"This won't cost money. But . . . don't freak out."

Her expression has gone more serious. "I'll freak out if I want to freak out."

I moisten my lips. "I want you to do a small watercolor for me. Of anything. Like I used to have." My bedroom in our old apartment was covered with paintings she did for me: the two of us flying on a magic carpet, me with our neighbor's horse-like Great Dane, the flowering trees in Tompkins Square Park . . . When we were homeless, we put our stuff in a storage facility, and when we couldn't pay the fee, everything was sold or junked. Her paintings were the most painful of all the things I lost—her paintings and our sewing machine.

"A watercolor?" she says stiffly.

"A small one. No big deal."

Acting nonchalant, giving her time to think, I turn to a page that shows a beautiful ancient ruin perched on a cliff over a blue-green ocean. "Ooh," I say. "What about . . ." I read the caption. "The Yucatán, Mexico." I look up, show her the page. Her lips are a tight line, pressed together. And pale. Her entire face is pale. *Shit.*

"It was only a suggestion." I close the magazine. "The painting. I just thought—"

"Indigo, I'd rather not talk about it now." She brings a hand to her forehead.

"But—"

"I've got a terrible headache."

I stare at her. "You were fine a minute ago."

"Please." She stands up. "Do we have any quarters left, honey? I need coffee." Now she's pinching between her eyes.

God, it's not like I asked her to jump off a bridge! A surge of anger rises in me. I try to tamp it down, reminding myself how bad she feels about having canceled the show and how she probably just associates that failure with painting in general. I hand her my last three quarters, hoping I don't need more for the machine. After she's left for the bodega, I release my clenched jaw and pick up the magazine again, flip it open, and transport myself onto a hammock on the beach in Mexico, imagine the breeze as I sway, the sound of the waves . . . my frustration and anger floating out to sea.

A little over a week later, I'm at the end of my shift at the Fud, thinking with exhaustion about going to the studio when I clock out. For the time being, I've set aside my plan to get my mom to take over—she hasn't mentioned making a painting for me, and I haven't brought it up again, either. So I've gone to Wolfwood every day except one and finished the second piece. All I want is to take the rest of the day off, but I also know there's no room in the schedule to do that. There are six weeks left, and six more paintings. I'm at my register, thinking about all of this, when I notice Kai standing two back in my line. Seeing him sets off a surprising flush of happiness. So much for keeping my distance.

He reaches the register and hands me a can of seltzer.

"You stood on line to pay three bucks for water?" I ask, bemused.

"Tastes better with the umlaut."

I can't help smiling as I ring him up.

"My wasted money will be worth it if you can take a break, join me outside," he says, putting his card back in his pocket.

I consider a second, conflicted, and finally say, "My shift is over in ten minutes. If you want to wait . . ."

When I get outside, he's sitting on the bench in front of the store, in the sun, looking at his phone. I sit next to him, even though the bench is for customers only, not staff. These shoes are worn down and my feet are aching.

"Sun feels good," I say, tilting my head back. The A/C is freezing inside.

"Mm. I think I might be sick if I stand up. Avocado seltzer was a mistake."

I look at him. "I thought you got lime. What the hell is wrong with you?"

"In my defense, I thought I got lime, too. Then I tasted it."

"The umlaut didn't help?"

He laughs full on, then puts a hand on his stomach. "Ugh."

I close my eyes and lean back. Not that I can spare much time. Need to get home and check in with my mom, eat, then go to Brooklyn. I'm gathering momentum to tell him I need to get going when I sense someone standing next to the bench. Shawna, my boss.

"Indigo," she says. "Sorry to be a jerk, but not with your shirt on, okay?"

I sigh. "I know, I know. Sorry."

"No biggie. Have a good rest of the day." With a cheery wave, she heads inside.

I stand reluctantly. "Can't sit on the bench in uniform. Which way you walking?"

"North," Kai says, pushing himself up. His biceps strain lightly against the sleeves of his tee. "New comic store. Not far from your block."

We head toward Essex Street.

"Beautiful day," he says. "Perfect for Coney Island. Wanna go?"

I glance over at him. "Right now?"

"Isn't the roller coaster calling to you? Indigo, come risk your life on meeeeee!"

"Sorry," I say, smiling. "Another time, though."

He narrows his eyes. "I can't tell if you're lying or not."

"Why would I lie about wanting to go to Coney Island?" Not that I can afford it or that I think I should spend time with Kai, but it doesn't mean I wouldn't want to. In fact, going there with him right now sounds fantastic.

"I don't know," Kai says. "Maybe you're worried I'm not tall enough to ride the rides, but you don't want to bring it up."

I laugh. "Can we just put this whole subject to rest? How tall are you?"

"Five-nine."

I raise my eyebrows. "Maybe on your player stats."

"Five-eight-and-a-half?"

My eyebrows stay raised.

"Five-seven is really just like five-eight."

"Five-seven," I say, suspecting it's more like five-six-and-a-half. "Okay. So without heels I'm only four inches taller. Big deal. No more jokes or derogatory statements need to be made." It's not like I care about his height at all, but I have a feeling it's a real issue for him, even though he jokes about it.

"So, no Coney," he says. "How about . . . Ravi's having a party soon. Y'know, a first thing at the new place. Nothing crazy, his parents will be around."

"Oh. Um, when is it?"

"Next Tuesday. Midweek, since everyone is away on the weekends. On the early side. Super chill."

"Tuesday? I think I have something."

"Is it because of the other day?" Kai asks. "I promise Fiona didn't mean anything bad. Or if it's that you feel like we're an annoyingly tight group, we're not. We've been friends a long time, but we don't even have that much in common anymore. We're . . . a dysfunctional family who prefers when there are non-family members around so we don't drive each other nuts."

"So, you want to use me," I say. "A diversion."

"You are very diverting."

I can't tell whether he's flirting or whether this is the same sort of teasing banter we traded when we were younger. I can't tell whether I'm flirting, either. Does it count as flirting if you always joked around, and you're just kind of acting like the kids you used to be?

"Honestly, though," he says, "I probably won't know a lot of people there. It'll be Ravi's friends from school." Before I can ask, he adds, "We didn't go to the same high school. He went to boarding school."

"Oh. Well, thanks for the invite. I'll let you know."

We've started walking up Avenue A, nearing a spot where there's always a small group of people hanging out on the sidewalk. All look unwashed and strung out. As we're approaching, a skinny guy with a sore on his face and too many clothes on for such a hot day calls, "Hey! Kid!" right at us.

I sense a jolt of surprise from Kai. "Hey!" he calls back, gives me a quick look, and jogs over to the guy. Possibilities flash through my mind: he's Kai's dealer, Kai's his dealer . . . Not that either seems likely, I just can't think of anything else.

I don't stare but keep glancing over, trying to figure it out. The guy is animated, like he's explaining something complicated, hands moving up and down. Kai has his hands in his pockets and isn't nodding or anything like that. No money is being exchanged. After a few minutes, Kai gestures over at me, fist-bumps, and then heads back.

We walk for half a block in silence.

"Shoot," Kai says, stopping. "I'm sorry. I just feel like I should call my dad. Do you . . . You okay going on without me?"

"Yeah, of course. Everything okay?"

"I mean, I don't know what my mom's told yours . . ." He must see the confusion on my face, because his expression changes. "That was Hiro," he says. "Sorry, I assumed you recognized him."

I don't get it right away, then my jaw drops. That was his brother? His brother who is only in his early twenties, who used to be so cute and athletic and funny? That run-down, vacant-eyed, skinny old guy was Hiro?

"That was Hiro?" I say inanely.

"He's in and out of rehab," Kai explains. "I don't know the last time my dad heard from him, and I feel like I should tell him I saw him, now, in case . . . I don't know, in case it matters."

"Of course. I can wait . . ."

He shakes his head. "I might end up walking back, if my dad wants me to give him some cash. He said he's got a new place and needs help with rent." Kai looks skeptical. "Or might see if I can get him to take a cab with me somewhere. To my dad's office or whatever. I don't know. Maybe my dad won't want me to do anything. My parents are always changing their minds about how to help him."

"I'm so sorry." It's the best I can offer.

He nods, and gives a brief, sad smile. "Anyway, hard to see him, but I guess every time I see him and he's semi-okay, it's a win."

I want to give him a hug but worry it might seem like pity, and I know that's the worst feeling, when people pity you. It's like they're saying they're glad they're not you. So instead I find myself resting a hand awkwardly on his shoulder. Through his thin T-shirt I can feel how warm and toned and alive his body is, and—*whoa*—an intense, electric fizz surges through me. His lips part slightly, as if he's about to say something.

"Okay, well . . . see you soon," I say, withdrawing my hand quickly, before the fizz short-circuits me or something. And with a final small smile and wave, I walk toward home.

Later, lying in bed, I send Kai a text. One I'd want to get if I were him.

> Me: Hope everything went ok with Hiro. Dont worry I won't tell my mom or mention it in front of your mom

He writes back almost immediately.

> Kai: Thanks it is hard but don't worry okay to talk about it, not a secret or anything

Kai: He's sick. No shame

Oh. Of course, not like I think he should be ashamed. I'm just not used to people being open about stuff like that.

Me: I really hope things turn around for him

There's a brief pause, then:

Kai: When your mom was in the hospital and had bad head pain or whatever did they give her opioids?

I don't answer immediately, too surprised he knows about my mom's illness. But of course he does. It was a major crisis. Annika visited her in the hospital. Still, I feel an uncomfortable tightening, like he's too close. At the same time, I also feel an unfamiliar sensation of wanting to tell him more, wanting him to know the truth about the direction our lives took after she was sick. There's something about Kai that makes me feel safe. (And something else about him that makes me feel very unsafe, in that electric-fizz sort of way.)

With everything about my life so tangled up with my mom's, though, the truth about some things isn't mine to share. Even if I found someone I wanted to share it with. Not to mention that the whole story leads to me forging paintings for his mother's gallery.

Me: Don't think she took opioids. Not that sort of pain. If she did wasn't a big deal and def doesn't take them now

Kai: Shes lucky. They gave them to hiro. Took them for some soccer injury and never got off not like he was an angle before that did plenty other stuff but wasn't so hooked, and now its everything

Kai: *angel

Me: Thts terrible

Kai: Its true, you should pity me a lot, so much that you come to r's party. You wouldn't want to disappoint someone with sad story right? Like watching the olympics you have to root for the athlete with the sad backstory

I laugh, then cover my mouth, aware of my mom sleeping on the other side of the room.

Me: Ill try. really

Chapter Sixteen

The sisters and I have finally reached the area of Wolfwood where I think we'll find that shelter I spotted. It was a much longer journey than we anticipated—the landscape messed with us even more than usual, shifting around like pieces in a slide puzzle. No matter how vigilant we all were, and how closely we followed my hunches, we were attacked over and over. I've reluctantly accepted the fact that I can see glimpses of the future but can't change it. What I see is what's meant to happen. And there's also a lot that I *don't* see.

The fact I can't use my powers to spare the sisters from pain is a constant pulse of guilt in my veins.

The area we've reached now is an expanse of mangroves, with turquoise water holes the size of small ponds scattered throughout. One wrong step and you're in the water, at the mercy of vines that can drag you under and drown you.

"If things haven't changed too much," I whisper, "the little hut should be right on the other side of that." I point out a shimmer of blue through the foliage ahead of us. "If you want to wait here, I can scout it out."

"You shouldn't go alone," Scarlet says. I know she says this because she thinks it would be safer for someone to come with me, but underneath that, I can hear it's also coming from suspicion. Ever since that big attack, she's been wary. Like it's somehow a problem that I saved them, instead of proof of my loyalty.

No wonder I feel guilty all the time, constantly aware of her mistrustful gaze.

"I'll go with you," Lila says. She turns to Scarlet. "Don't try to stop me."

For once, no one argues. Lila and I head out, creeping lightly, holding on to safe branches and stems when we can, knowing that the ground might give way into a deep pit of water at any moment. A tingle in my limbs tells me we're getting closer. The air around here is dead, which is a surprise. I'd think he'd shelter among monsters, for protection. Then again, the shelter did look old.

"Do you think there's a chance it's a portal home?" Lila asks me. "Like Azul said?"

I consider whether there's any reason to lie and decide not to. "No, I don't."

She nods, seemingly having had the same thought.

"Tell me again what he looks like." She's whispering, but there's a thrill in her voice.

"Long blond hair. Sharp cheekbones. Intense blue eyes."

"Like a wolf."

I don't bother telling her that wolves usually have golden eyes, not blue. Lila has a fascination with him that's more romantic than the others. Probably because of the way I've described him. But I'd be lying if I didn't describe him as handsome.

"There," I whisper, pointing. Ahead, an area of thick swamp grass is woven together to cover the side of the small shack. Thin branches bend to form an arch over it, adding to the camouflage. Hard to believe I saw it from so far away, when I was up in that tree. Like I knew to look for it. Maybe I did, in a way similar to my premonitions.

"Wait here for now," I tell her.

Lila hesitates, then gives a slight nod. "Be careful."

I high-step over a crisscross of roots, hanging on to branches, knowing how close the water is. I come up on the shelter from the side, my breath shallow as I ease my way around the circular structure. When I'm right next to the entrance, I raise my blade. I peer around the doorway, step inside. It takes a moment for my eyes to adjust. The air is almost water itself, it's so heavy, so thick. Musky. It smells like animal, not plant. Webs of thin rope hang from the walls onto the floor, a pile of filthy netting next to them. A small object sticks out from under the ratty fabric. It glints. Metallic. I reach out tentatively, touch the metal with my bare foot.

Something in the air shifts.

All of a sudden, it's like a veil is lifted. I see the ropes as they used to be: two hammocks, surrounded by a pristine, gauzy netting that hangs from the ceiling. I see shoes on the floor, sandals. Cold bottles of beer. And someone in one of the hammocks. Him. He's talking, but I can't hear what he's saying. I turn my gaze—someone is in the other hammock, too. A girl with long dark hair, long thin limbs. Familiar. She reaches out to him. They touch hands. They're in love—I can feel it. Their desire is as thick as the heat.

I smell her happiness—round, sweet.

He tilts his head and looks at me. Our eyes lock.

I startle, blink, and it's gone, all of it, except what's here now. The old rotting ropes. The dirty fabric. I hook the tip of my blade on the netting and lift it an inch, revealing the object underneath. Curved silver. A bracelet. I bend down to pick it up, and as I do I notice something else under the netting. I lift it a little higher.

Two blue eyes stare at me.

His head. Decapitated. Blood pouring out of his neck. I drop the fabric, suck in a breath, stumble back. Blood floods the shelter, covering my feet. Thick, warm, deep red blood. His head floats on top, still staring at me, eyes glowing through the thin netting.

Terrified, I turn and run. Grab Lila's hand. Keep running.

"What happened?" she says, stumbling a bit as she's pulled along. "What's wrong?"

Even if I wasn't breathing too hard to answer, I have no idea what I would say.

Sitting on the edge of her hammock, bare feet on sand floor, Zoe can't stop shaking. The thin light blue airmail paper trembles in her hand. Words wobble in front of her eyes:

Dear Colin,

    I hope you get this, what with the shoddy mail system down there. Not much to report from here. Your mother and I are well. The reason I'm writing is to let you know we're not going to wire you this quarter's allowance. We've decided it's time for you to come home to Chicago, finish school, and join the firm.

    You're almost 24 and have been given every advantage. All those studio visits we set up, all the favors we called in. The rent we've paid. None of it has led anywhere, except running away to Mexico, alone. I'm a collector and I know what it takes for an artist to make it. Art is a product, like anything else. (Just ask Koons.) Simply put, no one wants your product. I'm sorry for being so blunt, especially because I know you've tried hard. Probably too hard. I talked to J. Deitch after the studio visit, and he said you were a competent painter, but it takes more than that. You can throw a rock and hit a "competent painter" in SoHo.

We'll get you into a good business program after your BA. You can settle down, meet somebody, and build that part of your future. (Needless to say, your mother has ideas for that side of things.) Hopefully, you haven't fallen back into any bad habits. Your sister says you didn't look healthy the last time she saw you in New York. We've already been through that with you.

See you soon,

Dad

Zoe doesn't know which part of the letter is the most upsetting. Finding out he lied about his age (almost twenty-four!) . . . lied about the gallery people and how he was supporting himself . . . that his parents don't even know about her! Here she was, thinking he might propose, and his family doesn't even know she exists. And then there's how reading this must have affected Colin. God, it makes Zoe feel like her own insides are being torn out. Of course he got so upset when she was mean about his mural idea, after getting this letter. Why, why, why did she say all that?

Worst of all, what if he listened to his parents? What if he's flying to Chicago right now?

Zoe is still shaking when Lila finds her for dinner. She can't tell the sisters about the letter. This isn't the Colin she wants them to know. And she doesn't want them to know that he's been lying to her, either. She's humiliated. Humiliated that she knew so little about him. And she can't begin to admit that he might have abandoned her. Saying it out loud might make it true.

She tells Lila she's not feeling well, that she maybe ate something bad. She says she'll see them later. In a bit, Itzel comes down and offers her plain rice, but she's not hungry at all.

Hours pass. She stays in the sweltering, airless cabana, waiting for him to come home. Praying that he will.

Chapter Seventeen

t's the night of Ravi's party. When the door to his house opens, I'm greeted by a uniformed housekeeper—not the same one who took the camera from me. She steps aside for me to enter and then says, "One minute, please, miss," in a European-type accent, before she disappears off to one side through a doorway, leaving me standing alone. I stare after her in confusion, already feeling like coming here was a big mistake.

A couple of hours ago, I was at home, completely torn about whether to come. Kai and Ravi and their friends live in another world—another *galaxy*—and I didn't want to spend the party awkwardly trying to pretend I'm one of them or answering questions about my broken face. On the other hand, what sort of dope would say no to going to Tania Bawa's house?

While I was plucking my eyebrows and debating, my mother, out of nowhere, asked if I knew what had happened to the supplies at the studio. Completely caught off guard, I stumbled through an answer about how the gallery had let us keep it all there. "Why?" I asked.

"I'll need stuff if I do a painting for you," she said.

Somehow, I managed to keep my excitement in check. "So . . . you're thinking about it?"

"I don't know." She crossed her arms. "Maybe."

I could tell she was going to. She wouldn't have brought it up if she wasn't. And I know, I just know, that when her brush touches the paper and she remembers how good she is, and how much she loves it, her whole outlook on painting Wolfwood will be transformed. I was so excited and relieved, I decided to say fuck it and go to the party, take my chances. I'm on schedule with the third painting and can spare a couple of hours.

But now that I'm here . . .

The housekeeper returns momentarily, holding a pair of fuchsia silk slippers, and says, "Your jacket and shoes, miss?"

It takes me a beat, then I realize: She wants me to wear the slippers. I guess it's a no-shoe house? I don't wear shoes at home ever, but it didn't occur to me for a party. The polish on my toenails is old and chipped. I have a raggedy Band-Aid on that big blister. But the woman is staring at me, and what can I do? I take off my sneakers, thankful no one else can smell them or see the cheap label. I hand them to her, mumbling an apology, take the slippers (which are clearly new), and then hand her my jacket, too, flustered by the logistics of holding and exchanging things and hoping the jacket doesn't smell like basement and then thankful the slippers actually fit. (Do they have a whole warehouse of new slippers here? Are the housekeepers trained to guess shoe sizes?)

"This way, miss."

I shuffle behind her through the grand entranceway—dark wood floor, high ceiling, white walls with massive abstract paintings in vivid colors. We reach what I first think is a closet over to one side. An elevator. A fucking elevator, in a private house. Jesus. I step in tentatively and, for a moment, just stare at the pearly buttons before remembering that she said fourth floor. The door closes and the elevator ascends smoothly and silently. Nothing like the one in Josh's building, with its wheezing and jerking. The top half of the walls are decorated with shaped mirror tiles, so I can't escape my reflection and second-guess my outfit: high-waisted red shorts with a halter top that's really a vintage bathing suit. It leaves my back mostly bare and has this wild novelty pattern of planets and little astronauts and spaceships. A gift from Parker at the consignment store because it had a hole in the butt. The label has come out but Parker said it was some French designer. Maybe it's totally wrong, though. Maybe people are going to be really dressed up. I have no idea what sort of party this is. Or why I'm here.

And, shoot, I left my lipstick in my jacket pocket. And my phone! I was so rattled by the whole slipper situation.

The door glides open, revealing a vast space—one room spans the entire floor of the building, with multiple seating areas, a pool table, a giant monitor on one wall where a video game is being played, art everywhere. The light in the room is low, and there are maybe fifteen or so people, spread out in small groups, some sitting on couches, some playing pool. EDM pulses in the air, not too loud.

I now see that Ravi is one of the people playing the video game. But where's Kai? I scan the groups and don't see him. No one has noticed me. I could leave. I should leave. What was I even thinking? Without Kai, forget it. In this moment, it becomes clear that the main reason I wanted to come was to see him.

As I'm about to turn back around, I hear "Indigo!" and realize Ravi has spotted me. Damn. He sets down his controller, stands, and strides up to me in his easy but regal way, wearing a fitted black tee and purple track pants. He gives me a hug. I'm not quite ready for it, so I stiffen and then hug back.

"Hey," I say, hands safely in my pockets now. "Your house is . . . incredible."

"Thanks. I'm in the middle of a game, but let me introduce you to a few people." I follow him over to an area where three girls and one guy are sprawled on a huge couch and love seat. Ravi introduces us, but I'm nervous and forget their names as soon as he says them. He goes back to his game, leaving me stranded. I glance around, not sure what to do. Sitting down seems like the least awkward option, and there's a tray of small sandwiches on a coffee table right here, so I'll be near food. I pull up a small white stool and balance on top of it. My legs must have grown since I last looked. They're endless. Cartoon legs. They should be retractable.

One girl is wearing an over-the-top Victorian-style dress—a Look, for sure. And she's the only one not wearing slippers, I guess unwilling to sacrifice her lace-up booties. The others are more low-key: a striped romper on one, jeans and a smocked tube top on another, the guy in khakis and a tee that says EXETER SQUASH.

A voice comes from my side. "Miss?" Another woman in the same black uniform (housekeeper #3, I presume) is standing next to me. "Something to drink?"

"Oh, no thank you. I can get it myself."

The girl in the romper waves away that suggestion. "There are too many places stuff might be. They have, like, five kitchens."

"Not five!" Ravi calls.

The woman is still looking down at me.

"Um, Coke, thank you," I say, hoping that the expression in my eyes telegraphs that I'm not one of these rich kids, I'm like her, and I know how hard it can be to wait on entitled people.

Victorian Girl picks their conversation back up. "All I'm saying is why should I have to compromise my morality to take a class?"

"Let's not get dramatic here!" the one in the tube top says. She pops something in her mouth. "Want an edible?" she asks me.

"Oh. No thanks." I would like one of the sandwiches, but they're laid out in a fancy pattern and it's obvious no one has taken one yet, so I'd feel a little weird.

The guy turns to me. "Jess wants to take the Late Twentieth-Century Jewish Filmmakers class next semester, but there's a Woody Allen unit, so her parents might sue the school."

"You get it, right?" Victorian Girl—Jess—says to me. "Who wants to be a part of canonizing work by someone so reprehensible?"

All I know about Woody Allen is that he made movies and is either really old or really dead. "Um, well, yeah, I see your point."

"Just admit it matters who made something," Jess says to the one who offered me the edible. "I'll drop the subject if you admit you can't fully experience it without caring who made it."

I know they're talking about something different, but as I take a sip of the drink that appeared next to me, I can't help thinking about Wolfwood and how I agree, it does matter who makes the art. Otherwise I wouldn't even be hiding it. It matters who paints the scenes. It matters that I'm choosing colors, all of that. That it's my vision for the drawing brought to life, not my mother's.

I wouldn't feel guilty all the time if it didn't matter.

"Fine!" the girl who offered the edible says. "If it'll get you to talk about something more interesting, I admit it. I can't believe we're even talking about this at a party."

A noise comes from above, startling me. I look up, to my left. Do a double take. It's Kai—*he's here!*—hanging off some sort of bar that's attached to the ceiling. A trapeze. He's upside down, hanging from his knees. I have no idea what he's doing, but I can't believe how relieved I am to see him. He's looking down at me, clearly amused that I didn't notice him till now. I'm not sure how I missed him, except that there's so much to look at in here, and I wasn't exactly expecting him to be hanging from the ceiling. He's not a bat.

"Hey there," he says, chipper.

"What are you doing?" I ask, smiling way too wide. His tee is partly tucked into his pants, but one side is hanging down so I can see a glimpse of smooth skin on his torso.

"Hangin' out."

The girls all groan. "It was bad enough the first time, Kai," Jess says.

Ravi calls to him: "You really should get down. My dad would shit. Liability and all."

Kai swings a bit and then flips neatly down onto the rug. His beanie falls off. He grabs it and pulls it back on. I waste no time standing up and joining him. "I don't know how I missed you," I say, looking up again. "How'd you even reach it?"

He shrugs. "Flew."

We wander closer to the painting that's nearest to us, a massive, full-length portrait of a striking Black woman in a white gown, with a floral background that looks like brightly colored wallpaper. I'm pretty sure it must be by Kehinde Wiley, who did that incredible portrait of President Obama. Unbelievable. On the side table next to it is another tray of small sandwiches in an elaborate pattern. My stomach cramps at the reminder.

"Can I ask you something?" I say quietly, leaning down a bit so I'm closer to Kai's ear.

He looks expectant.

"Why isn't anyone eating the food? Is it just for decoration or something?"

He laughs. "Sort of. No, but seriously, I guess just because no one's hungry yet?" He lowers his voice. "And those sandwiches are kind of gross—they serve them every time we're at Ravi's, I have no idea why. I think it's a British thing. We'll order pizza at some point, I'm sure. But there's nothing wrong with the sandwiches, if you want one!"

"Nothing wrong with them. They're just gross."

"Aside from that, they're great."

I take one of the small blue napkins and pick a sandwich that looks like sliced cheese. "This isn't my usual party environment, so I just wanted to check they weren't sculptures or something."

"Not your usual environment?" Kai feigns shock. "Your friends don't all have elevators in their houses?"

"Elevators are undependable. My friends have staff who carry them from floor to floor, on those pillow seats." I take a bite. Cheese and mayonnaise? Not gonna complain about free food, but who makes a sandwich of cheese and mayo?

"How is it?" he asks.

"As reported."

We smile at each other, and I take another sip of my drink. Something feels different since the last time I saw him. Am I imagining that there's a crackle in the air between us? Every time we share a look I feel it spark. Maybe it's just me. Maybe when I touched his shoulder that time and felt all fizzy, I got zapped. But, at the very least, I feel like we're more comfortable with each other. Like actual friends. I ignore the voice inside me telling me that even being friends with him is too dangerous. The voice telling me I should have stuck to my plan to keep my distance.

"Are Fiona and Natalie coming?"

"Natalie's here," he says, looking around and then pointing to the other end of the room where the glass doors open onto a balcony. A few people are out there smoking. "Not sure about Fiona. She and her girlfriend had something else to do first."

"She has a girlfriend?"

"Yeah. And for what it's worth, I'm not in love with her." He rolls his eyes. "I had a crush on her in, like, third grade. Ravi won't let it die."

It makes me annoyingly happy to hear this. I finish my sandwich and ball up the napkin, not sure what to do with it. "So are you a gymnast or something?" I ask, thinking not only of him flipping off the trapeze but of that IG photo of him doing a handstand.

"Diver. Similar."

"You're the worst host," someone says from over by Ravi. She's standing next to the couch, arms crossed. "You said we could have next."

"My little sister's the only one who plays that anymore," Ravi says. "You really want to?"

"Yes!" some other girls say, and then one of them calls out, "Who wants to play *Dance Off?*" A few people raise hands.

I look at Kai. "Want to?"

"I'd embarrass you."

"I'm sure you're not that bad."

"Oh, no," he says. "Because I'd kick your ass."

I laugh. He doesn't realize that Grace and I were obsessed with a version of it, when I lived with her family. "You can try," I say. "We all have dreams."

We hang back and let the others go first, dancing in pairs, following the choreography on the screen and getting scored through some scanner process that's way more advanced than what we had at Grace's. When it comes time for one of us to take on the reigning winner, I gesture at him. "Age before beauty."

It's no contest between him and the skinny girl who seemed like she'd beat everyone. The song is Janet Jackson, and the choreography is a lot of fast footwork and gyrations, and he looks kind of hilarious but also like he could believably train to be a back-up dancer, no joke. At the end, I clap and raise my eyebrows at him.

"Ready?" he says.

I take off my slippers, happy the light in here is pretty dim so no one can see my feet well. I stand a few lengths away from Kai in front of the screen and stare down at him, this time standing as tall as possible to be as intimidating as I can be.

"Not fair," he says, grinning, as the first beats sound.

It's slow at first, easing us in—side step, shimmy, side step, shimmy, punch, punch, jump, kick change, punch, punch, jump, kick change . . . over again, arms added now. I'm getting the moves, watching my score—jump, kick change, jump, kick change. Hands in the air, eyes on Kai. We're dancing apart but playing together. Crackle crackling. Booties shaking. Watchers cheering. Scoring even. Kai gets hot, wipes his brow. Side step, shimmy, side step, shimmy. Hands in the air, hands in the air. Shake-shake-shake-shake, *boom*!

We laugh and catch our breath during the awkward extended side-step ending.

There are hoots and cheers when our final scores flash.

"Sorry," I say to him. Our scores were so close, it was the wipe of his brow that did it.

"About what? You think I couldn't have beaten you if I really wanted?"

"Not a chance." Don't have to be rich to dance well. Love that about it.

People seem to have lost interest, and no one wants to take me on, which is fine with me. We collapse on a nearby couch, a small, velvet-upholstered one with embroidered pillows in the color palette of Tania Bawa's designs.

"That's the painting I hung the other day." Kai nods toward a smallish abstract canvas nearby. "If you want to compliment me on my skills."

"The height is masterful. Not to mention it looks remarkably level."

He chuckles.

"So what's the deal with you and the gallery?" I ask. "You said you don't really work there, that time we saw each other, but it seems like you do?"

"Yeah, I don't officially have a job or anything. I just . . ." He pauses, eyes on his hands. "Hiro's not allowed in the apartment, but this one time I was alone, and he got past the doorman late at night, and he was at the door and I let him in. It was the wrong move, but it was raining out and I didn't know what to do, and he ended up taking some shit, of course. So I'm working off some of the money to replace it."

"Why?!" I say, indignant on his behalf. "That's not your responsibility. I can't believe your mother's making you."

"She's not making me. I want to. I knew I shouldn't let him in. And I'm not working off *all* the money. Just some."

"Of course you let him in. It was raining. And nighttime." This seems awfully harsh of Annika, no matter what he says.

He shakes his head. "Nah, I knew what would happen."

Before I can say anything else, Ravi appears with a "Hey, kids," and sits on my other side. I have to scooch over. My leg brushes against Kai's. Our arms press together, skin against skin.

"You guys looked cute out there," Ravi says. "Like Karlie and Christian." For once I actually get the pop culture reference someone's making, since it relates to *Project Runway* and the incredibly tall model host who towers over the designer mentor. "When are you leaving?" he asks Kai.

"Rude," Kai says, which is what I'm thinking, because I'm assuming Ravi means when is he leaving the party, but then he grins and adds, "Friday." He turns to me, "I'm going to Japan. Annual trip with my dad."

"Wow. How long for?"

"Around two weeks. We visit family in a couple places."

"You're gonna miss all the fun," Ravi says. "Indigo promised to show me all her favorite places in the hood, which she has not done yet."

"Sorry about that," I say. God, I was hoping he'd forget. *Here's the cheapest laundromat, Ravi. And the bodega where they give me free coffee 'cause they like me.*

A couple of girls have sat on the floor by us, along with another guy. I wasn't introduced to any of them, but with Kai here next to me, I don't feel awkward. One of the girls says, "So, Ravi, you like living here? Or do you miss our thrilling Upper West Side?"

"The park," Ravi says. "That's all I miss. Food and the whole scene are much better here. Neighbors are better, too." He nudges me.

"Cute block," the other girl says.

"Yeah," Ravi says. "Would be better if the asshole on the corner didn't keep telling me to 'go back to where I came from.' Otherwise it's great."

I know exactly who he's talking about. "White bearded guy with a dog?" I say.

Ravi nods and leans forward, elbows on his knees. "I feel like asking him where he wants me to go back to. Uptown? Or London? That's where my parents are from, technically." He huffs. "Obviously I know what he really means. And not like I haven't gotten it before. But hearing it every single time I walk that way makes me want to punch the guy."

"You should," one of the girls says.

"Yeah, well . . ." Ravi leans back now. "Whatever. The guy's homeless, sleeping on a piss-smelling street corner, so . . . you know." He shrugs.

My body tenses slightly. "Know what?"

"Oh, just, who cares what he says? Doesn't matter."

"He's still a person," I say. "What he says matters." The air around us gets a bit brittle as everyone keys in on me.

Ravi knits his brow. "Are you defending a racist?"

"No, definitely not. But his crime is being a racist. Being homeless has nothing to do with it." I can't read Ravi's expression. "I mean, no matter who says it, it's toxic. Toxic, racist shit. When you write someone off because they're homeless, you're opening the door to write them off in other ways."

My face is burning after I say it. All these people staring at me. And while the boy appears white, the two girls have skin the same shade as Ravi's. But this isn't something I could let slide. The biggest jerk in the world could be homeless and it wouldn't make him any less of a *person*. A person in a shitty situation he didn't ask to be in.

Finally, Ravi says, "Okay, yeah, I feel you."

His tone is genuine, and the tension in the air dissipates as quickly as it came.

"And I really am sorry he's such an asshole," I say. "Didn't at all mean to imply it was okay. If anything, the opposite."

"No worries," Ravi says. "Forget it."

"It was a good point," one of the girls says to me. "But, fyi, guys, more respectful to say 'unhoused.' Not 'homeless.'"

I almost laugh. The irony, her telling me that. I use "homeless" because it's the word that feels true: What I didn't have was a *home*. Also, while I hope she corrected us out of actual respect, it's infuriating that a lot of people seem to care more about the language than the "unhoused" individuals themselves.

"Right," I say. "Thanks."

"Should we order from Lombardi's?" the other girl asks the group. "Please. I've got the snackies."

"Why can't you ever call it 'the munchies' like a normal person?" the first girl says.

They all start to discuss, and I become aware of Kai, sitting on my other side. I hope he understood the point I was making. I hope

I wasn't being an asshole, saying all that as a white girl. He's leaning forward now, conferring about pizza.

"Anyone have topping requests?" a guy asks.

I have no idea how the money would work for this, whether if I make a request I'll be expected to pay, so instead of being part of the discussion I mumble something about needing to get my phone. I do want to get it, in case my mom texted about anything. (She thinks I'm at Grace's.) And I need a breather from the group, too.

I head over to the elevator and press the call button. When the door opens, Fiona is inside, along with another girl, taller and curvier, whose hand she's holding. "Indigo!" Fiona says. She drops her girlfriend's hand to hug me and exclaim how happy she is I'm here, then introduces me to the girlfriend, Saskia, who says Fiona told her all about me, and even though they both seem genuine, I can't think what she would have told her except that my face is messed up. Flustered, I step into the elevator and press a button, relieved when the door closes and I'm left alone.

After a short descent, it opens to reveal an unfamiliar room, not the entry floor. Without thinking, I let myself be pulled in by the riot of color on the walls. My eyes start to make sense of it, and I realize it's maybe Ravi's mother's studio. Or, at least, a home studio, if not her official one. There's a blue lacquer desk, an orange glass chandelier, a sitting area of modern armchairs, floor-to-ceiling bookshelves filled with art and design books, an entire wall covered in fabric swatches, sketches, notes . . . It's like being inside a kaleidoscope. I take a few steps forward and then a few more.

A folded purple garment rests on a nearby chair, and I can't stop myself from gently picking it up. My jaw drops a bit when the silk jersey unfurls. It's a short tank dress in a deep plum color, with almost-neon-yellow racing stripes on one side. Midway down, one of the stripes splits away and wriggles to the hem haphazardly. Such an unexpected detail. The armhole on the opposite side has fuchsia piping. The sportiness of the style contrasts with the expensive silk jersey that drapes like water. I've never felt something this luxe. I have an incredible urge to press it against my cheeks.

"Can I help you?"

Startled, I turn around. Tania Bawa is standing in front of the elevator. I didn't even hear the door open.

"Oh, hi," I say, hurriedly putting the dress back on the chair, fumbling with it as the watery silk starts to slide toward the floor. "I'm sorry. I'm a friend of Ravi's. I didn't mean . . . I guess I pressed the wrong elevator button, and it was impossible to resist coming in. All the color. I'm sorry."

"We should switch the lock settings on the lift," she says. She has a smooth voice and what sounds like a proper British accent. She's wearing wide-leg lime-green silk pants and a white linen tank. Thick-framed tortoiseshell glasses. Her black hair pulled back in a tight knot.

"Sorry," I say again, sheepish, and begin to walk out.

Then I realize that this might be my only chance to talk to her. and why should I feel bad, anyway? All I did was step into the room and pick up a piece of clothing off a chair.

"I'm Indigo," I say, trying to sound more composed. "I live on the block. I know Ravi through Kai. My mom's an artist, she shows at Annika's gallery."

Tania Bawa doesn't respond, just looks at me with an unreadable expression.

I plunge ahead. "I love your designs. Your aesthetic. Everything about it. The color combinations are amazing. The shapes and cuts, too."

"I see. Vintage Chloé?" she says, studying my weird top.

I look down at it, as if I have to check. "I'm not sure. The label was cut out. I do a lot of upcycling with clothes I thrift. I'm into that whole movement. Always had to figure out a way to make stuff fit me, you know? And the environment. I'd like to . . . well, my dream is to be a designer who makes really affordable, stylish clothes with recycled fabric, so people don't have to go to fast-fashion places."

Jesus, I can't shut up. I never, ever get like this!

She doesn't seem put off, though. Reserved, but not annoyed. "Are you at FIT?"

"Still in high school."

The pause in conversation is probably the right time for me to leave, but I don't. "The dress is beautiful," I risk saying, just to keep things going. I look toward the chair.

"Doesn't drape quite right," she says. "It's a sample. I gave it to a friend, but it didn't do for her." She shrugs.

"The colors remind me of my mother's paintings. There's a lot of violence in her imagery, but it's contrasted by the lush beauty of the colors." I laugh nervously. "I mean, that's probably what I read somewhere, but it's true."

"What's her name?"

"Zoe Serra. She has a show coming up this fall."

"That rings a bell. Have Annika be sure to contact me about it."

"I will. And sorry again for coming in here." I start toward the elevator.

"You can try it, if you like."

I pause. "Try it?"

She nods at the dress. "Take it. The colors are right for you. Maybe it will work better."

I don't know what she means.

"I'm sorry," I say. "Take it where?"

"Home. I'm not going to do anything with it."

She's giving me the dress? I'm literally speechless. Unable to form a word.

"Don't get your hopes up," she says. "It might not hang right."

"But . . . it's so beautiful. You don't want to sell it? At a discount or something?"

I can tell from her face that was the wrong thing to say, but I'm so overwhelmed. I know from *Vogue* that if this were in perfect condition it would cost hundreds of dollars. And aside from that, I've never even touched anything so beautiful.

"Just leave it if you don't want it," she says. "Either way." She walks over to the desk. "And let Ravi know if you need a recommendation for school. I'll look at your portfolio."

"Thank you," I say. "Thank you so much."

She raises her hand in acknowledgment.

Chapter Eighteen

Back upstairs, I sit with Kai, Fiona, and Saskia, so shocked by what just happened that I barely notice what's being said. I eat three whole slices of pizza (Ravi's treat), but even those hardly register in my train of thought: *I own a dress by Tania Bawa. I own a dress by Tania Bawa.* A bit later, when Kai says he's beat, I immediately offer to head out with him. Fiona tries to convince us to stay, but Kai just tells her she should've gotten here earlier, and we exchange hugs with her and Saskia, like I've become part of this equation.

We say goodbye to Ravi together. "Huh," Ravi says, looking between us with a quick lift of his eyebrows.

"You're so predictable," Kai says. "We're just taking the elevator together."

"Is that what the kids are calling it these days?"

Kai rolls his eyes.

I thank Ravi for the party and check one more time about the dress, which is in a little brown bag that one of the housekeepers got for me. I keep waiting for someone to tell me I'm being punked.

"Totally fine," Ravi says. "She won't even think about it." He looks between us again and adds, "Take care of my boy," as he tugs on Kai's beanie. I don't know him well enough to understand the attitude he's giving off. His words are jokey, but there's definitely something cool in his tone.

We step into the elevator, surrounded now by endless versions of ourselves.

"So, was it horrible?" Kai says, as we begin the descent. "Are we as bad as you thought?"

"I was never thinking you were horrible. I had a good time." Honestly, I'm not sure if I did or how I feel about any of it (except the dress and the pizza and dancing with Kai). What does it mean that I think it's completely messed up that some people have so much money, but that I'm also happy I was able to pass as part of the group?

"If Ravi seemed standoffish, it's just that he's probably confused why you'd be leaving with me instead of hanging around to see if you have a shot with him. Not a situation he's used to."

I laugh.

During our slow stroll down the block, he fills me in on backstories and gossip about a couple of the kids I met. (Victorian girl, Jess, is apparently his "archnemesis," because he always came in second to her at middle school spelling bees.) When we reach my stoop, he hops up a step and faces me. We're about the same height now—he's maybe even a smidge taller. His stance is a little wide. Solid. Like he's sure of the place he takes up in the world and won't concede it to anyone else. Instead of seeming arrogant, though, it's just . . . hot.

"Is this better?" he says, looking straight into my eyes.

"I thought we were past these comments," I say. "And better for what?"

He doesn't answer. Our faces are only about a foot apart. Breathing the same air. His eyes are clear and bright and kind and have that spark that never goes out. His lips look soft and smooth. I want to know what sort of kisser he is. I want to lean forward and taste him. But ... he's Annika's son. And rich. And if he wasn't Annika's privileged son, he's still not someone I'd want as a meaningless hookup. I like him too much for that. No way in any universe do I have room in my life for an actual relationship, whatever that would even mean.

I force myself to back up a step. The moment breaks.

"Okay, so ... get home safe," I say.

He hops onto the sidewalk. "See you in a few weeks."

Japan. I'd forgotten. "Have an amazing trip."

"Thanks." He smiles and starts down the block.

I feel a tug of disappointment, and also the sudden desire to clear the air, make sure we both know where things stand.

"Kai?" I say, when he's a few paces away.

He turns.

"I'm not sure what's going on ..." I walk toward him, moving my hand between us. "But I feel a crackle, you know? And—"

"A crackle?" he says, amused.

"Yeah. And I really like you and would love to be friends. But there's this guy I hang out with on and off. Casual, y'know? If you and me were hanging out, I'd want it to be more than that. And maybe you would, too? But I don't have the space right now to start something that would be an actual . . . thing."

He stares at me, eyebrows raised. "Wow. That was . . . a lot. Of assumptions."

I laugh awkwardly. He's right, of course. "I don't know how much of it needed to be said, if any. I like to just get stuff out there. Sorry if it was way off base."

"Well, thanks. For the honesty."

"Sure." We exchange uncomfortable smiles.

As I walk up the stoop, I can't help feeling that that was some seriously dishonest honesty. *I like to just get stuff out there* . . . How hypocritical of me to say that when I'm keeping so much from so many people, Kai included. But it's not like I can tell him I need to keep a distance because I'm scamming his mother.

"Indigo?"

I turn back and see he's coming toward me again. I meet him halfway.

He hesitates, biting his lip, then says, "It wasn't that I wanted to help him. I was scared, that's all."

I furrow my brow. "Sorry, what?"

"I didn't . . . It wasn't really that I wanted to help my brother, when I let him in the apartment. I mean, not in that moment, with him at the door. Wanting to help wasn't the main thing." He folds his arms against his body, as if he's cold. "I was scared of him. That's why I let him in. I'm a pussy and I was scared he'd break in or hurt me later or something. He sounded so angry. It wasn't because I wanted to help him."

I sit with it for a minute. "That's so understandable, Kai."

"Honestly? Sometimes I wish he would just . . . disappear. Most of the time I don't, of course. I want him to get better. But sometimes I think he'll never get better, and then . . ." He stares off at something in the distance. "Makes me feel like shit."

"Of course. But it doesn't make you a bad person. Sounds really normal to me."

"That's what my therapist said. That it's good to acknowledge messy emotions. And to know I can't save him. Her whole thing is that I need to know it's okay to not even try. Just to back away." He meets my eyes now.

"Well, I mean, not quite. You have to keep trying, even if you know it might not work."

"Not at the expense of your own sanity. Or safety. It's like that oxygen thing in a plane." He must see the confusion on my face. "You know, if you're crashing, you put on your own oxygen mask before your kid's."

I've never flown, but that doesn't sound right. I think it'd be impossible not to want to put it on your kid first.

"Anyway," he says, "when you love people . . . it can make things hard."

"I guess so," I say. Truthfully, I haven't thought of it like that before. Because love is what's supposed to be good, right? It's what's supposed to help us get through stuff, not make it more difficult. But obviously he's right.

Our eyes stay locked on each other's. This time, neither of us seems to want to be the one to walk away. We end up in a fumbling, hesitant dance into a goodbye hug. And once his warm body is against mine, I have to force myself not to run my hand down his back to the curve of his lower spine, and not to bend my head so I can rest my face against his neck and smell his spicy warmth. I concentrate on the tautness of his muscles under my fingers. On the rhythm of his breath. I don't know how long we stand here, but it's not a normal length for a hug like this that's supposed to be platonic.

The pull I'm feeling toward him—physical *and* emotional—is so strong, I'm relieved he's going to be away for a while. Even trying to keep it less complicated, it's still feeling like I won't be able to stop it. Like we're two marbles rolling down the opposite sides of a "V" toward that point at the middle.

Finally, we step apart.

He clears his throat. "I figured honesty deserved honesty. You know, about Hiro. So, there. That's the truth of it."

Honesty. Right.

My mother just murmurs a half-asleep greeting. I pull the curtain around my bed, turn on the little lamp, and take out the dress—the only thing that could possibly take my attention from the memory of Kai's body pressed against me. I spread it out on the mattress as carefully as if it were a spiderweb. I expected that I'd want to try it on right away, but I actually don't want to quite yet, in case it doesn't fit or doesn't look good. Right now, I want to imagine that it's perfect. I want to picture myself wearing it and looking like it was made for me. Hell, even if it wasn't made for me, I'll figure out a way to make it look like it was.

This dress is mine. How is this possible?

An issue, though, is where to keep it. All my clothes except underwear and nightclothes are hanging neatly on a rack that's clearly visible when my curtain is open. I don't have a closet. And this color and fabric—my mother will notice it hanging there, I'm sure. She'd never believe I got it at the thrift store. If it were sold used, it would go for at least a couple hundred dollars. I can't explain to her that I was at Tania Bawa's house. She still has no idea I've gotten friendly with Annika's son.

I fold it up neatly and put it in my plastic drawer with my underwear, even though that feels like sacrilege and I hate to think of it wrinkling. Just a temporary solution.

Then I get in bed and try, unsuccessfully, not to think about Kai.

As I'm drifting to sleep, I get a text.

Kai: The cackle is real

And a second later . . .

Kai: *crackle!!!!!

I'm pretty sure I'm still laughing when I fall asleep.

Chapter Nineteen

'm on a weird high from the party; that's the only explanation for what I do the next day. I'm high from the attraction I feel to Kai, from the dress and meeting Ravi's mother, from the fact that nothing went wrong . . . I'm as high as my mom dancing on top of a cube-shaped sculpture.

Because I could just leave well enough alone. Instead, when I'm checking my email at the library before work, I send a message to Annika, eagerly sharing the news that Tania Bawa wants to know more about my mother's show. I'm excited, thinking it could be another sale. With the type of money she has, maybe she'd buy more than one! In my enthusiasm, I perhaps slightly exaggerate Tania's interest.

My high continues through work. When my shift is over, Naomi lets me borrow her phone to go online. A reply from the gallery is waiting. Diana tells me that Annika wants to hang framed *Wolfwood* pieces in the office as a preview, for the rest of the summer—one each, in both the downtown and uptown spaces— to help build excitement and also so she can show them to Tania, who she'll be having lunch with in a couple of weeks. Not the piece on reserve for the Millers (the first one), two *different* pieces. So we should bring all the paintings that are finished to Su-Jin Lim, the framer, on Sunday at 11:00 A.M., and after they're framed Annika will choose which to hang.

I stare at the screen, not sure what to say. I've finished only the Millers' piece and one other. I'm not even halfway done with the third.

I text her while I'm walking home.

> Me: Got your email. I don't think that many are ready for framing. Zoe works on several at a time like I said before
>
> Diana: Given how soon the show is I'm sure many are finished. None of this should be a surprise. If this is a problem I need to talk to Zoe directly

I don't answer.

> Diana: Please confirm its not a problem. Or should Annika or I get in touch with Zoe
>
> Me: Not a problem

I stop walking and look up at the sky, picturing the days until then. I have Fud shifts on Thursday, Friday, and Saturday, and I promised Trinity I'd be at her place on Saturday morning. That doesn't leave me enough time to finish the third piece, not painting at the rate I've been going. Sooo . . . either I bring the first and second paintings to the framer (which will make Diana or Annika insist on talking to my mom), or I don't go to work and basically live at the studio, painting as much as possible, or . . .

... I tell my mother what's going on and get her to help. We can work in shifts. She can be there when I'm at the Fud. We can finish the third one in time to take it to the framer on Sunday.

My body floods with dread at the thought of talking to her. Confessing what I've done. I've been planning to do it, of course, but not tonight!

Get some balls, Indigo. You're never going to want to do it. She'll know you were just trying to help. She loves you and she'll forgive you.

I arrive home with all the eagerness of a prisoner arriving at their execution. We make rice and beans. She's excited because a new juice store where she applied contacted her for references. I feign enthusiasm when really my mind is searching for an opening, trying to guess what approach might work, anticipating her reaction and remembering how badly our other talks went, when I tried to get her to do the show.

"You're sure he's okay with it?" she says, talking about Marcus, Jaden's dad, who's agreed to be a reference.

"Completely."

"It's so nice of him."

I nod and spoon rice onto our plates. Neither of us says anything else as we set food on the table and fill our water glasses. After we sit, I know I need to get it over with.

"Mommy?" I say, looking her in the eyes.

"Mm?"

"Um ... so, the thing is ..."

Her smile falters. She can sense something's coming, something that will disrupt this fragile moment of hope for the future. And shit, who am I kidding? Why would I tell her now, when she's just got good news about a job possibility? Why would I ruin things for her? She's going to freak out, and we're going to fight, and she'll probably need days to cool off before she agrees to help with the paintings—if she agrees at all. There's no way she'll be ready to help as soon as I need her to. I have other options, and telling her is not the right one. "Um, I'm just . . . really proud of you," I say. "With this whole job thing."

She doesn't smile, exactly, but I can tell how pleased this makes her. "I haven't gotten a job yet. Haven't even gotten an interview!"

"I know. But even just doing all the applications, taking that risk, is really great. Especially for, y'know, a washed-up old lady."

She laughs and reaches for my hand. "Thanks, honey. That means a lot."

Not the right time. I'll make this work on my own.

I call the Fud and tell them that my grandmother died, that I'll be out of town for the funeral, and that I'll be missing my next shift and will check in after that to let them know. I'll probably have to cancel the ones on Friday and Saturday as well, but no point in doing it now when a miracle might occur. (Who knows, maybe the framer will postpone the appointment or something.) Losing the money from even one shift is pretty much a disaster. I'll have to figure out a way to make up the lost income. But that's a problem for Future Indigo. The third painting is the problem I need to solve now.

Early Thursday morning, I leave a note for my mother, telling her that I've gone to work and that I'm going to spend the night with

Grace's family, and that I'll check in when I can but not to worry if I don't pick up the phone. I'll have the ringer turned off while I'm painting—don't want her to panic.

I arrive at the studio with an extra-large coffee, packets of free saltines from the soup bar at work, a ramen cup, and a bagel. I figure they should last me awhile.

Every other time I've painted, I've set an alarm, because I've always had somewhere else to be. Now I don't have to. I can just paint until I get hungry or have to sleep.

The longer I can keep at it, the better. I don't give too much thought to how long that might be.

1989

The sun is just rising over the rippled metallic ocean when Colin returns from Cancún. Zoe hasn't slept all night, dragged back into a darkness she hasn't felt since before she met him. When she finally sees Don Eduardo's car pulling up the dusty road, she's like sand inside a clenched fist being released and spilling onto the beach. She almost collapses in relief.

As she hugs him fiercely, he explains that the car broke down, that he slept by the side of the road, waiting for the Green Angels, the mechanics who patrol the highways. He doesn't seem tired, though, just excited about what's in the car: a video camera and boxes of blank videotapes, along with endless packs of batteries. He tells Zoe that he's done painting. He's come up with an idea for a series of video sculptures. He doesn't tell her details yet, just says it's so much more where art is going and talks about different video shows they saw together at galleries in New York. He's still working stuff out, he says, but this is the perfect place to film the sort of footage he has in mind. Individual works that will be played on monitors in sculptural arrangements. Of course, they don't have a TV—or even electricity—so he can't work on it here, aside from getting the raw footage, but he says that doesn't matter. This is just the first stage.

He's talking so quickly about all of this that Zoe can barely keep up. And she's distracted by the idea of him not painting anymore. Painting is what he does. But she lets herself trust his excitement.

The sisters emerge from their cabana toward the end of his explanation. As Lila jokes about wanting to star in his movie, Scarlet watches him cleaning empty beers off the passenger seat with a judgmental expression. But when she starts to say something, Azul gives her a big-sister look, meaning *not your business*, and she keeps quiet. Thank goodness—Zoe doesn't want anything ruining Colin's mood. He's laughing, happy, practically vibrating with this new energy. Who cares if he had a few beers while driving? He's fine!

Although Zoe feels guilty about having read the letter, she now knows what she needs to do: show him that there's someone in his life who believes in him, by supporting this new project. Show him that his father doesn't know anything. It's like she's discovered the tiny baby bird of vulnerability inside, and she needs to cup her hands around it and nurture it until it flies. It feels like a big responsibility. Somehow it makes her love him even more.

Chapter Twenty

When I ran away from the little hut, away from the Wolf's decapitated head and all that blood, I grabbed Lila and we took off the way we came. Since then it's been nonstop attacks—vines snagging our ankles, pulling us into water holes; grenade-throwing flowers making us dodge and weave through explosions.

Now, we've finally found Scarlet and Azul, crouched together where we left them, a few of the Others patrolling the area.

Scarlet stands up. "That took long enough!"

I bend over, hands on my knees, breathing heavily.

"It was a shelter!" Lila says. "An old one. Just like Zoe said. It—"

"Well, was there anything in it?" Scarlet asks, impatient. "Did you go inside? Was he there?"

Azul lays a hand on Scarlet's arm. "Let them talk."

"I went inside," I tell them, once I've got my wind back. "It was a trap. There was a monster hiding. Other than that, nothing. Some old fabric, that's it."

A monster is a weak excuse for why I freaked out and ran, but it's the best I can come up with. What I saw in there—everything from the girl in the hammock to his decapitated head to the blood covering my feet—was in my imagination. There wasn't a drop of blood on me when I reached Lila. I don't know who that girl was or why I pictured her with him. I must have imagined the bracelet, too. There's nothing like that in Wolfwood. It was all just products of my confused mind. Nothing that the sisters need to know.

"Not a portal," Azul says, sounding disappointed.

"And no clues?" Scarlet asks. "About where he is now, or how to get home?"

I shake my head. She looks almost pleased that my hunch was wrong.

"It's still good we checked it out," Lila says, defensive. "We'd have kept wondering."

"Well, now that we know, it's time to move on," Scarlet says.

"I need to rest." Lila sinks cross-legged onto the ground.

Scarlet starts to object, but Azul stops her. "We've got Others stationed around a perimeter, and we haven't had any trouble. This would be a good time to sleep."

Even though there's no nighttime in Wolfwood, we still sleep occasionally. Or, at least, the sisters do. I stay awake and guard them. Now, we all settle onto the ground, keeping close to one another. Lila rests her head on my lap. Azul sings a pretty song, a lullaby, like she always does. Scarlet keeps a rock clutched in her hand. Eventually, their breaths turn deep and slow.

As I'm scanning the foliage around us, one of those black-and-white visions flickers in my mind. Me, back at the little hut, alone. Why would I go back there alone? That doesn't seem safe at all. And ... wait. Something else. I see the shelter collapsing around me. It's a clear image. I'm standing alone in the middle of that hut, the roof and walls collapsing around me. It looks like the kind of dangerous situation my instincts usually protect me from. But I know by now that if I have one of these visions, it's supposed to happen. For everything to turn out right, that's how things are meant to go.

I carefully lift Lila's heavy head off my lap, stand, and creep quietly away, ignoring the accusatory stares of the Others.

There's a true calm in the air as I follow my intuitive map—no sense of a coiled spring or imminent danger. The landscape has shifted again; the shelter is now just a stone's throw from where the sisters are sleeping. I've barely traveled any distance at all when I'm approaching it from behind. Then, suddenly, from the other side: a rustle. I freeze.

Another rustle.

Then nothing. Stillness.

I move around to the opening. Step into the doorway.

The netting around the hammocks is clean and untorn, the hammocks empty. No sign of anyone.

On impulse, I set down my blade and climb into the hammock on the right, arranging myself as it sways slightly from side to side. Once I'm settled, I close my eyes. I can hear the ocean. No, there's no ocean here. It's the breath of the jungle. The air shifts above me. I look up. It's him, his blond hair glowing in the light from the doorway. I'm so happy to see him! He climbs into the hammock with me, and I adjust until we're fitted against each other. He's warmer even than the steamy air. I wrap my arm around him. Love fills my veins. I want to make him part of me. I nuzzle against his neck, inhale his warmth.

And I smell his shame—sharp, sour.

I pull back.

He presses something into my palm. A silver bracelet. I slip it on to my wrist.

I close my eyes. Tell myself not to question his shame. Tell myself I'm happy. Keep my eyes shut and block it all out. I drift into sleep.

When I wake up, I'm alone in the hammock.

He's standing nearby, holding my blade. He raises it above his head.

I flinch back, scared.

He brings it down on his own leg. Blood spatters the walls. He raises it again, hacks off his hand. Blood spurts from the stump. He raises it again. I want to stop him, but I'm paralyzed. I watch him chop and slash and bleed. Until, finally, I find my courage. I tumble out of the hammock, feet sloshing in blood. I grab the blade—he's too surprised to stop me.

My heartbeat thunders.

He stares at me. *Help me*, his eyes say. He gets on his knees, the pool of blood lapping at his shins. Yes, I need to help him.

I raise the blade and swing it clear through his neck, sending his head flying. It hits the wall and splashes into the red flood.

I scream and drop the weapon.

He's kneeling, headless, in front of me. A geyser.

I can't stop screaming. I wanted to save him, not hurt him. What have I done?

I squeeze my eyes shut and scream and scream until there's no more space in the air.

When I open my eyes, the shelter is back to its old, dilapidated state. Ratty fabric and rotted ropes on the floor and hanging from the walls. No blood. No body. I'm panting, struggling to regain breath.

I sense movement behind me and turn.

The sisters are at the open doorway.

A cracking noise splits the air above. Another black-and-white vision flashes: the hut being decimated. It's about to happen. Everything is about to implode.

I don't run. I could, but I'm not supposed to. I'm supposed to stand here and let the sisters watch this happen to me.

With a crashing roar and impossible quickness, the thatched roof collapses, walls sucked in, debris pressing against me as I shout, getting crushed, in my mouth, in my eyes, I'm on the ground, under the rubble, the shelter imploded, everything moving around me, pressing and cutting into my flesh, immobilizing me. "Help!" I call into the chaos. A searing pain cuts my arm. I'm moving. Being moved, pulled. By my arm. Scraping against the ground below and debris above, I'm pulled fast out of the rubble, now *whoosh*, I'm out of the pile and jerked up, hanging in the air, the vine cutting into my arm.

Thorns dig deeper and deeper. Pain I haven't felt before. White hot. And then the sisters are below, and Lila is screaming, too, and Scarlet has found my weapon and she climbs to me, the blade strikes, and I fall.

Something hard under my cheek. Scuffed wood. Floor. I'm lying on the studio floor. My head . . . pounding. I struggle up, sit. My arm throbs. My mouth, cottony and dry.

I close my eyes. Hang my head. Press fingertips to temples. I don't remember lying down. I remember . . . hanging from my arm, falling. That monster, it was holding on to me. Scarlet cut me down. I open my eyes and look at my arm. A vicious, bloody scratch wraps around it. I can't . . . what happened? My thoughts are all mixed up. Real world—last I remember in the real world was starting painting. How did I get on the floor? I must have . . . passed out? Is that it? But how did I hurt my arm?

I use the table to help stand. Gravity's working double.

Everything tips and sways. I brace my hands on the table. The painting swims in front of my eyes. I'm falling into it. Or it's coming toward me. I close my eyes again. Something isn't right. Something . . . I don't know what I'm thinking. I look at the painting.

Color everywhere. It's finished. The third painting is completely finished. The final vignettes show the girl in white—me—sneaking back to the shelter alone. Going inside, the shelter imploding around me. Hanging from a tree by my arm, the sisters below.

How . . . ? How is this possible? How did I get so much done? This was supposed to take me days.

My phone sits on the corner of the table. I flip it open. Messages waiting, lots. And it's 9:04. In the morning. I started ... when? Yesterday, in the morning. I stare at the phone. Another minute blinks past.

I painted for more than a whole day? No.

Yes, I must have. The painting is done.

Too heavy, head too heavy to manage any more thought. Body drained. I barely make it to the couch.

Bright sun blankets me when I wake up. For a moment I think I'm back in my sunny bedroom in our old apartment. Then I remember. As I move to sit up, all my limbs protest with pain. My arm—I hold it up, see that bloody scrape. Memories of before I slept start to come back. Memories of Wolfwood, which should have disappeared by now. Cutting his head off with my blade, blood everywhere. The hut imploding. Hanging from my arm. The sisters underneath me, screaming. The pain of those thorns cutting into me ...

Then waking up on the floor, the third painting finished. That's right—I painted for so long I finished the whole thing and then passed out. I look around the room, yellow with sun. I must not have slept very long—this is still morning light.

I stand and find my phone on the desk. All those missed calls and texts, still waiting for me. And, wait ... it's 11:11 A.M., the following day.

Jesus. I painted for an entire day and then slept through another?

Like a sudden monster attack, hunger grabs me. Vicious. I find the bag of food, tear open the ramen, and inhale the noodles, raw, along with the leftover coffee, now cold and stale. I don't even care how disgusting it all tastes. I just need to get something inside of me.

My head isn't working right yet. Drained. Like my phone, which is giving me the low battery message, down to 1 percent.

I have fifteen voicemails, twenty texts. My mother, my mother, my mother, the Fud, the Fud, the Fud . . .

I fumble nervously with the buttons as I try to retrieve the messages. The first voicemail is my mother saying I should call her back. Then one from a collection agency we pay for my mom's debt. And then right as my mother is speaking again, the phone dies.

I slurp down a fresh coffee and devour the stale bagel on my train ride home, still ravenous despite my anxiety about what my mom wants. All those calls! She's hurt or sick, we were kicked out, Annika called her, she called Grace . . . So many very possible possibilities. Not to mention the Fud. I can't get fired. I can't.

And then I start worrying about that hut and what I saw there—how I had that vision of chopping his head off—before snapping back to reality. *Fuck*. Why aren't the memories leaving me, the way they usually do? I can see it all clearly, like I was really there. I know their names now: I'm Zoe, the girl in white. The sisters are Lila, Scarlet, and Azul. (Although nowhere in my mother's captions does she give the girls names, so are these really their names or just ones I've made up?)

I can't think about the throbbing wound on my arm without my heart trying to escape my chest. I just don't understand. Was I acting it out or something? I'd stopped worrying too much about the strange experience of how I paint, but this is different. This is too weird. How could I actually get injured?

Thank god I finished the piece, at least. I'm done. Never going back. This really, really has made me see that it's time to talk to my mother. I don't even care how mad she is. She's doing the rest of the paintings.

Although, all those calls . . . Who knows what situation I'm even coming home to.

I open the basement door and hurry in. She's standing by the hot plate. "I'm so sorry!" I say. "My phone died. What's going on?" I drop my bag and rush over to her without even taking off my shoes.

"Honey, I was so worried!" We hug tightly, then I pull back, my hands on her shoulders.

"What's going on?" I ask again. Nothing about her expression is telling me her mood.

"You didn't hear the messages?"

"No, just that you wanted me to call. My phone's totally dead. What's wrong?"

"Nothing. I got an interview!"

"You . . ."

"They want me to come in for a real interview, for the juice job! We only talked a couple minutes on the phone, about stuff like availability, and then they asked me to come in, tomorrow!" Now her face is all lit up.

"That's so great, Mom!" I laugh a little, letting out the tension. "God, seeing all those messages scared me."

"Sorry. I was excited. And nervous. I know it's silly—it's just a juice place. Will you help me decide what to wear?"

"Of course. Um, Grace and I didn't get much sleep or eat much. And I need to answer some calls I missed. How about I do that, take a shower, and then we get slices? My work shift isn't till two." (If I still have a job . . .)

"Perfect." She smiles.

I can't talk to the Fud in front of her, don't want her to know I missed my shifts Thursday and Friday and lied about a fictional grandmother dying. So I plug my phone into the charger and send Shawna several texts saying I thought I'd been clear that I'd be missing two shifts, not just one, and I'm so sorry that in my grief I must have confused her, and I'm so sorry I screwed them, etc., etc., etc. She responds immediately—angry, of course—but ends up telling me that she'll give me a pass this time, given the circumstances. *Phew.*

I stay in the shower long past the hot water disappearing, letting the icy spray clear my head. Waking up for real now. As I come back to life, I let myself get excited about the fact that I finished the paintings in time for the framer and that my mother has an interview. Once they meet her, they'll give her the job. She'll be pumped because of that. And I'll tell her that there's more good news: We can still do the show and make all that money, and three of the eight paintings are already done. She'll feel good about herself and thrilled that I figured out a way to make this happen, and she'll be happy to help me.

I refuse to think about the bloody scratch on my arm. Refuse to think about the lingering memories. Cuddling in the hammock. Chopping his head off. Doesn't matter. I won't be painting again.

Chapter Twenty-One

At the studio the next morning, I don't look at the three paintings, knowing I'll just start worrying about mistakes I don't have time to fix and not wanting to think about Wolfwood anyway. The paintings are inside the foamcore storage folder—the remaining blank pieces of paper moved onto the worktable—and all I need to do now is somehow get this enormous, unwieldy thing to Tribeca.

It's about six feet long. Am I really going to take it on the subway?

I guess I am.

Unfortunately for me, it's a windy summer day. By the time I've walked to the station in Bushwick, braved the annoyed crowd in the train car, transferred to a different line, and walked all the way west to reach the small brick building in Tribeca, on the far side of Manhattan, I feel like one of those plastic bags you see caught in a tree, getting battered this way and that, literally pushed in the wrong direction at one point on a block that's a wind tunnel.

Incredibly, I make it to the framer's address only five minutes late.

I compose myself before ringing the doorbell. As I wait for her to answer, the anxiety kicks in. Annika said this woman framed the old *Wolfwood* pieces, too. If she sees these and knows something's wrong, will she say something to the gallery? The image that I sent to Diana for the ad had been photoshopped. The framer will be the first person to see them for real, up close. The only person who'll see them naked, without frames to improve them.

I catch myself—*you're just making up stuff to worry about*. Even if they are terrible, I'm sure she won't tell the gallery. That's not her job.

A short, silver-haired Korean woman opens the door, introduces herself as Mrs. Lim, and ushers me in. She leads me through a large workspace, explaining what Annika already told me, that she framed all of Zoe's earlier pieces. "The frames we used then were quite simple," Mrs. Lim says, "but a special sort of wood. Have to see if I can get it again, if we decide it's best. I'll show you other options that might be just as good."

"You want me to help pick?" I know nothing about frames.

"Of course."

She brings me over to a large table, but there's not enough room on it. As she's clearing it off, the doorbell buzzes.

Mrs. Lim hurries to answer it. "Hello, hello," she says. "Just getting started."

She stands back. And Annika walks in.

Annika.

It's suddenly hard to breathe.

Did Diana tell me she was coming? No, no, she didn't. No one told me.

She's going to know. Seeing them up close like this, unframed? She's going to know my mother didn't do them.

Annika walks over to me and pockets her cell. "Where's Zoe?"

"Home," I say. "We didn't . . . I didn't know you wanted her to come. I didn't know you'd be here."

"Of course I am. We need to decide on the framing together. Zoe needs to approve it. Why did you think otherwise?" She's clearly annoyed.

"I'm sorry. Could . . . could I text her pictures of ones you're choosing between?"

Annika looks at her watch. "I suppose you'll have to."

As we gather around the table, I think about how to make this work. Okay, okay. I'll . . . I'll just fake sending the texts and getting answers. No problem. Although . . . that's presuming Annika even thinks the paintings are good enough to frame. *Annika is about to see the paintings.*

My gut roils. I want to run.

It had to happen sometime.

Mrs. Lim finishes clearing the table and I lift the folder onto it. Saying a prayer, I flip open the top.

The instant I see it, I'm bombarded by memories: the shelter imploding, the sisters' screams filling the air, the pain in my arm as I was dragged by the vine, the smell of my blood soaking my dress . . .

I give my head a tiny shake to clear it, wanting to be solidly *here*, standing with Annika and the framer, my feet on a wood floor, my nose smelling lacquer and sawdust, looking at the third painting. A painting that's a firework explosion of color, of sinuous shapes and dynamic motion.

Annika doesn't say anything, just stares at it. In the pulsating silence I again start to key in on the mistakes, one after another. And then I notice something else. There's no scene where I—where *she*, Zoe, the girl in white—imagines being in a hammock with the Wolf. No scene of her imagining cutting off his head. I've never kept memories like this, so I didn't realize that things happen while I'm there that aren't even part of the story.

Annika circles the table slowly, studying the piece from all sides. She lifts up her glasses and leans closer.

Finally, *finally*, she starts to speak. "It's been so long since I've seen one in person. Look at how gorgeous . . ." She presses her hand against her chest. "The colors, the detail, the . . . *life*. Zoe turns paper into a living object. Know what I mean? You can feel the jungle, feel the air, smell the flowers. And the girls . . . Look at those eyes." She points at Scarlet, gazing out at us from under her thick bangs. "It's uncanny. Those eyes are painted so simply, but it's like they're staring out of the paper and seeing you."

She glances up. "It's not just me, right? You see how extraordinary it is?"

Mrs. Lim nods. "Just like I remember."

Is this really happening?

"And, you know," Annika continues, "I feel like the feminist themes of the work are going to resonate even more now than twenty-five years ago. The sisterhood. Girls fighting together. Turning those petals into armor, the symbolism. It's basically the Me

Too movement, violence wherever they turn. And instead of killing them, it makes them stronger." She pauses. "Of course, white girls inside a brutal, tropical jungle is more clearly problematic now. But I think since the white man is the villain, it's okay. The violence isn't originating with the jungle itself." She seems lost in her thoughts for a moment, before adding, "Aside from anything else, it's just stunning art. It's *alive*."

I don't know what's going on, but I feel like I'm going to cry. From relief, maybe? And I understand what she's saying. It's not that the painting is realistic in a photographic way, but it feels like there's a pulse of life in the fibers of the paper. Like the girls' pain and love and desire and desperation are woven into the physical object. *I* did that?

We stand around the piece in silence for one more moment, and then Annika says, "Let's look at the others."

They were in the folder in reverse order, so when we bring out the one underneath it, we're actually looking at the second painting. Annika murmurs many of the same things and then moves on to the first one I did.

"Not quite as good," she says. "Still gorgeous and dynamic. Just a little rougher in execution. Like here." She points to the spot where I had too much paint on my brush and flooded the area. "But you know what? I don't mind. I like seeing the artist's struggles in work like this. Too facile and you lose the sense of labor and humanity. We see Zoe's struggles like we see the girls'. Not too much, of course. Only hints if you look closely."

God. This couldn't be going any better. She even likes the mistakes! I can't believe it. I want to laugh. Or whoop or sing or dance.

"Your mother is a pain in the butt," she continues, "but this makes it all worth it."

Mrs. Lim reaches for a stack of frame samples. "Let me show you options. I think we might—"

"Hold on," Annika says, frowning. She lifts up the corner of the top sheet and checks the two underneath it.

"What's wrong?" I say.

"Zoe didn't sign them."

I blink. "She didn't?"

"No. She needs to before they're framed."

How could I have forgotten that? All artists sign their works! "Um, she lets me do her signature on forms for school and stuff. Can I just—" Annika stares at me like I've suggested I slit her own wrist and sign with her blood. "No," I say. "Of course not. It should be her signature. I'll tell her when I get home. They won't be put in frames for a while, right?" Mrs. Lim will have to build whatever frames we pick. She said she'd have to order the wood.

Annika takes an annoyed breath through her nose. "Just call her now and tell her. You said she's at home, right? Let's just get her here. She can help pick the frame and sign them. She should have come to begin with."

"I'm not sure if she's still home," I say. "She had something to do. An appointment."

"Well, she can come from wherever she is. This is ridiculous. I'd call her myself, but she won't pick up for me."

I take my phone out of my bag with a hand that's almost shaky.

I start to send a text and Annika says, "Don't text, call her. So she's more likely to hear it."

She's watching me, and I can't think what else to do, so I press the call button and hold it up to my ear, let it ring twice and hang up. "Voicemail," I say with an apologetic smile.

"Why didn't you leave her a message, for god's sake?"

My phone starts to ring.

"There," Annika says. And before I know what's happening, she's taken my phone out of my hand and flipped it open and held it up to her ear. "Zoe, darling. It's Annika."

There's a pause, and I have to rest one hand on the table to steady myself while reaching toward the phone with a silent plea for Annika to give it back to me. But she doesn't.

She just says, "No, no, this is Indigo's phone. We're here together at Su-Jin's and I—" Pause. "Su-Jin Lim, the framer. Didn't you—" Pause. "Oh, I thought Indigo had told you. We're here to pick the frames and get Su-Jin started, and the pieces haven't been signed, it turns out, and I'd also like your input on the frame choice, so—Of course. She's right here." She holds the phone out to me, saying, in a harsher voice, "Tell her to hop in a car now. I can't stay long."

I take the phone, wetting my dry lips.

"Hi, Mom!"

"Indigo? What's going on? Why is Annika answering your phone? Where are you?"

"Are you done with your appointment? How did it go?"

"Terrible. What is going on, Indigo?"

I turn my back and start to walk across the room, toward the exit. "Didn't I tell you? The meeting with the framer is right now. And Annika wants you to come sign the three pieces and help pick the frames."

"What three pieces?"

I check to see if they can still hear me. They're looking down at the frame samples and seem to be talking to each other. I turn my back again and walk a little farther.

"Mommy," I say in a desperate whisper, "I'm sorry. I'm so sorry. But please, I'm begging you, just go along with what's happening and I'll explain later."

"Explain what? Indigo, what three pieces is she talking about? Why are you even *with* her? What the hell is going on?"

I swallow. Half-truths won't work anymore. "I never canceled the show. I did three of the Wolfwood paintings myself. Annika thinks you did them. Please, I'm begging, please, for me, please come here and sign them."

Silence.

"Mommy?"

"I don't understand . . . You told me you canceled it."

"I know. I lied. I'm sorry, I'm so sorry."

"You did the paintings? What do you mean? How?"

"From your drawings."

"And Annika thinks I did them? That's impossible."

"They look like yours."

"But . . . but I don't want to do the show. I told you. I don't want to do the show!" Her voice is panicky.

"I know. Just . . . I thought you might change your mind. We need the money so badly, Mommy. This isn't how I meant for you to find out."

I can hear her ragged breaths. "Jesus Christ. This is . . . Fuck! What should I . . . Where are you?" I don't know if I've ever heard her say the f-word before.

"The framer."

"I know that!" she shouts. "I know you're at the framer. The address, Indigo. Give. Me. The. Address."

Chapter Twenty-Two

I spend half the time we wait for her in the bathroom, close enough to being sick that I lean over the toilet. Why didn't I tell her before now? Did I really think I could keep going without something like this happening? I stare at myself in the mirror and try to set my face in a way that masks the physical panic surging through my body. I focus on redoing my lipstick, forcing my hand to stop shaking as I paint a meticulous shape with perfect edges. I recap the lipstick, stand up straight, and close my eyes for a brief second. Then go back out to wait.

The doorbell buzzes.

I barely recognize the woman Mrs. Lim lets in.

She's dressed for her interview in a black short-sleeved button-down and blue skirt. Her hair is back in a sleek knot. Her face is lightly made up, bringing it to life. Even in the midst of everything going on, my heart kind of breaks that she looks this nice for an interview at a juice store.

Her expression is completely neutral.

"Sorry you had to wait for me," she says as she nears us. "I got mixed up."

"Zoe, darling!" Annika says. "It's been so long." They share a hug that looks surprisingly genuine on Annika's part, stiff on my mother's part. When they break off, Annika asks, "How *are* you? Okay?"

"Fine, thanks." My mother doesn't even glance at me. She walks up to the table and looks at the piece, then the one under it, while Annika talks about how much she loves them.

Her face is blank. Scary blank.

"So," Annika says, "we need you to sign, and then we'll show you what we've narrowed it down to, for frames. Also, I have wonderful news." She pauses to smile at me. "Paige Droste of the Whitney Young Collectors Council, who Indigo met and spoke with, is going to bring the group by your studio for a talk and lunch in late August." My blood drains to my feet. "Now, before you say anything, Zoe darling, I know you don't like people in your studio. But that's weeks of time to prepare, and you can get a massage or take a Valium or whatever you need beforehand. You could even have Indigo there with you if you like. I'll make sure it's perfect and elegant."

"I didn't 'meet with her' meet with her," I say, clarifying, although what difference does that one detail make.

My mother still hasn't even looked at me. She just stands there, that same blank expression on her face.

Since it's clear she isn't going to reply, Annika keeps going. "I'm sure you'll get used to the idea before the date arrives. Anyway, from a purely crass point of view, these paintings are going to make you a lot of money. Now let's sign the pieces and choose the frames. I'm late for another meeting."

There's a horrible pause where my mother keeps standing there, silent. I have no idea what she's thinking or feeling, like she's rescinded my access to her emotions. Finally, she turns to Mrs. Lim.

"Do you have a pencil I can use?"

After we say goodbye to Annika, my mother walks down the sidewalk with furious strides. I hurry to catch up with her.

Should I say something? I don't even know where to begin. At least she went along with it. She came through for me. Maybe this won't be that big a deal. Maybe I should just explain how it happened and that will be it. She'll be angry for a day or two and then we'll move on.

"I'm so—"

"Don't!" she barks, stopping and turning to face me with a look of fiery intensity. A look I've never seen before. "When were you going to tell me?"

"Soon! I wasn't going to do them all. I wanted . . . I wanted you to take over."

"How did you do them?"

I don't answer immediately, and she says, "The paintings! How did you do them, Indigo?" Her voice rises, like she's trying to contain herself but can't quite.

I check to make sure Annika isn't walking behind us. "I already told you. Copied the drawings, like you do."

"No, how did you do them so *well?*" Her eyes are boring into me. The injury on my arm pulses, a warning. I know beyond a doubt that I shouldn't even hint at what happens when I paint.

"I don't know. I got into a flow. A rhythm."

She keeps staring at me for a long moment, then closes her eyes and puts her hands on her head. "Why?" she moans. "Why would you do this?"

"To help you. To help *us*. Just to get it started. Because you couldn't."

Her face stiffens at this. I shouldn't have said it.

She starts walking again.

"It's good, Mommy," I say, following her. "Annika liked them! Aren't you—"

"Don't, Indigo! Don't say anything else."

We walk home without speaking, my mother about ten feet ahead of me. When we reach the building, she heads down the stairs by the trash cans, unlocks the basement door, and then turns to me: "*Don't* come inside." She slams the door behind her.

I wait for a minute, halfway down the steps, my chest heaving from walking so fast and from the furious pounding of my heart. Not sure where else to go, I head back up, past the trash cans, up the stoop and inside the building. I hear it while I'm still in the entryway on the first floor. Wails. Primal. Desperate.

A chill spreads through me. I walk down the interior stairs to the door to our apartment. I sit on the floor in the damp, airless space, hugging my knees into my body. I'm shaking now. The wailing stops, replaced by a new sound. Choked. Desperate.

My mother, sobbing.

I've only seen my mother cry once.

She was the one who found me at the homeless shelter when I got beat up. She found me huddled next to the toilet, pants still down, blood pouring out of my mouth and nose. But that wasn't when she cried. She screamed for someone to get an ambulance and knelt down next to me and used her hoodie to wipe up blood until another woman started handing her damp paper towels. The whole time, she was saying soothing things to me, telling me I was okay, everything was going to be okay, that it was just some cuts.

She didn't cry in the ambulance, either, or at the hospital. She held my hand and talked to the doctors, distracted me when we were waiting for tests, and made sure that my pain was under control and that the police didn't interview me until I was ready.

She didn't cry when we said goodbye, the first night I went to stay with Grace's family. I did, but she didn't.

It was while I was still staying at Grace's that I got my new teeth put in.

My mother was the one who was there with me at the oral surgeon, waiting for me while it was happening. I was thrilled to finally be getting permanent teeth. When I came out, I flashed my mother a wide smile. They felt weird—way too big and foreign— but I had teeth again! She gave me a weak smile back, hugged me, and whispered, "I love you, Indi." We went outside. We sat at the bus stop. And, after a couple of minutes, I realized she was shaking. Then I realized she was sobbing, quietly, tears running down her face. I didn't know what to do. I had never seen her cry before.

"What . . . what's wrong?" I asked, feeling totally confused and helpless.

She just shook her head. She couldn't even speak.

"Mommy?"

Still nothing. At that point I was really scared.

"It's my fault," she finally said, between sobs.

"What?"

"I did this to you."

"Did what?"

She gestured at her own mouth. "Teeth. The teeth."

I didn't understand at all. "Aren't you happy I got them?"

"You . . ." The sobs were really choking her now. "You shouldn't have fake teeth," she managed to say. "You're only thirteen! It's my fault. We shouldn't have been there. You shouldn't . . . this shouldn't have happened to you. You could have died!"

Now she was crying about it? "But I'm fine!" I said. "Mommy, I'm totally fine! These teeth are way nicer than my real ones were. No bumps on the bottom. And so white and nice. I'm fine."

"It's my fault," she repeated. "It's all my fault. We shouldn't have been there."

She couldn't stop crying. The bus came and went. People stared at us. I had my arm around her, telling her it wasn't her fault, that everything was going to be okay, that my new teeth were great. That we were going to get a new home soon. That everything was totally fine. But I couldn't get her to stop crying. I was terrified. And lonely. It was the first time I realized I was a completely separate person from my mother, alone in the world. And all I knew was that I needed to fix this for her, fix it for us, so we could be together again.

I started making money after that: washing dishes at a diner we went to a lot, bussing tables, cleaning Parker's consignment store, babysitting. Luckily, enough people in our area of the East Village knew me that it wasn't too hard to find opportunities. Sometime later—four or five months—I got all dressed up, figured out how to take the PATH train to Hoboken, found the Asslord's office, and proposed that he let us rent out the front section of the basement, instead of wasting it on storing the useless junk that was piled down there.

I was fourteen. Probably he wouldn't have listened to me if I wasn't already five-foot-ten and wearing heels and makeup. But I was and he did. And being able to tell my mother that we could have a home again was the best moment of my entire life.

I wait in the hallway for a long time, the muffled sound of her sobs through the door making me feel just as scared and lonely and helpless as I did sitting at that bus stop. I can't miss my closing shift at the Fud, though, not after accidentally missing that other one. So when I can't stall anymore, I quietly open the door and go inside to get my uniform on. My mother's on the couch. She doesn't move. I don't risk saying anything, just change my clothes and go.

When I get home at night, she's not here. I lie in bed for hours, tension keeping all of my senses at high alert. She finally comes back, heads straight to the bathroom, and throws up. I go to her, but she tells me to leave her alone. The vomit reeks of alcohol. It makes me gag, but I don't leave. I get down next to her and hold her hair back while she cries and heaves, and I tell myself everything's going to be okay. It's all going to be okay.

1981

When Zoe's mother was sick—really sick—nine-year-old Zoe thought she could save her. She made paintings on huge sheets of paper, colorful scenes of herself and her parents doing their favorite things: picnicking, sledding, riding the carousel... Zoe hung the paintings around her mother's hospice room, convinced that they would do what all the surgery and chemo and radiation hadn't done, by reminding her mother why she had to stay alive.

After her mother died, Zoe's father took her to Paris to visit the art museums—something extravagant to distract them. As she lost herself in Van Gogh's sky and Monet's poppies, Zoe knew that when they returned to New York, her mother would be waiting for them. Zoe's paintings would have brought her back. She knew it.

When they arrived at JFK and her mother wasn't there to greet them at the gate, Zoe still didn't let herself believe anything was wrong. When they got to the apartment in Queens, Zoe told herself her mother was at work. She refused to go to bed that night, explaining to her father that she wanted to wait up for her mother to get home. Oh, Zozo, he said.

Something about his tone of voice, the devastation in his eyes... That was the moment Zoe realized: She had failed. Her mother was really, truly gone.

The world dropped from under Zoe's feet.

Later, Aunt Donna sometimes said that if Zoe hadn't acted out so much during the following year—in trouble at school, angry at home, refusing to go to church—her father wouldn't have had a heart attack. Donna would still have her brother if it weren't for bad Zoe. And Zoe knew she was right. Of course she was. No one else Zoe knew had lost both their parents.

Only her.

Chapter Twenty-Three

I don't want to get out of bed in the morning. I don't ever want to get out of bed again, the weight of everything so solid on top of me. A concrete blanket, too heavy to move. But I know the danger of giving in to that impulse—I've seen how the blanket gets even heavier—and I fight against it.

When I come out of the shower, I'm shocked to find my mother sitting on the couch, awake. Her face looks so strange and waxy, her lips so pale, and for a moment I worry she's going to be sick again.

I'm not even sure where to begin with my apology, my explanation, but she speaks first.

"I don't want the money," she says, her voice flat.

"What do you mean?" I sit on the coffee table in front of her. Her eyes are flat, too, as she stares off at nothing.

"I refuse to take any money from it."

"I . . . I don't understand."

She meets my gaze. "You do the paintings, the money is yours. We can use it for rent—other than that, it's yours. For college, whatever you want. Like you're paid for any job."

She wants it to be mine? Potentially thousands and thousands of dollars? Is she not even going to mention that I've been lying to her? Isn't she *mad* at me? I can't tell how she's feeling at all. There's no color in her voice or expression in her eyes.

"But . . . it's not like I'm doing all the work," I say. "You did the drawings. You made it all up. I'm just, like, an assistant. We need to pay off your debt. And . . . I can't do the rest of the paintings. I don't have time. Can't you—"

"We're not having that discussion again," she says tiredly. "If you want to do the paintings, agree to keep the money yourself. That's it. The only way this is happening."

I should be relieved that she's saying she'll let me do them. I should be happy that she's speaking to me at all. But this wasn't the point. I don't want to do the rest of the paintings myself!

She isn't going back on this, though. That's obvious.

"Okay, fine," I say. "I'll . . . take the money." If it's my money, I can do what I want with it, including pay off her debt.

"One more thing," Her dull gaze sharpens now—a sign of life. "Has it brought back your nightmares?"

I wasn't expecting that, so it takes me a beat to answer. "What? No."

"Don't lie to me, Indigo. I can't handle more lies."

"I'm not," I insist. "You'd know if I had nightmares. We sleep in the same room."

"And when you're painting, it doesn't . . . upset you?"

My breath hitches: Did it happen to her, too? Did she feel like she was actually *inside* Wolfwood? I want to ask, but clearly I can't. What would she say if she knew I'd hurt myself that last time? If I showed her the scrape around my arm?

"Upset me?" I say. "No. I barely even see the images. I just sort of break them down into abstract sections."

"If I find out you're lying, or if you start having nightmares, I will cancel the show. Don't think I won't." Her voice has sharpened, too.

I try to focus on the good part of what she's saying. "So, it's okay?" I ask tentatively. "You'll go along with it? You'll pretend you did them?"

There's a long, weighty silence as she just sits there. Then she closes her eyes and shakes her head. "I should've died, shouldn't I? It should've been me." She hits herself in the head with an open hand. "Piece. Of. Shit." She hits herself again and again. Hard. "Piece. Of. Shit."

"Mommy, stop!" I say, coming out of momentary shock. I grab her arms and she struggles against me, fighting to get free, and as we tangle, our words tangle, too, her blaming herself and me trying to calm her down:

"Terrible mother—"

"No, you're not—"

"Can't take care of—"

"Stop, Mommy—"

"—should have died."

"Don't say that," I beg, thinking she must mean when she was sick in the hospital. "Please. Please don't say that." Nothing is worth this. Nothing in the world. "I can tell Annika. I can cancel it, like I should have. I'll confess everything, tell her it's my fault."

She stops fighting, but I keep my grip on her arms. "No," she says. "No, I want you to have the money. Please, Indigo . . . let me give you this. It's all I have to give you. Please."

We hold each other's eyes, our breath ragged.

"Are you sure?" I ask.

She nods.

"Okay," I say, gently releasing her. "But . . . you'll have to pretend they're yours. You'll have to go to the opening and do that visit with the Whitney people, stuff like that. So, I'll need you. I can't do this by myself. Okay?"

She hesitates, then nods again. "Annika can never find out," she says. "No one can. No one can know I'm so bad."

"Of course not. But you're not bad, Mommy. You're not."

She purses her lips, clearly not agreeing with me.

I take one of her hands in mine, cold and bony. "You'll want to paint again, right? I know you don't want to paint Wolfwood, but something else?"

She doesn't answer. I think she doesn't believe in herself enough to say it out loud. She has to want to. She loved it. Dancing on that sculpture. Articles written about her. How could she not want to go back to that life? And even after I was born—our times in the studio, she was so full of energy and passion for her art. So full of color.

"You will," I say. "I know it."

Everything has changed. She's not going to take over the paintings, like I wanted, but at least I can stop lying to her about it. I can spend as many hours at the studio as I want, not worrying about making up excuses. No more sneaking around. No more guilt.

I should be happy. I should be relieved. But all I feel is dread.

Chapter Twenty-Four

When I return to Wolfwood, I'm lying on the ground, my head in Lila's lap, my white dress stained red. Azul is singing softly. Scarlet is pacing around us.

"You lost a lot of blood," Lila says, when she sees I'm awake. "You've been unconscious for a while."

My arm is bandaged with a scrap of her purple dress. Memories flash in my mind. The hut being attacked with me inside it; the woody vines writhing like a mass of snakes, tearing through the walls. That one vine pulling me out, then hanging me from that tree, cutting through my arm. It hurt me, but it also saved me, in a way. Before Scarlet cut me down.

I push myself up to sit, the injury throbbing. We're in an area of tall trees and bare ground, the air steamy and rank. A group of Others is stationed around us. Scarlet and Azul are now crouching on either side of me.

"We've been worried," Azul says.

"Why did you go back to the hut if it was a trap the first time?" Scarlet asks. "Going back wasn't part of any plan."

She's right. I snuck away while they were asleep. "I felt bad that we didn't find any clues when Lila and I went. I thought maybe I missed something, when the monster scared me."

"And?" Scarlet presses. "What'd you find? You were screaming bloody murder. Scared us to death. But when we got there, you looked fine—until the vines attacked."

I lick my dry lips, thinking about what happened before the attack. Or, I should say, what I *imagined* happening. Because none of it was real, was it? Like the time before, it was all in my imagination. Climbing into that hammock, adjusting my body to fit against his, the cool metal of the bracelet slipping on to my wrist . . . Not real, and not details I can share with the sisters. I'm terrible for even imagining that intimacy with the Wolf, the one who's trying to kill us.

"I didn't find any actual clues. But when I got there, I had this vision of him. He stole my blade, and I thought he was going to attack me. I grabbed it and killed him. I cut his head off."

I say it like it was a good thing, but at the same time, I'm filled with the emotions from when I did it: Horror. Guilt.

"What does it mean?" Lila asks.

"I'm not exactly sure," I say. "But . . . I know what we need to do next."

It's true. My premonitions have gotten clearer than they were before the attack. What needs to happen is all mapped out. Not the connective tissue of it, but the important moments.

"What?" Azul says. "What do we need to do?"

I glance at Scarlet uneasily, anticipating her reaction. "The opposite of what we've been doing. Instead—"

"What?!" Scarlet says, cutting me off. I knew she wouldn't like this, since she's been leading us.

"Instead of looking for a way out and getting attacked wherever we go, we need to find somewhere safe and stay there," I say. "Build a home."

"A home?" Scarlet is incredulous now. "In Wolfwood?"

"Not a home," I say quickly, realizing I shouldn't have put it like that. "I just mean a hut like the one that was destroyed. In a safe spot. And then stay there, instead of always being on the move. We stay there, safe, and let *him* come to *us*."

"No," Scarlet says. "We can't stay in one place. We'll never find the Wolf *or* the way out. If anything, moving more quickly sounds better. Not letting anything ever pin us down. Right, Azul?"

I'm assuming Azul will agree with Scarlet. Except for sleeping, she doesn't like to linger anywhere. But her brow is furrowed.

"The thing is . . ." Azul hesitates. "What if there *is* no way out? I mean, no physical exit." She looks at her sisters with a pointed intensity.

"We're stuck here forever?" Lila exclaims.

"No," Azul says. "Maybe the *only* way out is to kill the Wolf."

"What do you mean?" Scarlet sounds skeptical.

"Maybe there's no way out *except* killing the Wolf, which would end Wolfwood."

What she's saying is right. I know with certainty.

"Oh my god," Lila says, eyes widening. "Because if he made this place, and he's dead . . . *poof*. It disappears. And we go home."

I don't see this part of things, can't picture how it happens, but my bones know it's true. When the Wolf dies, Wolfwood dies, too. I already knew this, didn't I? I feel like I'm being reminded of something I forgot, not told something new. But if I knew it, why wouldn't I have said something?

"We were told from the start, those words written in the dirt—'Kill the Wolf,'" Azul says.

"We should've listened." Lila shakes her head.

"It's not like we haven't been looking for him," Scarlet snaps. "We just never found him. If we had, we'd have tried to kill him. That's been the plan. And now we keep looking. Stick with the plan until it works."

"No," Azul says with finality. "Like I said before, we need to trust Zoe's hunches. So . . . we stay in one place?" she asks me.

"And let him come to us," I explain again.

"Why would he?" Scarlet says. "He could have found us any time before now! He always knows where we are."

I don't know the answer to this. It's like I know certain things with utter clarity, and other things I'm looking at through a smudged window in the dark.

But I do know that what we do next is build the home where we'll be safe. I see it. It's what I want, what I *need* to happen. "He'll come to us," I promise. "And we have nothing to lose by trying it. We'll find a safe area, use whatever materials are around. It doesn't have to take a long time. If it doesn't work, we'll go out looking again."

Azul stands up. "We're doing it." She meets Scarlet's eyes. "Just for a little bit. See if it works." The three sisters have one of their wordless conversations, and after a moment, Scarlet gives a small nod.

"We build a home," I say.

"A shelter," Scarlet clarifies.

"Can it be a tree house?" Lila says. "With a cool ladder and stuff?"

"Absolutely not," Scarlet says. "Simple, so we finish quickly. First, we need to find somewhere safe to build." She takes charge immediately, as if it were her idea. "Are you okay to walk, Zoe?"

I slowly and carefully stand, a vision of the near future clear in my head. We're going to get attacked, and I'm going to get hurt again, but I have no choice. I need to follow along, let Scarlet lead. "Fine," I say. "Let's go."

We walk for a while, and I try my best to keep up, but my arm hangs limp and heavy, and I can't use it to brush aside branches, like I usually would. And then as we're entering a new area, I hesitate.

"What?" Scarlet says. I see myself getting bitten by an orchid, its teeth tearing through my dress and scraping my flesh. I see the blood, and I'm scared of the pain in a way I don't remember. But I also know this is part of the plan. I have to do what Scarlet says. I need her to see me get attacked. So I keep walking and don't say anything when the trees come together over us, blotting out the sun. Don't say anything when I sense the flowers growing around us, getting bigger by the second. Don't say anything when I know I'm about to stumble off the path and be shoved by a muscular leaf right into the jaws of a pearl-pink orchid, saliva dripping from its petals, teeth tearing into my flesh, just like I knew they would.

The alarm on my phone is screaming and so is my side. My left waist pulses with a hot pain. I lift my shirt to find a red mark where I was bitten, speckled with blood. Panic seizes me—*it happened again*—and I see the scene in my head, that flower biting me, but I take a few deep breaths to push the panic away. Who cares, right? It's weird, but it was already weird, and I have to keep doing the paintings. I let go of my shirt, covering it back up. Not a big deal, not a big deal, not a big deal.

Fuck.

Chapter Twenty-Five

Instead of eating my stockpile of saltines at the studio and painting for longer, I bring home fried chicken for dinner. Not enough for two, but with extra biscuits to fill it out. The chicken smells so good I can't stand it. It blocks out the rancid perfume that followed me here from Wolfwood, along with the injuries and flashes of memory that are as vivid as any memories from the real world.

Something changed the last time, when I painted for more than twenty-four hours—no doubt now. Maybe I was in there for too long, was sucked in too deeply, so the division between here and there became thinner. What does that even mean, though, if "there" is just in my mind?

When I walk into the basement, I'm expecting my mother to be in bed, to have to cajole her up with the temptation of a good meal.

I'm not expecting what I actually find. She's crouched in the bathroom, scrubbing the impossible-to-clean toilet with a flimsy sponge. Impossible because it's old and stained and we've bleached it a million times and it never gets better. It's the same toilet that was in the basement for workmen to use, before we moved in.

"That's as good as it will get," I say, standing in the doorway. She's not wearing gloves. Her hands look raw, her face gray.

"There are still stains," she says, voice weak.

"Those are old. They're always there."

"They're from when I was sick."

"No, they aren't. Seriously. There's nothing more you can do."

"But it's not clean yet. It's disgusting."

"I brought fried chicken. Let's eat before it gets cold."

She looks past me, toward the kitchen, then back at the toilet.

"How long have you been cleaning it?" I ask.

"I don't know."

"Well, you're done."

She drags herself out of the bathroom, eats two bites of chicken and then lies down on the couch. The fridge is broken again, and this time I can't get it to go back on, despite all my re-plugging and shaking and cursing, so I eat the rest of the chicken, which tastes like a soggy dishrag now. I'm too unsettled by finding her like that, scrubbing. Like if I hadn't come home, she'd have literally scrubbed the toilet till her hands were torn apart.

I know I should stay the night. The whole point of coming home, of not spending more hours painting, was to be with her. But the smell of the dishrag-chicken grease mixed with the cleanser from the bathroom and the rancid smell of Wolfwood is making me sick, making it impossible for me to distract myself and impossible to stop picturing her scrubbing like that, stop hearing her sobs from yesterday, stop seeing her hitting herself, all of it playing over and over on a loop.

In a way, I'm glad that Kai is in Japan, because the only thing I want to do is to talk to him. I want to take a walk with him along the river, tell him what's happening, tell him how worried I am, how scary it is to see her like this. Like how he talked to me about Hiro. And I want him to hug me tight and tell me it's going to be okay, that it's not my fault. But that's obviously out of the question—would be out of the question for me to share that stuff about my mother with *anyone*, let alone Annika's son.

No, better just to forget about everything for a while.

Seeing Josh doesn't help. The sex doesn't take me out of my head like it usually does, and I get distracted by the tenderness of my injuries, memories of Wolfwood flitting through my mind. Still, I go through the motions, hoping I'll click in.

Later, I wake in the charcoal-smeared dark, hear a child crying, and sit up in a panic. *Lila! Did I leave her alone? Was she attacked?* But no, no, it's a much younger kid, maybe even a baby. And there are walls, windows. I'm here, Josh's apartment. Not Wolfwood. I put a hand on my chest to calm my heart. Not in Wolfwood.

Josh sits up and rubs his head. The light outside is hesitant, watery. Early morning.

The baby is still crying. *Baby.*

"Your daughter is here?" I whisper, shocked.

He stands and stretches. "Crib's in my folks' room." He starts shuffling toward the hallway.

I reach for my clothes. "Sorry, didn't know."

"Not a problem. If she won't go back down, you can meet her."

"No," I say automatically, wriggling into my shorts. "That's okay. I gotta go."

He turns around. "It's early."

"I just . . . I gotta go. I'm sorry." This is messed up. I don't want to meet a guy's daughter. No way.

I'm gone by the time he gets back.

⟳

"What happened to you?" Shawna asks, looking at my arm while handing me my paycheck. We're in the employee room before my shift starts. Naomi is here, too, putting on lipstick at the mirror near our mini-lockers.

I run my hand over the red scraped area as if it will make it go away.

"Not sure," I tell Shawna. "Hadn't really noticed." At least she can't see my waist.

"Indigo, is everything all right? Missing that shift and stuff . . . not like you."

"I'm fine. I mean, except for the fact my grandmother died." My tone is snappy and defensive. I'm too exhausted to deal with her questions. And I'm still feeling bad about the goodbye text I sent Josh on my way here, even though it was nice, and way better than just ghosting him. Of course I knew he had a kid. But, somehow, hearing her like that . . . it was too much. I don't want to be some sort of potential stepmom-type person.

Shawna grimaces at me. "I'm sorry about your grandma and I'm glad you're fine, but missing shifts and all of this"—she gestures at my arm—"*not* fine. Maybe you could wear something long-sleeved under your T-shirt—which, not to be rude, could do with a wash." With that, she leaves.

My cheeks flush. She's right. I haven't had a chance to wash my tees since I last worked, and it's so hot that when I walk here I sweat like crazy.

"Bitch," Naomi says quietly.

"Seriously," I say, embarrassed that Naomi heard, even if she is on my side.

I take my check out of the envelope, and immediately regret looking when I see how little it's for. But why should I be surprised, given that I missed those two shifts? Shit. Even if this show happens, we need money until the pieces start selling, and that's still weeks away . . . I'm going to have to make up the difference somehow. I need to pull myself together.

I apply cover-up to my injury as best I can and take my spot at my register.

Chapter Twenty-Six

Next, it's my left wrist. A violent twist that leaves a thick bracelet of a bruise. Then I go several sessions without anything, before I'm dragged across the jungle floor by my hair. That one leaves a faint scrape on one cheek and a sharp ache on my scalp, like the time I had lice so bad I scratched till I was bloody. I'm lucky that I'm never hurt as seriously as the sisters and the Others. What would happen, I wonder, if I was skinned or gutted like they are? Since not everything that happens in my imagination is shown in the paintings, I can't totally predict what injuries I'll get next. As far as I know, anything could happen.

Before I started getting hurt, I'd somehow convinced myself that imagining I was *in* Wolfwood when I painted was sort of normal— or, if not normal, nothing to worry about. No way to keep believing that now. During the few hours I'm in bed each night, I stare up at the ceiling, obsessing about it, wondering what I'd look like if someone found me painting, if I'm acting it out and, if so, how I paint at the same time. Or is it even weirder than that? Do I actually *go* somewhere? Do I go to Wolfwood? It's so real to me now—how can it be in my imagination? (*Don't be ridiculous, Indigo! There's weird and then there's . . . impossible.*) And of course all of that makes me wonder again whether my mother used to go there, too, and if that's why she doesn't want to do the paintings. Maybe it scared her too much to go back? Or she didn't want to get hurt?

I've kept my injuries hidden from her—not difficult, given that she's barely gotten out of bed since the toilet-scrubbing incident. I've been telling myself it's like hibernation, what she's doing, sleeping all the time. And that while she's hibernating, she'll build up her creative energy. Regain her color. But I know that isn't true. If anything, the couch is erasing what little of her is left. Fading her pencil-sketch self line by line.

In the fourth and fifth paintings, we've been searching for a spot to build the shelter. But the landscape keeps shifting, and the monsters keep attacking, and because it's what's supposed to happen, I keep going along with it instead of trying to figure out a better plan. I spot the Wolf a few times, always up high, looking down on us, but the sisters still never see him.

We finally find a good spot to build: an open area of safe grasses, no monsters close enough to reach us. First, we gather bamboo for the frame of the structure. When we've made a good start on that, I offer to gather palm fronds for the roof. There's a stand of tall trees we can see rising over the bushes that surround us. Leaving the sisters working on the frame for the hut, I go on my own, a group of the Others following behind me for protection. I pass through the bushes and notice their strange white berries. Pluck a few for Lila.

Walk carefully past some shifty pink flowers with bulbous eyeballs at their centers. And in a few minutes I've come to the area with tall trees, trunks made of woody vines all twisted together, with more vines—thinner ones—hanging like curtains. The foliage here blocks the sun and there's movement among the hanging vines. A subtle sway and writhe. Some are wrapped around other plants, choking them. I keep my blade at the ready, but none of them attack me. I've never been attacked when I'm alone. Not once. Among the trees I find a palm that's safe to climb. Because of all my injuries, it's harder than ever to haul myself up.

When I've climbed high enough to break into the open, from dark to light, it's as if I've stepped from one world into another. The smells change, the air changes. My body changes, all pain gone.

A noise comes from above. And I see him, sitting on a branch, on the chaka tree next to my palm. Our eyes meet. I shimmy higher till the branch is in reach. I swing onto it, scoot farther to sit next to him. His body is wiry and taut as I press my side against it. His familiar musky smell melts through me. The rhythm of my breath syncs with his. I rest my head on his shoulder and imagine a home, here in the trees. I turn to look at his beautiful face. A vine is wrapped around his neck. A noose. It jerks up a bit. He chokes, grabs at his throat. *Help me*, his eyes say. His desperation cuts my heart. Yes, of course I'll help him.

With a swift, forceful motion, I shove him off the branch. He plummets; the noose slices his head off. His body thuds onto the ground and blood fountains out of his neck. The jungle floor becomes a sea of red. His severed head floats on top, screaming.

Why? Why did I do that? I didn't want to kill him.

I throw myself off the branch, plunging down.

Crack. I hit, crumple on the ground. Breath knocked out. My ankle, sharp pain. I inhale shakily. Sit up and see: There's no blood on the jungle floor, no headless body or screaming, decapitated head. Just a group of Others, circled around me. Their creepy, dead-eyed stares a few feet away, so close I can feel their cold breath. They never express emotion, but I feel their hatred. Their anger.

What did they see? They couldn't have seen him, could they? The two of us sitting close, my head on his shoulder. No, they couldn't have seen it because it wasn't real. I don't love him like that. Of course I don't.

Did they see me fall off the branch? A jump.

I look from face to face among the Others, seeing the sisters but not the sisters, seeing their hatred.

"What?" I say, even though I know they won't answer. "The tree pushed me. I thought it was safe. It wasn't."

Creepy stare after creepy stare, they all say nothing. I try to get up, but my ankle won't support me.

The Others tighten their circle.

1989

Trying to be supportive, Zoe embraces Colin's new obsession with his video project. This is what a real artist is like, she tells herself. Passionate. Single-minded. So what if she barely sees him during the day? He's creating!

And she has the sisters, so she's not lonely. Now Lila is the one who paints with her in the mornings, sitting on the back of Zoe's bike, arms wrapped around her waist, as they search out the best spots. They usually go somewhere in the Sian Ka'an preserve—with its jungle, forests, wetlands, mangroves—Zoe helping Lila make illustrations of the endless plants and flowers for her homeschool project. When they identify berries called white indigo, Zoe points out that it would be a beautiful name for another Lopez sister, Indigo.

Still, Zoe misses her time with Colin intensely, and when he tells her one morning that he's going to be in some of the videos he's making and asks if she'll film for him, she's elated.

The filming spot that Colin brings Zoe to is one of the hidden cenotes. He leads her to the edge of the water, in the brush, and points the video camera through the leaves. It's simple, he tells her. All she has to do is stand here and film him while he's in the water. She should stay as steady as she can, and then move around and film him as he swims back to the small wooden platform and climbs out. It needs to be a long shot, no breaks. Zoe asks what he's going to do, and he says not to worry, just to keep filming. No matter what, don't stop filming.

Zoe holds the camera up, nervous she'll drop it, eager to see what Colin has planned. He swims out, not too far. He treads water for a moment, staring at Zoe, at the camera, before disappearing beneath the surface. Zoe keeps the camera trained on where he went down. The water is so clear she can see the dark shape of him. What feels like a long time passes and he doesn't come up. She keeps filming. He still doesn't come up. Zoe starts to get concerned. Is he okay? The seconds tick by. Is he moving? She can't tell. Minutes have passed. Entire minutes, she's sure. Her pulse is racing now, loud and fast in her ears. Is it possible to hold your breath this long? No, it's not possible. It can't be. Something must be wrong. She knows she's not supposed to stop filming, but this is different. He needs help! She's about to toss the camera and jump in when finally—finally!—he breaks the surface, coughing, gasping, spitting water. The camera shakes as Zoe films him heaving for air, making terrible noises. He swims to the platform and hauls himself out of the water, his face ashen. She keeps filming as he collapses on his back and lies still, taking in gulps and gulps of air. After his breath evens out, he signals her to stop. He empties a few rocks out of his pockets. Rocks, to weigh him down.

I hope you got all that, he says. I think that's the longest I've ever done it.

Zoe's stomach lurches up her throat. She leans to the side and vomits out all her fear.

Chapter Twenty-Seven

T he fifth painting is done," I say, when I get back from the studio. "Ahead of schedule." I'm home early—I finished the piece and it didn't make sense to start another one. My ankle hurts too much to stand up for that long. Not to mention, I've painted faster than expected. It only took me thirteen days to finish these last two pieces and now I have a cushion of two days in the calendar. I came home to catch up on cleaning and then go to Trinity's. I've worked it out with her so I can be there sewing as late as I need to, making up whatever money I can.

My mother doesn't respond, of course. Doesn't acknowledge me at all. I should be used to her silence by now, but the pain hits fresh every time.

I'm not sure what else I should be doing to keep her from disappearing. When I'm here, I pretend everything is normal. I turn on the lights, make meals (although without a fridge and with less money than usual, that's become harder than ever), and carry on one-sided conversations. I know she's been through times like this before, but this feels different. Worse.

I take off the ratty button-down I was painting in and put on a long-sleeved tee, to hide my bruises and scratches.

My phone buzzes—work or the gallery, no doubt.

Kai: You home?

Kai? My heart leaps. I haven't heard from him since he went to Japan. I respond eagerly.

Me: yup. You back!? How was trip?

He doesn't answer right away, so I resume my other "conversation."

"I've been thinking," I say, picking up a dirty glass off the table. "A couple times Mr. Ryan has mentioned we've missed stuff in the hallway. Maybe you could walk up and down every day, to make sure there's nothing I need to do?" Since she doesn't have the energy to clean, I've been trying to take care of both our own apartment and the building. I haven't stayed on top of it, though, and the Asslord is losing his patience. Earlier today, Marcus warned me that Mr. Ryan had sent around an email to the tenants encouraging people to tell him if the building isn't "up to par." It's hard to hide my frustration that I have to worry about this from my mother, but I try. The last thing I want is to make her feel even worse.

My phone buzzes again.

Kai: Look out front window

The front window? How would Kai know what's out there?

Then it hits me: Maybe he's out there himself. Oh, crap. I rake a hand through my hair. This is the kind of small building where it's obvious the apartments all have front-facing windows. But we have only the tiny ones behind the trash cans—ones that clearly don't belong to a real apartment.

I bite my cheeks and stare toward the street, as if a big window is going to open up in the mostly underground wall.

    Kai: ?

Split-second decision, I do the only thing I can think of: hobble up three flights and knock on Marcus and Jaden's door. Marcus is surprised to see me, but only chuckles and says, "Sure," when I ask if I can look out their window for a second.

"In-deeee!" Jaden screeches from his high chair.

"Hey, cutie!" I say, as I limp over and look down and see Kai, Ravi, Fiona, and Saskia. Kai is carrying a blow-up dinosaur that's as big as he is. When he spots me he makes it so the dinosaur is waving.

I get another text: Xtinct concert. Come!

A concert?

    Me: Don't have ticket

    Kai: Outdoors free no tix!

Free.

Obviously, I shouldn't go. I should clean the hallways, clean the apartment, work for Trinity, stay with my mother, sleep, and should, should, should . . . But here is what I see: the four of them smiling up at me, the early-evening sun gilding their faces, breeze ruffling Fiona's otherworldly hair and the skirt of her long, multicolored dress, a cooler bag on Ravi's shoulder, probably containing a picnic. (I'd even settle for those cheese and mayo sandwiches.) They want me to come—I can see the hope in Kai's eyes from all the way up here. Suddenly, the shoulds and shouldn'ts don't matter. Suddenly, I'm not tired at all. Fuck it. I finished that painting. I deserve a night off.

I head back downstairs wondering what to wear, what to wear, what to wear? *Who do you want to be, Indigo?* I want to be Fiona and Saskia. I want to be one of them, standing in the sun, out with my friends for the night, beautiful and nothing to worry about. I need to figure it out quick, and the first thing that jumps into my brain is the Tania Bawa dress. If it fits me, that is. I haven't tried it on yet, not wanting to ruin the fantasy of its perfection. I'll be so crushed if it doesn't work. I throw off my shirt and sweats and hesitate only one moment, wishing I was putting the pristine silk on clean skin. I don't have time for a shower—they're waiting for me now—so I carefully slip the silk jersey over my head. It feels like whipped cream sliding down my body.

I look in the mirror. Whoa. It's better than I even let myself imagine. Almost magic, the way the cut hugs my curves. The closest I'll ever come to looking like a celebrity. And because of the type of fabric, it's barely wrinkled at all. I'll have to wear my jean jacket and some light leggings to cover my bruises, which sucks, but still. I'll wear sneaks and make it a rougher, dressed-down look.

I hurry to the bathroom and do my makeup as quick as I can, rush back out, make my mother a peanut butter sandwich, see Kai texted again, grab my bag. "I'm meeting people," I tell my mom, who's still curled on the couch, facing away from me, "but I made you a sandwich. Just don't leave it out, okay? There was mouse poo on the counter yesterday."

Staring at her backbone visible through her thin shirt, I feel the string around my heart pulling tight. If it winds tight enough,

I won't be able to leave. Another text comes and I remind myself: There's nothing more I can do for her here.

⌒

"Welcome back!" I say to Kai as I walk down the steps, trying to hide my limp. He looks different. He's not wearing the beanie and his hair has grown in. More color on his face, tawny under his dark freckles. Healthy. God, so good to look at. It's been less than three weeks, but it feels like months since I've seen him. I lean down to give him a big hug. And, oh! He smells delicious. Like suntan lotion and candy. (I pray that the fresh deodorant I put on is all he smells on me.) His body feels so firm and alive. I don't want to let go, and it seems like he doesn't want to, either, but we do.

"Wow," he says, eyes wide as he checks out the dress. I hold out my arms. My jacket is unbuttoned, and the richly colored fabric shimmers in the sun.

"Totally wow," Fiona says, while Saskia murmurs agreement. Looking at us, a stranger might think I belonged with them.

"I thought you just lived with your mom?" Ravi says. I follow his gaze up. Marcus is walking past the window, holding Jaden. Clearly visible—a Black man and a toddler, *not* a white mother. In the same window I was looking out of.

"Oh," I say, thinking fast. "Yeah, those are our neighbors. They're friends. Hanging out." I smile brightly. "Should we get going?"

⌒

When we arrive at the park, it appears that everyone in Manhattan had the same idea for what to do tonight. The line literally disappears over a slope in the distance. After deciding we probably won't get in, Ravi tells us to wait a minute while he "sees what he can do about it."

We watch him stroll toward the ticket booth area. "Ravi's gonna Ravi," Fiona muses.

The air vibrates with the rustle of leaves above us. I scan the trembling green canopy, on edge, picturing an oak reaching down and wrapping its branch around me, dragging me up into the sky. I feel naked without my blade for protection.

"What're you looking at?" Kai asks, pulling my attention back. He has his arm around Darrell (the dinosaur).

"Oh, just . . . nature. Haven't been to a park in a while."

"You need to get out more." He grins.

"Guys!" Ravi calls, beckoning us to come his direction. As we walk down the leafy path, I force myself to keep my eyes down. Shove my hands in my jacket pockets. When we reach Ravi, he explains, "We can go in the other area if we buy subscriber passes. They're good all summer. There's a nicer area to sit in and food and shit."

A subscriber pass to some fancy area?

"Sorry," I say. There's no point in pretending. "I can't. You guys should go without me."

Kai glances at me, then says, "Yeah, I'll just wait on line. Summer's almost over, anyway. Passes won't be good much longer."

"You can't be serious," Ravi says to him. "Look at the line. And you love Xtinct. You're the main reason we're here."

"Dude, you know I'm still paying my mom back."

"Which you shouldn't even be doing." Ravi crosses his arms.

"Don't fight, boys," Fiona says. "Sas and I will buy passes, Ravi."

Saskia nods. "The money benefits the park, I think, so that's cool."

"How 'bout I pay for you guys?" Ravi says, looking between me and Kai. "You can't ditch us on your first night back—house rules."

"Thanks, Rav," Kai says, "but that's way too generous."

With that, Ravi's expression closes off. "Okay," he says with a shrug. "Good luck getting in."

Kai hands Darrell over to Saskia, and the three of them (four, including Darrell) head off toward the subscribers' entrance.

"You should go," I tell Kai. "It's my fault it took us so long to get here." I couldn't fake my ankle being okay. Had to tell them it was sprained and walk slowly.

"Nah, they're fine without me," he says, gazing toward the back of the line. "Do you want to wait, just in case? Or want to . . . watch a movie or something? My mom's place isn't far. Might be a better plan."

An alarm bell blares inside me. Kai's *apartment*? That's where his bedroom is. Not that we'll necessarily be *in* his bedroom, of course. (I'm going out on a limb and assuming there are other rooms in the apartment.) Still, I'll know it's there. Lurking.

I consider the smarter choice: going home to finish the long list of tasks I should be doing. But . . . the girl wearing a dress like this, out with a friend she hasn't seen in weeks, doesn't go home before they've done anything. When I left the basement, I was giving myself this one night.

"Sure," I say. "Movie sounds good."

And, shit, god help me at the effect his adorably pleased grin has on my body.

Chapter Twenty-Eight

My doubts worsen the closer we get to his place. As we take the elevator up, I keep asking myself whether this is a mistake. Does he think we're here to hook up? Most guys would. We had that conversation, after Ravi's party. Am I giving a mixed signal by coming over? Should I say something again?

Laughter and delicious smells seep into the hallway as we approach the apartment. "Damn," Kai says, taking out his key. "Forgot my mom has people over. Sorry." He may be sorry, but my immediate thought is *Phew, a buffer.*

When the door opens, the sound is like an East Village bar on a Saturday night. But it's not frat boys or basic twentysomethings with identical blow-outs. It's Annika and a long table full of women, from young to almost elderly, a mix of skin tones and styles. One of them is climbing onto her chair. Dark brown skin, box braids, a midthigh white tank dress, and elbow-length red patent gloves. She stands on the seat, getting everyone's attention. "It's like this," she says, and gracefully ripples her arms. "Right?"

"Yes!" another one says. Youngish, white, with a platinum fauxhawk and a caftan-style dress. She climbs on her chair, too. "And then, after he drinks, more like . . ." She does the same arm movement, except way goofier. Everyone laughs.

Annika notices us. "Darlings!" she calls. "Come say hello!"

At the same time, a small black dog under the table sees Kai and skitters over, tail wagging madly.

Kai scoops up the dog and gives me an *I guess we have to* look. I'm not hesitant at all. I want to know who all these fabulous women are and to see what smells so incredible. We got slices on the way home, Kai's treat, but my stomach is a bottomless pit these days.

"Darlings," Annika says again when we reach them. "Everyone, you know Kai."

"Of course we do," the one in the caftan says from her perch on the chair. "We love Kai!" All the others hoot and cheer in agreement. Kai looks half appalled, half delighted.

"And this," Annika says, holding her arm out, "is Indigo Serra, daughter of Zoe, who should have been here tonight but is probably toiling in the studio, as usual. Isn't that right, darling," she says to me. "And don't you look gorgeous, in one of Tania's."

I smile and avoid the question about my mom, just giving them a wave and a general "Hi!"

"These," Annika says, "are some of the most glorious and smart and influential and soon-to-be-influential people in the art world. This is Lulu—she shows with the gallery—and Shian, and Margot, and . . ." She goes around naming each one. I'd guess the oldest is about eighty and the youngest are the two on the chairs (now sitting down), who I gather are artists. Every single one looks confident and magnetic, each with her own distinctive style and glamour. The table is covered in ceramic dishes of food—lasagna, vegetables, fish, chicken—two big wooden bowls of salad, the remains of a loaf of fresh bread, and bottles and bottles of wine. If I have to be an adult one day, I want it to be like this.

"We can't wait for Zoe's show," one of the women calls out.

"She was my inspiration in art school," one with a jet-black pageboy says. "Standing on that Serra sculpture, such a fuck you to minimalism. Love *Wolfwood*!"

"Can't wait for those girls to get that fucking Wolf!" one of them calls out, and they start a chant: "Get the Wolf! Get the Wolf!" Someone bangs on the table with her fist, rattling the dishes. They all cheer. *Jesus.*

"We will," I say. "Promise!" Only after I say it do I realize my phrasing might have seemed strange.

"Want to join us, you two?" Annika says over the din.

"That's okay," Kai says quickly, probably scared he's going to be dessert. He's clutching the dog like a shield.

"I do these potlucks about once a month," Annika says to me. "Zoe is on my list, but she never comes, of course."

I picture my mother sitting at the table, laughing, eating, drinking wine, enjoying the admiration of younger artists, knowing she's made a difference in the world, knowing her own self-worth.

"You and your mother should join us at the next one," the young artist in the white dress says to me. "It'd be an honor to meet her."

I force a smile. "We'd love to."

"Yikes," Kai says, when we get into his room.

"Can't handle it?" I joke.

"Wouldn't even pretend I could." He grins and sets the dog down. "This is Miss G, by the way." She approaches me cautiously and sniffs my hand, then lets me rub her soft head for a bit before trotting to the closed door. "Fine, fine," Kai says, letting her out. "Food is more interesting, I know."

His room is tiny, barely enough space for a full-sized bed, desk, and dresser. He doesn't sit, so I don't, either. Luckily, there's a lot to look at, so I can pretend not to notice that his bedroom has a bed in it. I also need to be distracted from thinking about all that food, which I can still smell in here. There'll have to be leftovers. Maybe if I just bide my time . . .

"Don't you want to take your jacket off?" Kai asks.

"I run cold," I lie.

One wall of the room is entirely covered by built-in shelves filled with row after row of books and a lot of little knickknacky things: miniature action figures, clay pots that look like a kid made them, seashells, awards . . . framed photos going way back. A really cute one of him and Ravi as kids, with Ravi's front teeth missing. One of him and Hiro, arms around the shoulders of two other Japanese boys, on a baseball diamond. Knickknacks cover the top of his dresser, too, and the wall space is filled with posters and photos, a lifeguard certificate, a comic-book-style BAM! in a funky bubble.

"I have to clean this place out," Kai says, perching on the side of the bed with his laptop. "Drives my mother crazy."

"I like it. It's very you."

"A mess?"

"No, just . . . you care about the past. Like, you remember stuff from when we were little." I study the rows of book titles. "Have you read all these?" I recognize some of the authors' names but don't know much about them: Octavia Butler, Haruki Murakami, George R. R. Martin . . .

"Most of them."

I can't imagine how he ever could have had enough time. Or what a big gap there is between everything he's read and what I have. Between what he knows and what I do. I actually went to great public schools when I was younger—the Earth School, especially—but my high school sucks. Even if I had the time and energy to keep up with the work, I don't think I'd have learned much.

"Ideas of what to watch?" he says, scrolling on the laptop.

"I'm blanking," I say. "Give me options." I don't really feel like watching a whole movie—I'm too tired—but I also don't want to be alone with Kai in his bedroom with nothing to focus on except him. Especially not with the way his T-shirt hugs his back muscles as he leans over the computer.

While he makes suggestions, I turn my attention to photos and stuff pinned on a bulletin board. There are notes about a couple of colleges on it—SUNY Purchase and Binghamton.

"Are you taking a year off?" I ask, remembering that Ravi mentioned something about Kai's college applications getting messed up.

"Oh. Yeah." His eyes stay on the screen. A moment later, he adds, "Only got into one school. No scholarship. And I didn't realize how much Hiro's treatment had eaten up my parents' money. So I'm gonna apply to state schools for next year—avoid huge student loans."

I'm surprised money would be a factor in anything for him. I mean, not that this apartment is anything like Ravi's house, but still . . .

After we choose a slasher flick, he says, "Sorry it's so tight in here. Okay if I set it up at the end of the bed?" Meaning we'd be sitting next to each other up by the pillows. On the bed. Kai's bed.

"Um, yeah, whatever works."

I settle in next to him, a gap of less than a foot between us, making an effort not to feel that warm crackle. There are a couple of soft pillows behind me and the light is low. I remember how tired I am. By the time the movie starts, I'm already having trouble keeping my eyelids open.

I wake up to him nudging me. "Hey," he says quietly.

"Did I—" I wipe at my face. Credits are rolling on the screen. "Oh, shit. I missed the whole thing?"

"Deader than the many victims."

"You should've woken me up sooner."

"Figured you must need it. And"—a smile plays at the corners of his mouth—"you looked cute."

"Cute?" If there's one thing I'm not, it's cute."

"That's your opinion."

I must've been even more spent than I realized, to fall asleep so quickly.

"You're welcome to crash here for the night," he says, then adds, "I mean, I'll sleep in Hiro's room. Unless . . . would your mom mind?"

I rub my eyes, too comfortable to care about the implications of staying over. "She won't mind. She'll just think I'm sleeping at the studio."

"The studio?"

Fuck. "I mean, she's probably sleeping at the studio and doesn't even know I'm out. I can text and let her know. She won't care."

"Oh, okay. So . . . you want to stay?"

"You don't mind sleeping in Hiro's room?"

"Not at all."

When I come out of the bathroom, revived after using a new toothbrush he opened for me and washing my face with apricot mango face scrub and drying it with a fluffy towel, and having changed into sweats and a long-sleeved loaner tee (both way too short), he's tucking a fresh sheet into his mattress.

"You didn't have to do that," I say, even though I'm thinking how nice it is that he did.

"I wasn't going to make you sleep in my old sheets."

I bend down and help tuck. The sheets smell like laundry looks like it smells on TV commercials: flowers and grass and breezy air. Not a heavy, sickly flower smell, like in Wolfwood. After we finish, I sit on the end of the mattress. He sits next to me.

"Were you really scared of me when we were younger?" I ask.

He appears to consider this. "More like . . . scared and fascinated at the same time."

"Like a horror movie?"

"Ha. Exactly. What'd you think about me?"

I hesitate, because honestly, I don't remember having very strong feelings. "I thought you were funny. And weird for following me around."

"You had a crush on Hiro, didn't you?"

"No, not—" We meet eyes and he raises his eyebrows, and I laugh.

"It's okay," he says. "Everyone did. Between him and Ravi, I've mastered second fiddle."

"If you've mastered it, I think that makes you first fiddle."

"Touché."

We're silent for a moment. "Any news from him?" I ask, figuring it's okay since he's been so open about it all. "Hiro, I mean."

He shakes his head. "Not since I ran into him with you."

I nod, smooth down a ripple in the comforter.

"So, you scare me. What scares you?" he asks.

What scares me? *My mother never getting out of bed, the Asslord's name on my phone, not having enough money at the store, having to drop out of school, Annika finding out I'm painting* Wolfwood, *Kai finding out I'm painting* Wolfwood . . .

"Oh, you know . . ."

"Nothing," he says. "I knew it."

Right.

"Sorry we had to leave them, at the park," I say, to change the subject. "Ravi was pissed."

Kai shrugs. "He's used to getting his way. But buying the passes wasn't an option."

"Does it bother you that those guys kind of treat you like you're younger?"

"Nah. It's just . . . whatever, my role in the dysfunctional family. I'm sure you have a role in your friend group, right?"

I bite my cheeks. "Not really."

Kai doesn't say anything, and I find myself wanting to tell him more.

"I've kind of grown apart from my one closest friend," I begin, obviously not mentioning that it was because I was lying to her about being homeless, "and we didn't have a set group like you do. It was more like people would come in and out and it would change depending on our classes and stuff. And me and her didn't end up at the same high school, so . . ."

"Yeah, that's hard. Ravi and I were definitely closer before he went to Exeter."

"You still seem close."

"We are, in that way you get with people you've known most of your life." He shifts so he's sitting against the headboard and his legs are on the bed. "But I feel like I've changed a lot in the last few years, and he still sees me as the old Kai. We'd definitely do some damage to protect each other, though. No question there."

"How have you changed?"

"Stuff with Hiro, you know? I guess before that I was pretty oblivious. I thought . . . I thought everything would be okay, that if something goes wrong you fix it? You know, typical privileged attitude. And now, Hiro . . . Every time our door buzzer rings, I think it's the police saying he's dead."

He pauses, but he doesn't seem finished, so I don't respond.

"And the thing is, there's nothing I can do about it. Like I said before. It's out of my control. I can do things to help him, but I can't save him. Nothing my parents have done has helped, even though they've thrown so much energy and almost all their savings at it.

"And it's so hard not knowing how to help. Like, in the beginning . . ." He stares up at the ceiling. "In the beginning, I just kept his secrets, you know? I knew he was getting into stuff, and I didn't say anything. I thought that was loyalty, right? And that he'd reward me by keeping it under control. Like, I bargained with him. 'Okay, I won't tell if you promise you're okay.' But, you know . . . his promises meant nothing. I was a real idiot." He draws a breath. "No, not an idiot. I'm not supposed to say that. I'm supposed to remember that I was doing my best in a difficult situation."

"Ravi doesn't get it?" I ask.

"He does. But he's so defensive of me—he gets pissed at my family when Hiro's problems mess up my life. And he wants me to be as mad as he is. Which I get. I *was* mad, for a long time. And now, I don't want to be, more than I have to. A little mad is okay. A lot of mad . . . sucks."

"Sorry if I kind of acted like that, too, when I said your mom shouldn't make you work off the money. You know, at Ravi's party."

"Oh, no worries." He shifts the pillow behind his back. "So . . . how's that guy you're hanging out with?"

I forgot I ever mentioned Josh to him. "Right. Yeah, not hanging out with him anymore."

"What happened?"

I shrug. "He's a good guy. We were just at different places with stuff."

"Sorry to hear it."

"Wasn't a big deal."

"Okay, not sorry to hear it." He smiles. There's an awkward moment where the crackle zaps the air.

I start talking to cover it up. "I'm scared of a lot of things."

"Took you a while to come up with something."

I grin. "No . . . I'm scared of . . . I'm scared that my mother . . . I love my mother, so much." I pause. "But she gets really overwhelmed by stuff, and there's a lot that I feel like I have to take care of and make okay. To help manage it for her. And she gets so mad at herself, that she needs help. She . . . doesn't like herself very much, and she gets really upset. That scares me." My heart is pounding, like footsteps running down a hallway. I don't talk about her with people. It feels like I'm violating some primal law. But hearing him share stuff about his family makes it seem somehow okay.

"How do you manage it for her?" He sounds interested and concerned, but not judgmental.

I try to think of examples that don't make her look bad or give anything away. "Like . . . Well, you know I have to take care of business-type stuff, with the gallery, and also with the landlord, or health-care-type stuff. And I get worried I'll mess it up, but also worried because she's being so hard on herself. It can be a lot." I want to use the word "depressed," but I don't, since my mother doesn't use it herself.

"So," Kai says, "is she one of those artists who's just all about their work? That's all they can really focus on? I've met a couple like that. Like, bad at life, but then geniuses in the studio."

"Um, yeah. I guess."

"Sounds like you're kind of the parent."

"No. She does parent stuff." She used to, at least. Not at the moment. At the moment, Kai's right.

"Well, you're not going to be there too much longer, I guess. If you go to college, and then wherever you end up after that, she'll have to start doing it all for herself?"

"I haven't thought that far ahead." I assume that if the paintings sell and I can afford to go to college, I'll go to community college and live at home. I can't imagine leaving my mother.

"I hate that you have to worry about her so much," Kai says, "but sounds like you're a good daughter."

We've migrated so that we're both stretched out on the bed, on our sides, a couple of feet between us.

"Not always." I'm the reason she's disappearing: Lying about canceling the show, working on the paintings behind her back—it's what led to where she is now.

Even talking to Kai like this. It's a betrayal.

"You're better than me," he says. "I called my mother a fucking asshole the other day."

My mouth drops open. "Annika? You did not."

He laughs. "I did."

"I'm sure it didn't go over too well."

"No, it did not. And I was being a total dick. But at least she heard me."

It's so weird—even though I haven't said the whole truth, and even though I feel guilty, it also feels good to have shared this, to have someone else in this space with me. That's what it feels like. Like the truth of my life is a space that no one gets in, and even just cracking the door a bit and talking to him through it, maybe touching his hand, it's letting in air and I can breathe better.

We turn onto our backs and gaze up at the ceiling in silence. I'm sleepy but also hyperaware of his body, energy, breath. My own body is tingling, on the verge of trembling . . .

"If you could be anywhere right now, doing anything, where would you be?" he asks.

I don't have to think long. "We'd be lying just like this, except on a beach with really, really soft sand, listening to the ocean, which is a gorgeous turquoise color, and there's nothing around, just this huge sky and sun and air—like, all sky—and there'd be nothing else to do until it's time for lunch, which would be this huge plate of tropical fruit and milkshakes. Really thick milkshakes. And fries."

I feel him shift and glance over. He's on his side again.

"So, you'd be with me?" he says.

Oh, right. I just said that, didn't I? "I don't have much imagination," I joke.

"Haha. You know, we have ice cream. And fruit. So we could actually make this moment pretty close to perfection for you."

As he says it, out of the corner of my eye, I see something stirring on the floor. "Watch out!" I cry. I sit up, anticipating a vine—a quick, thorny one—leaping out and grabbing us.

"Jesus!" Kai yelps. A cat darts from the corner of the room, hides under the bed. "That's Will," he says, laughing. "You scared us both half to death."

"Sorry," I say. A cat. Not a monster. Obviously. "I didn't even realize he was in here. I didn't even know you *had* a cat."

Kai peers under the bed and murmurs reassuring words to Will, before sitting back down next to me.

"I guess that's another thing you're scared of," he says. "Cats."

I smack him with a pillow. "He was being sneaky!"

Kai holds my wrist for a second, and there's a pause where the air is charged from our skin touching. Crackling like crazy, sparks flying from an outlet. Before I know what I'm doing, I lean closer, and he leans closer, and I give a little nod. Our lips touch and it's the spark that starts the fire, my body melting like chocolate in the heat. Until . . .

. . . I remember all the reasons this can't work. I pull back. His eyes are so bright and beautiful. His lips flushed pink from the flames.

"That was nice," I say. "Really nice."

"But . . ." he says, "a one-off?" Clearly, he read something in my face.

"At least for now," I say quietly.

He bites his lip and nods, then says, "I think it's all clear out there," his voice a bit funny. "Should we see if there's any dessert left over? Or fruit and milkshakes?"

He doesn't have to ask me twice.

After breaking the tension by stuffing our faces with chocolate cake and ice cream with fresh berries, we stay up way too late—him on the chair, me on the bed—talking about progressively sillier stuff, like which would win in a fight, a rat we saw in the park or his dog, and watching baby goat videos online, which is profoundly foolish since what I need most in life is sleep. I don't even notice the hours passing. A couple of times we laugh so hard my stomach muscles ache. When we finally go to bed, I reluctantly set my phone alarm for pretty early, so I don't sleep away any of the day. For now, though, I'm going to enjoy sleeping on a good mattress, on a bedframe, with soft, clean sheets and a comforter and a fluffy pillow under my head, a belly full of food, Advil for my ankle. The kiss in my memory. Real life can wait.

1989

Zoe is haunted by the memory of Colin gasping for air.

After she threw up that day at the cenote, he tried to explain what he was doing with the video. He talked about the history of performance art, body art, Chris Burden's "danger" pieces. (Burden got nailed to a car!) He told her that important art requires bravery of all kinds, sometimes physical. He told her he'd been practicing holding his breath, that he knew what he was doing.

Still, since then, she's kept herself busy with the sisters, hoping that he won't ask her to film him again. When the sisters go on full-day expeditions, Zoe joins them. They drive to the ruins at Chichén Itzá and Cobá, to climb soaring pyramids under the blistering sun. During long rides in the Jeep, deeper and deeper into the jungle, Zoe starts to hate it when the three of them talk about what they're going to do next, when they leave Mexico, something they plan to do soon. Azul has "wanderlust"—wants to see more places before college starts—and Scarlet wants to leave so they can stick to the plan they told their parents. (Lila, however, tells her sisters that she's staying in Tulum as long as Zoe and Colin are there.)

Zoe is so desperate for the sisters to stay, she organizes activities for coming days: a boat trip with a local fisherman; an afternoon with Itzel's grandmother learning about Mayan cooking, followed by dinner with Itzel's family; a trip through Sian Ka'an with a naturalist . . . anything to distract them from making firm plans to leave. She can't lose her pack.

The sisters stay, but, before too long, Zoe's other fear comes true: Colin asks her to film him again. And, despite what happened at the cenote, she can't bring herself to say no. She's promised herself she'd support him. She reminds herself how much he needs her.

This time, he has her bury him in a grave-sized pit in the sand and film him as he claws his way out, emerging coughing and sputtering and frantic. Before doing it, he promises her that he knows exactly how deep it should be—but that doesn't make it any easier to shovel clumps of sand onto his face. Burying the person you love alive is not something anyone should have to do. The next time, it's a noose made of vine, hanging from a tree in the forest. Even though he never loses consciousness, it's horrifying, seeing him dangling there like that, panic plain on his face. On their way back to the cabanas, Zoe feels dirty. Disgusting. She can't deny what's going on anymore. Colin is taking this too far, in an attempt to prove himself. She wants him to know that she understands him, that she knows what he's fighting against. That he can count on her and confide in her. Without thinking it through, she gives in to an impulse.

She tells him she read his father's letter.

Chapter Twenty-Nine

I emerge from Kai's room bleary-eyed, hoping I'll be the only one up, but find Annika in the open kitchen, with the smell of coffee in the air and a spread of breakfast food on the island: bagels, cream cheese, lox, tomatoes, granola, yogurt. My mouth literally waters. The sky is a brilliant blue outside the huge windows. The whole place is flooded with light, like we're actually part of the atmosphere. You could never feel dirty in here. Nothing could ever sneak up on you, no thorny vines or people who want to hurt you. And it's so quiet! At home, there's always something: constant traffic, the *beep-beep-beep* of a truck backing up, garbage cans clanging, neighbors talking or shouting, dogs barking. In Wolfwood, there's the rustle of gigantic leaves, the distant screams of Others being hurt, the heartbeat of the jungle . . .

Here, nothing.

"Good morning, darling," Annika says, cheery. "Sleep well?"

There's maybe a little innuendo. And while she's not *entirely* off the mark—*Kai and I kissed, holy shit*—I still find myself wanting to set her straight.

"Yes, thanks," I say. "Is Kai up? I hope he didn't mind not sleeping in his own room."

"Not yet. He's an early riser, like me, but not this early."

Even though I should get going, I accept her offer of coffee and food, happy that she's preoccupied with her phone while I eat, since my brain is too fuzzy to handle conversation. After inhaling one bagel—thick with cream cheese and piled with lox and tomatoes—I start on a second. Eventually she sets her phone aside.

"How's Zoe?" she asks. "Relatively speaking."

"Okay." I get up to refill my coffee mug, hoping she'll leave it there.

"Feeling all right about the Whitney visit? I talked to Malcolm yesterday—you know, the curator you met—and I think he'll come, too, even though he doesn't usually go to those young collector events."

A familiar buzz creeps into my legs, the one I always get when I think about the upcoming visit. I have seventeen days to help my mother go from where she is now, emotionally, to talking with fancy collectors at her studio—something she'd hate even at her best.

"So, um . . . how does that work?" I ask, sitting back down. "Like, does my mom really have to be there? Because, you know, she gets uncomfortable with people being in her studio, and I think maybe it would be better if she's not there when they make the visit."

Annika raises her reading glasses onto her head and stares at me. "The whole point is for her to be there." She pauses. "I understand your mom better than you think. I know how devastating it was when we couldn't sell those other works after *Wolfwood*. I understand her self-doubt."

When she says this, she looks me in the eyes, and I have a fleeting moment of thinking maybe she would understand, maybe I could talk to her.

But then she says, "I also know Zoe's a strong woman, and she's got to just suck it up and do what's best for the show."

Right.

The noise of a door opening pulls my attention. Kai zombie-walks out of Hiro's room and heads straight for the coffee, giving us a wave that says he's not awake enough to talk yet. God, he looks adorable when he's morning-rumpled. No, not adorable. *Hot.* Despite everything going on, I feel the full-body flutters of what is now a major, major crush. Maybe more than a crush.

"To be very clear," Annika continues, "she needs to be at the visit. That's what they're coming for. The whole point." She spreads a thin layer of cream cheese on a cracker, slowly and deliberately. "Zoe has to understand that there are ways she can talk about the work, about the origins of *Wolfwood*, without going into some big confession. She can talk about it in more general terms."

"Confession?"

"I mean, she doesn't have to get personal or go into details about her life. You know, trauma, whatever."

"What do you mean, trauma?" Does Annika know something I don't?

"Oh, I just meant . . . if she's talking about where all the anger and violence and everything come from, she can talk about it in any way she wants. She doesn't have to say, 'The Wolf is a jerk I knew in college'."

"She didn't go to college," I say, feeling lost.

Annika waves me off. "I was just making that up as an example. She always seemed like she didn't want to talk about the work because she felt like we were trying to be nosy. That there was something she was . . . processing. And I'm just saying that she can talk about it in ways that get to the emotional heart without sharing anything too personal. That's all."

I tear my bagel, not liking this conversation. The story in *Wolfwood* doesn't have a specific real-life meaning behind it. That's why my mom doesn't like talking about it—because she has nothing to say. She just wanted to be controversial. That's what she's always told me.

"She can also just talk about returning to the paintings after all these years," Annika adds. "How her perception of the series has changed . . . She was so young before. Such a mess, frankly. She really got herself together when she had you." Annika chuckles. "In some ways. Not in her ability to return a phone call."

I'm not sure how you can describe someone who had all that success as a mess, but I guess Annika means the partying.

"Anyway," she says, "I'll send someone over beforehand to set up light refreshments, very elegant, and have whoever it is help transport the works to Su-Jin afterward."

"The framer?" I stiffen. "Do they need to go to Mrs. Lim the same day as the Whitney visit?" That's five days earlier than the date that I've been aiming to have them all finished!

"It's a big job," Annika says. "We need time for the framing and then the installation." She turns to Kai. "You can handle the Whitney setup and transport after, yes?"

He nods. "Mm-hmm," he says sluggishly.

So much for being ahead of schedule. Now I'm three full days behind. I bite my cheeks, hard.

"All you'll have to worry about is Zoe," Annika says to me. "We'll take care of everything else."

Kai rides the elevator down with me so he can walk Miss G. "She'll scare away any cats," he jokes. I smile, but it's forced. Luckily, there's another tenant in the elevator with us, so we aren't awkwardly alone in the small space.

As we walk toward the subway, we bump into each other now and then, just small moments, like we're magnetized and being pulled together. My mind is elsewhere, but apparently my body can still maintain a different focus.

"Everything okay?" he asks. "You seem stressed."

"Fine. Just tired."

"How's the ankle?"

"Much better, thanks." Luckily, it is.

"You know," he says, "I was thinking about what you said last night, about your mom . . . and, like I said, lots of artists are disorganized. So if you're doing too much and need her to take over dealing with the gallery, just tell her not to worry. Diana's used to it. No big deal if your mom waits a few days to answer something. Would knowing that help with her anxiety?"

As he talks, guilt rises up and weaves between my ribs. In the morning light it's so clear: it's dangerous, how safe Kai makes me feel. That whole scene last night, lying in bed with him, never should have happened. Let alone the kiss! I got too close to him. I let down my guard. And it needs to end here. Which opens up a hollow inside me, because all I want is to do it again. Telling him those things made me feel so much less alone. And kissing him felt so *right*. But it was wrong. A betrayal. Both betraying my mother and betraying him. Sure, I told him my emotional truth. But I outright lied to him, too, while acting like I was being so open.

"Thanks," I say. "I think I gave you the wrong impression, though. It's not a big deal. My mom's great."

"Oh, I didn't think . . . I was just saying, since it sounds like you're kind of stressed—"

"I'm not."

"Okay," he says. "Wanted to throw it out there, that a lot of artists they deal with are difficult."

"Yup, good to know."

"And if there's anything you need help with, just ask."

"I'm fine," I say, waving him away. "But thanks. I appreciate it."

I wish more than anything there was something he could do. I feel that so, so strongly, walking here with him. Like if we could really rely on each other, we'd both be stronger.

But we can't.

When I get home, my mother is making her way back to the couch from the bathroom. She's bloodless. A skin bag with bones in it.

Dirty hair. Unwashed clothes. Even at her worst, she never would have let herself look like this before. Her erasure is almost complete.

"Mommy," I say, somewhat in shock. "You need help." It comes out before I mean to say it, the urgency taking away all caution.

"Not now, Indigo," she says wearily.

"Maybe . . . maybe I should call someone . . . A doctor." We have Medicaid . . .

"I'll be fine."

"Someone to talk to you, at least. To make sure you're okay."

To fix what I've broken.

She lowers herself onto the couch. "I know you're worried about that visit, the Whitney. But I'll be better by then. I promise." It seems like an unbearable effort for her to even get the words out.

"It's not the Whitney. I just want you to be okay."

She doesn't respond to that.

I wish there were someone else she was close to. A friend. A sister. Anyone. I wish Lila and Scarlet and Azul were with us. I can't do this alone. I need help.

"I brought you a bagel." A weak offering, but something, at least.

"Thanks, honey. I'm not hungry."

⁀

Even if she didn't look so fragile, I'd know better than to ask my mother if Annika was right about Wolfwood, that there's more behind the story than just wanting to be controversial. She'd tell me it means nothing, no matter what the truth is. But now that the thought's in my head, I can't forget it. And it seems so obvious. Of course the story must have come from somewhere. Why else would one of the girls be named Zoe? I need to know: Who is the Wolf?

The only evidence I have about my mother's life when she was young is a manila envelope of photos. I sneak it into my bag before heading out to the studio. I've pored over the photos plenty of times before, curious about relatives I've never known, but as I lay them out on the studio worktable now, I try to see them through a new lens, looking for signs of trouble.

Most of the pictures are from before her parents died. She seems like a happy kid: laughing while her dad held her in the air, grinning widely on her little red bike. She had birthday parties and Christmas trees. Went to Central Park and museums. They had a nice apartment in Astoria, Queens, crowded with books and toys. In one picture, she's painting at an easel in the kitchen. There's what I think you call a prayer card from when her father died, with a photo of him on one side and a psalm on the other. I'm mostly studying his face, looking for traces of my own, when something catches my eye. The date he died. It says here January 13. But the date my mother always goes drinking is June 4. Maybe she drinks on the date of her mother's death, not her father's? (I've always thought it was strange that she drank on the anniversary of one of their deaths and not the other. I figured it was because the day her father died was when she became a true orphan.)

Nothing in the envelope gives any hint about who might be the Wolf. Or Lila, Scarlet, and Azul. My mom doesn't have sisters and has never talked about girlfriends or cousins. I've never known her to be close to *anyone*, except me. Whoever the sisters are, the Wolf must have hurt them, too? And this story is about them getting revenge, together. All of this hurt leading to one final takedown and escape from the guy.

Maybe the Wolf is my father.

Oh, Jesus. For a moment, a brittle chill in my bones makes me think it must be true. Then I realize she started painting this series more than ten years before she met whoever my father is, so it couldn't be him. Thank god.

Maybe . . . maybe it doesn't matter. Maybe it's better if I don't know.

I'm here now, and this is where I can make a difference. This is where I win. Whoever the guy is, Wolfwood is where I take him down for her.

Wolfwood is where we get our revenge.

I've wasted enough time thinking about all of this. I shouldn't have wasted *any*, now that I'm behind again, from not factoring in enough days for the framing. Need to put everything else aside and push myself even harder.

A chant rings in my ears, punctuated by the sound of fists on a table: *Get the Wolf! Get the Wolf!*

Chapter Thirty

Zoe!" Lila breaks through the circle of Others crowded around me. Seeing her fills me with relief.

The Others have been pinning me with their accusatory stares, ever since I jumped off that branch where I imagined sitting with the Wolf. The branch where I imagined pushing him to his death. I've tried to get up, but the pain in my ankle is too sharp.

"Thank god the Others were protecting you," Lila says, squatting next to me. "A monster could've gotten you easily." She turns to Scarlet and Azul, who broke through the circle right behind her. "We never should've let her go alone."

"She wasn't alone," Scarlet says. "They kept her safe, better than we could have."

"I had another vision of him," I say. "Before I got hurt." As Lila helps me up, I explain what happened. Not my emotions, of course—not the pull I feel toward him and my horror at his death— just that I climbed the tree and hanged him with a noose made of vine. I tell them I pushed him off the branch and the tree pushed me. My pulse accelerates as I tell the lie.

"Maybe that's what we should do," Azul says thoughtfully. "Hang him. Sounds dramatic. Ceremonial."

With Lila supporting much of my weight, we start on our way out of the area. Because I can only hobble, our pace is slow. The Others have dispersed into a more fluid wall around us, spreading out and guarding against attacks. Now that the sisters are here, I realize I was paranoid before, thinking that the Others were being threatening when they surrounded me. Of course they were just protecting me.

We're quiet as we make our way through soaring palm plants—ten feet high or so—with fronds that wriggle like Medusa's snakes. A canopy of serpents. I hold my blade ready, but with one arm around Lila's shoulders, I won't be much help if something happens. Soon, though, we see light up ahead and find the open, grassy area where we've started building.

Since I've been gone, they've constructed a section of one wall.

"So," Scarlet says, in her take-charge tone. "We still need those palm fronds for the roof. And have to start tying together the next wall segment."

"Zoe can't do much, with her ankle," Lila says.

"I can tie bamboo," I say.

"Okay," Scarlet says. "You and Lila do that. Azul and I will get fronds."

The two of them head back into the brush. When Lila calls, "Be careful!" guilt spikes inside me, the way it does whenever I know I'm letting the sisters walk into pain. This mission doesn't end well for Scarlet. I see what's going to happen, and there's misery ahead. *But this is how it has to go. It will all work out in the end.* As usual, I make myself feel better by remembering that.

After they've gone, Lila uses sticks and some long grass to make a splint for my ankle. I can put weight on it again. As thanks, I give her the white berries from my pocket.

"White indigo," she says. "Edible!"

White indigo. Something about this strikes a note inside me—a quivering high note—but I don't know why. She pops a berry in her mouth, chews, and sticks out her tongue, now a deep blue.

We begin pulling out grass to lash around bamboo, that note still vibrating inside me, uncomfortable.

Suddenly, Azul appears from the brush. She calls to us, breathless: "Scarlet!"

It's all she has to say. We drop what we're doing. In the splint, I can move almost as quickly as usual. We follow Azul through bushes and trees and vines, to the scene I already knew was coming. It's even worse than I foresaw.

Scarlet is suspended in the air, arms held up and out by branches, legs held down and apart by roots. Her dress is torn, exposing most of her midriff.

Flowers—pink ones, like anemones, with writhing petals and gaping yellow mouths at their centers—are spitting poison at her. Every time it hits, it sizzles, like water drops on a hot pan, leaving her skin flame-red and blistered. Ruptured. Oozing pus. The air is heavy with the smell of toxic burning. Her eyes are rolled back in her head. She pulls against the restraints.

Her wails of pain sound as if her soul were being ripped out.

"How do we do this?" Azul asks, voice desperate. "It's coming at her from all sides! We'll get hit, too."

"We'll have to cut her down as fast as we can," I say. "No other choice."

"Not you," Lila says. "If it gets in your eyes, you could be blinded. For good."

The Others have begun fighting the monsters, and when poison hits them in the eyes, they're incapacitated, rolling on the ground in agony.

"I'm helping," I insist. I look around, find large-leafed plants behind us. "Shields!" I chop off the biggest leaves I can find, quick as I can—one for each of us.

Holding them up like riot gear, we duck and run toward Scarlet. Poison hits the shields, sizzles, smells like burned rubber. A spray hits my feet. *Fuck!* A thousand wasps stinging one spot of skin. Finally, we reach her. I hack at the root holding her right leg. Azul and Lila use rocks on the one trapping her left. *Thwack, thwack, thwack* . . . I raise my arm and chop over and over, cutting through the thick, fibrous beast. Trying to ignore the heart-stopping pain when I'm hit. Scarlet is quiet and limp. Unconscious. My blade cuts through the last bit of the monster's flesh. Her right leg is released.

I look up, ready to strike the branch holding her arm. There, hanging loose on her wrist: a silver bracelet. The one I thought I imagined. Before I can grab it, Azul is beside me. "Our rocks aren't sharp enough—the root is too thick. Use your blade. We'll do the arms." No other choice, I switch to that side, hack at the root with all of my muscle. *Thwack, thwack, thwack* . . . When I venture a look, the bracelet is gone. Azul doesn't have it—both hands are gripping her rock. Did I imagine it? I must have. In all the blur I imagined it.

With one last *thwack*, we've cut Scarlet free. We cover her with our shields as we hold her and run, our bodies unprotected, my mind detached from pain that's too great to handle. Her limbs won't bend. She's rigid.

Back at our clearing, we lay her on the ground. Her skin is even redder than her dress, purple almost. No sign of healing, just volcanic blisters and pain and pain and pain. My own skin is blistered in spots, too. Azul and Lila have already recovered.

"How did you avoid getting trapped like her?" I ask Azul quietly. There's a hush among us as we stare at Scarlet helplessly, waiting for her wounds to heal. It's hard to bear, seeing her like this.

"I got distracted," Azul says. "We lost each other for a moment. It was my fault. I should've stuck with her."

"It's not your fault." *I'm the one who knew what was going to happen.*

"She had something to tell me," Azul continues. "Was calling to me, really urgent. Like she'd found something important. But before I reached her, she was attacked."

Lila stares at Scarlet, thinking. "Maybe she saw the Wolf."

Azul raises her eyebrows. "Maybe."

They turn their attention from their sister to the clearing around us, scanning the open space and trees beyond.

I don't know what Scarlet saw, but deep inside, I know: she couldn't have seen the Wolf.

Chapter Thirty-One

I put strict rules on my interactions with Kai. I let myself text him, but even that I have to limit because of my phone plan. I let myself do it only at night, during the rare few hours when I'm in bed or on the sofa at the studio, where I'm sleeping more often these days, so I don't waste time on the subway. I remain upbeat with Kai. I don't mention my mother or tell him anything that's upsetting me or go into anything too serious.

> Kai: Were you there for the "skating" party my mom let me and H have at the gal where we all skated around in sockfeet?
>
> Me: omg yes! Hiro was the dj right?
>
> Kai: Ok yes mostly but I never got credit for the songs I asked him to play. some of the best were my choices
>
> Me: you still remember not getting credit? Lol sad
>
> Kai: living in the shadow of an older sib is rough, what can I say

I'm sure he didn't mean that in a more complicated way, but obviously it has lots of layers. Still, I want to keep this light.

Me: why did you ask about the party

Kai: oh right. I'm going to organize one for my little cousin's bday. Want to come be chaperone?

Me: Totally! If the timing works I'd love to

Of course, though, it turns out I'm busy on the day of the party, and the other couple of times he suggests stuff, too. I promise him I'll be less busy once school starts. That I'm just working hard now so I'll have some savings for fall. If everything goes okay, I won't have been lying.

I don't let myself do anything else to jeopardize the future, either. No more missed shifts at the Fud, even if that means I'm working over twenty hours in a row between there and painting. By cutting back on sleep and pushing my studio hours to the limit, I'm slowly inching toward being on schedule to finish by the Whitney visit. Making good progress with the sixth painting.

Hard as I'm working, though, it's not enough to stay on top of everything in the real world. Not with my mother having faded to almost nothing. Every small thing that she used to do and doesn't now is another chore piled on top of me.

One day, I come home midday after an early Fud shift and the hallway smells strongly like pine cleanser. I follow the stairs up, hoping maybe the smell is coming from inside one of the apartments. But I find a woman cleaning the woodwork in the hallway, which is supposed to be our job. She says the Asslord hired her. I go out on the stoop, where my mother won't be able to hear, and call him, stomach tight.

I have some idea what's coming, but it's even worse than I expect. I go cold when he tells me: Since we won't be responsible for the cleaning anymore, he wants $300 extra for our rent. Per month. Three hundred dollars. And that's with us still taking care of the trash. Rent is due tomorrow; I can't possibly have it by then, so I have no choice but to beg for extra time. He loves it when I grovel—gets off on the power he has over us. Still, he gives me only four days.

Back in the apartment, I take out the plastic envelope where we keep our cash and count what's in there, praying that there will somehow be more than the last time I checked. I count the bills over and over, waiting to find one stuck to another. But of course that doesn't happen. Which means I have to raise $300 in four days.

I don't know how we'll make next month, either, but next month is next month, and all I can do is put out one fire at a time.

Think, think, think, think . . .

Even though I can't spare the time, since I'm still playing catch-up at the studio, I text Marcus to see if he needs any extra babysitting hours from me, but he and Jaden are on Martha's Vineyard for the week. I ask Shawna for an advance on my next paycheck. Ha. Trinity doesn't pay enough to make it worth it. And there's no way I'm borrowing from anyone, not when I don't know how I'll ever pay it back.

While my mother sleeps, I search the basement for anything we could sell, examining the few vases and dishes and knickknacks and jewelry we own. Nothing that has any value other than sentimental. Nothing except . . .

No.

No, no, no, no, no.

Do I have a choice?

I gently hold the liquidy silk jersey of the Tania Bawa dress. It's just an object, I tell myself. Just pieces of fabric sewn together with thread. Nothing magic about it. I set it aside on my mattress. Next, I take my mother's dress off the rack, the one she's wearing in the *New York* magazine photo. It's a vintage designer dress, in surprisingly good shape. Definitely worth a little money. I can't even bring myself to look at it, just rest it next to the Tania Bawa one and go find a clean bag to carry them in.

They're inanimate objects that shouldn't have any importance. It's vain to care so much about them, to care about what I look like.

I tell myself these things, but I know they're not true. It's not vanity to feel transformed by something you wear. Not selfish to feel connected to my mother's neon days. Not shallow to care about a dress that's also a piece of art, like the Tania Bawa is. They mean something to me, these sewn pieces of fabric, beyond what I look like in them. It's what I feel like inside myself.

It's not selfish to want something. To treasure it. I may not have money, but I'm allowed to want. I guess I'm just not allowed to *have*.

I handle them very gently. Wrap them first in cut paper grocery bags, like birthday presents, my arms slow and heavy. Carry them to the consignment store in my cleanest tote.

As Parker unwraps and studies them, I bite my lips. "You've been holding out on me, kid," she says. "These are fabulous!" I manage to ask if she can forward me some money now, since they're so salable, but she says no. She says she'll hang them in the window, though, and that pieces in the window sell quickly when they're this good. I fake a smile and walk out, arms wrapped tight around me, telling myself it's nothing, that I'll be able to buy whatever dress I want after the paintings sell.

Still, I make it only two blocks before I turn around and hurry back. I jog, in fact, suddenly desperate to get there.

Parker is arranging my mother's dress on one of the store's mannequins.

"Sorry," I say, a little out of breath. "I just . . ." No way to explain this truthfully, that I can't give away every bit of my mother's old happiness. It's not worth the money. "I don't think I want to sell that one. Not yet at least. Sorry."

"No problem," Parker says, unzipping it. "Never want you to do something you'll regret."

She hands it back and I clutch it to me. Not this one.

Parker sells the Tania Bawa dress as quickly as she expected, and I just make rent. Since it's a couple of days late, the Asslord makes me go all the way to Hoboken to drop it off at his office, instead of leaving it in his mailbox at the building. The train fare and time aren't things I can spare, but I have no choice. And handing the envelope to his assistant doesn't give me any relief or satisfaction. It doesn't change the fact that the rent has been raised a ridiculous amount and I'll need more money in a month than I can imagine making. (To live in that shithole!)

I do the only things I can. Start spending less on food than I ever have. Keep reminding myself that there's an end in sight. An end to the hunger and exhaustion. An end to my mother's hibernation. An end to all the lying. And I keep painting whenever I'm not at work.

It takes Scarlet longer than usual to recover from the last attack. The poison burned her eyes and the inside of her mouth, so she can't see or speak. When I'm with her, all I can do is whisper, "I'm sorry, I'm sorry," even if she doesn't realize the reason I'm sorry is that I knew what was going to happen and didn't stop it. While she lies shielded from the sun by a makeshift canopy, we gather the materials for the shelter. Going in shifts, always leaving someone to stay with her. Every trip involves a battle. Every battle involves more pain. I wish I could avoid the attacks when I see them in my premonitions. But I can't. The sisters have to know that I'm one of them. That I get hurt here, too.

Despite the injuries, sometimes when I'm in the real world, ringing up groceries or talking pointlessly to my mother's back, I'd rather be in Wolfwood. I'm never hungry there. I have friends I love who love me. I know, with certainty, what we're supposed to be doing and how to save them. I know that even though we're getting hurt now, we're going to win in the end. Fiction, not real life.

1989

Colin's jaw goes slack when Zoe tells him she read the letter from his father. She keeps talking, assuring him she loves him, she doesn't care how old he is, she's so sorry his father is an asshole, and she understands how he must feel, why he needs to prove himself, but his father is wrong, about everything. Colin's paintings are amazing. He is amazing.

As she talks, Colin just stares at her, eyes freezing over, face becoming a mask.

After a pulsing quiet, he says, much too calmly, You think you know me? You don't know anything.

He turns his back and walks away, taking all the air with him.

From then on, he stops speaking to her. Stops looking at her. Like she doesn't exist. His silence is a sharp, solid thing lodged in Zoe's chest. She spends her days with the sisters but is aware of it with every painful breath. She would much, much rather they'd had a huge fight than have him shut her out like this. And she doesn't blame him for being so angry. She can't believe she told him she read the letter. What a stupid mistake! She wouldn't want Colin to know her dark secrets—that she couldn't save her mother and caused her father's heart attack and has no one who loves her. Of course Colin wouldn't want her to know his! She should have just kept it to herself and supported him like she promised herself she'd do. Why did she tell him?

She's too ashamed to share any of this with the sisters and isn't sure what they notice on their own. He's being perfectly friendly with everyone else. More friendly than usual, even, as if to make it more painful for Zoe.

After four days of the silent treatment, Colin borrows Don Eduardo's car again and takes off. He apparently told Lila that he was going to Cancún for more equipment, but Zoe fully expects him not to come back. A comforting fantasy takes shape in her mind: She'll go wherever the sisters go next. She'll stay with them and everything will be fine. They'll let her do that, won't they? She won't have lost her whole wolf pack? But, to her shock, Colin returns home later that same day—with more video equipment, just like he said. A second video camera, because his next piece needs to be filmed simultaneously from two different angles. With Zoe sitting right there, he asks Lila if she'll help and suggests maybe Azul could help, too.

Before Lila can answer, Zoe grabs his hand. Let me do it, she says.

She doesn't care what the video is, doesn't care how dangerous it is. She needs to be one of the people who helps. There's an excruciatingly long moment of eye contact, where she can tell Colin is evaluating. Can he forgive her? Can he trust her? Zoe tries to telegraph everything in that one look: I'm so sorry. I do know you. I know you don't care what your father says. I know how strong you are. I believe in your art. I trust your judgment. Important art requires bravery. I understand.

Finally, he says okay.

Chapter Thirty-Two

One night, I'm taking the subway home from Wolfwood, and as I wait for the train, my hunger is like the rats on the tracks, big and sharp-toothed and gnawing, gnawing, gnawing. I pace up and down the narrow, filthy platform, feeling like there are eyes on me. Monsters everywhere. Not only them, but the Others, too. Everyone is always watching. I avoid the edge of the platform.

I think about what happened today, while I was there, in Wolfwood. I'm anxious about it—anxious in a way I'm usually not. Scarlet recovered, finally. She told us that right before she was attacked, she came across the wreckage of the old shelter. She thought maybe there'd be materials we could use in our hut. But she found something else, something she wanted to show Azul, and was running to find her when she was attacked. "A bracelet," Scarlet said, touching her wrist. "I found a silver bracelet. None of you saw it when you were helping me?"

My breath caught. I turned my eyes to the fronds I was weaving for our shelter's roof so they wouldn't see my surprise. Until then, I'd been telling myself I'd imagined the bracelet, that I must have. And for some reason, I didn't want the sisters to know that I'd seen it.

"You're probably just remembering something from home," I said. "There's nothing like that in Wolfwood."

"Maybe," Scarlet said. "But I can picture it so clearly. Simple, with a dark yellow stone and some geometric decorations. And . . . it had an inscription, I think."

I didn't know anything about an inscription. Still, her words tugged at something inside me.

"Zoe's right," Lila said. "No way there's something like that here."

Later, when the sisters were sleeping, I snuck past the groups of Others that were guarding us. I started digging near where Scarlet had been attacked, expecting my hand to hit something cold and hard and small. Metallic. When it touched something else—spherical and smooth, the size of a small melon—I hesitated.

Somehow, I knew what it was. Even though I didn't want to see it, I finished digging it out.

A skull, caught up amid a tangle of the thin netting.

A vision flashed: his head, pouring blood. Eyes staring at me. Blood everywhere.

As quickly as possible, I wrapped the skull in the hem of my dress and took it to bury it somewhere else, far away, in case the sisters came back to look for the bracelet. No monsters attacked me. I saw no one. But I felt eyes on me the whole time. And when I got back to where the sisters still slept, the Others guarding them watched me like they knew what I'd just done.

Now, sitting on the subway, my gaze darts from the elderly woman across from me, to the hipster couple next to her, to the man in a Con Ed uniform, to the woman with a child. Why do I feel so guilty? Why do I feel like they're watching and judging me? And whose bracelet is it? I try not to think about the skull. Try not to remember those scenes of his head floating in a sea of blood. Or the way I feel about him when I'm with him. Try not to think about what any of it means or why I hide so much from the sisters.

My desperate hunger and my Wolfwood worries keep gnawing at my gut. On the walk home from the station, I pass McDonald's and can't stop myself: I go inside. Waiting in line, I count out the change in my pockets and scrounge for anything extra in my bag—all I come up with is $4.06. I read the menu over and over, wanting everything and nothing sounding quite right, nothing sounding like enough.

"Gonna order or what?" the guy behind me says.

"Yeah." I move forward. "Um, Big Mac."

"Four thirty-six."

"I thought it was $3.99?"

"Tax."

"Um, then wait . . . Just a Quarter Pounder."

"Jesus Harry Christ," the guy in line mutters. I want to scream at him. I have no rope left. I just need to eat. I need strength to fight.

The cashier hands me my burger. I turn around, scan the restaurant for a table.

That's when I see her.

Eating by the windows. Crew cut, pug nose, pale skin. Chunky rings on her fingers. I swing back around, hands shaking. Drop my tray on the counter. It's the woman from the homeless shelter, the one who beat me up. Did she see me? *Run!* my brain screams. But she's sitting too close to the exit. "Bathroom?" I ask the cashier, even though it's the last place I want to be. He points, and I hurry on rubber legs and slam the door shut behind me, lock it, and lean against it, shaking. Did she see me?

Monsters everywhere.

I let down my guard.

What if she saw me?

I glance around for a plunger or soap holder, a weapon of any kind. There's nothing. Nothing in my bag, either. Only my phone. I curl my fingers around it. I want my mother. Would she come if I call? Would she help me? *Rattle, rattle.* The door handle jiggles, someone's trying to get in. I back away, sit on the toilet, curl up as small as possible, arms wrapped around myself.

Rattle, rattle. I close my eyes. Hold my phone tight, don't bother dialing; the Mom I need isn't there. Eyes shut, I whisper: *Go away, go away, go away . . .*

One more *rattle,* then . . . nothing.

Silence.

Slowly, my breath starts to even out. My body stops trembling. I don't know how long I've been sitting when a knock comes at the door. "Someone in there?" A young person's voice. Not hers. "Hello? Anyone in there?" Another knock. The handle rattles.

"One second," I call back. I straighten up, splash water on my face, and try to walk on normal human legs when I come out. "Sorry," I say to the kid as I pass him.

The restaurant isn't big—from the hallway, I can see the table the woman was sitting at. Empty. No one wearing the bright orange tee she had on. She's gone. I wait for a moment, just to be sure. Tension drains out of me, making me weak. Finally, I emerge from the hall and head toward the front.

"Don't you want your food?" It's the cashier, indicating my abandoned tray, shoved to the end of the counter. I grab the burger, leave the tray. I need to get home.

Outside the door, I look left and right, and . . . wait . . . there's a woman in a bright orange tee, untying a shaggy dog tied to a lamppost. It's the woman from the restaurant. Definitely. But . . . she's not the woman from the shelter. She's similar. Same type of face. Crew cut. This woman is younger, though. Much younger. I stare at her to be sure. Blink, as if clearing my vision. I was so positive it was her! But no, it's not. She looks my direction. Her eyes pass right over me. No recognition.

Not a monster.

I take a deep, slow breath.

Not a monster.

As I navigate my way through the East Village nighttime bustle, I eat my Quarter Pounder, not really tasting it, despite my hunger. I'm losing my mind, aren't I? Thinking I saw her, out of nowhere. In the four years since the shelter, I've never had that happen before. My brain is breaking. I turn onto my block, so tired that even making it from here to my building seems like too much effort.

"Indigo!" I startle at the voice. Ravi is standing in front of me. "I've been calling you from across the street. Didn't you hear me?"

I swallow my bite. "Hey," I say, forcing a smile. Of course I run into him *now* of all times. "What's up?"

He works his jaw, as if there's something he wants to say but doesn't know how to say it. I can already tell it's something I'm not going to want to hear.

"You sold the dress?"

The dress . . . *Shit.* It takes me a moment to manage a response. "How'd you find out?"

He makes a face like it's a silly question. "Dude, it was hanging in the fucking window."

Right. I should be mortified. I *am* mortified. But I also feel kind of flat. I'm spent, emotionally, after all the adrenaline. Too drained to truly care about anything.

"I'm so sorry," I say. "I didn't want to. I just . . . needed money."

"You needed money and *that's* what you did? Why didn't you ask your mom? Or borrow?"

"Wasn't sure I'd be able to pay it back. Did you . . . tell Kai?"

"No. I'm not a total asshole. I wanted to talk to you first. It was a real bitch move, Indigo."

I bite the inside of my lip. I *am* sorry, but I'm also annoyed I have to stand here and listen to him when he knows nothing of what my life's like.

"And what's up with your arms?" he asks.

I'm wearing the button-down I was painting in, sleeves rolled above the elbows. Scattered bruises and scrapes—old and new—decorate my skin.

None of your business. "Went camping with a friend. Poison ivy, hiking . . ." I start unrolling one of the sleeves.

"You look really strung out." His eyes narrow. "What's going on with you?"

From the way he says it, and the way he was looking at my arms, I wonder if he thinks I'm using. "Nothing," I say. "Just working too hard. That's all."

"Kai doesn't need someone else lying to him."

"I'm not!"

Ravi raises his eyebrows.

Fuck this. "Don't know what to tell you," I say. "We can't all be millionaires. Maybe you're just not used to knowing someone with a normal life. I must have something going on 'cause I need money? 'Cause I'm eating at McDonald's instead of Bareburger? Is that it?" I hold up the remains of my Quarter Pounder.

"No!" he says. "God, no." I can tell I've hit a nerve. Good. "I'm not a total asshole," he says again. "I just don't want you hurting Kai."

I feel my spine lengthening, my skin thickening. I fight monsters, I remind myself. I imagine Lila, Scarlet, and Azul standing behind me, having my back.

"I really am sorry about the dress," I say. "But I gotta go." I brush past him, not waiting for a response.

Chapter Thirty-Three

After the strangeness with the bracelet and the buried skull, everything starts happening as it should inside Wolfwood. We finish building the shelter, a huge relief. The sisters are safe now. I've done what I needed to do. I can't see how everything ends—this is pretty much the last of what I can envision—but it feels like I've done the best I can to take care of them.

It's cozy in our little hut. We wove two hammocks from vines, with room for two of us in each. I wanted the sisters to *want* to be here. Lila and I take one hammock, Azul and Scarlet the other. I try not to think of that vision I had, a long time ago, of being in a hammock with him, feeling affection for him. Try not to think of the bracelet or him pressing it into my hand. Or his head on the floor. None of it matters.

At first, it seems like the sisters appreciate the quiet and safety, able to relax for the first time since they—since *we*—arrived in Wolfwood. And for me, it feels like a home, like we're a family. I have no desire to leave. But after we've been here for what feels like a couple of days, they start getting antsy.

"How long are we supposed to wait?" Scarlet asks, pacing around the small space. "I don't want to stay here if nothing's ever going to happen. I'd rather risk dying out there, fighting. Doing something."

"Maybe he's here and we just can't see him," Azul says.

We left a couple of small spaces between the bamboo to monitor outside, but our vision is severely limited. Azul stands, peering out.

"The whole point is to stay safe inside," I say.

"The whole point is to lure the Wolf here and kill him!" Scarlet says.

"Maybe I was wrong to say this was a good idea," Azul says. "Maybe I was wrong about needing to kill him to get home."

"We've talked about this," Lila says, braiding my hair to match hers as she talks. "What we were doing wasn't working. So we're trying this. Seeing what happens. Like you said, Azul, Zoe's intuition is always right."

"We know nothing about him," Scarlet says. "Why do we think he'd come here? And how come Zoe's the only one who's ever seen him?" She and Azul are working each other up, the confined space of the shelter trapping and amplifying their frustration.

"My vision is better," I say with a shrug.

"Maybe he comes to you." Scarlet gives me a pointed look.

"What do you mean?"

"Maybe there's something about you that draws him. You're different than us, right?"

I cross my arms. I don't like where she's going with this.

"Okay," I say. "Maybe you're right. Maybe I should leave you all in here and go out and try to draw him to us."

"Maybe you should," Scarlet says.

"No way," Lila says. "You're the one who should *stay* here, Zoe. You're the one who doesn't heal like we do!" She turns to her sisters. "Isn't it better to be in here than to be out there getting hurt?"

"No," I say. "Scarlet is right. I should see if he'll come to me."

"I'll go with you, then," Lila says. "I want to see him."

I shake my head. "I'm going alone. If there's some reason he only comes to me, maybe I need to be alone."

"It's dangerous!" Lila says, then begs Azul, "Tell her not to!"

But Azul just says, "Lila, let her go."

I emerge from the hot, airless cabin into the even hotter, sun-drenched air and walk a few feet before I stop. What if the sisters decide to leave while I'm gone? The way they were just talking, I wouldn't be too surprised. I can't risk that happening. So without thinking about it, I find a wide stick and wedge the door shut from the outside. They won't even know they can't get out unless they try, which they shouldn't be doing. For their own good.

I walk the perimeter of the clearing. The landscape has shifted. Now all the area around us is dangerous. There aren't any safe spots. It's like the monsters have gathered to surround us. I keep my blade raised; nothing happens, but jaws are chomping and poison is dripping and vines are writhing.

And wherever I go, I see him. I see him climbing trees and jumping into the air. I see him sinking in a clear pool of water like a stone. I see him beautiful, and I see him bloody. Standing in the sun, and hanging from a noose. As I walk around the shifting jungle,

I see him everywhere. But it's all just visions. I can't find any sign of the *real* him.

I don't know how long I wander. When I return to the shelter, it takes me a moment to make sense of what I see. The Others have gathered in the clearing, circling up around the shelter. Not one deep. Not two deep. An entire army, assembled in the grassy open area, in all states of injury and dismemberment. Forming a human (inhuman?) barrier all around us.

I push my way through. The sisters are in front of the shelter, building something.

"What were you thinking?" Scarlet yells when she sees me approaching. "Trapping us like that!?"

"Trapping you? I was keeping you safe."

"Locking the door from the *inside* keeps us safe," Azul says. "From the outside it traps us!" I've never heard her raise her voice like this before.

Even Lila is looking at me like I betrayed them. But why? The whole point of the shelter was to stay in it! To stay safe.

"How did you get out?" I ask.

"The Others let us out," Scarlet says.

This is very strange. The Others don't do things like that. All they do is protect us and fight the monsters.

"What are you making?" I look up at the skeletal structure they've begun to build.

"A gallows," Azul says. "To hang the Wolf."

"You're the only one with a blade," Scarlet says. "So we need options, right? What if he shows up and you've gone AWOL?"

I swallow. I don't like the way they're looking at me. When I locked them in, it was no different from the things I've done to save them during attacks. All of it is about taking care of them. Saving them. They should see that.

Lila and I meet eyes, and I can tell that she does see it. She understands.

She comes over and hugs me. "Don't do it again," she murmurs.

"So?" Scarlet says, hands on her hips. "Did you see him?"

I shake my head.

"Didn't think so."

I don't want to know what she means by that. And I have the horrible sensation that even though this is all what's supposed to happen, everything is going wrong.

Chapter Thirty-Four

When I finish the seventh painting, I think I'm in good shape. Six days left—enough time to do the last piece, at the manic rate I've been going. But then it hits me: I don't have the final sketch—the one that was missing when I brought the portfolio of drawings to the gallery, all those weeks ago. I've been so focused on getting through the ones I've been working on, I haven't even thought about it.

I check in the portfolio again—it's definitely not there. I check in the large foamcore folder with the watercolor paper—not there, either. The boxes that are out here at the studio are all too small to hold it, but I rummage through them anyway and find only notebooks and some old art supplies. I search all around the small room with the desk, like I did when I was looking for paintings the first time I came out here. Nothing.

Worry grows inside me as I search. What if there isn't a final sketch? If she never did it, or if it got lost? I can't do one myself. I can copy, that's it. And even the copying takes intense concentration. I don't have time for this!

I'll have to get my mother to draw a new one if I can't find it. She'll have to. She can't say no, not when I'm this close to finishing.

I stare out the window for a moment and try to quell the storm inside me. No reason to panic before I even ask if she knows where the drawing is.

The basement is dark. I tug the string, and the light bulb illuminates a worse situation than I expect. Piles of unwashed clothes. Used glasses and mugs all around. Roaches on the wall by the fridge, not even bothering to scatter. I haven't been here often enough to keep up with cleaning. When I am here, I'm so hungry and overwhelmed I usually go straight to bed. The best cure for hunger (other than food) is sleep.

I promise myself that as soon as this last painting is finished, I'll do a major cleanup, top to bottom.

My mother is where I knew she'd be: on the couch, facing the wall. I put my hand on her bony shoulder and gently shake her.

"I'm asleep," she mutters.

"I just need a minute. It's important."

She manages to turn over and look at me. Her face is hollow and puffy at the same time. Pillow wrinkles map across her cheek. I can't let myself be distracted by the pain of seeing her like this.

"The last drawing," I say. "Where is it? The Whitney visit is in six days, and I have to be finished by then."

"The last—?"

"The drawing for the final painting."

"With the others, I guess." Her voice is so faded I have to strain to hear it.

"It's not there."

She hesitates. "I don't know then."

"Did you do one?"

"Yes."

"So, where else could it be?"

Her brow furrows. "I don't know . . . It was so long ago."

"Are you *sure* you made one?"

"I told you. Yes." She sounds like she's telling the truth.

"Do you think it could be here?" I say, looking around the room.

"I don't know, Indigo. I'm sorry." She turns toward the back of the couch again.

We don't have any real closets. We don't have under-bed areas. All we have are a few boxes stacked in the corner and small plastic sets of drawers. I search through everything, not hopeful, and as I expected find nothing.

I sit on the coffee table and rest my head in my hands, trying to keep my shit together.

"Would you have thrown it out?"

"No." Her faded voice is muffled by the cushion, almost inaudible. "But I didn't want anyone to see it. Maybe I hid it."

Hot tears of frustration build behind my eyes as I scan the room for somewhere it might be hidden that I haven't already checked. There's nowhere.

"You're going to have to do it over."

"I'm not doing it over." She pushes herself up a little now, so I can hear her better. "Did you look in the books? The journals and sketchbooks?"

"In them? No. Just in the boxes." The ones at the studio.

"Maybe it's in a sketchbook. '89 or '90. Where I started the ideas . . . for Wolfwood."

~

When I open the sketchbook, several pieces of paper are trapped between its pages. One is bigger than the others and folded up. Yellowed from age. I carefully unfold it and spread it out on the worktable. It rips a bit as I do, the thin paper accustomed to being creased. Oh my god, the rush of relief and elation I feel at seeing the familiar faces and setting and handwriting . . . Thank god, thank god, thank god.

I text my mother immediately: FOUND IT. THANK YOU!!!!

I scan it quickly, anxious to see how the sisters and I are going to get out of this, anxious to see how the Wolf will finally be taken down. Is there a scene outside of Wolfwood? Back at home? Do I get to stay with the sisters, or do I end up somewhere else? I hate the thought of being separated from them.

My eyes skip from moment to moment, not understanding what I'm seeing. The final image, the last vignette . . . it's not of the Wolf being killed, or the girls finding the way out or back home. It doesn't make sense.

The final caption: THE BETRAYAL IS REVEALED, THE REAL WOLF EXPOSED.

It's Zoe who's hanging from the gallows.

Zoe.

Dead.

Zoe is the Wolf.

My hand has gone to my own neck.

1989

The video that Colin wants Lila and Zoe to help with involves driving the Jeep in the middle of the night. When Scarlet hears, she says no way—neither girl is insured to drive it. End of discussion. Lila is furious. Zoe expects Azul to mediate, as usual, but instead Azul is firmly on Scarlet's side.

In private, Colin asks Zoe if she'll talk to Scarlet and Azul, explain that there's nothing unsafe about what they'd be doing. One of the girls will stand on the side of the road with a camera, he says, filming as the Jeep approaches in the distance. The other will drive the Jeep, just at the speed limit, nothing dangerous. She'll drive straight, far enough that the camera can capture the taillights disappearing. They'll film right before dawn, when it's still mostly dark and the road will be empty. That's all the girls will do. One will film, one will drive. Perfectly safe, no reason to worry about insurance or anything.

And what about you? Zoe asks him. What will you be doing?

He looks her in the eyes and says, Filming from another location.

Zoe feels herself making a choice by not pressing him to explain anything else, even though she knows he's holding back. Obviously, there's more to the video than he's saying. But that look in his eyes is clear: You're either with me or against me. And she's with him. She has to be.

So she talks to the sisters. She says she knows that Scarlet doesn't love Colin but that he did stop pursuing the mural idea after Zoe talked to him about it. That he's passionate about the videos. She tells them how safe the filming will be. When Scarlet and Azul both still say no, Zoe makes another choice: She hates to share her problems, but she confesses that Colin has been angry at her, and if she can help him with his project, he might stop being upset. She begs them. As she does, she finds herself starting to cry.

At this, Azul hugs her. Okay, Zoe, she says. We'll do it. Don't worry.

Scarlet still looks skeptical but doesn't contradict her older sister.

In the end, it's decided that all the girls will go. Zoe will be the one filming on the side of the road; Azul will drive, since she's the insured one; Scarlet will be in the Jeep supervising; and Lila will be there just because she refuses to be left behind.

It's agreed that if the weather is good, they'll do it tomorrow.

That night, Colin climbs into Zoe's hammock with her. He thanks her for getting the sisters on board. He tells her that he got her a present in Cancún, the first time he went, and says even though it was supposed to be for her birthday, he thinks he should give it to her now. Zoe's heart is beating unreasonably quickly, but she can't pinpoint the emotion. It should be excitement—and happiness and relief that he seems to have forgiven her for reading the letter. Is that what it is? Excitement? Why does it feel more like fear?

Wait for my birthday, she says.

That's three weeks away. She tells herself that Colin will have finished his videos and everything will be back to how it used to be by then. Eighteen will be her best birthday ever.

Chapter Thirty-Five

You have to change it," I say, hearing my own panic. "You have to do another drawing, one that shows the right ending." My phone is pressed against my ear. I'm pacing back and forth in the studio, the drawing spread out on the worktable.

"That is the right ending," my mother says.

"No, you don't understand. One of the girls can't be the Wolf." What I really want to say is: *I wouldn't do that. I wouldn't have tricked them like that. I love them.*

And I *can't* paint that.

"Indigo, that's the story. That's how it ends. It's the truth."

"There is no truth!" I snap, making no attempt to hold back my emotion. "This is made up. It can be anything you want. You always told me it wasn't *about* anything anyway."

"Fine. This is what I want. I need to go now, okay?"

"But it's not what other people want! You know, people who are excited for the show." I think of them, those women at Annika's— *Get the Wolf! Get the Wolf!* The press release the gallery sent out, all about the feminist themes, the sisterhood.

"I never promised anyone a happy ending."

"It doesn't make any sense, Mommy. The whole story is the girls coming together and winning. Not about one of them betraying the others. They've been gaining an army to fight the monsters and kill the Wolf!"

It's all true—we do need a different ending for the show, to give people what they want. Obviously, though, that isn't the real problem. I can't tell her the real problem—that I can't paint this ending. I can't risk painting myself hanging. I mean, Jesus, what if my neck broke! Or I stopped breathing?! And I won't do that to the sisters, either. I can't have them thinking I've been working against them this whole time. It makes me feel sick just thinking about it.

"I'm too tired to keep talking about this, Indigo. Sometimes the wolf is among you."

No, it's not! I want to scream. I know because I'm living it, and there's no way I'm letting it be a story of betrayal. It's my story, too.

Somehow, I hold it together and don't say any of that.

After we hang up, I go into the other room and press my face into the musty couch pillow and scream. I scream and scream, anger and frustration about everything in the world coming out of me all at once. I scream and scream and scream and scream and scream.

The only solution is for me to draw a new one myself.

First I write out a series of possible scenes so I'll know what to draw, which is hard enough. I've never made up a story like this. Still, at least I know what sort of thing is supposed to happen. They're supposed to kill the Wolf and then get out, so we see them happy in the real world. Or . . . that sounds difficult, showing the real world, integrated with the scenes in Wolfwood. Maybe I'll just show that they find the way out? Even that is hard to picture, though. It can't just be a door with a big sign that says EXIT. My imagination doesn't work this way. Ask me to turn a plain T-shirt and track shorts into a red-carpet dress, sure. Not this.

After thinking and sketching and getting more and more frustrated, I realize that maybe I should use most of what happens in my mother's original drawing and only change the last quarter, where the sisters find out that Zoe betrayed them. That way I'll be able to fill a big chunk of the paper with stuff I can copy, and at the end, instead of hanging me, they'll hang the Wolf. Resolved, I lay out a fresh sheet of watercolor paper and go through the hours-long process of copying most of what's in my mother's sketch. When I get to the part where I have to create new scenes from my imagination, my hand feels like it's forgotten how to draw. The girls are stiff and out of proportion, the gallows ends up too big and doesn't fit on the paper, the monsters look like houseplants. I erase and start that section over but don't get it right the second time, either. Or the third. Eventually, there are so many layers of graphite and erasing and graphite and erasing it's all a grubby gray color that I won't be able to paint on.

Over the next couple of days I barely sleep. A frenetic energy courses through me, keeping me going hour after hour, at work and at the studio. I ruin multiple sheets of paper, drawing and erasing and drawing and erasing until the surface isn't salvageable. At some point, I realize I can't waste any more time and need to start painting. As is, I'm going to have to miss shifts at the Fud and cancel babysitting to have any hope of finishing. So I start on a fresh piece of paper, copy the bulk of it, leave the last section blank, and begin painting, praying that by the time I've painted these parts, I'll have had an inspiration about how to finish it.

I really can't envision how any of this ends, in Wolfwood or here in the studio.

Chapter Thirty-Six

Two hours before the Whitney visit, it's become clear: I'm not going to make it.

I wasted so much time trying to draw a new ending that I've finished painting only about two-thirds of the final piece. There's still one scene that's already drawn that I need to paint—one of the vignettes that corresponds to my mother's original sketch—and then there's that blank white area. Blindingly white. I'm scared of messing it up by turning it grubby and gray like the other pieces of paper I've ruined.

I have no idea what I'm going to tell Annika. It's not just the fact that the painting isn't ready to be taken to the framer now. The problem is way bigger than that. The problem is that there's a good chance I won't *ever* be able to finish this piece. I've spent hours and hours trying, and it's clear that I'm not good enough to draw a new ending myself. So . . . where does that leave me? All my hard work can't be screwed up because of this. It can't. But what possible reason can I give that the eighth and final painting isn't going to be in the show?

The excuse I concoct will have to be simple enough that I can get my mother to go along with the lie, since she and Annika will both be here today. Last night, I was sick to my stomach, knowing I needed to remind her about the visit. She's barely moved in weeks: Was I really expecting her to come out here and talk to rich collectors? But when I sat on the edge of the couch and rested a hand on her hip and said, "You okay to be at the studio for the Whitney visit tomorrow at noon? I need to spend the night out there painting, so you'll have to come on your own," she just pressed her mouth into a line and nodded.

"You know how important it is, right?" I said, wanting to make sure I was very, very clear. "This is the one thing I *need* you to do for me."

She nodded again and said, in a voice barely stronger than a whisper, "The dress is in the bathroom?"

I'd chosen a simple black sheath for her to wear, something that looks elegant despite being nothing special. I hung it in the bathroom so the steam from the shower would take out the wrinkles.

"Yup," I said. "And I cleaned up your red sandals, too."

When I left, she was asleep. I texted this morning to make sure she was up, but not too early. The less time she's awake, the less time she'll have for second thoughts.

"Ms. Serra?" someone calls out now. "Indigo?"

Kai. He's here already? Shit!

"Hey, Kai! One second!" I call back, reaching down and pulling a sheet of newsprint from below the table to place over the unpainted area. But it's too late, the door to this room is opening and he's standing there, seeing me. I hastily position the newsprint, blocking his view of the unfinished part.

"Oh, hi!" I say. "How'd you get in?" I reach for a couple more pieces to cover the rest of the painting, then turn around and lean against the table, smile tight.

"The gallery has a key. I knocked for a long time but no one answered. What's going on?" he asks, clearly confused.

"Just . . . cleaning up and stuff."

"Where's your mom?" He's walked over to the table. I'm standing in front of the unfinished section of the piece, resting a hand on the newsprint.

"Oh . . . she's on her way. I came out early to make sure everything was ready. We're not hanging the final one in the series today, so I'm just protecting it."

He's not looking at me or at the newsprint-covered painting, though. I follow his gaze to the palette where I was mixing my colors, which is freshly used. Next to it, the glass jar where I wash my brushes—the water inside swirled with pigment. Neither of us says anything, but my mouth has gone dry. I wonder if he can smell the sick perfume of Wolfwood that's still lingering in the air: the iron tang of blood and the sweet rot of flowers.

"I thought we'd set up the food and wine in the other room," I say. "If you want to start arranging it, I just need to change." I indicate my red-and-pink dress, slung over the door. "I'll come out and help in a sec. When we're done in there, we can hang the pieces in here." My voice is overly cheery.

"Okay, sure," he says. After he's gone, I take the dress down and close the door, leaning against it for a moment to gather myself. Then I calmly take off my button-down and sweats and put on the dress, with my usual leggings and a thin cardigan to hide my injuries. I also empty the water jar and put the wet palette on the shelf under the table.

With what I hope is a convincing smile on my face, I join Kai in the other room, where he's clearing off the desk.

"Thought we could set stuff out on this," he says, not meeting my eyes, "but I didn't know what to do with all the papers, so I just . . ." He indicates a pile on the floor.

"No worries. I'll deal with that."

My breath is uncomfortably shallow as we straighten up the room to prepare for the food and wine delivery. I'm not sure what I'm most anxious about: Kai seeing whatever he saw in the studio, the painting not being done, the Whitney people coming, my mother having to talk to them . . . I texted her to check that she's on her way and she didn't respond, which didn't surprise me but also didn't do anything to relieve my worries. Kai and I bustle around in silence occasionally interspersed with stilted small talk. The most personal we get is when I apologize for never finding a time to get together. I explain that I've been really busy. He just replies, "Yeah, no big deal."

Annika arrives shortly, a large bouquet of peonies in her hand, hair freshly styled, and face impeccably made up. Her smile disappears when I tell her Zoe isn't here yet.

"She'll be here by noon," I say. "She's . . . stuck on the subway."

"The subway?!" Annika says, incredulous. "The most important studio visit of her career and she took the *subway*? For god's sake, why didn't she just take a car?" She stares at me as if expecting an answer, but then just says, "Never mind. As long as she gets here."

With that, she sets down her purse and flowers and snaps into drill sergeant mode, watching as Kai and I hang the paintings, barking orders: "Higher on your side, Kai. No, stop! Too high." "A little to the left. No, too close to the other. Back right." Thank god, she agrees about not hanging the last one and doesn't ask to see it, too focused on making everything look good. The food and wine arrive; she micromanages the setup of those, too, down to how we arrange the paper cocktail napkins.

Throughout all of this, every beat of my heart is a prayer that my mother truly is on her way. I call her once, twice, three times. At 11:55, I get the text.

Mom: I'm so sorry. I can't

Did I really think she would come? I don't know. I guess I did. Because the feeling when I get her text is the shocked whoosh of blood draining to my feet, leaving me light-headed. Annika can see it on my face. "What?" she asks me.

"Um . . . she's not going to make it," I say quietly. The group from the Whitney is clanging up the stairs as we speak—the studio door is open to the hallway and their steps reverberate like a countdown.

"Not going to make it?" Annika echoes. Her mouth hangs slightly open in shock.

"Hello, hello!" Malcolm's voice rings out from down the hall.

"In here!" Annika calls to him. "Last door on the left!"

"I can talk to them," I say quickly. "I know all about her process and everything."

"Don't be ridiculous," she snaps, eyes flashing. "No one wants to hear from a teenage daughter."

And now the room is full of Lilly Pulitzer and Tory Burch dresses and collared shirts tucked into pressed khakis, diamond rings and pearl studs, everyone a lot preppier and less artsy than I expected. Kai and I offer them wine, pour and hand out cups, smiling, and I hope that no one notices I'm shaking, an aftereffect of Annika's restrained yet obvious fury. She's conferring with Malcolm and Paige in the corner; I can't hear what she's saying. Soon, everyone except me and Kai has filed into the room with the paintings.

I catch Kai giving me a funny look. "What?" I ask.

He shakes his head. "Nothing. You just seem . . . weird."

I shrug, mumble something about not sleeping well, and move over to the doorway between the rooms, pretending to be interested in what's going on in there.

As Annika and the Whitney curators talk to the group about *Wolfwood*, my mind spins, once again trying to come up with a way to explain to Annika that there won't be an eighth painting. Time is running out: I have to tell her before Kai takes the paintings to the framer at the end of the visit. But by the time they finish the presentation, I still haven't come up with anything. Now, collectors are drifting out to get more snacks and wine, looking at the paintings on their own, chatting with each other ... Annika is in sales mode, going from person to person and animatedly discussing the work in ways that I can tell are designed to subtly lead them to buy one. I wander into the studio room to pick up abandoned napkins and empty cups. I hear the screams from Wolfwood, smell the gore ...

I bite my cheeks as my eyes stray to the sheets of newsprint spread across the worktable.

Everyone is milling around the crowded room. People bump against the table as they walk past each other. No one realizes the unfinished last painting is there, barely covered by those thin top sheets. Vulnerable. And it occurs to me: There isn't going to be a last painting, which will be impossible to explain to Annika. But if there's *another* reason the painting can't go to the framer, a reason that *is* explainable, well, she'll just have to do the show without it. Right? I don't have much time to decide whether this is a good plan, and it could definitely screw things up even more, but I have no other ideas, so I just have to do it and pray it makes things better, not worse.

I go back into the other room. Kai is preoccupied showing some woman which of the hors d'oeuvres are vegetarian.

When I'm sure no one's looking, I pour myself a plastic cup of red wine, then walk back into the studio room, wine held at hip level, out of sight. Can I really do this without it being obvious? Everyone is chatting in twosomes or looking closely at the work.

I place the cup on the table and separate the sheets of newsprint a bit so a sliver of the painting is revealed. While looking in another direction, I tip over the cup, then quickly walk away, leaving the cup on its side, not even glancing at the result.

No one notices at first. I spiritedly engage in conversation with a woman and man who are studying one of the pieces. Then:

"Oh!" The gasp is loud. "Oh, oh no, is this . . . ?"

We all turn and look. The dark red has spread across one side of the newsprint. The woman who noticed has lifted a corner and you can see the painting underneath, also wet.

I rush over. "Crap," I say, feigning alarm. I grab paper towels and start mopping it up. "I should have told my mother to move the painting. We didn't want people to see the last one."

Annika is at my side.

"Oh dear, oh . . ." She looks at Malcolm and Paige, who both appear frozen with dismay, and says, "Please, don't worry," then turns to me, desperation in her eyes. I can tell she doesn't want them upset, doesn't want them to feel responsible.

"It can be fixed," I say, still blotting.

"Are you sure?" the woman who noticed the spill asks. She's standing close, hands clutched.

"Yes," Annika says, "Zoe is a master. Please, everyone . . . no worries about this. Please keep chatting. Everything is fine."

Despite Annika's attempts to revive the gathering, the group files out not long after the "accident," everyone looking subdued and slightly guilty, probably all wondering if they're the one who knocked into the table and spilled the wine.

Annika assures Malcolm and Paige over and over that this isn't a big deal, not to worry. She says she'll meet them at the restaurant where they're all having lunch.

The moment it's just me, Annika, and Kai, she says, "Well, fuck. This is a disaster." She lifts a paper towel, revealing the ruined painting. I'm standing between her and the unpainted section, so all she can see is the stain on the painted part.

"I guess we'll just have to end the show with the one before this," I say.

"What are you talking about?" She turns to me, confused.

"Well, the works are going to the framer. This one can't be fixed. So . . . I guess it's too late." *Gee, too bad!*

She shakes her head. "Not an option. We'll bring the frame for this one to the gallery and Su-Jin can put it in there last minute. So there's time. If Zoe can't fix it, she'll do it over."

"But . . . I thought today was the deadline?" I say, moistening my dry lips.

"Yes, but this is an extraordinary situation. And it's only one piece."

"That's . . . that's kind of a lot to ask of Zoe. To fix it or redo it or whatever. She didn't ruin it. Maybe the story ends with the girls about to find the Wolf, staying safe in the shelter they built. Who says it doesn't?"

"I say it doesn't," Annika snaps.

"It's my fault it was on the table. Not Zoe's."

Annika starts typing on her phone, dismissing me. "She can have the time to fix it, obviously. But anything else is a ridiculous suggestion. She's already disrespected me beyond measure by not showing up today. I don't even want to talk to her about it. Just get it to us."

"But I don't know if she'll be able—"

"Are you kidding me right now?" Annika stares at me. "Forgive me, Indigo, but you are not your mother, last time I checked. And you have absolutely zero to do with what is happening here. I am truly sorry about the accident. But she *will* fix it, and she *will* deliver it, and then the show *will* open with all eight of the paintings, like we agreed. I'm not doing the show without it. Do you know how lucky she is that I'm even taking this chance on her comeback? Do you?" There's almost literal fire coming out of her eyes, the icy blue gone hot with fury.

"Yes," I say, swallowing. "I do."

1989

The sky is the purple of a ripe plum the morning they film Colin's final video. They all stayed up on the beach like usual, drinking, listening to Azul play guitar, Lila skinny-dipping in the dark, dragging Zoe into the water with her.

Now, as dawn approaches, Colin squats in the middle of the road, camera raised. He's explained the plan more fully: He'll be filming from this spot as the sisters drive toward him from the distance, and when the Jeep comes close, he'll dodge out of the way. It will be spliced with footage that Zoe will have filmed from the side, to make it look like the Jeep almost hits him, when in reality he'll have moved sooner than that. He's set up a flashlight next to him so the girls will see him and know when he's moved. They'll just keep driving straight, same speed, until they're out of view.

No one seems worried, but Zoe's heart is racing, like it was the night before. She drank more than usual to try to calm herself down—it didn't work.

The girls drive away, their taillights shrinking smaller and smaller. As they disappear, Zoe has an urge to call after them, to tell them not to do this. It's too late for that, though. She needs to stop worrying. Everything will be fine. She turns to Colin, who explains they'll start filming before the Jeep reappears, to capture the first pinprick of the headlights. He tells her to keep her eyes and camera on the Jeep the entire time so the shot follows it as smoothly as possible. He calls her a pro, says she knows what to do.

The last thing he says is: Okay, start filming.

Chapter Thirty-Seven

T hat went well," I deadpan as soon as the door closes behind Annika.

Kai doesn't smile. He goes straight to the worktable and lifts the paper towels and newsprint, exposing the entire painting, unfinished section included.

He turns to me. "What's going on?"

I don't know what to say. I stand there, staring at him, mouth open.

"When I showed up," he says, "were you . . . were you trying to finish her painting for her or something?" His brow's tightly furrowed, like he's saying it but can't believe it might be true.

I still don't answer.

"Or is it even worse than that?" he says. "Ravi is convinced . . . I mean, he doesn't know what, but he's convinced there's something you're not telling us. He talked to me after he ran into you." Kai crosses his arms. "He's not even sure you live in that building."

"What?!" I say. "Of course I do! And I'm not using, if that's what he told you. Seriously. You have to believe me."

He hesitates. "Is it something with your mom? Is she not okay or something?" Despite his obvious suspicion, there is such concern in his voice. Such warmth. Like he's wrapping his arms around me.

I don't know what to do.

I don't want to betray my mother, to share truths she wouldn't want shared. But I'm so tired. I'm so tired of lies. They've become as much a part of me as my skeleton, and they're heavy as lead.

I sink down on the floor, rest my back against the wall. Kai sits next to me, quiet. Waiting. Maybe if I was thinking at full capacity, I could come up with a story, an excuse. But not now. Whatever happens, happens. Finally, I start.

"I didn't know until June that she was having trouble with the paintings." I go from there, sharing the basic details about our money problems, our tenuous living situation, my mother's emotional struggles. My desperation to give her back her career. My intentions at the beginning, when I only wanted to start a painting and then get her to take over. The only things I don't tell him are how I do them, how deeply I enter Wolfwood, and why I can't finish the last one. I just say I ran out of time.

At the end we sit in silence.

Kai clears his throat. "So . . . you've done *all* the paintings? Your mother didn't do *any* of them?"

"Lots of artists have assistants who help with their work."

He raises his eyebrows. "Why would you have lied about it if you didn't think it was wrong?"

I don't answer that. "Please don't tell your mother," I beg. "Please. I know it's a lot to ask. But please."

"The other night, with Ravi—all your bruises and scratches. If you're asking me to lie for you, I need to know everything. I'm not kidding, Indigo." His tone has hardened into one I haven't heard from him before.

Again, I scramble for a plausible excuse. And again, I decide I have to at least give some of the truth. After a moment, I explain how involved I get when I paint, how deeply I enter my imagination. That I sort of pretend I'm really in Wolfwood. As I talk, I play it off like it's nothing important.

"You realize how strange that sounds," Kai says. "Like . . . not okay strange."

"I know. But I'm sure it's something that happens to other artists. Just part of the process."

His brow is deeply furrowed again. "So . . . is it . . . is it kind of self-harm?"

"No!" I shake my head firmly. "Not like that. It's not like I do it on purpose. I don't *want* to hurt myself."

"But you do it to yourself."

"No, it happens there," I say, and he blinks. "I mean, yeah, I do it myself, but not on purpose. More like it happens to me, when I'm attacked by a monster or something. I do it, but not. I mean, not that I'm really *there*." My explanation gets all jumbled as I talk. I'm so tired and confused about what he can know and what he can't. And I don't even know myself how the injuries happen, so how can I explain it to him?

He rubs a hand across his forehead. "None of this sounds right. You're scaring me, to be honest."

I stand up, my back to him. Cross my arms and stare at the wall, eyes burning. "I knew you wouldn't understand. You have no sense of what it's like to work, no idea what it's like to hold down jobs and try to save your mother and save your friends and pay the rent and have it all piled on top of you. You have no idea what real life is like!" Even as I say it all, I know it's not true. Sure, he doesn't know what pressure I'm under. But he knows some things. His life is real, too.

"That has nothing to do with this," he says. "I just think you sound like you're working too hard and are too stressed out and it's messing with you. That you need to sleep and eat. What you're saying about getting hurt . . . it's not healthy. And what 'friends' are you trying to save?"

Shit. Did I say that? I must have meant the sisters.

"Not important," I say. I turn to face him. He's standing now, too. His jaw is stony. His eyes have lost their usual brightness. "I'm so sorry I lied, Kai."

"Yeah, it really fucking sucks," he says. "And, you know, I can't believe you think this is your responsibility, that you're willing to do something so extreme for your mother, not even worrying about what it's doing to you."

"I'm not just doing this for her. It's for me. Once it's over, and she's painting again, I can go back to . . . I don't know, I can have my own life. That's all I want. I just want her to be okay and for us to have some money, so I can have a life. I haven't had one for so, so long, Kai." I swallow, throat tight. "There are things you don't know, about what we've been through. Really hard things. And I promise

I'll tell you at some point. But right now, I just need you to know how important it was for this to happen."

I'm not quite ready to tell him all about being homeless and what really happened to my face. I've never said those things out loud to anyone. "It's not like I could have just . . . let this opportunity slip away. I was drowning even before this. This was the lifeline."

He's quiet for a moment. "Doesn't your mother care that it's beating you up to do them? What's wrong with her that she'd let you get hurt?"

"Nothing is wrong with her," I snap. "She doesn't know . . . I mean, I haven't exactly told her. She'd be worried."

"Well, yeah!" He starts pacing. "Wouldn't she want to know? So she can help?"

"She'd just feel bad. She has a lot of self-hatred. It doesn't make her productive. It shuts her down."

"So you're protecting her by hurting yourself."

I don't respond.

"Parents should be parents," he says. "They should protect their kids."

"Like your parents protected Hiro?" The minute I've said it I know I shouldn't have, but I can't stand him being judgmental about my mother. Of course, I'm angry at her myself. Angry she let me do this. Angry that I always have to put her life first. Angry that I'm responsible for keeping us afloat. Loving her and worrying about her don't mean I'm not also angry at her.

But it's one thing for *me* to be angry, and another thing for someone else.

"That's totally different," Kai says. His back is to me as he starts taking a painting off the wall, so I can't see his expression. "And if you're gonna go there, what about my mother? She's relying on this show. What if . . . I don't know, what if someone found out? And she got in trouble?"

"No one will find out if we don't tell them," I say. "And I'm doing this so there *will* be a show. Why are we even talking about this? It's just one more painting."

"Honestly?" he says. "I'm worried about you doing it any longer. Even finishing this one. Or redoing it. It seems like you're on the edge here. I don't like it. And I don't like . . . I don't like being responsible for this secret."

"I don't like it, either," I say. We're both moving paintings from the wall to a pile on the floor now, but he keeps avoiding my eyes. "I'm so close, though, Kai. And if the show is a success . . . it will change our lives in a way nothing else could. Please," I repeat, "please let me have this, Kai. You don't understand. I need to save her. I need to do this." I hesitate. "I know that it's terrible for me to ask you to keep this from your mother. I know that. But . . . it's my entire life, really. Everything is on the line."

He meets my gaze now. "So what's going on with the last one? You got all the way here. Why isn't it finished? I don't believe that you ran out of time."

I'm the one to glance away this time. I shake my head. "I can't do it. It's too hard to explain why."

"Try. Try to explain."

I inhale slowly. "Just . . . it's not the ending I want to happen, and my mother won't change it."

"What's wrong with it?"

"You've heard everyone. They think this is some big victory story. It's not. And it's . . . brutal."

"Brutal like you could get badly hurt?"

I nod. "I mean, I'm sure I'd be fine. I'm just being a wimp." *Or maybe I wouldn't be fine . . .*

He hesitates, too much behind his eyes for me to read. "I'm not sure what to say. I don't think you should do it, but I don't think you should have done any of them, so . . ."

"Are you going to tell Annika?"

"I don't know. I don't want to know this!"

I bite my lip. He stares at the floor, rubbing the back of his head.

"Look," I say. "I don't want you to think . . . I don't want you to think I don't realize how weird this all is. And how wrong. I do. And these injuries? They scare me. I wouldn't be doing it if I saw any other solution or thought there was any chance my mother would just finish this last one or change it. I've asked her. She won't."

He meets my eyes again. "It must be scary. The whole thing, I mean. Everything with your mom."

I don't want to listen to his sympathy right now, because it's making my throat swell and what I need is to keep my shit together.

"Yeah. But I'm not easy to scare," I say, lightening my tone. "You know that."

"Right." His expression closes off and he gestures at the paintings. "Anyway, I gotta pack up and go."

"Wait," I say. And before I know what's going to come out of my mouth, I ask, "What about, you know . . . us?"

His brow lifts. "Us?"

"Can we keep being . . . whatever we are? Friends?" I shift on my feet.

"I don't know, Indigo. What are we even? I haven't seen you. You've been lying to me in almost every breath. Don't mistake my . . . sympathy, or whatever, as meaning that I'm not pissed."

What was I thinking even bringing it up? I don't need to be dealing with this right now. "Okay. Well . . . If you can't keep all this from your mom, I understand. But could you just sleep on it? I'm going to stay here, keep working, in case. And we can talk tomorrow?"

"So you're going to do that last one? Even with the injuries?"

"I have to," I say, not clear what part of this he doesn't understand. "I have no choice."

1989

Zoe presses the record button. Moments later, the Jeep's headlights appear in the distance. At first, it looks like they're driving slowly, but as the lights get closer they seem to go faster. Zoe tenses, wishing they would slow down. Still, she tries to do what Colin said. She tries to keep her eyes and camera on the Jeep. When it's close enough for Zoe to make out a figure—Lila—leaning out the open side, a sudden clatter makes Zoe turn her head toward Colin.

She doesn't understand what she's seeing. The flashlight is rolling toward the side of the road, away from Colin, as if it's been tossed, and Colin is lying down, not squatting. Zoe looks back to the Jeep, can't tell whether the girls see him. The Jeep isn't slowing down. Zoe doesn't know what's happening. Do they see him? Does he have time to move? Why is he lying down? Why hasn't he moved yet?

It all happens so quickly. Zoe can't judge anything and can't make any rational decisions, all she can do is what she does, which is shout loudly, jump into the road, and wave her arms wildly for the girls to stop.

Chapter Thirty-Eight

O nce Kai is gone, I look closely at the damage for the first time. The wine mostly stained an area of darker, more opaque colors, which I think can be fixed by lifting up and redoing some of the paint, and also by making it so there isn't such a clear border around the stain. I might be able to salvage it. God knows I don't want to paint the whole thing over. I stare at what's left to finish: the white section with a partial drawing and then that total blankness.

Maybe I've missed the obvious. I never struggle with the painting when I'm actually inside Wolfwood, since I'm not even aware of doing it. Maybe I need to change the ending from within there, instead of trying to draw a new version when I'm out here, in the real world. Just start painting, and when I get to the spot with nothing, where the drawing cuts off . . . see what happens. Do what I want to do while I'm in Wolfwood and hope that I'm able to paint it without any outlines drawn on the paper. Even if I make a mess of the painting, I'll be no worse off.

But what if I can't change the original version and I end up getting hanged?

I could take precautions against getting hurt. Wear something to protect myself. It's hard to know if that would make a difference, though, when I don't even understand how the real-world injuries happen.

Despite the danger, I think this plan is my best choice. Drawing a new ending hasn't worked.

Having a course of action makes me feel better.

After making the decision, I pour myself a small cup of the leftover wine and sit on the couch. Even though I don't want to, I can't help thinking about Kai and how upset he was and how much it hurts that he might not want to be friends anymore. I close my eyes and try to forget about everything for a moment, just breathe in the humid air of the jungle around me. I take a sip of the wine. Ugh, dusty and sour. I put it aside. Take one final, deep breath and force myself to get up and deal.

Before anything else, I need to repair what's reparable in the painting. Technical work like this means I don't get lost in Wolfwood, so as I do it, I keep getting distracted by the ping of texts coming in. Kai, Kai, Kai. I read the first: Look Im trying to get less upset but its not working. I don't read any of them after that. I put my phone on silent. Fixing the piece is tricky, gently lifting up some areas of paint by rewetting and blotting, adding layers of paint to blend over the edges of the stain, making some areas more opaque. It's a delicate process that takes a couple of hours. Finally, though, I think it's good enough that I can move on.

I steel myself and consider the rest of the paper. That blank space, waiting to be filled.

There's a big drugstore not too far from here. Maybe I could get some sort of neck brace, in case I do get hanged. Except . . . I don't have the money and I'm not going to risk getting caught shoplifting. Anyway, I'm not going to let them hang me. I'm going to do things differently.

Despite that resolve, I check around both rooms to make sure there's nothing that could be used as a makeshift noose. The only fabric is my extra clothing. I change out of my cardigan, dress, and leggings and leave them in the hallway, put on the shirt and sweats I was painting in before. Now there's really nothing I could use—no fabric or rope of any kind. (*Not like there are knives in here, either, Indigo, and you still get cut.*)

A shudder goes through me. This isn't worth risking my life.

I play out the alternate scenario. Would Annika really cancel the show with no final painting? I think she might, given her anger and her insistence that showing it without an ending would be ridiculous. The whole press release was about how long people have waited to find out what happens. As if it's the final *Game of Thrones* or Harry Potter or something.

Without this money, it's very clear what's going to happen to us. We won't be able to afford our rent, not with the increase. There's no way. Not if I go back to school in a couple of weeks. Not with all the time I've taken away from Trinity. Not with the $18,000 we'll owe the gallery for using the studio. If Annika is angry enough, she might demand that money back immediately. She could sue us. And win.

My phone is lighting up again. Kai. I turn it off entirely.

And then I go to Wolfwood.

Chapter Thirty-Nine

Lila and I are in the shelter alone when Scarlet yells for us to come outside. I don't want to go out there. I know what she's going to show us, and I have no idea how I'm going to explain it. Hiding in here won't change anything, though: I'll have to face Scarlet eventually.

I follow Lila out the narrow doorway, my legs weak.

Scarlet and Azul are standing next to each other. The clearing is still crowded with the army of Others. Scarlet's hands are extended. She's holding the skull.

"Whose is it?" Scarlet asks me. "The Others found it. Buried."

His blue eyes flash then blink away.

"How should I know?" I meet Scarlet's eyes to avoid looking at the dark holes in the skull where his just were. The Others must have seen me bury it. That doesn't explain why they would have dug it up and given it to Scarlet, though. Despite all I know about this place, the motives for what the Others do remain a mystery to me.

"It's his, isn't it?" Scarlet says. "Whoever he is—*was*—he's already dead. You know he is."

She's right, but I don't say anything.

"I don't understand," Lila says.

Scarlet turns to her. "It's his skull. He's not even here, really."

"The Wolf?" Lila says, and Scarlet nods.

I lick my lips, my mouth dry.

"But . . . if the Wolf is already dead, why are we still here?" Lila asks. "Why does Wolfwood still exist?"

Scarlet pins me with her gaze. "He's not the real Wolf."

"What are you talking about?" I say, swallowing.

She looks disgusted. "I remembered more about the bracelet."

"The one you imagined? From home?"

"No, the one I *found*," she says, spitting the word. "I remember the inscription. It said *For Z, my wolf.*" She pauses. "You're Z, aren't you?"

Suddenly, I can't breathe. Everything is spinning and blurring, truth and lies spinning and blurring in my head. *For Z, my wolf.* The air, thick as cotton in my lungs.

"You're the Wolf, Zoe," Scarlet says. "Admit it. You're the one who trapped us here, and you're the one who needs to die."

"What?!" Lila exclaims. "No, she's not! Take it back, Scarlet!"

"Lila," Azul says somberly. "Scarlet's right."

Lila looks at me, confusion and uncertainty plain on her face.

But no, I'm not the Wolf! I can't be. All I want is to save them. All I want is to keep them here, safe. Together. I love them. Look at all the pain I've endured to protect them.

I can't say it, though. Words don't come. The Others are closing in around us. "Tell them you're not!" Lila begs me. But I can't. There's only one thing I can do.

In a sudden burst, I take off, squirreling my way through the surprised Others, running across the grass into the jungle, brushing past bushes and flowers and trees that normally would attack us. The monsters let me go, just the snap of branches as I run through them. Behind me, I hear screams. The Others are coming, but the monsters aren't letting them get through. They're attacking with glee. Still, some of the Others make it past, and more are joining, and the rhythm of their feet on the ground is picking up pace. Occasionally I look back, see a bloody, bandaged girl with fury in her eyes close on my heels. I turn forward quick, speeding on. Heartbeat a thundering drum. Screams all around, filling the air.

From nowhere, an Other—no, more than one—bursts out in front of me. I stop, glance over my shoulder. More coming. I run left, scrabbling under low branches. Trip, landing on my face. A branch pulls me to my feet. I run.

"Wolf!" The cry comes from behind.

The Others have found their voices.

They're too close. And I've run where there aren't monsters to protect me.

"Wolf!"

I turn, blade out. They're upon me. I stab Scarlet in the heart. Slash Azul's hand off. Decapitate Lila, her lovely head dropping on the ground. *It's not really them. It's not really them.*

I keep running.

The cries behind me grow. Ahead, there's an area of yellow flowers with jaws. I push hard, fast as I can. Once surrounded by the flowers, I stop. The army of Others descends. It's a battle. Me and my blade, the flowers and their teeth, the Others and the scrappy weapons they've amassed. A tornado of blood and screams and flying flesh and arms and legs and torn flower parts. No air. Just mayhem. Pain. We should win. The monsters and I should win. But then, as I raise my hands to strike, my blade is wrenched from my grip. My arms are yanked down and behind. They've got me. The Others have me tied up, disarmed and helpless.

The carry me on their shoulders, back to the clearing.

A sea of Others surrounds the shelter. They part to form a path and let us through. In front of our little home, the sisters have finished building the gallows. The Others set me on my feet next to it.

"You're going to die," Scarlet says to me. One of the Others hands her my blade. "But before it happens, I want you to confess. For Lila."

"I'll never believe it," Lila says, shaking her head. "She wouldn't have done it."

"She did," Azul says gently. "And now she has to confess."

I won't do it. I have to make them understand there's something wrong here. I wouldn't have done this to them—trapped them here like this. Wolfwood doesn't belong to me. It can't.

The Others gather around us in a crowd so thick it's a new organism, not separate bodies. One huge, bloody mass of fury. Circled around us, staring at me. Waiting. Inching in closer. Slowly, like they don't want me to notice. Shrinking the space around me.

"Confess," Scarlet says.

Wolf. Wolf. Wolf. Wolf . . . A low chant from the Others.

I won't confess. But I can't deny it. My mouth doesn't work. I'm frozen.

All I'm allowed to do is confess. Then I have to die. I see it happening. I see my body hanging from the gallows, and I know that's the only way this is allowed to end. Now that they've figured it out, there's no going back. There's no life for me with them. I know that. But I keep fighting against it, trying to talk, trying to say anything other than *Yes, I am the Wolf*. There has to be another way, a way for us all to be safe and happy. Another explanation. It doesn't make sense. I need to prove that they're wrong, that I wouldn't have betrayed them.

But nothing else is in my brain, no option for anything else I could possibly do. The only choice is to confess and let them execute me. That's justice. It's the inevitable end.

Still, I fight it.

"Confess!" Scarlet says again.

Wolf. Wolf. Wolf. Wolf.

All of a sudden, the entire landscape, the Others, everything I see, shimmers like a reflection in water, and—

A flash of light blinds me.

I blink and blink. Shapes and colors re-form. But I don't understand what I'm seeing. I'm seeing myself with the sisters.

I look down. See nothing. No body, that is. No *me*. I'm not here. I'm invisible.

And Zoe and the sisters are standing in front of me.

Zoe, my mother.

Scarlet steps closer to her. "Confess!" she barks again, not seeming to have noticed what just happened.

"Yes," my mother says. "I am the Wolf."

"No!" I scream, but my voice is air. No one hears me.

"You trapped us?" Azul says, moving closer now, too. "This is all your creation."

"Yes."

"And the way out is for us to kill you," Scarlet says. "Is that right?"

"Yes," my mother says. "Kill the Wolf."

Scarlet turns to Lila. "Do you see?"

Lila doesn't answer. She's crying too hard.

Scarlet tears off a strip of my mother's white dress and wraps it around my mother's eyes. A blindfold.

Azul guides her to the gallows, has her climb up the ladder. I'm screaming, but, still, no one hears. Scarlet hands my mother's blade to Lila and climbs up to the platform, behind my mother and Azul. Lila stays below, sobbing. Scarlet ties the noose made of vine around my mother's neck. Azul leads her to the edge of the platform.

"Please don't hurt her!" I beg. "Don't hurt my mother!"

I have to save her. I *have* to.

But I can't. I'm powerless here.

"We're not going to push you," Scarlet says. "We want you to step off yourself."

"One step is all it will take," Azul says. She's crying now, too. "You're right at the edge."

My mother nods, and the sisters climb back down. Even Scarlet looks upset.

"Please!" I scream soundlessly. "Don't do it, Mommy!"

She turns her head toward me, as if she's finally heard. But then she shifts forward—

"Wait!" Lila shouts. "Wait!" She moves closer to the gallows, all her attention on my mother. "I don't understand why you did this, Zoe," she says. "But I forgive you. I love you, and I forgive you."

"Lila!" Scarlet grabs her arm. "What the hell are you doing?"

Lila shakes off Scarlet's grip and turns to her sisters. "She's letting us go home. Taking her own life so we can live. Before we go, I want her to know."

"But . . ." Scarlet seems flustered.

"I love her," Lila says. "And she loves us. No matter what she did."

The sisters look between each other for a long time, having one of their wordless discussions. My mother stands motionless on the platform, jaw hanging slightly open below the blindfold. I'm watching it all, silently begging her to stay where she is.

Finally, Azul takes Lila's hand and nods, then looks up at the gallows and says, "I want to go home, but I wish we didn't have to leave you, Zoe." Then she tells her that she, too, forgives her.

My mother still doesn't move. Just that hint of confusion and shock on her face.

Scarlet scans the army of Others circled around. All their injuries. The fury on their faces. She presses fists against her forehead and clenches her eyes shut for a moment. Turns around and looks up.

"Like Lila said, I don't understand it," she tells my mother. "And I'm angry. But we've been with you . . ." She wipes her cheek. "We've been with you a long time. I forgive you, Zoe. I do."

My mother's jaw has gone completely slack. She's at a loss for words.

"Isn't there another way?" Lila says, stepping even closer, the blade in her hand, long and sharp. "I don't want you to die."

Yes. Maybe Lila's right. Maybe there is another way, now that they've forgiven her. There must be!

My mother's chest rises with a deep breath.

She finds her voice. But all she says is "I'm sorry."

Lila lunges forward, shouting, "Don't!"

My mother takes a step and plunges down.

1989

Later, waving her arms is the last moment that Zoe remembers as part of a sequence of events. The rest of it is just images. Flashes. Sensory fragments. But she knows what happened. Her shouts spooked the sisters. Azul looked toward her voice and swerved in Zoe's direction, overcorrected, and swerved toward Colin. The shouts startled Colin, too. He sat up but didn't have time to move. The Jeep hit him, ran him over, lost control, ran off the road, flipped and flipped and flipped, then burst into flames.

High-pitched wails. The toxic smell of burned flesh. A pool of blood on the asphalt. Colin's head, Colin's head, Colin's head . . . The broken-doll angles of a body. A scorched leg. The blood. All the blood. Everyone's blood.

Everyone's blood except Zoe's.

Chapter Forty

A *thud* jolts me out.

My breath is heavy, like I've been running or I'm scared. I grip the table. They were chasing me. The Others were chasing me. It's all so real: the chase, and then my mother there, standing on the platform, blindfolded, and the sisters forgiving her, and my mother stepping off the edge. I press a hand against my heart. *I'm not in Wolfwood. I'm safe.* And the painting, spread out in front of me, is finished. I blink, surprised. It has the same ending as the original sketch. The hanging. I shift to look closer. Wait . . . there's something different . . . Yes, Zoe is hanging. But Lila is in motion, holding the machete in the air. Different from the original drawing. Seeing it, I remember more now. I remember the blade streaking toward the noose the moment my mother stepped off. I remember Lila slicing the machete through the vine. Here in the painting, it shows the split second before she got there—Lila lunging forward.

My foot nudges something solid. I look down next to me.

My mother. Lying on the studio floor.

Chapter Forty-One

For a moment, I freeze. Then everything's a blur. I drop down. "Mommy," I say. "Mommy!" She doesn't move. Red marks on her neck. Nothing around it. Paintbrush on the floor, near her hand. What do I do? I don't know, I don't know. I can't think. 911, right? 911. I find my phone, drop it, pick it up, call 911. Questions I can't answer. How? How long? I don't know. I don't know. Breathing? I don't know! Pulse? I can't tell! I need help. I need help. I need help. Please. It's coming, he says. I hang up. He told me to wait, but I can't. What if it's too late? I press on her chest. Once, twice. . . . My own lungs hurt. I press again, breathe into her mouth. Every breath, I pray. Please. Take it, take my breath. Just come back. Come back.

Soon—or not soon, who knows—three strong men, one strong woman, blue uniforms, bright yellow stretcher. More questions I can't answer. I'm shaking. Light-headed. They're telling me I did good. I need to breathe deep. Calm down.

"Could someone else have been in here with her?" the woman asks. "Before you found her?"

I shake my head. "Is she alive? Is she okay?"

"She's alive," one of the men says. "We're taking care of her."

She's alive. Thank god. Thank god. She's alive.

⌒

I'm separated from her at the hospital. They tell me she's stable, not to worry. Not worry? Right. I answer questions about insurance and medical history, trying to focus, trying not to scream at them to shut up and let me be with my mom.

While I sit on the hard chair in the waiting room, I read my texts and listen to my voicemails and piece together why she came out to the studio. Kai was trying to reach me to tell me that he thought I really needed to tell my mother, that I shouldn't keep painting. But I didn't pick up—he called over and over—and his last message said he was sorry, but he was too worried about me and he was going to tell her himself, that she'd want to know. Then messages from my mother, telling me not to do it, that it was her story and her ending and it wasn't safe and it was her responsibility. Telling me to wait, that she was on her way. I barely recognize her voice—so different from the faded one I've gotten used to. This voice is vivid with the colors of fear and determination. So that's how she ended up coming and finishing the painting herself, the real Zoe, while I stood on, helpless.

⌒

Finally, someone brings me to see her. Outside the curtain, a doctor tells me that at first she didn't remember what had happened. Then when asked if she might have choked on something, she told them yes, that was it. He says it explains her slightly swollen throat. The red marks the EMTs noted are gone, he says. She grabbed at her neck, probably, when she was choking. And she hit her head on the floor when she lost consciousness. There was a bit of blood and swelling.

I gently pull aside the curtain and step through. She looks so small and old lying on the bed, hooked up to a couple of machines and tubes in her nose, skin so sallow under the lights. "Indigo," she says, voice scratchy. And it's the first time I really believe: She's alive. She'll be okay. I bend down and hug her, face wet with tears. "It's over," I say. "It's over."

1989

Like the moments after the accident, the following hours and days, and even weeks and months and years, are confused and sporadic in Zoe's memory, with huge gaps. Huge stretches of the deepest darkness.

After help came, she somehow got from the scene to Itzel's family's house, the only place that seemed safe. She stayed with them. They took care of her. Helped with the authorities' questions and with arrangements. At some point, though, Zoe had to go back to Don Eduardo's. Had to pack up everything in the cabana. In Colin's stuff, she found a small bag from Cancún.

Inside it, a box. Inside the box, a silver cuff with a piece of amber, golden like her eyes. Inscribed: For Z, my wolf.

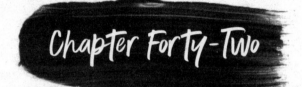

Chapter Forty-Two

The doctors keep her overnight—she has a migraine, and they want to monitor her because of the head injury. I confide to a nurse that I'm also worried about her emotional state, and the nurse has me tell one of the doctors, who says they'll do a mental health evaluation before releasing her. I never find out what they ask her or what she says. Just that she's ready for discharge the next morning, with instructions to follow up with her primary care doctor. Unrelated to the "choking" incident, she was dehydrated and underweight.

We don't talk about Wolfwood at the hospital. We don't even say its name. The afternoon she comes home, we sit together on the couch, and she tells me the story, words and tears streaming out of her after being held back for so many years. She tells me about the loneliness of living with her aunt, the thrill of falling in love with Colin Wolf and running away to Mexico. Her friendship with the sisters, Colin's moodiness, his video project. The accident on June 4, 1989. I try not to show too much shock or horror, because it's so clear she blames herself and I don't want her to feel like I'm judging. Inside, though, I *am* shocked. Not shocked at anything she did or didn't do. Shocked that she was part of such a tragedy and that I knew nothing about it. All those lives, gone. And all these years, I hadn't known about this event that has *everything* to do with her life now. With *my* life now. It's clear she was too ashamed, too sure that the accident was her fault, to talk about it. As if she were confessing to murder. I understand, but I also don't.

"You did what anyone would have done when it seemed like the Jeep might hit him," I say. "What were you supposed to do, just stand there and film while they ran him over?"

"He probably knew what he was doing," she says. "He would have moved in time, if I hadn't distracted him."

"But it looked like he wasn't going to, right?"

She hesitates. "Still, I'm the reason they were all out there. It wouldn't have happened without me. I convinced them. And I could have tried harder to convince Colin it was too dangerous. Instead I just went along with him."

"You were afraid he'd leave you. You'd already lost so much. And you thought you were helping him. Supporting him."

"That night wouldn't have happened without me."

It's clear that there's nothing I can say right now that will wipe away decades of guilt. And no matter how unfounded it sounds to me, I wasn't there. I didn't see all that blood. Who's to say how it would have affected me if I had? Or what I would have done with my grief?

"How did you end up painting Wolfwood?" I ask.

She tells me that after coming back to New York, she was plagued by visions from the accident. When she started sketching, Wolfwood came out of her like it was telling itself—an outlet for all the blood and guilt. A way of confessing and giving the sisters revenge. In this fictional version, my mother tries to keep the sisters in this dangerous place, but they figure it out, and she's the one who's punished. She's the one who dies, not them.

She says she was focused on making the paintings, not on showing them. But she was living in a group loft, and Annika came to look at the work of another artist and immediately offered my mother an exhibition. She hated profiting off her guilt, so she wired a lot of the money she made to Itzel's family, who had helped her after the accident. "I couldn't make up for the trauma I brought to them . . . to Tulum itself," she tells me. "The accident was traumatic for the whole town. But the money was something, at least." She says she would have sent some to the sisters' parents, too, but she left Mexico before the American consulate in Cancún had located them, and once back in New York, how was she supposed to find a couple with the last name Lopez, whose first names she didn't know and who lived off the grid, in a time before the internet? The girls' passports had listed an address in Ohio, but according to directory assistance, there was no one by the name of Lopez in the town anymore.

The money that wasn't sent to Itzel's family, she spent on drugs and alcohol, mostly, to try to block it all out.

"But you were so happy during those years," I say, confused.

"Whoever said I was happy? I was either high, blackout drunk, or in Wolfwood."

"But . . . dancing on that sculpture. In the magazine."

"That was a photoshoot, honey. They told me what to do."

A photoshoot?

"At the clubs . . ." I say. "You danced there."

"Indigo, I was completely wasted, looking for people I could have sex with so I'd feel even worse. Nothing about it was fun."

I have a hard time recalibrating. My entire image of what her life was like during all that success was completely wrong. Although, when did she ever say *anything* about it? We didn't talk about her past at all. I've always somehow known not to ask her questions, the same way I've always known not to tell people certain things about our life.

"And then," she continues, "I got pregnant. And you were my chance to do something right. To *create* a life. So I stopped painting Wolfwood. I couldn't keep going there, getting injured all the time, especially knowing how it ended. And I couldn't . . ." She swallows. "Like I've said, I couldn't have this baby girl at home and then go watch the sisters being tortured."

It must have been so hard, putting aside all that trauma to be there for me. "And you couldn't explain to anyone why you stopped."

She nods. "I tried to go back, for the show. But I was too scared of seeing them—scared I'd start seeing blood all the time, like I used to." She pauses. "I didn't think it could happen to you. I always tied it to the drugs. And just . . . the trauma of it all. *My* trauma. So I didn't think . . ."

"Well, also, I lied to you," I say. "You asked if it upset me. I said no." She doesn't respond to that, just keeps looking into the middle distance.

"Did the same thing happen to you with other paintings?" I ask.

She shakes her head. "Only Wolfwood." The air pulses with the strangeness of it. "My other paintings . . . the series when you were little . . ."

"*Home Safe?*"

"Painting those made me happy. They came out of *love*. And I always thought . . . I thought that's why they didn't sell. That it was karma—I didn't deserve to be happy."

"You know that's not true, don't you?"

When she doesn't answer, I say, "The sisters forgave you. You heard them, right?"

She wipes her nose. "That wasn't supposed to be part of the story."

"Listen to me," I say, taking her hands in mine. "Lila, Scarlet, Azul—I *know* them." I feel the truth of it as I say it. "They wouldn't want you blaming yourself. They wouldn't want you punishing yourself. I promise. I've been with them for weeks. When they forgave you? They meant it. And Lila cut you down! She saved you."

My mother's brow furrows.

"You don't remember that?" I ask. Clearly, she doesn't. "If you look at the painting, it's a bit different from the sketch. Lila's raising your blade. And I remember—I saw it. She cut you down as soon as you . . . were hanging."

"She did? But . . . why?" My mother sounds skeptical. Confused.

"They didn't want you to die."

Her brow is still knit tight, as if she's not sure she believes me.

Now that the discussion has gone here, to that moment my mother stepped off the gallows, noose around her neck, there's something I need to ask. I wish I didn't have to, but I need to know. "Mommy," I say, "why did you step off the platform? Did you *want* to die?"

She hesitates, then shakes her head. "No. I just . . . wanted them to live. And for it to all be over."

My muscles release a bit of tension, but still, she risked her life.

"You need to talk to someone," I say. "Someone who can help you process what happened in Mexico."

"I have you."

"No," I say firmly. "You need someone other than me. Someone professional."

She stares down at our hands, still entwined. "What if they agree it's my fault?"

She's worried a therapist will justify her self-blame? "Mommy, they won't. I promise."

I can't tell if she believes me. After a minute, she says, "You heard them, too? You heard the sisters forgive me?"

I lean over and hug her fiercely. Rub my hand down the back of her hair, like she used to when I was little. I don't understand how Wolfwood works, whether that was all in her imagination, or my imagination, or . . . somewhere else. But it doesn't even matter. Yes, they forgave her.

We sit in silence for a little bit, and my thoughts switch from her past to our future and what happens now.

"We need to tell Annika," I say. I can't ask Kai to keep this secret. Not to mention that I'm sure my mother won't go to the opening or anything like that, and I'm sick of making excuses.

"No," she says immediately, burying her face in her hands. "I can't."

Before today, I'd have offered to do it myself. But even though I'm the one who decided to do the paintings, I can't take full responsibility. Not anymore. "I can't do it for you," I say. "I'll do it with you, though."

She looks up at me now. "How are you so brave? You didn't learn it from me."

My first thought is that she's right. Then I think back to when we were kicked out and she let me go to Grace's while she faced the shelter and streets on her own. And even further back, when she gave up everything to go to Mexico. Her determination to be an artist. Having a baby on her own. Changing her life completely to take care of me. Getting out of bed in the morning, despite living with this much guilt. Finishing the final painting, to save me. Going to Wolfwood, even though she knew what might happen. Confronting her monsters.

I did learn it from her. My mother is the bravest person I know.

Chapter Forty-Three

In the end, though, her bravery and my resolution to make her take responsibility for things only go so far. She can't make herself come to the gallery to talk to Annika. It's not like I can force her, so I go alone. We call her from Annika's office and put her on speakerphone, making her a part of the conversation.

We tell Annika a very simplified version: that the paintings are based on a difficult time she couldn't face and that I did them for her. My mother says she's sorry she didn't talk to Annika much earlier, when she first had trouble painting. I apologize for my part, making sure to own up to the fact that I did it at the beginning without telling my mother, that I lied to her about canceling the show.

Annika is so taken aback that it's hard to judge her emotion—not like at the studio, after the Whitney disaster, when she was so angry at me. She says she needs to think, that she'll let us know. But she also says that Kai should get the final painting from the studio and bring it to the framer, in case the show goes ahead as planned. That's a good sign, at least.

I'm a little bit shaky as Kai walks me out of the gallery, but relieved, too. So relieved.

It's not just the fact that we might still have the chance of making money—that she didn't cancel the show automatically—it's the lightness of not carrying all these secrets alone.

Kai comes with me down the block, out of the view of the gallery's plate glass front. We pause on the sidewalk at the corner, like there's an unspoken agreement we'll talk here before he goes back to the gallery and I walk home. At this moment, I have no idea what our relationship will be when we go our separate directions. I've apologized over text a million times, but he's been clear about how upset he is that I lied to him for so long.

"I'm so sorry, again," I say. "Whatever you decide about . . . you know, being friends, I'll understand."

He gives a wistful smile. "Privacy, I'm cool with. But secrecy and lies, no. So . . . I guess it depends if you think stuff really will be different now."

I nod. "I do. I mean, all I can do is say I'm really, really going to try. And I feel different. I feel . . ." I look up at the hazy blue sky, trying to think of how to put it. "I feel like everything shattered, and now I can put stuff back together the way that I want it to be, not the way that it was. And I can promise I'm done with how it was before. So, if that's enough . . ." I bite my cheeks.

After a moment, he says, "Honestly? I wish we could go back in time, start over. But since we can't . . . Yeah, that's enough."

Happiness blooms in my chest. I can't believe what I'm about to say, but I'm going to say it. "Kai? I need you to see where we live. I need to share that with you. And I need to tell you the truth about . . ." I gesture at my face. When he looks confused, I add, "You know, how it got broken."

"You mean how it got fixed?" he says. "Because, I mean, it's pretty much perfect."

It's so obvious he really means it—he isn't just playing.

We're standing at the edge of the sidewalk, and I step off the curb so I'm on the street, our eyes almost the same level now.

"Is this better?" I ask, face inches from his. After the words are out there, I'm scared that maybe he doesn't want this, that he now thinks I'm too unreliable to be more than friends, too damaged to get closer than that.

But he doesn't miss a beat. "Better for what?"

We both grin. I lean forward to touch his lips with mine. Gentle. Simple. A promise of more later when we're alone. We linger in it, though, the kiss spreading through my body like hot liquid. I smell the spice of his skin and hear a small murmur from his throat. Our hips press into each other. He moves against me. I part my lips. Now I'm the one murmuring.

"Can I come home with you right now?" he whispers.

I laugh. "You can. But it's not that sort of visit. My mom will be there." Saying it out loud, picturing what he's going to see, makes me want to take back the invitation. But I don't let myself. "Still want to?"

He sighs. "Yeah. I want all the sorts of visits."

"Me, too," I say. And I lean forward to kiss him for just one . . . more . . . minute . . .

Things happen and change so quickly, everything that's broken reconfiguring and re-forming. Kai's visit, telling him more about my history . . . it all feels monumental but not in the traumatic way I thought it would. Yes, we live in a shithole. Yes, we used to be homeless. Yes, he's kind of shocked. But the upshot is him saying no one should have to go through that or live in a place like this. He obviously doesn't see it as a reflection of who we are, what we deserve, or how hard we work. (Not to mention that throughout his visit, I somehow manage to be preoccupied by thoughts of kissing him, which I obviously don't do, since my mother is right there, pretending to be asleep.)

I'm still getting used to the unfamiliar sense of having opened up my life when Annika gets in touch—much sooner than I expected. She's going to show the paintings, with amended publicity. She's going to call it a collaboration: story by Zoe Serra, paintings by Indigo Serra. She's going to lower the price but hasn't yet decided by how much. It's an unusual situation and she needs to talk to a couple of people, see what feels right and fair to everyone—to collectors and to us. She says it's not necessary for anyone to know the circumstances of the collaboration, and we can just use the explanation that my mother's illness a few years ago compromised her physical abilities, but that all the images are directly based on her original sketches.

She also says that even though she's still working out the price, and nothing is definitely sold, she's willing to advance us a small amount of money now, if our situation requires it. My jaw drops when I read that. She's worded it in a very businesslike manner, and just a week ago, I never would have wanted to admit to her that yes, our situation requires it. But now, I'll have no trouble taking her up on it. Even if she gives us a fraction of one of the paintings, we'll be able to pay rent for the coming month. I close my eyes and sit for a moment.

I don't ever want to lose sight of the fact that if this all works out, and we climb out of the deep, dark hole we've been in, it will partly be due to luck. It will be from hard work, yes, but also opportunity, something that is never guaranteed. *Thank you,* I whisper, not even really sure who I'm thanking. *Thank you, thank you, thank you.*

Chapter Forty-Four

A couple of weeks later, something happens at the Fud that feels like fate. Like one last opportunity to be seized.

Naomi arrives at our shift frazzled, hair not as perfect as usual, no lipstick. During a lull between customers—sorry, I mean "guests"—I ask her what's up.

"I'm totally screwed," she says. "You know my roommate Jordan? The one I actually share with, not the other two girls in the place?"

I nod.

"She ghosted me. Like, moved out, no warning, no nothing. And I'll be on the hook for her rent next month if I can't find someone, and it's not like I want just anyone sleeping in the same room as me."

As she's talking, I get the strangest sensation. It has never, ever occurred to me before now that I would move out on my own any time soon. Even when I fantasize about going to school for fashion, I always assume I'll go somewhere in the city and live at home—that I *need* to live at home, to take care of my mother. But as Naomi talks, I start thinking . . . maybe what I need is the exact opposite. And maybe this opportunity is the answer (if Annika will forward me a little more money). It's a shared bedroom, so not a lot of privacy, but I'm comfortable with Naomi. And who knows, it could be fun to live with her and two other girls. The main thing, though, is that it will give me distance. Space. To live my own life. To breathe.

I need to move out—now, not on some magical day when my mother is "happy."

Since everything exploded, I haven't been able to tell whether she feels better or worse. She cries all the time, tears dripping down her face even when she's not actively sobbing, like a broken faucet. And she still isn't ready to talk to someone. When I got a list of therapists who charge on a sliding scale from Marcus, she just thanked me and set it aside. But while the crying makes it seem like maybe she's doing worse, there's something else going on, too. She's painting. Smaller pieces—lots of them. It's great, of course. It's what I've wanted! I should be thrilled. And I kind of am? But I'm also obsessed with analyzing them, scared of what they might show— signs of self-hatred or guilt or suicidal thoughts. (A girl holding an armful of light entering a dark tunnel: Is she bringing hope, or on the way to being extinguished?)

The crying, the refusal to get help, the paintings . . . worrying about it all leaves me with a constant thrum of anxiety, an anxiety that serves no purpose and that won't go away as long as I have no distance from her.

I don't tell Naomi I can for sure do it, but I ask her to hold off on looking for someone, just for a couple of days, until I can figure out the money stuff. It makes me feel good, how excited she gets about the possibility.

That evening, after my shift, I sit down next to my mother on the couch. I can feel myself starting to talk myself out of it, like those times when I chickened out on telling her I was painting Wolfwood. Not this time.

"So," I say, "something came up at work, with a friend." I go on and tell her, and simply say that it's a really great situation: I won't need to get approved or live with a roommate I don't know. The rent is affordable since Naomi and I will share a bedroom. And it's not too far, just a few blocks southeast from us, closer to the river.

"Once we have enough money from the paintings selling, I'll help you find a place and move out of here, obviously," I say. Nothing is finalized except the Millers' sale, but that's a good chunk of money we're definitely getting. Annika thinks there are at least five other likely sales, too. I called her on my way home from my shift, to figure out if this could work.

My mom is quiet for a moment. "You're moving out." Her voice is toneless.

I nod, my throat getting tight. How can I be doing this to her?

"I think we both need it. I can't live my own life while I'm so caught up in yours. And you can't live your own life while I'm living it for you."

She purses her lips over and over. I have to hold myself back from saying so many different things: promising her I'll be over here a lot, telling her again she needs therapy. Or saying the whole thing is a terrible idea and I won't do it.

"Okay, well, I'm going to take a walk," I say, to remove the temptation.

I end up walking for miles, all the way south to Battery Park City, where I stand and stare out at the moody, steel gray water and the Statue of Liberty. I don't get home until hours later, petrified about what I'm going to find.

She's lying on the couch, of course. But she sits up when I come in, instead of keeping her back to me. I sit next to her, close, so our bodies are touching. We're both looking straight ahead, as if it's too painful to look at each other.

"I don't want you to go," she finally says. "But . . . I understand. And I'm happy for you, that you can live with your friend." She reaches over and takes my hand. Her skin is cool and soft. "The most important thing for me is for you to be happy, Indigo. I wish I'd been able to take better care of you but . . . I just couldn't."

I'm so shocked she's said it, I almost don't know how to respond.

"And you'll let us use Wolfwood money on a new place for you, right?" I say. Up until now, she's been maintaining that she doesn't want to use the money on herself, that it wouldn't be right.

She nods and squeezes my hand, then lies back down and turns away from me. I can feel myself wanting to lie down and spoon against her, to soak up her pain. Instead, I stand up and go over to my own area. The string wrapped around my heart hasn't snapped, but I do feel like it's now got a bit of give.

Chapter Forty-Five

The *Wolfwood* exhibition is almost over, and I haven't been to the gallery to see it yet. I haven't had even the slightest desire.

But Annika is trusting Kai to close up the gallery one night—a big deal for him—and he and I have plans to walk along the High Line elevated park at sunset, so I decide to meet him there. Once the show ends and the paintings go to their new homes, I might never see them again. And I suppose I am a little curious about how they look, framed and formally exhibited.

When I arrive, I text Kai. He unlocks the door, lets me in, kisses me—a hungrier, more passionate kiss than our first ones, any hesitance replaced by pure desire. After we've pried ourselves away from each other, he looks me up and down and shakes his head.

"How is it remotely possible that this wasn't designed and made specifically for Indigo Serra?" he asks. I smile, warm from the compliment.

He means the dress. The Tania Bawa dress. Turns out Ravi bought it when he saw it at Parker's store, not wanting his mom to know it was there. After my whole situation came out, he gave it back to me, refusing my offer to pay him when I have some cash. Kai said I should accept his generosity, that there were no strings attached, Ravi just genuinely wanted me to have it. So I did. Thanked him by giving him that tour of the hood, realizing I had plenty to share about where I've grown up.

"I'm going to finish putting stuff away in the back," Kai says "then call my mom so she can make sure I remembered everything. Won't take long."

"I'll be here."

First, I stand in the middle of the space and take in the pieces from a distance. I have to admit, they look amazing all together. There's so much energy in the room. So much rhythm and pace and flow from one painting to the next, the colors all working together. I'd never noticed how the compositions build up to the last one. The Others increase in number until, in the last piece, there's more space dedicated to them than to the actual monsters. Then the explosion of energy in the final battle scene. And the contrast between all of that and the pared-down image at the end, with Zoe, hanging. Lila in motion next to her. When my mother drew them, I doubt she did this all on purpose. From the sound of it, she was just drawing, not worrying about technical aspects. But seeing them like this . . . whether she did it on purpose or not, the compositions are brilliant.

After soaking in the view from here, I approach the first one I did and study it from close enough that I can see details and subtleties—the good and the bad. It's true, the frame does make everything about it appear that much better. As I stand here, the chill of the gallery air gives way to something hotter and heavier. I hear distant screams. Can feel Lila's body jostling around on my back, can hear Azul's rich voice as she sings a lullaby. Smell the burning flesh. Moving to the next, I hear the explosions of the grenades, and in the next, my cries for help as the hut implodes around me. I move through the story, the sensations coming back, stronger and stronger. I don't want to look at the final image, but something compels me. As I do, one of the Others turns her head and spots me, her eyes narrowing as she realizes who it is. Then another notices. And another. They're coming toward me, the army of brutalized bodies. Next to them, a thorned vine writhes like a sea serpent, heading my way, too. I should move, but I can't. My injuries burn under my clothes. The Others get closer. An orchid shifts its giant, toothy maw toward me. The serpent vine darts out, wraps itself around my neck, squeezes while the Others lunge and grab my limbs, pulling me, *Get the Wolf! Get the Wolf—*

"Ready to go?"

I swing around, heaving, and see Kai waiting. My hand is at my neck.

"Indigo? You okay?"

Hearing my name from his lips grounds me.

"Yeah, Just . . . not good memories. Still too real."

He nods. "Let's get out of here."

"Definitely."

He walks over to a hidden panel on a side wall and turns off the lights one by one, until the only ones left are the flickering fragments from the alarm system and the red glowing EXIT signs.

There aren't any wolves in Wolfwood, but there are monsters. I'm seventeen years old when I tell them goodbye.

Acknowledgments

No doubt, this book would have been written more quickly had Indigo secretly ghostwritten it for me. Alas, I was on my own. But I was never without support, and I owe an enormous debt to the following people.

To my agent, Sara Crowe: My eternal thanks for your steadfast belief in me, your always excellent guidance, and your friendship. And to the entire team at Pippin Properties. I'm so lucky to be a Pip.

To my editor, Maggie Lehrman: Thank you for your enthusiasm about Indigo's story, your keen feedback, and (not least) your patience and kindness. And to everyone at Abrams/Amulet who had a hand in the process: Emily Daluga, Amy Vreeland, Hana Nakamura, Deena Fleming, Chelsea Hunter, and Maggie Moore. And to artist Tran Nguyen, for the absolutely stunning cover illustration.

To all my readers along the way: Jandy, I'm not sure if you remember that it was during a conversation with you that the idea for the book came together, spurred by something you said. Combined with the many, many discussions over the years and your spot-on reading of the draft . . . What can I say? My appreciation of you is stratospheric. Katie, your friendship makes everything better, and your eagle eye undoubtedly had that effect on this book. I can't thank you enough. Daphne, Marie, Jill, and Eliot—your insightful comments on the early draft were absolutely essential. I consider myself unbelievably fortunate to have you in my life. And my Beverly Shores crew—especially my fellow pommers, Katie, Mary Winn, and Rachel—not sure how I would have made it through the pandemic years, let alone written the book, without you.

Heartfelt thanks also to my friends and family who may not have given specific story-related feedback, but who were just as important to my process, by making me feel loved and supported and by helping me keep at least one foot in the real world. And thanks to my dearest Boog for the memories of Tulum.

My only regret about this book is that I didn't finish it in time for my mother to read it. I don't know what she would have thought of the story, but I do know that she would have been proud.

About the Author

MARIANNA BAER is the author of *The Inconceivable Life of Quinn*, which *Publishers Weekly* called "a delicate, complicated, and engrossing exploration of the collision between real life and the inexplicable" in a starred review. She's a graduate of Vermont College of Fine Arts with an MFA in writing for children and young adults. She lives in Brooklyn, New York.

★ "A delicate, complicated, and engrossing exploration of the collision between real life and the inexplicable."
—*Publishers Weekly*, starred review

DIVE IN TO THE MYSTERY OF
The Inconceivable Life of Quinn